"I don't believe we're facing terrorists," Mack Bolan stated

"No?" Makhdoom set down his cup. "Then what?"

"True believers."

"I do not understand the difference."

"Terrorists lash out. There is no real objective that they can hope to achieve other than killing. True believers have an objective, however mad it may be. I believe the people we're facing have a higher purpose than just lighting off a nuke and killing as many people as they can."

"What is that higher purpose?"

"I don't know." Bolan stared at the Pakistani special forces captain. "But God help us if we don't stop it."

Don Pendleton's Mack
Bolan®
Lethal Tribute

A GOLD EAGLE BOOK FROM
W☉RLDWIDE®

TORONTO • NEW YORK • LONDON
AMSTERDAM • PARIS • SYDNEY • HAMBURG
STOCKHOLM • ATHENS • TOKYO • MILAN
MADRID • WARSAW • BUDAPEST • AUCKLAND

First edition May 2005

ISBN 0-373-61505-1

Special thanks and acknowledgment to
Chuck Rogers for his contribution to this work.

LETHAL TRIBUTE

Printed in U.S.A.

...we wrestle not against flesh and blood, but against principalities, against powers, against the rulers of darkness of this world, against spiritual wickedness in high places.

—Ephesians,
6:12-13

My path has taken me face-to-face with the event horizon of human evil. I have dedicated myself to War Everlasting and to staring into the terrible place and telling the evil no. I will take down the deceivers.

—Mack Bolan

Dedicated to the world's Special Forces

CHAPTER ONE

Haji Pir Pass, Pakistan-Kashmir Border

Musa Company was moving.

Mack Bolan shadowed them in the inky black of the cloudless night.

The ugly rumor at the Pentagon was that Pakistan had lost control of several of its nuclear warheads. Such a happening had long been an established fear in the West, as nuclear security protocols in Pakistan were a fluid situation at the best of times. The Pakistani government vigorously denied through both public and private channels that any warheads were missing. They claimed the CIA had its own agenda, had fabricated lies so that the United States and her United Nations lackeys could invade Pakistan and wrest away her sovereign power. Such action would, thus, lay Pakistan open to the political and military machinations of their true nemesis, India.

Nuclear warheads passing from Pakistan into the disputed region of Kashmir was a worst-case scenario for a catastrophic meltdown between the two nuclear nations. One that could light a fire throughout all of East Asia.

The rumors in Washington were confusing. Some sources

claimed that ultra-fundamentalist factions in the Pakistani government and military had engineered the grab. Other rumors indicated the warheads had been taken, humiliatingly, right out from under the Pakistani military's nose.

Bolan watched Musa Company move, and he began to think that Pakistan was as worried as the West.

Named for the Prophet Moses, Musa Company was Pakistan's elite counterterrorist unit. They had received training from the British SAS and in the past had sent personnel to the United States for special warfare and airborne training. Bolan had suspected that whoever came down through the Haji Pir Pass would be involved in transporting and security for the weapons. His first guess had been that the grab had to have been an inside job.

But Musa Company wasn't transporting nuclear warheads.

They had been instrumental in quelling rioting and dissension between Pakistan's fractious factions. Musa Company would be the last unit to betray their country and to let Pakistan's nuclear weapons loose into the world. Their loyalty was unquestionable. Nor were the men below passing themselves off as travelers or pilgrims. They carried no baggage and they were well off the roads. Bolan had watched as they had perilously engaged in a night jump down into the high crags of the pass. They now moved through the nearly vertical terrain, wearing night-camouflage body armor, night-vision goggles and carrying Heckler & Koch MP-5 SD-3 silenced submachine guns. They moved as silently and swiftly as wolves.

Musa Company was definitely on the hunt.

Bolan judged by the way they were fanned out and leap-frogging from cover to cover that their quarry had to be very close. They were being very careful, as they were very close to the disputed border with India. Indian armored and airborne troops were barely two miles away and always on alert. The disputed area was a flashpoint, any mistake could easily lead to a renewal of war.

Bolan subvocalized into his throat mike sat link. "Bear, what have you got?"

Back in Virginia, Aaron and his entire cybernetic team worked furiously. They were directly linked with the "Puzzle Palace" within the National Security Agency. Unless Musa Company had gone rogue, they had to be in touch with someone. "Striker, we are detecting radio communications. Very narrow bandwidth. We are adjusting values. One moment." Bolan waited while Kurtzman made his moves. Pakistan had nothing much in the way of sophisticated communication satellites. The best they had for special operations was a narrow bandwidth radio using security encryption protocols.

A secure radio channel was far from secure when Aaron Kurtzman and his team were on the job.

Kurtzman paused a moment as several of the National Security Agency's most sophisticated Signal Intelligence satellites tried to break in to eavesdrop on the Pakistanis' conversation. "We have it triangulated. One contact point is right below you. Everyone in the Musa Company team is individually wired. The second transmission point is a signal station. Definitely Islamabad. Their orders are coming straight from the capital. NSA says they are using encrypted audio."

Bolan nodded to himself. Whatever Musa Company's orders, they were receiving them in real time and they were coming straight from the top. "You've broken in?"

"One moment, Striker. Encryption broken. We're in," Kurtzman confirmed. "Patching you in passively."

Bolan's earpiece crackled as he was connected to the Pakistani secure radio frequency. The Puzzle Palace had done its work. Whatever encryption code the Pakistani military was using wasn't up to the giant supercomputers in the bowels of the NSA building. Bolan listened as voices spoke in the quiet, clipped tones of soldiers giving and receiving data across a military channel. Bolan frowned slightly. He had been in Pakistan before and could speak enough words in the dominant language to get by as a tourist. He didn't recognize the language being spoken. "Bear, that's not Urdu."

"Confirmed, Striker. One moment." Pakistan was a large country split by mountains, deserts and river valleys. The people of Pakistan spoke several major languages and had innumerable dialects. "Switching translators."

Bolan watched Musa Company creep forward, disappearing and reappearing from behind rocks and boulders below. They were slowing as they approached their target.

"Striker, they're speaking Sind. Patching in standby translator." Halfway across the world Kurtzman sat in Virginia and opened a satellite conference call with the NSA translator in Washington, D.C. "Translator is in. I am squelching the dialogue on your end."

The sound of the Pakistani commandos faded from Bolan's earpiece and was replaced by a woman's voice speaking with an English accent. "Striker, this is Translator 2, I am receiving."

"Affirmative, Translator 2. What are they saying?"

The woman listened for a moment and began translating. "Musa—Approaching objective. Islamabad—What are your observations? Musa—No movement. No activity observed."

Bolan crouched in the rocks, scanning through the electro-optical sight of his sound-suppressed M-1A scout rifle. Musa Company was converging on something.

"Musa—Objective in sight. Islamabad—What do you see?" The translator spoke clearly and rapidly in Bolan's ear. "Musa—No movement. No apparent sentries."

Bolan scanned for an objective, but the craggy, boulder-strewn terrain showed nothing but rock peaks and shadows.

The translator's voice rose slightly. "Musa—Bunker found!"

Bolan's eyes slightly widened and he strained to see a bunker entrance. It was more likely to be a fortified cave. The mountains of Kashmir were riddled with them. "I'm moving closer."

"Affirmative, Striker," Kurtzman replied.

Bolan picked his path through the piled mounds and erupting knife edges of rock. "Bear, what can you see?"

"Observation satellite shows twelve individuals below you. Moving in concert."

That was Musa Company. "Anything else? Any sign of hostiles?"

"Nothing, Striker. Just you and the team below you."

Bolan scanned everything in a 360-degree arc. His spine spoke to him. "Bear, there's someone else out here."

"Satellite shows nothing but you and Musa Company, Striker."

"There's someone else out here, Bear." Bolan trained his sight back on the area Musa Company surrounded. "I can feel it."

Kurtzman was silent a moment. Through long, hard experience he had learned that a Mack Bolan hunch was to be heeded at all costs. "Acknowledged, but we don't see them, Striker. Satellite shows no motion and no anomalous heat sources. If they're hidden, then they are hidden but good."

"Translator, what are they saying?"

"They are not saying anything." The translator unsquelched the Pakistani transmission and there was nothing except silence. "They've stopped transmitting."

Bolan gazed hard at their position. "Bear, any motion?"

"Negative, Striker. Musa Company has come to full stop."

Bolan let out a long breath. Whoever was in command of Musa Company didn't like it, either.

Something was wrong. The translator spoke again. "Musa— We are going to breach the bunker. Islamabad—Affirmative."

Bolan waited long moments. There was a sudden quick flare of light in his night-vision goggles. Bolan recognized the hissing crack of flexible-shaped charge detonating.

"Musa—Sending in Number 1 section. Islamabad—Affirmative."

Half of the Musa Company team disappeared underneath an outcropping while the other half held down the perimeter.

"Section 1—We are inside. No hostiles detected. Islamabad—What do you observe? Section 2—Extensive underground complex. Catacombs, very old stonework. Believe complex predates target occupation. Islamabad—Any sign of the packages?"

Packages. Bolan raised a bemused eyebrow at the code word. His hunch had been right. Musa Company was hunting the same thing he was. If Musa could make a successful retrieval and get the warheads back in Pakistani government hands, Bolan might just be able to call his own mission a wrap.

"Section 1—No sign of packages. No sign of targets. Signs of recent habitation Proceeding. Islamabad—Affirmative."

Bolan grimaced. Musa Company was no one to mess around with. If the bad guys had gotten wind that the elite commandos were on their trail, they would have hauled ass into India already and the nukes would be gone.

"Section 1—Zia? What happened to Zia? Zia, report! Islamabad—What is happening?"

Bolan's instincts began to clamor up and down his spine again. "Translator 2, what are you hearing?"

"Intercommunication between individual Musa Company soldiers, Section 1 and 2 and Islamabad. It's becoming…confused." The translator's voice rose just slightly as she translated. "Section 1—Zia! Where is Zia? All units hold position! Section 2—What is happening, Falzur? Islamabad—What is happening? Section 2—Falzur! Falzur! Where is the sergeant! Islamabad—Report!" the Translator swallowed. "I am having difficulty keeping things in order—"

"Keep translating!" Bolan ordered.

"Musa—Section 2 hold positions! By God, I said hold positions! Islamabad—What is happening? Report! Section 1—Where are they coming from! I can't see any—"

Kurtzman cut in. "Striker, satellite reception shows multiple radio transmission points in Musa Company are now off the air."

Bolan's blood went cold.

The translator broke in. "Striker, I hear gunfire."

"Give me audio."

"Patching you in, Striker."

Kurtzman unsquelched Bolan's end. The soldier's eyes flared under his night-vision goggles. Someone was firing a semiautomatic handgun as rapidly as he could pull the trigger. The sound was followed by the crack of a hand grenade.

People were screaming.

The translator's voice was rising close to panic. This wasn't the sort of mission she had been trained for.

"Islamabad—What is happening! Report! What is happening? I order you to report!"

For a moment there was nothing but silence.

A voice spoke in tightly controlled Sind and the translator spoke over it. "This is Section 2, all contact lost with Section 1. Repeat, all contact lost with Section 1. They are not responding. We are holding position outside. What are your orders? Headquarters—Try them again."

Section 1's commander spoke slowly and clearly. It needed little translation. "Section 1, any unit, report. Repeat, Section 1 this is Section 2, any unit report."

Nothing but static came back.

Section 1 was gone.

Bolan watched Section 2 through his night optics. They were arranged in a crescent around the hidden opening of the catacombs.

"Section 2—There is no response. We are holding position. What are your orders?" The pause on the line was lengthy. "Islamabad—Section 1, withdraw to primary extraction point. Section 2—Affirma—"

The translator stopped as the transmission was cut off. Bolan didn't need translation. He had the man in plain view. The man in Section 1 who was transmitting levitated from where he crouched. His arms flailed and with a convulsive jerk he floated up and over the rock he'd been crouching behind and disappeared.

Section 2 began firing in all directions. One soldier rose. He heaved and flailed. His silenced submachine gun fell from his hands as he stumbled backward like a spastically moonwalking marionette. He dropped from sight in a crevice between two boulders.

"Bear! What do you have!"

"Movement, Striker!" Kurtzman was also perplexed by what he was seeing via satellite. "Anomalous movement! Musa Company is in a fight with something, but we can't see it!"

"Bear!" Bolan watched as another man from Musa Company was seized by the invisible and dragged into darkness. "Give me something!"

"Striker, there is nothing! I repeat! Satellite does not pick up any hostiles! All we— Jesus!"

Bolan watched as the waist, legs and then boots of a Musa Company commando were dragged behind a boulder and disappeared.

"Striker, this is Translator 2." The woman's voice trembled. "I have nothing. No Musa Company units are transmitting. Only headquarters is on the channel, demanding to know what's happening. It sounds like they are panicking back in Islamabad."

Bolan watched through his night optics. Nothing moved but the wind whistling through the rocks.

"Striker, we have nothing." Kurtzman's voice went flat. "Musa Company is gone."

Bolan's skin crawled.

"Striker?"

Bolan strained all of his senses out into the darkness. "Receiving you, Bear."

"Get the hell out of there."

Bolan adjusted the gain on his optics. "I see movement."

"Confirmed!" Kurtzman was adjusting his own optics from their vantage two hundred miles up in space. "Looks like one of Musa Company, staying low in the rocks and maintaining radio silence."

Bolan watched the man crawl through the mountain terrain. His submachine gun was cradled in his hands and his head whipped back and forth fearfully. The Executioner's instincts tingled as he felt the watching presence of the enemy. Something else was out there and it was observing the man from Musa Company, as well. Bolan had ugly thoughts of cats tormenting mice before the kill.

"Bear, can you patch me in to him?"

"I cannot recommend that course of action, Striker."

"Can you do it?"

"Striker, has it occurred to you whatever the hell is out there achieved total surprise because they were listening to everything that Musa Company was saying? We compromised their secure channel. I'm thinking someone else did, too. Right now I think—and I emphasize *think*—you're anonymous because we are communicating via satellite. The minute you transmit on the Musa Company radio frequency you are fair game, Striker."

"Do it."

"Striker, I cannot recommend against this strongly enough—"

"Do it!"

Kurtzman acquiesced unhappily. "Patching you in, Striker. Link achieved, you are on the Pakistani secure mission net. The minute we unsquelch you, you are active. Do you want the translator?"

"No." Bolan turned on his radio and spoke in English. "Surviving Musa Unit Section 2! Move due north! Now! As fast as you can! I will cover you!"

There was a split second's hesitation, then the man rose and bolted for his life. Bolan's eyes slitted as something blurred behind the man in his optics. The Executioner pulled his trigger repeatedly and the M-1 A rifle bucked against his shoulder. Bolan couldn't tell if he had gotten any hits. There was nothing there but shards of rock and boulders the size of men. The Pakistani ran as if hell were on his heels.

Bolan snarled silently. He could feel the enemy. They were all around.

The Musa Company soldier suddenly staggered as if he had run into an invisible wall. His submachine gun flew from his hands as he toppled to one side and then staggered backward. The air around him blurred. Bolan fired three quick shots directly behind the tottering Pakistani.

The Musa Company soldier seemed to be walking backward against his will toward an outcropping.

Bolan spun the sound suppressor from the muzzle of his rifle and aimed just above the Pakistani's head as he squeezed the trigger repeatedly.

The M-1 A scout ripped into life. Without the suppressor the rifle spit flame in a meter-long muzzle-blast. The rifle cycled through the remains of its 20-round.

Bolan's position was revealed to the world by the strobing fire of his rifle.

"Striker!" Kurtzman's voice thundered in Bolan's ear. "You're lit up like Christmas!"

Bolan knew it all too well, but the gambit paid off.

The Pakistani stumbled forward, clutching his throat, seemingly released from the grip of the invisible entity. Bolan slapped in a fresh magazine of full power 7.62 mm ammo and began engaging the unseen. His weapon pounded out rounds like a jackhammer out of control as he laid down covering fire to either side of the Pakistani as he began to run again. Bolan's weapon finally clacked open on empty. He shoved in a fresh magazine and slid a rifle grenade down over the muzzle of his weapon. The grenade clicked into place on the launching rings that the Cowboy had machined into the weapon back in Virginia.

"Musa!" Bolan transmitted as he raised his rifle skyward and fired. "Take off your goggles!"

The rifle boomed against Bolan in recoil and the grenade shot up into the night sky. Bolan ripped off his night-vision goggles as the French Night-Sun illumination munition detonated like a star going supernova. The burning magnesium flare burst into five-million candlepower brilliance. The lunar landscape of the pass was thrown into a shadowless white incandescence. Bolan flicked off the power to his rifle's light-gathering optics and snapped his rifle down. His muzzle tracked from rock to rock as he searched the unforgiving glare for targets. Bolan began to feel a mounting sense of dread.

There was nothing.

Bolan had been betting that whoever was out there was wearing night-vision equipment, and the intense flare of the burning magnesium would have solarized their optics and temporarily blinded them. Bolan had also hoped to find his enemy blinded, stumbling and exposed by the sudden supernova of light.

Nothing moved.

There was no movement other than the running man from Musa Company. No sound other than the ragged panting of the runner in Bolan's earpiece, his boots crunching into sand

and rock, and the stuttering hiss of the burning flare as it slowly floated to the ground on its parachutes.

Bolan began to engage nothing, firing rapidly into any dark crevice sheltered from the vertical glare of the grenade. He fired for effect, but nothing fired back. Darkness draped down the slopes of the hillsides as the burning grenade drifted low in the sky. The Pakistani clawed his way up the slope. His right hand filled with a Browning Hi-Power pistol. He caught sight of Bolan, who waved him forward and then crouched back down among the rocks.

A moment later the Pakistani piled into Bolan's position. He collapsed against a boulder in a fit of ragged coughing. The world plunged into darkness once more as the grenade fluttered sputtering to the ground. It landed among blades of rock and sent strobing pulses of light out from the crevices like a beacon. There were only scant seconds left of light. Bolan pulled his night-vision goggles back over his eyes and powered up the optics of his rifle.

"Who the hell are you?" the Pakistani wheezed in excellent English.

Bolan saw no reason to lie. "An American."

The muzzle of the commando's 9 mm pistol leveled at Bolan's skull. "How do I know you are not…" The Pakistani's voice trailed off. He lowered his pistol as he considered the destruction of his unit. The answer was obvious.

Bolan answered him anyway. "If I'd wanted you down, I'd have taken you down."

The Pakistani commando glanced at Bolan's telescopic rifle and accepted the truth of the statement. Bolan's teeth clenched as his eyes told him nothing was out there and his spine told him the enemy was closing in. "You're Musa Company."

"Captain Mahmoud Makhdoom." The Pakistani captain prudently turned his back to Bolan and watched the rear.

Bolan swept his scope across the landscape. There was still nothing to see. "What hit you?"

The Pakistani shuddered and shrugged at the same time. *"Djinns?"*

Bolan raised an eyebrow without looking up from his scope. Captains of highly professional special forces units didn't often blame supernatural beings for their misfortunes. Bolan didn't scoff. What he had seen with his own eyes and, more to the point, what he hadn't seen, had set his own skin to crawling.

"We have to get out of here."

"Indeed." The captain's hands were shaking. He had lost his entire unit and he, himself, had been assaulted by the invisible opponents.

"Striker!" Kurtzman was far from panic, but his voice had gone up a register. "What is your situation?"

"Situation…" Bolan searched for a way to summarize what was happening. "Bear, this situation has gone *X-Files*. Enemy unknown. Nature unknown. Numbers unknown. I am with Captain Mahmoud Makhdoom of Musa Company." Bolan shook his head bitterly. The nukes were in unknown hands and there was no way to get his hands on them. "The nukes are gone. We are extracting."

Bolan turned to Makhdoom. "You do have extraction?"

"Helicopters will come if I call for them, but I was maintaining silence until you broke into our channel. Our primary extraction point was the plateau above your position."

Bolan gazed out into the dark. "I think the *djinns* can hear you."

Makhdoom nodded unhappily. "I believe you are correct."

Bolan considered the plateau he had crossed earlier in the evening. It was three hundred yards upslope, and an ugly climb. The only alternative was to stay where they were and wait. "Do it."

Makhdoom spoke rapid Sind into his radio. Bolan could feel invisible ears pricking up and taking notice of the transmission.

The Pakistani nodded. "The chopper is coming, with gunship escort."

Bolan took out his two white-phosphorous grenades and pulled the pins. "Go!"

Makhdoom bolted from cover and began to claw his way up the rock slope. Bolan hurled his grenades off to the right and left. The grenades detonated and the incandescent flare of magnesium was replaced by hellish heat of burning phosphorous that shot up into the sky in streamers trailing white smoke. Bolan burned a magazine in an arc in front of him and began loping up the hill. He clicked in a fresh magazine and pounded up the mountainside.

Makhdoom's voice boomed. "Down!"

Bolan went flat into the rocks as a grenade sailed over his head and detonated with the whipcrack of high-explosive driving razor-sharp bits of metal at supersonic speeds. The fragmentation hissed and sparked off the rocks. Bolan leaped back up and climbed for the plateau. He passed the Pakistani and clawed on upward.

"Allah Akhbar!" The man from Musa Company roared in religious defiance against the unseen. He rose up and began unloading his pistol in rapid double taps in an arc across the way they had come. No cries rang out. No answering fire came back. Makhdoom was firing at shadows.

The shadows were closing in.

Makhdoom's pistol racked open on a smoking empty chamber. Bolan whirled. "Go! Go! Go!"

The captain turned and ran, reloading his pistol as Bolan pumped covering fire into the trail behind him. The big American searched for flaming figures, unnatural shadows, any break in the landscape, any movement at all.

There was nothing.

Every fiber of Bolan's being screamed at him that time was running out.

"Go!" Makhdoom roared. "I will cover."

Bolan and the Pakistani leapfrogged positions up the mountainside. Bolan clambered up beside the captain and stopped. "I think they're waiting for us up top."

Makhdoom's commando knife rasped out into his left hand. *"Inshallah."*

God willing.

Bolan smiled grimly. The man from Musa Company wanted payback. Voices spoke in Bolan's ear in Sind. Translator 2 spoke from Washington. "The helicopters say ETA five minutes."

The Pakistani spoke. "The helicopters will be here in—"

"Five minutes, I know."

An eyebrow rose above the captain's goggles. It was very clear that just about everyone had compromised his communications. "I see."

Bolan clicked his last rifle grenade onto the muzzle of his rifle. He had one hand grenade left, and he was nearly out of ammo for his rifle. Bolan ground the butt of his gun into the sand and pointed the muzzle skyward. The rifle boomed and the antipersonnel round shot skyward. Bolan took out his last hand grenade. Somewhere up in the dark the rifle grenade lost its upward impetus and nosed over and arced back down toward the plateau like a mortar round.

The rim of the plateau above flashed orange as the grenade detonated. Bolan hurled his last grenade up and over, and Makhdoom followed suit. The two grenades cracked and sent shrapnel hissing across the open ground. Bolan slapped leather. He filled his right hand with his .50-caliber Desert Eagle pistol and his left with a Beretta 93-R machine pistol.

The two men charged up the side of the mountain and went over the top to the plateau. The plateau wasn't really flat, but just an area of rolling rocky terrain rather than vertically falling hillside. Nothing moved other than a summer-dried shrub that one of the grenades had set on fire. Bolan and Makhdoom went back-to-back as they walked across the open ground.

Rotor blades thumped in the distance.

Something scraped on rock thirty yards to Bolan's left.

The Executioner tracked his pistols like a twin gun turret and flame shot from both muzzles as he extended them. Makhdoom showed his professionalism by covering the rear.

"Anything?"

Bolan scanned the darkness with his night-vision goggles. Nothing moved.

"No."

Translator 2 spoke. "They say ETA one minute."

The hammering of rotors shook the night sky.

Kurtzman came online. "Striker, your fireworks have been noticed. Satellite imaging shows Indian army gunships are taking off five miles east of your position."

"Affirmative, Bear, I—"

God's own flashlight speared the plateau with light as the Pakistani helicopter swept the broken ground with its searchlight. Bolan kept his eyes on the terrain around him. The light suddenly blasted him and the captain, and the sound of rotors slowed as the Mi-8 Hip helicopter descended to just a few feet above the ground.

Makhdoom jerked his head. "Go!"

Bolan didn't argue. He turned to board the helicopter.

Something flashed in his vision. It was for but an instant, but in the clouds of dust there was a flash of something. More a flash of nothing. There was a moment of totally incongruent space where the dust fluttered and coalesced against the rotor wind.

As if it were striking something that wasn't there.

Bolan fired both pistols as rapidly as he could squeeze the triggers. The Pakistani door gunner leaning out of the helicopter couldn't see what Bolan was shooting at but his PKT light machine gun ripped into life and green tracers streamed into the seemingly empty space.

Bolan stopped firing and strained to see through the whirling dust storm.

"What was it?" Makhdoom slapped a hand on Bolan's shoulder and roared in his ear over the rotor noise. "What did you see?"

"I don't know." Bolan kept his guns leveled. "Something. Nothing."

"I must apologize, given the debt I owe you." The uncomfortably warm muzzle of Makhdoom's pistol pressed behind Bolan's ear. "But you are under arrest."

Bolan had expected nothing less. He opened his hands and let his pistols fall forward from his grip, hooked only by a single finger through the trigger guards. "Captain, get us the hell off this hilltop and I'll be the one in your debt."

CHAPTER TWO

Islamabad, Pakistan

Bolan had been in worse cells. This one actually had a sunroof. Bolan peered up through the three iron bars in the ceiling. The late-morning sun threw shadows against the western wall of the cell, and he idly wondered what happened to the occupants when it rained. He ate the last bite of mystery meat he had been served and was wiping the remaining couscous from his bowl when someone hammered on the battered steel door of the cell.

"Prisoner! Step away from the door!"

Bolan was already sitting in a half-lotus position on the opposite side of the cell, but he decided cooperation was his best gambit for the moment. "I am away from the door."

A slot in the steel door shot back and a glowering, bearded face noted his location. "Do not move!"

"I won't."

Keys turned in the massive lock and the door swung open. A hulking guard with a pistol on his hip filled the entryway. He carried a three-foot length of roughly turned wood wrapped in leather. Bolan knew that such truncheons were most often used in the Middle East for beating the bottoms of the feet of prisoners. A man with collapsed arches was unlikely to make trouble, much less attempt any escape. The guards had taken his boots upon incarceration. Bolan eyed the club in the man's hands.

The guard should have brought backup.

The guard moved aside as Captain Makhdoom entered the cell. Bolan nodded. "Captain."

The Pakistani frowned. "You have put me in a very difficult position."

"I saved your life," Bolan countered.

"Yes." The captain nodded solemnly. "Which puts me in a very difficult position."

"I see." Bolan smiled in a friendly fashion. "How may I be of further assistance to you?"

"Um, yes." The special forces captain shifted uncomfortably. "The United States government denies any knowledge of your existence, much less any legitimate reason for you to be lurking, illegally, and armed, within the borders of Pakistan."

Bolan shrugged. It was a very old story.

Makhdoom shrugged in return. "And yet, my superiors have received—" the captain raised a troubled eyebrow "—intimations, from very, shall we say, oblique sources, that any consideration shown you will be appreciated."

Bolan kept the smile off his face. "I'm prepared to assist you in any reasonable fashion within my means."

The guard stared back and forth between Bolan and Makhdoom. His bludgeon creaked in his fists. He clearly yearned to do away with the pleasantries and beat Bolan into paste.

"Captain, may we speak privately for a moment?"

Makhdoom waved the guard away. "Corporal, you may wait for me down the hall."

The guard's face twisted in indignation as he gnashed his teeth and stormed from the cell.

Makhdoom's voice went grim. "I cannot vouchsafe your safety in this place. There are those who wish to see you dealt with severely."

"Captain, your government is missing some nuclear warheads. No one's safety can be guaranteed."

Makhdoom peered up unhappily through the narrow bars in the ceiling.

Bolan continued. "The United States government is aware of your missing warheads and is gravely concerned. You and I both know that whoever took them is most likely to be a dedicated enemy of the United States, Israel and Europe." Bolan gazed at the captain critically. "Unless of course, the weapons weren't stolen, but given away by members of your government to further the agenda of terrorists, or the liberation of Kashmir."

Makhdoom flared. "The warheads were not given to anyone! They were taken! Despite every security precaution!"

"Taken?" Bolan eyes narrowed. "You mean, by force?"

"Taken," Makhdoom affirmed. The anger in the Pakistani captain's eyes was tempered by a certain dread. "As my men were taken last night. As you and I were almost taken. The guards at the facility were taken by something unseen. The warheads taken by the unseen. The guards on duty were gone. The weapons littered the floor, unfired. No trace was left."

Bolan regarded Makhdoom. Pakistani special forces were nowhere near as sophisticated as U.S. Navy SEALs, the British SAS or the German GSG-9. The Pakistani government often used their special forces as shock troops and a number of their "sensitive" operations had turned into bloodbaths. They did, however, have a well-deserved reputation for toughness. Even Bolan had been disturbed by what he'd seen.

Makhdoom was genuinely afraid, and of more than loose nuclear weapons.

Bolan took the captain's gaze and held it. "If the missing

weapons can't be contained or accounted for, the United States and others may be forced to take action, drastic action, very possibly within your national borders."

Makhdoom stared into an ugly future. "There are those who say the first step in avoiding such a confrontation with the U.S. would be getting rid of you. Quickly and quietly."

"I'm sure it's been suggested." Bolan nodded. "But I believe we both know that your first, best recourse would be to go back to the site of last night's—" he considered the inexplicable events "—incident, pick up whatever information we can and proceed from there."

Makhdoom's head snapped around. "We?"

"You and I are last evening's only two survivors. We also have a mutual problem." Bolan opened his hands. "It's only reasonable that we pool our resources."

Makhdoom stared at Bolan long and hard. "Guard!"

The guard roared back into the room with his club cocked back in his hands for a blow. He seemed as giddy as a schoolgirl with the prospect of beating Bolan into oblivion.

Makhdoom let out a heavy sigh. "Fetch this man's boots. He is coming with me."

Northeast Pakistani Border

THE MI-8 HELICOPTER thundered across the sere mountains. It was summer in Pakistan and even up in the mountains the land beneath the aircraft was blast-furnace hot. Bolan sat back and enjoyed the breeze through the open doors. The flight of helicopters carried a full platoon of Musa Company special forces soldiers. A pair of Hind gunships flew in escort of the transports. Bolan wore tan Pakistani fatigues that didn't quite fit, and a steel-pot helmet woven with camouflage netting. Russian-made body armor of titanium plates sandwiched between spun fiberglass fabric encased his torso. Musa Company was no longer creeping around in the dark. It was in assault mode and wanted payback.

Gone were the silenced submachine guns, night-vision goggles and black balaclavas. Each man carried a G-3 automatic rifle with a 40 mm grenade launcher slaved beneath the barrel. One man in each squad carried a light machine gun and another carried a rocket-propelled grenade launcher. Every man was also festooned with a personal assortment of pistols, knives and grenades.

Bolan cradled his own weapon. The German G-3 was long and heavy, but it fired the NATO 7.62 mm high-power rifle round and was hell for tough. While dated, all of the Pakistani equipment was solid kit. Bolan could think of worse weapons, and worse people, for that matter, with whom to assault the unknown. He vainly wished he had his satellite link so he could communicate with the Farm, but that wasn't forthcoming. Everything he had brought into Pakistan had been confiscated. Still, the fact that they had brought him along, much less armed him, showed just how desperate the Pakistanis were. Bolan glanced up as the copilot leaned back in his seat and yelled at Makhdoom over the rotor noise. Bolan didn't need translation. He had been watching the terrain fly by beneath them.

They were approaching their target.

The Mi-8s dropped toward the plateau like stones. The Hind gunships clawed upward into the sky and orbited the site with their machine cannons and rocket pods ready. The red dust of the mountains flew up as the transports landed.

Musa Company debarked the Mi-8s and fanned out by sections across the plateau. Bolan leaped out behind Makhdoom. He had no orders other than to stick to the captain like glue. As Bolan examined the plateau, he could see spalling and bullet strikes scoring the rocks from the previous night's one-sided battle. Several spots were scorched by the high explosive of rifle grenades. The single, lonesome shrub lay blackened and burned.

Musa Company maintained radio silence. Makhdoom chopped his hand forward and his men went by sections, two by two, to the edge of the plateau and began to descend the mountainside toward their objective.

In the night the land had been a lunar landscape. By day the arid, vertical hillsides could have passed for a bad patch on Mars. The platoon swiftly descended. A man held up the spent flare and parachute of Bolan's illuminating round. They leapfrogged from cover to cover, constantly sweeping the surroundings, still encountering nothing. They stopped as they reached the area where Section 2 had been lost. Bolan scanned the recent battlefield. Brass shell casings and spent bullets lay in the sand and gravel, deformed where they had struck rock. There were no bodies.

There was no blood.

Makhdoom moved forward, his rifle at the ready. Musa Company followed. They swiftly came upon their target. Bolan examined the objective. Beneath an overhang of rock there was an opening in the mountainside. It was squared off, clearly man-made, and lined with stone. Just inside lay a heavy wooden door reinforced with iron bands. Its hinges were gone where they had been cut with flexible-shaped charge. Bolan stared at the square, black hole in the mountain.

It looked like the back door to hell.

Makhdoom's eyes burned into the inky blackness within. Bolan quickly looked around at Musa Company. They had joked of *djinns* on the flight in. Now no one was laughing. Each man here was one of the most trusted soldiers in Pakistan. Each had been briefed about the nuclear warheads that had vanished without a trace and the guards who had disappeared with them, their weapons scattered and unfired. Each man had also heard the radio tapes of the battle the night before, listening as half a platoon of Musa Company had been wiped out to a man, one by one, by an enemy unseen. They had heard the terror in comrades' voices as they had been taken.

Musa Company stared at the black hole in the mountain and their fear was palpable.

Bolan spoke very quietly just behind Makhdoom. "Captain."

Makhdoom didn't look away from the entrance. "Yes?"

"May I make a suggestion?"

The captain peered backward. "I am very open to suggestions at the moment."

"Have your men fix bayonets."

Makhdoom's mustache lifted. His lips skinned back from his teeth in a feral smile. He turned to let his men see it, then snarled in guttural English, "Bayonets!"

Two dozen bayonets rasped from their sheaths in a single motion. Makhdoom snarled again, "Fix!"

The bayonets clicked into place. Cold iron glittered in the afternoon sun. Musa Company's determination ratcheted up by a factor of ten. Few things centered a soldier's aggressiveness more than having his commanding officer give the order to fix sharpened steel to the business end of his rifle.

"Lights!" Musa Company pulled miniflashlights from their web gear and affixed them to clips on their rifles' handguards. "All sections, set rifles on full automatic. Maintain radio silence unless you see something to report. Sections 3 and 4 secure the perimeter. Sections 1 and 2—" Makhdoom stared grimly at the dark doorway "—follow me."

Bolan followed Makhdoom and Musa Company into the earth.

The passage into the mountain was square, and just large enough for men to walk two by two. Once inside, the heat of desert fell away as if they had stepped into what seemed to be an air-conditioned building—except that the air within was fetid, clammy and cold. Bolan played his light across the walls and examined the stonework. There were places upon the earth, old battlefields, ruins, places in the wilderness, which resonated with what had transpired. Bolan had long ago learned to trust his instincts, and to feel the vibe.

"This place is very old." Bolan didn't need to add that terrible things had happened here.

Makhdoom nodded as he shone his light ahead. Niches carved into the walls on either side of the passage stretched down the corridor facing each other. "I have seen the like before," he stated. "Before the words of Mohammed the Prophet reached these lands, there were many pagan sects. These niches probably once held idols, or the dead."

Bolan paused as brass shell casings glittered in the light of his rifle. He knelt and picked one up. They were subsonic 9 mms, fired from the weapon of Musa Company the night before. He glanced around, gazing at the niches. They were certainly large enough to hold a man, and it was clear that this spot was where many of Musa Company had met their doom. Bolan dug his bayonet into the dirt floor of a niche.

Musa Company held position while Bolan worked. Makhdoom nodded. "Trapdoors?"

"None that I can find." Bolan poked at the ceiling of the niche. It was solid rock. "Let's go a little farther."

Bolan and Makhdoom led, the points of their bayonets preceding them. The corridor opened into a larger, low-ceilinged room. They paused at the entryway.

"Your men didn't mention a room."

Makhdoom kept his muzzle covering the room ahead. "No, I do not believe any of them survived this far."

Bolan caught the smell of something he didn't recognize, a bare lingering of something that was both acrid and sickly sweet. The sense of dread solidified as Musa Company entered the room.

A disk of carved stone dominated the middle of the room.

Bolan approached it warily, playing his light across it. The stone was three feet tall and nearly six feet around. It was very old. In his rifle light Bolan could see that there were fresh scratches on the top.

"It is an altar." Makhdoom ran his finger along a scratch in the rocket. "Something was moved."

"More likely removed." Bolan tested the stone with his hands. The altar probably weighed several tons. Bolan checked the floor but he could see no sign that the massive stone itself had been moved or rotated. He and Musa Company moved farther back into the dark space.

The only sound was that of their boots and the wind moaning down the corridor behind them.

Bolan pointed. "There."

In the far corner of the room was an incongruously modern object—a heavy wooden pallet. Musa Company fanned out to surround the object. The pallet was of thick construction, meant to support something heavy. Bolan knelt without touching the pallet and gazed at the dirt around it. In the harsh light of the flashlight beam he could see that the pallet had sunk several inches into the dirt floor. The pallet had recently held something heavy, and whatever the load had been, it was gone.

"I think your warheads were here, Captain, perhaps as recently as last night."

Makhdoom shook his head wearily. They were too late. "And what of my men?"

"That's a good question." Bolan considered the passageway and the single room. "If I were you, I would get a platoon of combat engineers in here and have them go over every inch of the place. I'm thinking there must be a bolt-hole."

Makhdoom broke radio silence. He spent long minutes speaking with his superiors in Islamabad, then clicked off his radio with a sigh. "Combat engineers are on the way."

Bolan frowned at the room around them. "Whoever the

enemy was had to get out of here fast, taking three warheads and disposing of nearly two dozen bodies."

"Such a graveyard would take up half of this chamber." Makhdoom shrugged helplessly. "I see no sign of digging in the floor."

Bolan gazed around the room until his eyes fell on the pallet once more. He unclipped the light from his rifle and thoroughly scanned around its edges and through the slats for wires or booby traps. Bolan lifted the pallet and pushed it back to lean against the wall.

Beneath the pallet was the same gray dirt as the rest of the chamber. Bolan's eyes narrowed as he knelt and ran his fingers through the dirt. The walls were wet. If the pallet had been here for any length of time the soil beneath it should have been moist.

"We dig here."

Makhdoom's face tightened. "Twenty-three men cannot be buried in such a space."

Bolan stared back implacably. The Pakistani captain barked out a few words and his men broke out entrenching tools and began to dig. With the first shovelful one of his men looked and spoke in rapid Sind.

The soil was loose, moist and disturbed beneath the thin veil of gray dirt. Musa Company continued to dig. They didn't have to dig long.

"Bismillah!" A corporal jumped back in fear and outrage. The corporal had encountered a head. The head was wearing a black balaclava from a night raid. The men lifted the body out and more cries of outrage met the discovery. Makhdoom's face was stone. Many of his men made the sign against the evil eye at what they had found.

The body was one of Musa Company. The body's shoulders and hips had been shattered, the arms and legs broken, the body folded up around itself like a cricket. The body took up no more space than that of a child. They all knew what lay below.

Beneath the tiny space of the pallet, a full platoon of Musa Company had been mutilated and buried.

Makhdoom swallowed as another and yet another of his men were exhumed. "Have you ever seen such a thing?"

"No. Not exactly." Bolan watched as the doll-like bodies of Makhdoom's troops were pulled from their communal grave. "But I think I know someone who has."

CHAPTER THREE

Islamabad

"The Thuggees of Kali?"

Kurtzman was incredulous.

Bolan leaned back in the rickety wooden chair. He was back in his cell, but his satellite link equipment had been returned to him. The guard with the club stood glaring at him, and a man Bolan hadn't met before stood taping everything Bolan said. "I need everything you have on them."

"There is no more Cult of Kali, last I heard. The British wiped them out in the seventeenth century."

"Didn't Phoenix Force have a run-in with them some years ago?"

"Well, yeah, they did," Kurtzman admitted. "But the guys Phoenix hit were yahoos. There were less than three hundred of them, a sideshow revival movement, and the whole thing was organized by the KGB. They were little more than Russian stooges, manipulated into killing Americans and Europeans in India. It was a real cute setup. The Russians even had a mechanical idol of Kali with a high-frequency laser built in it to keep the faithful in line. The only people they were fooling were mostly illiterate tribesmen and some well-heeled psychopaths in Bengal. Even their high priest was a fake. Once he was exposed, his own people killed him and the cult disbanded." Kurtzman sighed. "Stealing nuclear weapons from high-security areas, turning invisible and taking out entire platoons of special forces troops just wasn't in their repertoire."

"These won't be a bunch of barefoot, illiterate tribesman. This will be the real deal. True believers, highly organized, well-funded." Bolan paused. "With a new agenda."

"Striker, are you sure?"

"I'm not sure at all. But we found Musa Company's lost platoon. Their shoulders and hips were broken and folded to fit twenty-three men into a mass grave barely big enough for six, and the autopsies revealed that each one of them had been strangled, to a man, and not a drop of blood was spilled."

"Well, from what I remember about Thuggee ritual killing, that fits, but—"

"It also goes a long way toward explaining how the men of Musa Company were being jerked up into the air and flailing like marionettes."

"Okay, but by invisible attackers? Who don't show up on night-vision or high-resolution satellite imaging? And for that matter, how did they make the bodies instantly disappear?"

Bolan ate a chunk of barbecued goat and followed it with a spoonful of garlic-stewed spinach. His food had improved with his status since morning. "Bear, I'm going to let you figure that one out."

"Uh-huh." Kurtzman had seen that one coming a mile away.

"As I recall, Thuggee means 'deceiver' in Hindi."

"That's correct."

"I think someone deceived their way into the Pakistani nuclear weapons site. They had to know the layout to make their attack. Invisible or not, they had people on the inside."

"Well, assuming the bad guys aren't supernatural in origin, I'd have to agree with you." Bolan could hear Kurtzman pounding keys on his computer. "Phoenix is deployed right now, but as soon as they are inbound I'll have the boys that were involved in the India mission get in touch with you. Meanwhile I'll send you everything on the mission I have on file, though it's going to have to be redacted for security unless you can guarantee a secure line."

"Right now I can't guarantee whether or not I'm going to be shot as spy. I'm going to give you Captain Makhdoom's fax number. Send everything you can that doesn't compromise the home team or national security."

"How do you feel about this Makhdoom guy?"

"He's good people, but he's a captain. A highly decorated special forces captain, but he won't have the final say about my final disposition, and my presence here has rattled the cages of a lot of people above his pay grade."

"I understand." Kurtzman stopped multitasking for a moment. "How's the food?"

Bolan smiled as he ate another bite and washed it down with mint tea. The food was excellent. Pakistanis knew a thing or two about goat shish kebob, but Kurtzman wasn't asking about the food. He was asking if Bolan wanted him to arrange some kind of extraction. Unfortunately, Pakistan was an ostensible ally of the United States. A U.S. raid on one of their prisons could strain that slender relationship to the breaking point. Frankly, Bolan was fairly sure it was something the U.S. was unwilling to risk. Not that it wasn't something the men from Stony Man Farm wouldn't gladly risk anyway if asked. "Food's not bad. I'm not missing home yet."

"Glad to hear it. It might be hard to get a Big Mac into Islamabad at the moment."

"Don't worry about it, just fax Makhdoom the files. I'm interested to see what he thinks of them."

"I'm on it. Kurtzman out."

Bolan clicked off his link and smiled at the guard. The man with the tape recorder took back the communications gear and left without a word. The guard slammed the door shut and the soldier tossed back the last of the tea, then stretched out on his bunk. Thin white clouds passed overhead as he looked up through the grille.

Bolan took a nap and waited to see what developed.

"THE Thuggees of Kali?"

Makhdoom was appalled.

Bolan leaned back in his chair. It was nice to be in a conference room instead of a cell. "You've heard of them, I gather."

"Yes, I have heard of them. Murderers and worshipers of idols." The captain flipped through the file of information that Kurtzman had anonymously faxed him. "The information you have shared with me is fascinating, but I do not see how it is relevant. The British East India Company wiped out the Thuggees more than a century ago."

Bolan shook his head. "Not all of them."

"Granted." Makhdoom closed the file. "But your file says that the Thuggees encountered were a rather pale revivalist movement and dupes of the Russians."

"This won't be the same group. As a matter of fact, I believe whoever we're dealing with is hard-core, old-school Thuggee."

Makhdoom blinked. "Old school?"

"Originals. The real deal. Probably a splinter sect of those who were originally operating and driven underground by the British. Their tradition has been practiced unbroken for possibly thousands of years. It is now resurfacing with a new agenda."

"I see." The captain nodded.

"But I believe they will have many of the same modes of operation and we can draw a lot of clues from studying what the U.S. team encountered."

Makhdoom flipped open the file again.

Bolan's voice hardened slightly. "The theft of your warheads was an inside job."

The captain frowned. "I suspect so, also."

"Perhaps we should visit the facility," Bolan suggested.

"The place where the weapons were stolen from is a high-security area, and secret. It has already been locked down and the people who work there interrogated, vigorously." Makhdoom raised an eyebrow. "And I suspect my superiors would take a dim view of a renegade American commando examining the premises."

"They have a dim view of me now," Bolan countered. "The weapons are already gone and the facility is in high-security lockdown. What could it hurt?"

Makhdoom stared ruefully out the window. The mysterious American had saved his life. Beyond that he was making Makhdoom's life a living hell and doing nothing to help his career prospects.

But avenging his men was more important to the special forces captain than his career. "Right!" Makhdoom threw up his hands. "Let us go look for Thuggees in one of my country's top-secret weapons facilities."

"Don't you need to clear that with your superiors?"

Makhdoom sighed with infinite fatigue. "Do you really think I should tell my superiors I am going to take a renegade American spy into one of our top-secret nuclear facilities and search for invisible, idol-worshiping assassins?"

"Well, yeah, you should." Bolan shrugged. "But only afterward, and only then if we produce results."

The captain nodded. "You and I shall get along splendidly."

Al-Nouri Weapons Facility

BOLAN WATCHED footage from the facility security cameras. The film was grainy black-and-white. It wasn't particularly well focused and the video appeared to have tracking problems. Most convenience stores in the United States had security video of better quality. What the footage showed was shocking in the extreme.

The weapons facility was a small, heavily fortified building within a large Pakistani air force base, comfortably outside of Islamabad in case India launched a surgical nuclear strike against the weapons stored there. The weapons themselves were stored in hardened underground bunkers. Underground rail tunnels led out to the airfields, which allowed the weapons to be rapidly transferred to revetted Mirage III/5B supersonic fighter-bombers. If the balloon went up between the two Asian superpowers, the French-made jets would scramble across the border to devastate the Indian subcontinent.

At least, that was the plan.

The current problem with the plan was that three of those nuclear warheads had vanished.

Bolan watched the footage for the fourth time. Bored guards armed with Chinese Type 56-1 assault rifles manned the internal checkpoints. One by one they swiftly rose onto the tips of their toes, flailing, struggling and clawing at their throats. Bolan counted seconds. Each guard went limp at ten and then dropped after another thirty. It took approximately nine to ten seconds to strangle someone unconscious and an approximate total time of thirty to forty seconds of strangulation to make sure that victim never woke up again.

Supernatural or not, whoever had attacked the Al-Nouri facility had strangled each guard in their way with clocklike precision. "Autopsies would show strangulation as the cause of death."

"Indeed," Makhdoom agreed. "Except that we have no bodies."

"The guards worked in pairs at the internal checkpoints within the facility. That would imply two-man elimination teams to eliminate them at the least, and four would be better."

Makhdoom shook his head in frustration. "Where are these 'elimination teams' you speak of?" He waved an angry hand at the monitor. "Where? I see nothing!"

"They're there." Bolan pointed at the screen. "We just can't see them."

"I can accept that they attacked the video system, somehow erasing themselves from the camera footage, but you and I were out in the pass. You saw what I saw, and with your own eyes you did not see what I did not see, as well. They were not observable in night-vision equipment, nor were they observable to our naked eyes, even in the glare of a magnesium flare." Makhdoom sagged in his chair. "Explain that."

"I can't. Not yet. But the answer is right here." Bolan hit the rewind button again.

"Did any guards survive?" he went on.

"Most of the guards in the facility survived. Indeed, most were unaware that anything had happened until after the warheads and the men guarding them were discovered to be missing."

"What about the men who were monitoring the video control area?"

"Gone." The Pakistani sighed. "Presumed dead."

Bolan let out a long breath. "There's a mass grave, like the one we found in the tunnels, probably very nearby. If they were transporting the warheads, they would neither have had the time nor the manpower to drag them far."

"Yes, I suspect you are right. I will have men sweep the

outlying area." Makhdoom leaned back in his chair. "What else do you suggest?"

"You say the rest of the staff here has already been interrogated?"

"Yes. Vigorously."

Bolan nodded. "I propose we speak to them again."

CHAPTER FOUR

Islamabad

The man in the cell wasn't happy. He didn't have a skylight. No one was bringing him barbecued goat kabobs. No one looked to have brought him anything but pain. His clothes were torn and bloodstained. His face was a misshapen lump of hamburger. A pair of guards stood over the miserable man, each with a tapered, leather-bound wooden club.

The bottoms of the prisoner's feet were masses of purple bruising.

This was the twelfth such prisoner Bolan had seen. Pakistani justice, both military and civilian, was primitive, corrupt and brutal. One's best hope was to be tried under Sharia—Islamic Law. The men Bolan had seen weren't being tried. They were simply being tortured for information. Even if they knew nothing, their apparent failure at keeping the nuclear weapons in their charge secure justified their punishment in the minds of their jailers. Most had been wearing Pakistani army uniforms and had been guards at the Al-Nouri Weapons Facility. This man was dressed in civilian rags.

One of the guards looked up, saluted and shrugged at

Makhdoom. He muttered a few words in Urdu, which Bolan didn't need translated. The prisoner had been tortured extensively and he had nothing useful to say. Makhdoom let out a long breath. He clearly wasn't pleased with the torturing of the prisoners, but neither was he raising any fuss about it. He had lost half a platoon of men and the fate of his nation could depend on what was discovered.

Whatever kid gloves of civility Makhdoom normally wore as an officer and a gentleman had come off in the past twenty-four hours.

Bolan examined the prisoner critically. He sat crumpled and hunched on the stone floor between the two guards, flinching with adrenaline reaction from his most recent beating and fear whenever either of the guards moved. He sniveled as one of the guards prodded him to demonstrate what a useless prisoner he was.

Bolan happened to be wearing the uniform of a Pakistani captain of special forces. His blue eyes were hidden behind dark glasses, even though they were in an underground cell. He had the reassuring weight of a loaded Browning Hi-Power pistol holstered on his hip. Bolan nodded at Makhdoom. It sickened him, but it was the only way.

Makhdoom nodded at the guards.

The prisoner shrieked as the bastinadoes of the guards fell upon him once more like rain. The beating went on for a few moments, then Makhdoom strode into the middle of it. He seized the prisoner by his shirtfront and slammed him against the wall of the cell. Spittle flew as Makhdoom screamed first in Urdu then in Sind. The man flinched and jerked as he was threatened with everything from castration to death. Makhdoom cut off his tirade and hurled the prisoner to the floor.

Bolan took off his sunglasses and strode forward.

The prisoner stared up into Bolan's burning blue eyes and cringed in terror. The man flinched and pressed himself into the wall as Bolan crouched and cocked his hand back as if he were going to backhand him.

Bolan's back was to Makhdoom and the guards. He didn't backhand the prisoner. Instead he quickly passed his right hand down in front of his face. The prisoner's eyes flew wide. Bolan whispered one of the two phrases in Hindi he had memorized this day.

"Greetings, Ali my brother."

It was an ancient greeting, that members of the Cult of Kali had once used to identify fellow members in strange cities. The prisoner's eyes flared wide at the words. Not with fear, nor with confusion, but with recognition.

Bolan had gotten a bite. He yanked on the hook to bury it deep and reeled the man in as he used his second phrase of Hindi. "Be strong. Be ready. We will come for you."

The big American suddenly stood and yanked the prisoner up with him. He snarled a phrase in Urdu he had learned long ago during a mission in Asia, something about the prisoner enjoying relations with goats and how he particularly enjoyed allowing the goats to assume the dominant position in the relationship. The guards laughed uproariously. Bolan grabbed the prisoner by the throat and shoved him across the room. The prisoner collapsed into a heap in the corner. Bolan hated this aspect of role playing, but it was necessary.

Bolan spit on the man and fell into step with Makhdoom as they left the cell.

"You have a remarkable gift with languages," the captain acknowledged.

"Thank you. You have a beautiful language filled with poetic metaphor."

Makhdoom smiled for the first time in seventy-two hours. "And now?"

"Now? Now I think it's time that you arranged a jailbreak."

"Ah."

Bolan cocked an eyebrow. "Do you speak Hindi, by the way?"

"I am a Pakistani special forces captain." Makhdoom smiled slyly. "Infiltration was one of my specialities."

Bolan nodded. "I was hoping you'd say that."

The Prison, 4:00 a.m.

"SO WHO IS THIS GUY and what's his story?" Bolan watched the bored guard pace outside.

"Atta," Makhdoom answered. The Pakistani captain flipped through a file on his lap. "Atta Naqbi. He is a technician, recently graduated from the American University in Egypt. His family fled from East Pakistan during the 1971 war. He had no criminal record and has been working at the Al-Nouri Weapons Facility for six months."

Bolan considered the information. What was once Eastern Pakistan was now known as Bangladesh. It was about half the size of Kansas and just as flat. Only unlike Kansas, Bangladesh was cut by the mighty courses of the Ganges, the Tista and the Brahmaputra rivers. When the snows of the Himalayas melted, Bangladesh was their final destination. Flooding was endemic. When the mountains didn't flood the land, the monsoons swept the sea-level nation with tidal waves. Swiftly approaching a thousand people per square kilometer, every disaster took a horrific toll in human life. Bangladesh was an autonomous nation, but she was heavily reliant on the help of India to survive. Of much more interest to Bolan, Bangladesh was also the neighbor of the Indian state of West Bengal.

The traditional home range of the Cult of Kali.

"What city is he from?"

"Chulna, it lies upon the Pusur River, in the Great Mouths of the Ganges," Makhdoom responded. "Do you know of it?"

"I've seen the Mouths of the Ganges," Bolan responded,

"but I've never been to Chulna. It's not on my mental map." Bolan cocked his head slightly. "How many kilometers is it from Calcutta?"

The captain grinned. "Why, less than one hundred."

"Does Mr. Naqbi still have family there?"

"Most of his family reportedly came here, to Pakistan. But we have spies in Bangladesh, and in Bengal. I am having it looked into."

"Does he speak English?"

"Fluently."

Bolan pulled his black ski mask down over his head. "Let's go rescue Atta."

"Indeed." Makhdoom pulled down his own mask. "Let us go rescue Atta."

Bolan and Makhdoom got out of the battered 1950s vintage Mercedes and approached the guard at the gate. The guard snapped to attention and saluted. Makhdoom returned the salute. "Corporal?"

"Yes, Captain?"

"You are dead."

The corporal dropped to the ground, flailed and made expiring noises.

"Less melodrama, Corporal."

"Yes, Captain," the corpse whispered.

Bolan and Makhdoom swept through the prison. Guards saluted and fell down "dead" in their wake like human driftwood. The two of them swiftly came to Atta Naqbi's cell. The guard outside the door stood and turned. Bolan whipped a knotted silk sash around the guard's neck. The guard went to his knees and made throttling noises as Makhdoom threw open the door.

Naqbi sat in his cell and gaped as Bolan apparently strangled the guard to death. Makhdoom ran in and yanked him up. The man could barely walk with his swollen feet. Makhdoom and Bolan took an arm each and strung him between them as they carried him out of the cell. Despite his pain and fatigue, Naqbi began firing off questions rapidly.

He wasn't speaking Urdu or Sind.

Makhdoom shushed him. Naqbi spent the next few moments quietly staring in astonishment at the seemingly dead guards strewing the floor of the jail. They gave Naqbi no chance to examine any of the "corpses" too closely. They spirited him outside and deposited him into the waiting car.

Bolan took the wheel and drove off into the night.

The translator spoke in Bolan's earpiece. "Striker, do you read me?"

Bolan reached up and tapped his earpiece twice in acknowledgment. His satellite rig was in the back seat and he was plugged into the satellite above. There was a microphone in the back seat, as well.

The translator began translating what Naqbi and Makhdoom were saying to each other in Hindi.

Naqbi was chattering a stream of questions, and Makhdoom was playing it close. They jockeyed back and forth with questions and counterquestions. Makhdoom was playing with a deck missing many cards. There had to be call signs and recognition signals, ones that neither Bolan nor Makhdoom knew. They needed to make the man admit something. The only gambit they had was that Naqbi had spent the past forty-eight hours being starved, beaten and sleep deprived and that he wasn't quite firing on all cylinders.

Makhdoom laid all the money down and rolled the dice. "Are the weapons safe?"

"What?" Naqbi shook his head. "Only the chosen ones could know of that! How could I—"

Chosen ones. Bolan grinned under his mask.

Hook, line and sinker.

"There have been problems," Makhdoom stated. "Somehow the Americans have become involved."

"Americans?" Naqbi gaped in confusion. "Impossible! What Americans?"

Bolan pulled off his mask, locked his gaze with Naqbi's as he spoke in English. "Me."

"Oh…" Naqbi's shoulders and arms clenched in upon himself like a spider that had just been stepped on. His face went as white as a sheet. "Goddess…" He shuddered with the enormity of his betrayal. He clutched his face with his hands. "I…am doomed."

"You're in a world of hurt." Bolan's voice was as cold as the grave. "Doomed is up to you."

"Doomed…" Naqbi was swiftly sinking into a robotic stupor of terror.

Makhdoom snapped him out of it with the back of his hand. The captain suddenly glanced up at the lightening horizon. From a minaret beyond the Christian Quarter, an Imam sang forth the call to prayer. Bolan listened as the call rang out against the orange light of dawn. He had fought Muslim opponents many times, but the unearthly beauty of the call and its message had never failed to move him.

Throughout Islamabad, the believers turned westward toward Mecca and knelt in prayer. Makhdoom removed a small, rolled rug from the back seat of the Mercedes. "I must go to prayers. Then we will have breakfast." His smile was expectant and ugly as he locked his gaze with Atta Naqbi.

"Then we shall have a talk. The three of us."

Islamabad. The Christian Quarter

MAKHDOOM CONTINUED to surprise Bolan. Christians weren't popular in Pakistan. That the man had friends in the quarter was interesting. It was the last place in the world one would expect to find a Pakistani special forces captain, much less an American commando and a worshiper of the goddess of death.

"The food here is outstanding." Makhdoom stated as he deftly slid a massive chunk of lamb from his kabob. The meat steamed in the morning chill and dripped with clarified butter. The captain closed his eyes with a delight bordering on the sensual as he chewed the tender meat and swallowed it. Most people Bolan knew from the Middle East did not take big breakfasts. Makhdoom had ordered them a feast under the rising sun. He smiled at Bolan as if he had read the American's mind.

"I was sent to train with United States Special Forces in 1989." He sighed as he speared another piece of meat with his knife. "The Prophet Mohammed, all praises onto him, says a man should be moderate in his eating. But I have been to Fort Bragg, and to my ruin I have learned the joy of a hearty American breakfast."

Bolan smiled. He had been to Fort Bragg. The boys there took their breakfasts with extreme seriousness. They often didn't know how long it would be until their next one.

Makhdoom raised a dry eyebrow at Atta Naqbi over the rim of his teacup. "The menu is not to your liking?"

Naqbi said nothing as he stared down at his plate. The sauce around his cubed lamb tongue was congealing.

"Perhaps the prison gruel was more to your taste?" the captain suggested.

Naqbi's shoulders twitched, but he didn't look up or respond.

Makhdoom snarled. "Idol worshiper!"

The man jumped in his seat and stared down miserably.

"Ah, I see the problem. Since you are an idol-worshiping disciple of death, you are a vegetarian. Would you care for some vegetables?" He shoved the plate of carrots, celery and cauliflower toward Naqbi.

Makhdoom spoke conversationally. "You know, Islam is the religion of love." He drank tea reflectively. "However, there are three people my religion tells me I must despise."

The captain withdrew his pistol and set it on the table. "Worshipers of idols, worshipers of fire, and those who engage in human sacrifice. Perhaps I should deposit you back into the prison and explain to the guards you are so far two for three."

"Atta, if you go back to jail, you're dead," Bolan opined. "Then again we could just turn you loose. You have any guess what would happen to you then?"

Naqbi clutched the tabletop to stop himself from shuddering. Everyone at the table knew what would happen to him. He was damaged goods.

He had been compromised.

"There is a third option." Bolan freshened Atta's tea, as part of his "good cop" role.

Naqbi glanced up for the first time.

"You cooperate. You help us. You produce results, and we cut you loose. With money, a new identity, and we drop you any place you'd like. Bora Bora, Argentina, South Africa, the North Pole, you name it."

Naqbi glanced at Bolan and actually met his eyes. The soldier didn't like what he saw there. He saw the absolute ruin of despair. "You think you can protect me from a god?"

Makhdoom straightened in religious outrage.

"Do you think you can protect yourselves?" Naqbi's shoulders rose and fell. "Kali will take us. She will take us all. We are all dead men." His head shook back and forth in a slow-motion movement of helpless horror. "She shall have our flesh, she shall have our blood, she shall have our souls."

"Speak not of demons!" Makhdoom snarled. "Only tell us where we can find their worshipers and the weapons they stole!"

"Kali is not a demon." Naqbi no longer looked at Bolan or Makhdoom. He was staring off into the middle distance, into his own personal vision of hell and horror, and he spoke more to himself than anyone at the table. "She is the slayer of demons. When demons ruled Heaven and Earth, and all the gods and all the angels could not stand before them, they summoned Kali. All powerful, all conquering, goddess of the destruction…"

Naqbi received the back of Makhdoom's hand. "There is no God but Allah, and Mohammed is his Prophet!"

"Goddess of the burning ground." The young technician was unmoved. The world around him ceased to exist. Bolan had seen such expressions before in the faces of religious fanatics in crisis. Naqbi was zombifying himself into his own little insular hell of despair. Given a few more hours, he would lapse into catatonic depression.

Bolan couldn't afford to let that happen. "What about your family, Atta?"

"My family." He glanced up with fear sharpened eyes.

"Maybe we can't stop a god—" Bolan shrugged meditatively "—but we can stop her followers from killing your family."

"I…"

"You have to make a choice."

Naqbi's eyes flicked about in mounting panic. Bolan nodded to himself. Panic in an intelligence asset was good. Turning into a stalk of broccoli wasn't.

"That's air in your lungs, Atta. That's food on your plate. Life is good. It's worth living. It's worth fighting for, even in the darkest moment. Your family is worth fighting for. But if you want to fight for them, you're going to have to help us. You can give up on yourself, that's your choice, but you have another decision to make."

Atta Naqbi looked as though he might throw up.

Bolan's burning blue eyes held Naqbi's implacably. "Do you want us to try to help your family?"

Naqbi vomited.

Bolan nodded at Makhdoom. "I'm going to take that as a yes."

CHAPTER FIVE

Rawalpindi, Pakistan

"This was the place of worship."

Bolan kept his eyes on Naqbi for a moment. The young technician was looking green around the gills and his hands were shaking. Once more terror ruled his darting gaze. Bolan noted the man's fear and was duly satisfied. He was terrified, and of more than just receiving a bullet through his brain from Bolan's gun. The soldier frowned as he scanned the surroundings for the hundredth time. The problem was that the enemy had to know that Naqbi had been incarcerated. If they observed even the most basic of security protocols, they would have to assume that the man had been compromised.

The city of Rawalpindi was less than twenty kilometers from Islamabad and a light industry center. Naqbi's place of worship appeared to be nothing more than a warehouse in the textile section of town. Makhdoom cradled a Russian-made Bison submachine gun and peered down the alley. "What do you think?"

"I don't like it." Bolan, too, held one of the Russian weapons. The stock had been removed for concealment and a laser sight had been slaved to the barrel. Both were modifications that Bolan didn't particularly care for. It was a cowboy gun, suitable for little more than slaughtering the unsuspecting in phone booths. But beggars couldn't be choosers. Operating while still technically under arrest presented unique logistical problems, and he would have to make do with what he was issued. Makhdoom was also operating on his own. He was fairly certain that some of his superiors had been compromised. Bolan was of the same opinion. Makhdoom had liberated the weapons, not requisitioned them, and no one except Kurtzman knew exactly where they were at the moment. The two of them were operating without a net. There would be no backup if things went south. Bolan hefted his weapon. The 64-round helical drum magazine, however, was comforting. Bolan turned to Naqbi. "How many guards?"

"Normally only a man or two at the door." He shrugged nervously. "Perhaps a lookout up on the roof."

Bolan held Naqbi's eyes and was half satisfied. The young technician was telling the truth, as far as he knew, but Bolan suspected there would be one hell of a lot more to security than a couple of bouncers at the door and some guy smoking cigarettes up in the shingles. There was still the matter of invisible killers who could wipe out a platoon of special forces troops without being seen or leaving a drop of blood in their wake.

That was weighing heavily on Bolan's mind.

It was weighing on Makhdoom's, as well. "So, we go in?"

"It's what we came here for. Leave the engine running." Bolan slid out of the car and kept his Bison beneath his drab overcoat. He spoke into his throat mike. "Bear, we are going in."

"Roger that, Striker," Kurtzman acknowledged. "You be careful in there."

"You!" Makhdoom jabbed Naqbi with the muzzle of his weapon. "Come!"

The cultist's shoulders slumped in despair as he slid out of the car. The three of them walked down the alley. Pigeons cooed in the eaves. The alley was empty and the sky above the close-set buildings cobalt-blue. The three warehouses faced one another, turning the alley into a cul de sac. No bouncers stood on the steps below the sheet-metal door. No lookout stood upon the roof. Bolan crossed the street and tried the door. "It's locked."

Makhdoom shot a glance up and down the street. "How do you want to play—"

Bolan's weapon stuttered in his hands as he put a burst into the lock. Naqbi nearly jumped out of his shoes. Sparks shrieked off the ancient metal and Bolan's boot sent the sprung door flying back on its hinges.

"Very well." Makhdoom nodded. "The direct approach, then."

Bolan strode into the murky interior of the warehouse. Dim light filtered downward in hazy beams through the filthy sky-lights high above. "You smell that?" the Executioner asked.

"Sandalwood." Makhdoom snuffed at the close air. "And *nag champa*."

The air was thick with the cloying, sweet scent of devotional incense. "Not the usual smell of a textile warehouse."

"No."

Naqbi's hand trembled as he pointed across the cavernous space. "The altar was there, and the idol behind it."

Bolan took out a flashlight and panned the beam at the far wall. The floor showed fresh scrapes where something very heavy had recently been dragged across the concrete. Other than that, the warehouse was as empty as the cavern above the pass. The lingering sweetness in the air was the only clue they had left. "There's a truck dock in back?"

"Indeed." Makhdoom shone his light around the room. "I am currently running a check on the building. This ware-house and the two next to it are owned by a reputable Pakistani cotton merchant. However, a year ago, he rented this space to another company. They are proving much harder to track down."

Owning all three warehouses on the block would give the enemy a nice quite zone of control where they could do whatever they wanted. It was also a fine tactical setup for an ambush. "The company will be a cutout." Bolan glanced around the room again. "They'll be some kind of—"

Bolan froze at the sound of a scraping noise. He and Makhdoom swung their flashlights around the room, but there was nothing to see but bare corrugated walls and the concrete floor. Bolan had known it was a trap, and expected it, but the unknown was an opponent as ugly as they came. An unbidden chill ran down Bolan's spine as the unseen came for them. Naqbi let out a whimper. Makhdoom clicked on the laser sight of his weapon. "Ready?"

Bolan reached into the pocket of his overcoat. He had reviewed the battle a thousand times in his mind.

And he had formulated a plan. "Now!"

It was time to see how the goddess of death enjoyed something a little stronger than the smell of incense. Bolan and Makhdoom ripped the pins from the CS tear-gas canisters and flung them to the floor. The riot grenades burst apart as they hit and the multiple skip-chaser bomblets skidded across the concrete hissing and spewing thick white smoke. Bolan and Makhdoom pulled their gas masks from under their coats and yanked them over their faces. Naqbi let out a shriek that was instantly choked off as he inhaled the riot gas.

Bolan shouted through his mask as the gas bloomed around them. "Back to back!"

"Striker!" Kurtzman's voice rose in urgency. "What is your situation?"

"Bear, I need absolute quiet!"

Makhdoom turned and he and Bolan covered each other

while Naqbi collapsed weeping and coughing between them. Bolan flicked on his laser and panned it across his section of the building. Once again he found himself searching for the enemies he couldn't see.

Makhdoom's snarl was muffled by his mask. "I see nothing!"

Neither could Bolan, but he knew the enemy was here. He listened for another rustle or scrape or any sound of movement. He particularly listened for the hacking or coughing of an enemy.

Naqbi screamed as Bolan cut loose with his weapon. The weapon shuddered in his hands as he ripped off a 20-round burst in a sweeping arc in front of him. The bullets punched holes in the corrugated sheet metal of the walls and rays of sunlight shone in bright shafts through the thickening gas. Behind him Makhdoom fired off a similar burst. When Naqbi wasn't hacking and coughing, he was screaming.

"Doom!" Bolan desperately tracked for targets. "Shut him up!"

Makhdoom cut off the hysterics by driving his boot into Naqbi's ribs.

Bolan stared into the gas. There was nothing he could see, but it was something suddenly missing that caught his eye. The shafts of sunlight came through the bullet holes in the walls and crisscrossed the room like lances of light. It could have been a trick of the conditions, but for a moment there seemed to be a shaft of light that stopped, disappeared and then resumed its course two feet away.

Bolan held his trigger down on full-auto. Flames stuttered from the muzzle of his weapon, spitting bullets in line with the laser sweeping the section of gas. The lines of sunlight broke and resumed diagonally toward the ground.

It was as if the invisible man had fallen.

Bolan tracked his weapon, spewing bullets through the projected path. Makhdoom's weapon continued to chatter in short, searching bursts. Naqbi's screaming and choking was suddenly cut off.

Bolan whirled.

The cultist was clutching at his throat and walk-flopping backward in a remarkable fashion across the warehouse. Bolan whipped his laser between Naqbi's flailing legs and fired off a burst. He suddenly collapsed backward as whatever was holding him up failed.

"Doom!" Bolan shouted. The attack on Naqbi had been bait and Bolan had taken it. "Look out—"

The unseen reached out and seized Bolan by the throat. His carotid arteries were instantly cut off and a hard lump crushed into his larynx. Only Bolan's body armor kept the massive blow he took to his kidneys from buckling him. Sick weakness washed through Bolan's arms and legs as he was dragged backward. His arteries and air pipe were relentlessly constricted as he was choked and strangled at the same time. Bolan watched helplessly as Makhdoom's back arched like a bow and the Pakistani's weapon fell from his hands as he clawed at his throat. Every instinct in Bolan's body screamed at him to fight the horrible grip on his throat as it bent him backward.

Instead Bolan let every ounce of his 200-plus pounds go limp. He hung himself as he dropped into the garrote. Something bumped into his back and a thick veil seemed to enfold him. Bolan's vision narrowed to blackness as he flipped the muzzle of his Bison submachine gun over his shoulder and burned his magazine dry behind him.

The grip on his throat weakened and Bolan ripped at his throat as he heaved himself forward. He dropped his empty weapon and his knife rang from the sheath on his belt. Fabric bunched beneath Bolan's hand and parted beneath his blade. Bolan sucked breath through the smothering filters of his mask. He couldn't quite get enough to fill his lungs, but his vision cleared.

In his fist Bolan held a thick gray piece of dully glittering fabric.

Makhdoom's knees buckled as his body began to fail him. Bolan lunged up and threw himself like an NFL linebacker at the empty space above Makhdoom's head. His bones jarred as he slammed into what he couldn't see. Bolan's vision skewed as he felt something veil him. Whatever it was couldn't stop the reinforced point of his combat knife. The blade punched into something solid and Bolan's lips skinned back from his teeth as he recognized the feel of steel grating on ribs. He smelled human sweat and beneath it the sudden stink of pain and fear. Bolan rammed the blade home and ripped it back out, stabbing three more times rapidly. He heard the groan of a wounded man. Bolan raised his knife for the kill.

His vision exploded into blackness lit with pulsing purple pin-pricks of light as something struck him in the back of the head.

Bolan rolled with the blow. His vision was tilting crazily, but his battle instincts had been hard won in conflicts on every continent on the planet. He rolled up to one knee and his hand found Makhdoom's weapon at his feet. He scooped up the automatic and sprayed lead in an arc in front of him. His vision darkened and he nearly buckled as he stood. Bolan shook his head to clear it and took several tottering steps backward. He was rewarded as he bumped against corrugated steel wall.

The warehouse wall had Bolan's back. His eyes glared out of the lenses of his mask as he swept his muzzle, looking for any sign of the enemy. Makhdoom was a few feet away. His hands were at his throat and his chest was heaving, trying to suck air past his mask and down his traumatized throat, but he was alive. Naqbi lay unmoving a few yards away. His eyes were rolled back in his head and his blackened tongue lolled out of his mouth.

Sunlight was pouring in from the back of the warehouse. The back door had been opened. Bolan fired a burst out the door and whipped his muzzle back to cover the rest of the room. The enemy had extracted. Bolan scanned the room again. He didn't believe the enemy had brought gas masks. Anyone in the room would now be weeping and choking. Bolan made a fist around the piece of fabric in his left hand.

Even if they were thickly veiled by something, they would be affected by the gas by now.

"Doom!" Bolan shouted. "Can you hear me?"

The Pakistani captain pushed himself up painfully. His choking and gagging was plain to hear, but his masked head nodded. He crawled across the floor a few feet and scooped up Bolan's weapon. He unhooked the spent drum and slid in a fresh one from under his jacket. He also picked up Bolan's fallen knife. The soldier covered Makhdoom as he tottered over and sagged against the wall. The two men kept their weapons aimed into the billowing gas.

"Atta—" Makhdoom's voice was a rasp "—appears to be dead."

"Yeah," Bolan wheezed.

"But we have learned something."

"Oh?"

"Yes." Makhdoom nodded. "Our enemies are not *djinn*."

Bolan managed a wry smile beneath his mask. "You're sure about that?"

"Yes." He held up Bolan's knife. The shallow curve of the Japanese-style fighting knife was stained to the hilt. The Pakistani's red eyes glittered beneath his mask. "*Djinns* do not bleed."

CHAPTER SIX

Islamabad

"You gave him a gun!" General Iskander Hussain's voice rose into a scream. He may have been named after Alexander the Great, but the incredibly short, fat, little man in front of Bolan and Makhdoom didn't meet the mark. When he stood up from his desk, he hardly seemed to have stood at all. He was capable of expanding in the horizontal plane. Hussain seemed to literally inflate with rage. Bolan thought he might burst the seams of his uniform, if he didn't burst a blood vessel first. He screamed in English for Bolan's benefit.

Makhdoom stood at ramrod-stiff attention. "Yes, General!"

"You took him to the Al-Nouri weapons site! You took him along on an unauthorized raid into Rawalpindi! You equipped him with automatic weapons and unauthorized war gas! An American saboteur and a spy!"

"A Pakistani ally, involved in a sensitive operation of mutual concern—"

"You gave him a gun!" Hussain's rage went apoplectic. "Did it not occur to you he could escape! Idiot!"

"Indeed, General, I did give him weapons. It was he who

generated the leads we have found so far. The act of arming him saved my life and the lives of my men. I do not regret—"

Spittle flew as General Hussain lost his English and began screaming so rapidly Bolan could no longer tell whether he was shrieking in Urdu or Sind.

Makhdoom clearly could understand. He stood like a rock but his cheek muscles flexed with tension as he was dressed down in ever-increasingly personal and inflammatory detail. The general gasped and stopped in midscream. He had to lean over and put both of his hands on his desk as he caught his breath from his outburst. He lifted his right hand after a moment and pointed an accusing finger at Bolan. "And you! You are—"

"Privileged to work with the officers under your command on a matter of mutual concern to my nation and our trusted friend, the Sovereign Republic of Pakistan," Bolan finished.

Hussain blinked and then began to open his mouth.

Bolan beat him to the punch. "Is it the general's pleasure to receive our report?"

"No! I do not wish to hear your bloody…" The general suddenly caught himself. "Yes! It is my pleasure to receive your report! Immediately!"

The general slammed his fat frame back down into his chair and glared at them in as menacing a fashion as he could muster. "I await! I am very interested! You have my undivided attention!"

Bolan swiftly sketched out the events in the Haji Pir Pass and everything that had happened subsequently at the Al-Nouri facility and then in Rawalpindi. He left nothing out other than his conversation with Kurtzman and exactly under what auspices of the United States government he was working for. Hussain's facial expression slowly went from rage, to confusion, to disbelief to just a blank stare as Bolan finished. Hussain gazed off into space a moment, blinked, then turned his gaze to Makhdoom. The general's head cocked slightly like a dog that has heard a noise it doesn't understand. "Captain Makhdoom, do you agree with the facts of this report?"

"I do, General," Makhdoom concurred. "All he says, I have seen with my own eyes and experienced personally."

Hussain's voice went flat. "You are saying our strategic nuclear weapons have been stolen by Hindu death worshipers who can turn themselves invisible?"

Makhdoom nodded once. "That is our current and best theory."

"I do not believe I can have you shot for being insane, Captain, but given your other offenses—"

"General," Bolan interrupted, "you have seen the videotape of the activity in the Al-Nouri facility when the weapons were stolen?"

"Of course." Hussain shook his head. "But—"

"Other than *djinns*, General, how would you account for the disappearance of the weapons?"

"The videotape could have been doctored," Hussain blustered, "or somehow overcome."

"We also considered that possibility. However, in light of what happened in Rawalpindi we have reassessed the situation. We have come to grips with the enemy, and I assure you that we are dealing with far more than a doctored videotape. You also heard the radio transmissions from Musa Company during the battle in the pass?"

"You were attacked by invisible Hindu stranglers?" It was more than Hussain could deal with. "This is what you truly wish me to believe?"

Bolan pulled down the collar of his shirt and exposed the purple bruising mottling his throat. "Yes."

Makhdoom pulled down his own collar. "The traitor, Atta Naqbi, is in the morgue. He bears similar marks, only he did not survive them."

"Assuming I were to buy into this fantasy of yours, Captain, tell me why? Why would Hindu idol-worshipers do such a thing?"

"Why do idol-worshipers do anything?" Makhdoom shrugged. "Except to please their heathen gods."

Bolan had a number of acquaintances around the world who worshiped idols, but he kept that to himself. "They have some sort of agenda, General. That is clear. They are also clearly well organized, funded and must have clandestine contacts high up within the Pakistani military."

Hussain began to purple again with outrage.

Bolan cut off the general before he could detonate. "For that reason, Captain Makhdoom suggested that you were one of the few members of General Staff who can be trusted. He informs me that your service record and your loyalty to your country are unimpeachable."

General Hussain ceased changing colors and relaxed back in his chair slightly.

This was an outright lie. Somehow, Hussain's spies within the military had found out about Bolan's and Makhdoom's activities, and he had sent his own bodyguards to summon them to his offices. However, Bolan had decided to give Hussain a full report for the simple reason that the general was such a blustering egomaniac that whoever the enemy was, they would clearly not trust his involvement in stealing nuclear weapons.

Hussain made his first intelligent remark of the day. "Do you realize how insane this sounds?"

"I wouldn't believe it myself, General, had I not seen and experienced what I had under Captain Makhdoom's command."

"This is all most unusual. I must admit I—"

"General, this is my suggestion. This conversation does not leave this room. Captain Makhdoom and I will coordinate our investigation through your offices. I will put you in contact with my superiors in the United States. If, indeed, members of the Pakistani High Command have been compromised, we must be able to present incontrovertible evidence to back up our accusations. When we have the proof we need, and the location of the stolen weapons, you will present the evidence to Military Command and the president."

Hussain blinked at Bolan.

Makhdoom looked at Bolan as if he were insane.

"I…yes." Hussain's brows furrowed. "This is a matter of utmost security. The traitors must be ferreted out. Our stolen weapons must be located. We cannot afford incompetence. This effort shall be coordinated out of my offices and under my direct command."

Makhdoom tried to keep the horror out of his voice. "General, I would like to assemble a picked team of men who I can—"

"No!" Hussain cut him off with a wave of his hand. "Nuclear weapons have been stolen, and it was clearly an inside job. Our enemy is unseen and has unknown contacts." Hussain began reciting back Bolan's report as if it were made up of his own experiences and opinions. He nodded to himself. "If we have traitors, they may well be members of the special forces."

Makhdoom blanched but said nothing.

"No, no members of Musa Company or the other special units. They often travel afar and who knows how they may have been corrupted."

It was Makhdoom's turn to start purpling.

Hussain was oblivious to Makhdoom's outrage. "My service record and loyalty are unimpeachable. I choose my own men for the same reason. I will assemble you a team from among the most trusted men in my personal bodyguard."

Makhdoom looked as though he wanted to shoot himself, if he didn't shoot Bolan and General Hussain first.

"The contents of this meeting do not leave my office. Do not report back to your headquarters, Captain. Go home. The American will be under your supervision and will be your responsibility at all times. Report none of this to your superiors in special operations. I will contact you in the morning and we will begin our investigation properly."

Hussain leaned back and steepled his fingers in deep thought. "You are dismissed."

"YOU ARE INSANE! Do you know that?"

Bolan shrugged. Makhdoom had maintained a granite silence in the car ride all the way back to his house. He had stiffly asked his wife to make tea and bring refreshments. He had sat like a statue and watched Bolan drink a cup of tea and eat a piece of cake. Makhdoom had observed the laws of hospitality.

Then he had exploded.

"You are an idiot!"

Makhdoom's wife, Zarah, was a lovely woman, and she looked on in horror as her husband screamed in rage at their guest.

"You turned our mission over to a man like Hussain?" The captain's knuckles whitened as his hands clenched into fists. "Hussain is a cabbage! No! He is less than a cabbage! At least a cabbage can be boiled and eaten!"

He shook his fists at the ceiling. "Of what possible use is Hussain!"

Bolan was getting the impression that Makhdoom had had one or two run-ins with the general in the past.

Makhdoom's roar shook the rafters. "Yet you have put us under his fist! Do you realize what you have done?"

"I do. What do you believe Hussain would have done had we not cooperated with him?"

Makhdoom spent several long moments collecting himself, then a few more considering the question. His hands fell to his sides as his reason overcame his indignation. "At the very least, Hussain would have raised bloody hell with my superiors over my conduct. Our investigation would have been blown wide open. For having taken you, an American, into the Al-Nouri facility, I could have been stripped of my rank. Regardless of the fate of my career, you would have probably ended up being thrown out of the country, though first you would have been extensively tortured. It is not outside the realm of possibility that you could be shot as a spy. Hussain is a toad, but he walks the corridors of power and he has the ear of the president. Though all he ever whispers into it is the word yes, if I am not mistaken."

Bolan nodded. "That was my take on the situation. I decided it would be better to stroke the man rather than buck him. I apologize if I acted out of turn or superceded your authority. It was a choice that had to be made on the split second, and I stand by my decision."

"Your actions were correct." Makhdoom sank down heavily into his chair and picked up his cup of tea. "I do not like them, and I fear their consequences, but at the time, they were correct. I do not begrudge them."

Two young men in their early teens appeared in the doorway of the living room. They were dark complected like their father but had the light brown eyes of their mother.

"Ah." The captain visibly brightened. "My sons. Muhjid, Kaukab, come and greet our guest."

The two young men entered and stared at Bolan wonderingly. Americans were a source of great debate among the Pakistani people. Most considered them godless, an enemy of Islam and unforgivable allies of the Israeli occupiers of the Holy Land. They were also supposed to be perverted, fabulously wealthy and famous. The two young men were somewhat cosmopolitan because their father had trained in the United States and he told very interesting stories about his experiences. They had also listened to their father roar at the stranger for ten minutes, telling him what an idiot he was.

The two young men nodded formally. "Greetings. Welcome to our home."

"Thank you." Bolan nodded to Makhdoom. "Fine young men you've raised."

Makhdoom puffed up happily. Zarah beamed. Makhdoom waved them away. "You may go. My guest and I have much to discuss."

The two young men ran off and Zarah disappeared back into the house.

"Nice family you have."

"Thank you."

"Get them the hell out of here."

Makhdoom glanced up from his tea. "You think they'll come here."

It was a statement, not a question.

"I would. We've gotten closer than anyone has to them. We bloodied them. They don't know who I am, but we have to assume they know you. They know we're after them." Bolan held up the strange, dully gleaming piece of fabric. "They'll want this back. They're coming. Sooner rather later."

"Muhjid! Kaukab!"

The two young men came skidding into the room at their father's call. Makhdoom pulled a large wad of notes from his wallet. "Take this money. Take the shotgun. Take the car. Take your mother out of the city."

The two boys' eyes widened.

"Do not dally! Evil men are coming. Take care of your mother. Go!"

Muhjid ran to the mantel and took a double-barreled shotgun off the rack and then a box of shells from the chest beneath it. Kaukab ran to find his mother.

Makhdoom rose. "My friend, I want you on the opposite

roof. I will give you binoculars and a rifle. When they come, I will be inside and act as bait. When—"

Zarah ran into the room. "There is a car out on the street."

"What kind of car?"

"A black one." She glanced fearfully from Makhdoom to his guest. "It is full of men."

Makhdoom picked up the phone. He clicked the old-fashioned receiver twice and grimaced. Most of Pakistan still used phone lines rather than cell phones. The phone line to the house had been cut. He turned to his boys. "My sons. Take your mother upstairs. Kill anyone either than myself or the American should they attempt to come up."

Muhjid and Kaukab went wide-eyed, but they hesitated only for a second. They took the shotgun and their mother and ran upstairs.

Bolan polished off his tea and rose. "We need guns."

General Hussain's men had demanded they surrender their submachine guns and had not seen fit to give them back.

"Follow me." Makhdoom strode down the hall and entered his study. Maps of the world covered the walls that weren't dominated by bookcases. In one corner was a small desk with a computer.

Opposite the desk was a gun cabinet.

He opened the twin glass panels and pulled out a pair of rifles. They were Lee-Enfield bolt-action rifles of WWII vintage. Sporting stocks had replaced the full wood furniture stressed for bayonet fighting. The barrels had been shortened to twenty-two inches and telescopic sights had been fitted. The old battle rifles had been customized for hunting, but both would still hold ten rounds of the powerful British .303 military ammunition.

Makhdoom checked the loads in both rifles and then tossed one of the weapons to Bolan. He removed a box of shells and dumped half of the cartridges into Bolan's hand, then thrust the rest in his pocket.

They had twenty shots each.

"They're not coming invisibly this time."

"No, not during the initial assault." Bolan flipped on the safety of his weapon. "But they may come sneaking up during it."

Something struck the front door a tremendous blow. The house shook and wood creaked and splintered. Bolan flicked the safety off of his weapon. "Here they come."

A heavy piece of pipe rammed the door off of its hinges.

"Here they go," the captain snarled. They walked to the end of the hall and pointed their rifles across the living room into the foyer. The iron battering ram crushed tile as it was dropped onto the floor and men in long coats waving short automatic weapons spilled into the captain's home.

The two hunting rifles thundered as one. The first man in shuddered and sagged as Makhdoom's .303 rifle bullet smashed in his chest. The second man's head erupted like a melon as it failed to absorb the 2200 footpounds of muzzle energy Bolan delivered into it with the precision of a trained sniper. He flicked the bolt of his rifle and chambered a fresh round. The men in the doorway were screaming in a language Bolan didn't recognize.

A line of bullets pocked up the wall beside the Executioner as the invaders behind fired their weapons blindly into the house.

"Amateurs," Makhdoom growled.

"They'll be coming through the back, as well."

The captain nodded. "Go kill them. I will stay here and prevent the ones in front from coming in."

Bolan strode down the hall toward the back of the house. He swept into the kitchen as a man crawled through the shattered window. He perched precariously on the sink, trying not to cut himself on broken shards of glass still in the window frame.

He had a single split second of wide-eyed horror before

Bolan blew him back through the window with a bullet through his sternum. The big American flicked his bolt open as the back door to the kitchen smashed inward and charged into the invaders. The throat of the first man in was torn away as Bolan shot him point-blank. There was no time to work the bolt of the ancient weapon for a second shot, but the dying killer had sagged into his companions and clogged the doorway. Bolan swung the butt of his rifle in a brutal arc and shattered the jaw of the second man. The third desperately tried to shove his machine pistol past his broken comrades.

Bolan lunged and rammed his rifle forward in a bayonet thrust.

No blade was mounted on the end of Bolan's rifle, but the steel muzzle and the front sight of his rifle rammed up through the assassin's teeth and crushed his upper palate. A muffled mewl of agony bubbled through the shattered remains of the man's mouth. The assassin's agony was cut short as Bolan whipped the butt of his rifle around and brought it into the killer's temple with bone-cracking force.

The soldier racked the bolt of his rifle and stepped over the men he had taken out of play.

Makhdoom's house was very typical of the Middle East and East Asia. The front of the house was a nearly blank wall except for a door and very narrow upstairs windows. Beyond the interior living space was a walled courtyard in back.

A man sat straddling the wall shouting into a cell phone and waving a machine gun.

"Igor! Igor!" the man shouted.

Bolan raised an eyebrow.

Igor.

That wasn't a typical Pakistani name. Bolan sighted and shot the man through the leg he had thrown over the wall. The assassin howled, clutched his shattered thigh and toppled forward into a rosebush.

Upstairs a shotgun boomed.

The fallen assassin was thrashing and howling in the rose thorns. Bolan shot him through the other leg. The man screamed as Bolan slung his rifle and picked up a pair of the fallen weapons of the men clogging the kitchen doorway. The weapons were Kiparis submachine guns. Bolan flicked their selectors to full auto. The man thrashing along the garden wall looked up and screamed as Bolan charged him with a weapon in either hand.

The man shrieked as the soldier vaulted him. Bolan dropped the commandeered weapons on their slings and caught the wall as he leaped. He swung his leg over the top and dropped to the street below.

Bolan ran down the back alley and rounded the corner of Makhdoom's house. A black Landrover was parked on the street with a man waiting behind the wheel. In one hand he held a cell phone into which he was talking rapidly. The other held a silenced handgun. He was craned around in his seat, and his attention was fixed on the front door of Makhdoom's residence and the pitched gun battle going on there. He caught sight of Bolan in the corner of his eye and whipped back around.

Bolan raised both machine pistols and held down his triggers. The windshield of the Landrover went opaque with bullets and then splashed red from the arterial spray within. Three men were in the doorway of Doom's house. A fourth lay dead on the stoop. They were spraying their weapons like firehoses into the house. Bolan raised his left-hand weapon and burned the rest of his magazine into the back of the rearmost assassin. Bolan dropped the spent machine pistol and raised the weapon in his right hand. One of the remaining killers spun, and Bolan walked a burst up from his belt buckle to his brain.

The fourth man leaped into the house as Bolan tracked his

weapon on him. Makhdoom's rifle thundered within, and the man staggered backward out the door again clutching his chest. Doom's weapon boomed a second time and the killer was smashed off his feet and sprawled in the gutter.

Bolan scanned the street and the rooftops opposite Makhdoom's house. People were shouting and screaming in the neighboring houses. But nothing appeared to be moving on the street.

It was what Bolan could not see that made him wary.

Bolan approached the Captain's door obliquely. "Doom!"

"I hear you!"

"You all right?"

"I am!" shouted back the Captain. "You?"

"The street is clear! I'm coming in the front door!"

"Come ahead!"

Bolan stepped across half a dozen dead bodies as he entered the house and entered the living room. The interior of the house was littered with corpses. Most had one or two high-powered rifle bullet wounds in their chests. One lay spread-eagled further in by the foot of the stairs. A shotgun blast had left his head and shoulders in ruins.

"Everyone all right?"

Makhdoom came out from the hallway. "Kaukab!"

The young man's voice came from the top of the stairs. "We are all right, father!"

"Stay where you are! Do not move from your post until I tell you!"

"Yes, father!"

Makhdoom stared around his bullet-riddled home. "Do you think the unseen ones come?"

Bolan looked around the living room. His eyes fell upon the low table where he had set his teacup. It was also where he had left the length of strange fabric he had cut from his own throat in the warehouse in Rawalpindi.

The fabric was gone.

"They were here, and they've left. They took what they came for."

Makhdoom straightened in shock. "The fabric! You left it out where they could find it!"

"I did." Bolan nodded. He reached into his pocket and pulled out a three-inch length he had cut from it. "But not all of it."

"But did they not also come for our lives?"

"That was what the muscle was for. I remember reading in the intelligence report on the Thugs that their religion forbids them to shed blood except in certain ritual circumstances. The goons were for us. But the Thuggees came for the evidence.

Makhdoom's smile turned feral. "So, they think they have what they came for."

"Yeah, and I need to get this to my people in the United States ASAP, and without General Hussain knowing about it."

"That I can arrange." Makhdoom glanced around again. The corpses piled around his house were just that, corpses. "But it appears we are without leads once more."

Mujhid's voice shouted excitedly from upstairs. "Father! There is a man! Thrashing about in mother's roses!"

"You saved one," smiled Doom.

"I figured we'd give him to Hussain." Bolan shrugged. "We have to let the General do something."

CHAPTER SEVEN

General Fareed's office

"I understand there was an altercation in your home, Captain."

"Yes, General." Makhdoom nodded. "But it was prosecuted to a fruitful conclusion."

"Yes, very well and good, and congratulations on taking a prisoner." The General smiled unpleasantly. Along with performing the function as military yes-man for whoever might be occupying the presidency of Pakistan, Hussain was also firmly entrenched in the highest echelons of Pakistani secret police. The prisoner's two shattered thighs had probably been the least of his discomforts during the night. Hussain's smile went smug as he regarded Bolan. "Our guest was correct. The weapons used on the attack on your residence were Kiparis OTS-02 submachine guns." Hussain paused dramatically. "Of Kazakstani origin."

Bolan met Hussain's smile. "And your prisoner?"

Hussain glowed with self-satisfaction. "He is of Kazakstani origin as well, as were most of the confederates, as far as we can tell. His name is Yusef Zagari, a gangster involved trafficking heroin from the poppy fields in Afghanistan and Pakistan that flow into the former Soviet Republics and Russia."

Bolan nodded. "He's muscle."

"Yes." Hussain savored the English slang. "Yusef is drug muscle. It is my belief he and his men are mercenaries, hired by our enemies."

General Hussain had a firm grasp of the obvious, but Bolan kept that to himself. "Excellent."

"There is more. We have learned of Yusef's contacts here in Pakistan, as well as their lair near the border." Hussain smiled again. "But first, I feel somewhat remiss about the incident that occurred in your home, Captain."

Makhdoom stared. It was the closest thing to an admission of error out of General Hussain in ten years of interservice conflict. Doom shook his head diplomatically. "It is nothing, General. Who could have known the enemy would strike so swiftly?"

"Nonetheless, we must be prepared for any eventuality." The General spoke with utmost seriousness. "Let me assure you that you shall not be caught outnumbered nor unprepared again." Hussain knocked on the top of his desk twice and gestured behind them. "Behold, your men."

The door to the General's office opened, and Pakistani men in plain clothes began filing into the room.

Bolan suppressed a smile. General Iskander Hussain may have picked his bodyguards for their loyalty and unimpeachable records, but it appeared the General also picked his bodyguards on the basis of body mass. Not one of the twelve men jamming themselves into the room was less than six feet tall or running less than two hundred and fifty pounds.

They were a brute squad. Pure and simple.

Hussain lifted a hand toward their leader. "This is Captain Ghulam Fareed. My most trusted man. You shall find him invaluable, as I have."

Ghulam was six foot five and tipping the three hundred-pound mark. His eyebrows met over the bridge of his nose forming a single coal black wing that dominated his Neanderthal brow. Startling green eyes peered out from the shadow beneath it. He measured Makhdoom and saluted sharply. The Captain's stars, jump wings and Special Forces badges he wore demanded respect even out of a pampered General's head goon.

Captain Ghulam Fareed regarded Bolan with open suspicion.

Bolan smiled. "Do any of them speak English?"

Hussain blinked. He hadn't thought of that.

"I speak English," rumbled Fareed. "So do Hossam, Farrukh, Iqbal and Asad."

Hussain nodded benevolently at his Captain and gestured at Bolan and Doom. "This is Captain Makhdoom. He is in command of this mission. You will follow his orders explicitly. You are authorized to requisition any weapons or equipment the Captain deems necessary. This is our American guest. You will render onto him any assistance he requires."

"Yes, General."

Hussain's smile widened. "And you will report all actions taken directly to me.

"Yes, General."

"Captain, I have also stationed some of my men in your home. Your family and residence will be guarded at all times."

"Thank you, General."

Bolan kept his sigh to himself. He and Makhdoom were now being officially babysat, and they would be watched at all times. He ran his eye over the massive examples of humanity filling the room.

Any kind of undercover operation was going to be extremely interesting.

Shoghot, North Pakistan

"WHERE ARE THE HEROIN DEALERS!" The suspect flew across the cramped tearoom, borne by the momentum of Fareed's fist. Cups and saucers shattered as he fell into a table and the patrons sitting around it shouted and screamed and ran in all directions. The Captain stalked across the room like some unstoppable bearded juggernaut and seized up the bleeding, half-conscious man.

Bolan rolled his eyes.

The undercover operation was proving to be extremely interesting. Interesting to the point that there was no undercover operation. Ghulam and his men had fanned out through the streets of Shoghot like a pack of rabid wolverines, and every minute more and more of the population was running for the trees.

The city of Shoghot was one of the northernmost cities in Pakistan. It was close to the border of Afghanistan, and many Afghan refugees had fled there and settled during the Soviet war in Afghanistan. It was also very close to the border of the disputed region of Kashmir. It was a transition point for heroin coming out of Afghanistan and running guns into India. Shoghot perched among mountains and glaciers of the Hindu Kush. The surrounding countryside was absolutely inhospitable. The heights were owned by warlords and the valleys infested with bandits. As the world went, it was a very rough neighborhood.

Captain Ghulam Fareed fit right in.

In fact, he acted like he owned the place. He was like some terrible scourge from the Book of Revelations that had been edited out the Bible for being too violent.

They had roared up to the outskirts of Shoghot in Pakistani Army Mi-8 transport helicopters loaded with weapons. The stub wings of the aircraft were festooned with rockets, missiles and gunpods. The only nod toward this being an undercover probe was that Fareed and his men had jammed their massive forms into some of the most poorly tailored business suits Bolan had ever seen. Pakistan was famous for its cotton and wool.

Ghulam Fareed and his men were sheathed in garish polyester.

"Where!" roared Fareed as he projected the man across the room. The Captain stopped a moment to adjust his horrifically ugly tie and then stalked after his prey once more. Already broken porcelain and furniture crunched beneath his size seventeen shoes.

The proprietor knelt weeping near Makhdoom, shaking his hands and intermittently pleading mercy and innocence. The teashop owner's innocence was highly debatable. There was a second shop below the regular tearoom. The patrons there smoked waterpipes, and the air reeked with the sweet stench of opium. The filthy back hallway lined with closet-size niches was a shooting gallery, strewn with the used needles of those who required their opiates stronger and introduced into their bloodstream by more direct methods.

The storage room in back contained bails of opium.

The proprietor whimpered and cringed as his best supplier was systematically demolished. Bolan had to give the Sergeant credit. The man was a force unto himself. When drug-dealer had drawn his pistol, Fareed had slapped it out of his hands and then slapped the teeth right out of his head. The drug dealer had then made the mistake of drawing an immense Khyber-style knife and invoking God. Fareed had broken the drug runner's wrist and then broken the sixteen-inch blade across his knee before resuming work.

Bolan and Makhdoom stood like stones and watched the ham-fisted hurricane that was Ghulam Fareed's work. The last patrons fled flinching beneath the gaze of Fareed's men as more crockery crashed. Apparently the proprietor understood English. Makhdoom spoke it for Bolan's benefit as he finally deigned to notice the man pleading at his feet.

"You, my friend, have drawn the attention of unreasonable men."

The proprietor flinched and threw a sickly stare in Fareed's direction. "...Yes."

"I, however, am a reasonable man." Makhdoom opened his billfold. The proprietor's eyes bugged as the Captain began fanning out American one thousand dollar bills. "Tell me that which I wish to know, and I shall recompense your inconvenience in any way you require within reason."

The proprietor's gaze darted back and forth between Makhdoom and Fareed like ping-pong balls.

He was clearly conflicted.

Doom shrugged. "However, should you not wish to cooperate..."

He sighed and glanced over at Fareed. The Captain held the hapless subject of his attention up by the lapels of his coat. The man's feet did not touch the ground. His head ricocheted against the wall repeatedly as the Captain shook him. Fareed seemed only a hairsbreadth away from sinking his teeth into the suspect and savaging him like a beagle with a bedroom slipper.

"That unreasonable man shall beat you until you die," Makhdoom stated.

The proprietor turned a sickly pallor as Fareed dropped his suspect and turned. The Captain's single massive eyebrow bunched as his green eyes glowed hatred at the teashop owner.

The owner went slack-jawed with fear.

"Tell me," queried Makhdoom. He glanced at the man lying unconscious on the floor. "If that man were conscious, would he able to tell me about the heroin trade within this city?"

The proprietor couldn't look away from Fareed, but neither could he meet Makhdoom's baleful gaze. He settled for gazing in fixed horror at Fareed's massive, hairy, bloodstained hands as they flexed into fists. "...I believe yes."

Makhdoom cocked his head inquiringly. "Could you?"

"I…don't…"

"Think very carefully before you answer. How you answer will be very important."

Fareed lumbered forward.

"I would like to cooperate!" gulped the man.

"Splendid. Splendid fellow." Doom rained United States currency down on floor by the proprietor's knees. Makhdoom took the man by the arm and raised him to his feet before he could begin to scoop up the money. "Come, my friend. Let us take tea together."

BOLAN'S STOMACH DROPPED as the helicopters fell like stones out of the sky. The fortress loomed ahead like a forbidding mountain sentinel. The crumbling brown walls of the fortress were ancient, and over the centuries they had been patched and shored up with a hodgepodge of brickwork, boulders, heavy timbers and rammed earth. The foundations of the fortress had been laid down by Genghis Khan.

The Russian-made Dshk-38 heavy machine guns emplaced in the battlements were recent additions. Yusef Zagari, the Kazakstani gangster Bolan had captured, had led them to the city of Shoghot and the opium den. Makhdoom had made the proprietor and several other drug kingpins in Shoghot offers they could not refuse.

That information had led them to the heights of Tirich Mir and the fortress of Ali Ul-Haq. In Northern Pakistan the crime did not matter—drugs, guns, prostitutes, slaves, anything that passed illegally across the borders with Afghanistan, Tajikstan, China or India—Ali Ul-Haq had his hand in it. Anyone operating on their own gave Ul-Haq his cut out of respect and fear. Ali was well connected in the highest reaches of the Pakistani government, both locally and in the Capitol. The Pakistani police left him alone. During the 1980s he had used

Afghan refugees from the war with the Soviets as muscle. He continued feeding their families and developing a fanatically loyal army of his own. He now gave that same refuge to Taliban refugees who had fled before the US Military might during Operation Enduring Freedom. He was well connected with the mafiyas of the surrounding former Soviet Republics. Ul-Haq ran his little corner of the Hindu Kush range like his own private hunting reserve.

Bolan smiled. Ali Ul-Haq's hunting license had been revoked. General Iskander Hussain continued to surprise. When Makhdoom had radioed the General the news of who their quarry was, both he and Bolan had fully expected to be told Ul-Haq was a hands-off situation.

General Hussain had declared open season on Ul-Haq. The General appeared to be taking his role as savior of the Pakistani Republic with great seriousness. He wanted the nukes back at any cost. Bolan also suspected that General Iskander Hussain was imagining such a move would a useful step toward the Presidency of Pakistan.

Hussain had sent Hind gunships.

General Hussain's political aspirations were of no concern to Bolan. That was the State Department's nightmare to deal with. Ali Ul-Haq was a righteous target in and of himself, and Bolan wanted those nukes back as much as Hussain.

He also needed more clues about the invisible assassins that had reached out for his throat.

Of even more immediate concern were the green tracers streaking upward from the walls of the fortress. Hail seemed to rattle on the Mi-8's airframe, and a ragged line of holes appeared down the middle of the troop compartment. Makhdoom roared orders into his radio.

The Hind gunships swept ahead of the transports like avenging dragonflies, their twin automatic cannons hammering in response to the ground fire. Fire blossomed beneath the stub-wings as the rocket pods rippled into life. 57mm rockets swarmed downward in smoking lines. The orange fire of high explosive erupted along the walls of the fortress. The anti-aircraft guns swiftly fell silent as the battlements were bombarded. The transports swooped down toward the inner courtyard. The door gunners hosed down the walls as the helicopters dropped to the cobblestones.

Captain Ghulam Fareed and his men had changed out of their leisure suits. They now wore camouflaged coveralls and Russian-made titanium body armor. Bolan jumped out beside Makhdoom, cradling his HK automatic rifle.

The fortress was already falling. Ul-Haq's stronghold was more for show than anything else. It was deep within his territory and made him inaccessible. His real defenses were the influence he bought and the murder of his rivals. It was well equipped to protect him from assassination or a misguided assault by a fellow warlord. Neither Genghis Khan nor Ali Ul-Haq had ever envisioned repelling a Special Forces helicopter assault.

Neither of the two warlords, ancient or modern, had envisioned falling under the wrath of Mack Bolan.

Bolan's rifle ripped into a crew of men trying to wheel a heavy machine gun around on the wall to fire down into the courtyard. The big .30 caliber rifle pounded them to pieces around their weapon. Makhdoom's hand slammed down on Bolan's shoulder, and the Pakistani shouted above the sound of gunfire and the aerial artillery barrage.

"There!" Doom pointed his rifle and the squat, round-shouldered shape of the fortress's central tower. "The keep!"

Bolan nodded as he shouldered his weapon. The HK bucked against him, and a man on the steps of the keep fell in red ruin with a five round burst through his chest. Bolan ejected his spent magazine and slapped in a fresh one. The door to the keep was small and massively constructed of thick oak timbers bound with iron. The structure itself was made of massive blocks of ancient stone. Each floor of the keep had narrow firing slits for the defenders. They had been designed to service bows and crossbows, but they worked equally well for automatic rifles and light machine guns. Charging across the open courtyard would be a suicide mission for anyone trying to breach the door.

"Doom!" Bolan glanced up meaningfully at one of the orbiting Hind gunships as it swept the walls of the last defenders. "We need that door blown and a rocket run on the keep to keep the gunners down while we assault!"

"Indeed!" Makhdoom roared rapidly into his radio in Sind. One of the Hinds dropped out of its low circling pattern and dropped out of sight behind the walls. It popped up again directly over Bolan and Doom's heads. Its five massive, fifty-foot rotors pounded the air of the courtyard into thundering vortices of smoke and dust and vibrated the very cobblestones. A pair of AT-6 Spiral guided anti-tank missiles sizzled off their launch rails trailing their guide-wires. The door disappeared in twin flashes of orange fire. The gunship pilot tilted the nose of his aircraft, and the rocket pods beneath his wings began breathing fire like some terrible pipe organ of destruction. Rocket after rocket hissed into the front of the keep. The guns in the firing slits went silent as explosion after explosion shook the tower.

Makhdoom sliced down his hand. "Attack! Attack! Attack!"

"Allah Akbar!" Captain Fareed did not hesitate. His war cry was taken up by his gang of thugs. "God is Great!"

Bolan and Makhdoom formed the sharp end of the spear as they charged the keep beneath the gunship's sheltering salvo. The door, the doorframe and about two feet of masonry to each side had been blown out and the breached tower oozed smoke. The world was consumed by the smell of brimstone and the stench of burnt high-explosive. Bolan threw a Chinese-made offensive hand-grenade into the smoking hole. Pale yellow fire flashed as the grenade detonated with a spiteful crack. Someone inside screamed.

Bolan and Makhdoom strode though the smoldering doorway with their rifles blazing. A pair of gunmen fell and two more threw down their weapons, pleading for their lives in Urdu. The first floor of the tower was done up like an opulent reception hall complete with Persian carpets and a gilt throne. Ul-Haq held court like an ancient pasha. Only, Ul-Haq was nowhere to be seen. Bolan glanced around as the prisoners were bound. The question of the moment was whether Ali Ul-Haq was the kind of modern warlord who would hide in the top of his tower or be burrowed down at the bottom.

Bolan was betting Ul-Haq was a top tower man.

"Doom! I'm going up top!"

"I will arrange it!" Makhdoom spoke into his radio. "Take Captain Fareed with you! I will meet you in the middle."

Bolan strode back into daylight. Fareed fell into step behind him. A pair of ropes descended from the cabin of a Hind gunship circling overhead. "We want Ul-Haq alive!"

"I know something of taking men alive!" Fareed rumbled.

Bolan grabbed a rope and scissored it with his feet. He waved his hand and the Hind began to rise up into the air. He kept his eyes on the firing slits in the tower and his free hand covered them with his rifle. The big American unclamped his feet as he cleared the crenellations at the top of the tower and his boots touched down on stone as the Hind delivered them. The ropes fell behind them as the Hind cut free and veered off. Bolan examined the top of the tower. It was littered with broken weapons and shattered bodies. The rocket and cannon runs had defoliated the tower of defenders.

A thick wooden hatch of the same construction as the front door below was scorched and scarred but still intact.

"Captain, tell the gunship we need that door blown!"

Fareed nodded and spoke into his radio. "We should take cover."

Bolan and Fareed ran to the crenellations. They hooked their ropes around the tombstone-shaped battlements and swung off the tower to put some stone between themselves and the assault.

The Hind returned to hover twenty yards over the tower. It tipped forward until it seemed to stand on its nose. The immense helicopter began rotating on its axis like a sixty-foot, eighteen-thousand-pound, slow-motion ballerina. The twin barreled 23 mm cannon mounted in the fuselage began to rain armor-piercing shells down into the door in vertical brutality. The Hind made one orbit on its axis and then veered off. One orbit was all that was required. The door was gone, as was about five feet of rock all around it. There was nothing left but a smoking crater.

Bolan regarded Fareed dryly as they hung in space from the battlements. "I did mention we wanted Ul-Haq alive."

"I had thought they would use a missile," Fareed grunted. The captain frowned deeply as he considered what might have happened to any living thing in the floor below them. "I should have been more specific."

Bolan heaved himself up onto the tower top and approached the smoking hole. He took out a grenade and pulled out the pin. "Hey!" he shouted. "Anyone alive down there?"

Automatic rifle fire answered from the floor below. Bolan leaned back as the gunman burned his entire magazine. "Captain, tell them we need to talk."

Fareed began to speak in Urdu. He was instantly interrupted by a long and furious speech in the same language. Fareed rolled his green eyes toward heaven as the man below ranted.

"He says that you and your crusader religion receive a thousand phalluses daily because Allah wills it."

"Really."

"Indeed." Fareed's brow veed dangerously. "And what he said of my wife and the nature of my relations with her shall be reckoned between myself and him."

Bolan nodded. "He is a profane and uncultural man."

"Indeed."

Bolan held up his grenade. "Tell him he'd better duck."

Fareed barked out a few words as Bolan opened his hand. The safety lever of the Chinese offensive grenade pinged away across the tower top. Bolan rolled the grenade into the hole and leaned back. The grenade detonated and smoke and dust erupted out of the hole. Com-Bloc offensive grenades tended to be concussive rather than shrapnel-oriented. The blast wave of the HE would have been horrendous in an enclosed, stone room.

"He still with us?"

Fareed shouted down the hole. No gunfire answered, but the voice half coughed, half shouted back in an enfeebled fashion. Fareed shook his head impatiently. "He is speaking of phalluses again."

"I see." A handgun popped twice and bullets sparked off against the crumbling lip of the hole. "What is Makhdoom's situation?"

Fareed consulted over the radio for a moment. "He says he is blocked from the top floor by a very heavy steel door of modern manufacture. He is bringing up an RPG-7 rocket, but he is not sure if it will breach it."

Bolan checked his web gear and cocked an eyebrow at Fareed. "Captain, do you have a smoke grenade?"

Fareed brightened immediately. "Indeed, a purple one, in case we needed to mark our position for more air strikes."

Bolan inclined his head at the hole. Fareed grinned uncharacteristically as he lobbed his grenade. Bright purple smoke began to billow up out of the hole in the top of the tower and the firing slits in its sides. Bolan and Fareed shifted so that the smoke didn't blow in their faces.

The man in the tower had no such option.

Bolan took up one of the rappelling ropes and swiftly made a knot. He held the rope loosely and gathered a few coils of slack as he peered into the swirling violet depths below. Fareed grunted and pointed with the muzzle of his weapon. "There."

A figure was dimly visible, thrashing its arms in the purple smoke and staggering toward one of the firing slits. Bolan swung the lasso twice in a short circle around his head.

"Ha!" Fareed's green eyes glittered as he watched in fascination. "American cowboy!"

Bolan cast.

Fareed clapped his hands in childlike delight as the loop snaked around Ul-Haq's head and Bolan yanked it tight. He grabbed the rope in his hairy hands and he and Bolan reeled up a thin, bald-headed man in a beautifully tailored Armani suit, hand over hand, into the light.

"Ali Ul-Haq!" Fareed seized the gangster by his crotch and his collar and pressed him overhead. "You wish to speak of phalluses and other men's wives?"

Fareed strode to the edge of the tower with Ul-Haq feebly flailing up in the air.

"Captain…" Bolan cautioned. He kept a hold of the rope in case Ghulam grew overzealous and flung Ul-Haq into the void.

"I have no interest in phalluses and other men's wives!" Fareed dangled Ul-Haq over the courtyard by his ankles. "I am interested in criminals from Kazakstan and several missing nuclear weapons!"

Ul-Haq began squealing incoherently as the blood rushed to his head. Below him his surviving men knelt on the cobblestones of the courtyard with their hands bound behind and rifles pointed at the backs of their heads. They squinted upward and watched as their leader was dangled in space. The gunships circled the smoking ruins of the fortress.

"Speak English! Dog! Lest you irritate my associate!"

"I do not know!" Ul-Haq screamed.

"You lie!" Fareed let go of one of Ul-Haq's ankles. The Pakistani gangster screamed in terror his hands clawed at empty air and the back of his head bounced against the tower wall. The captain's face contorted with the effort of holding Ul-Haq with one hand. "I grow weary!"

"I cannot!" Ul-Haq shrieked. "They will kill me!"

Bolan nodded. Ul-Haq knew something.

Fareed yanked Ul-Haq back between the embrasures. Ul-Haq now had his heels on stone, but his behind still hung out over the courtyard. Fareed squatted nose to nose with the gangster and his green eyes blazed with barely contained rage. He spoke very quietly. "Tell me. Who will kill you?"

Ul-Haq's voice was barely more than whisper. "I…cannot."

Fareed put his index finger against Ul-Haq's chest and pushed slightly. "Oh, do."

The gangster went deathly pale as he tottered squatting on his heels. He gasped a single horrified word. *"Djinns!"*

Fareed glanced up at Bolan, then back at his suspect. "I see. You believe if you speak to me the *djinns* will come, invisibly. They shall extend their will about your throat and strangle the life from you, won't they?"

"Yes!" Ul-Haq's head bobbed up and down frantically. "Yes! Yes! I have seen it!"

Bolan smiled. Paydirt.

"I shall strangle the life from you now!" Fareed thundered.

Ul-Haq screamed as the captain shoved him over the edge.

"Fareed!" Bolan took the rope in both hands and braced himself to take Ul-Haq's weight. His boots skidded a foot as he was yanked forward. Bolan put a foot against an embrasure to brace himself and hoped Ul-Haq's neck hadn't snapped. Bolan raised a questioning eyebrow at the captain.

Fareed stared up into the sky and began whistling.

The rope jerked in Bolan's hands with Ul-Haq's strangled struggles. He counted to ten slowly and then began to reel him back in. Ul-Haq flopped back on the top of the tower, his eyes rolling in his head. His face was purple and spittle flecked his lips. Fareed loosened the noose and Ul-Haq pulled air back into lungs in a tortured wheeze. The captain waited several moments until Ul-Haq appeared vaguely lucid. He stared down implacably as Ul-Haq gibbered and wheezed.

"You may speak with the American." Fareed took several coils of the rope in his hands. "Or you may speak again with me."

CHAPTER EIGHT

"Well, he's seen them." Makhdoom sipped tea in the ruins of Ul-Haq's fortress.

"Or at least encountered them." Bolan considered the intel they'd gathered from the gangster. "No one's really seen them, yet. Did you manage to get that sample out of the country?"

The captain smiled. "I sent it Federal Express, overnight, to the address you provided."

Bolan nodded. He'd provided the address of Hal Brognola's office at the Justice Department. The fabric should be in Bear's hands by now. It was the one clue they had that could bust things wide open. He looked over at Ali Ul-Haq. The gangster sat miserably on a low sofa, his small frame crushed between two of Fareed's guards. The men were even larger than Fareed and they kept their pistols jammed into Ul-Haq's ribs.

The gangster hadn't been able to give them too much they could act on, but his story had been fascinating.

He had been approached by Kazakstani gangsters. They'd know Ul-Haq had contacts high up in the Pakistani government; they wanted some very strange favors and were throwing around money. Vast amounts of money, and in U.S.

dollars. Ul-Haq's cunning and greed worked hand-in-hand, and while he wasn't the most powerful criminal in central Asia, he was one of them. He had quietly sent out feelers through his contacts in the Russias and found his instincts were correct. The Kazaks had a reputation for toughness and brutality, but they were throwing around far too many millions in American currency for gunrunners from a failing former Soviet republic.

They were being used as middlemen.

That didn't disturb Ul-Haq. Indeed, it was an opportunity. He had demanded more money. He had demanded contact with the people behind the Kazaks. When his demands went unanswered, Ul-Haq had kidnapped several of the Kazaks and made very unpleasant examples of them to show that Ali Ul-Haq was not to be ignored. He had decided to keep the money he had already been paid as a down payment of the full sum he demanded, and would take no further action until it was forthcoming.

It was at this point in the story that Ul-Haq had begun to shake uncontrollably, and not from fear of Bolan or the further ministrations of Captain Ghulam Fareed. Ali Ul-Haq had sat secure in his mountain fortress. He'd sat secure on ten million dollars U.S. and his Kazak hostages, and waited for the money to come.

The *djinns* had come.

One morning the men guarding the Kazaks in dungeons below the fortress had been found dead. The Kazaks themselves were still in their cells, screaming mad stories about the hideous deaths of the guards. Ul-Haq had tortured the Kazaks savagely but even the ugliest methods produced nothing but the same nonsense. On the second morning, not only had the new guards been found dead, but the Kazaks were dead in their locked cells, as well. On the third morning, the ten million was missing. That night Ali Ul-Haq had been in close council with his most trusted advisor when the *djinns* had come for him. His right-hand man had died, eyes bulging and tongue blackening, dangling in midair in front of his eyes in the inner sanctum of his fortress.

The message was very clear.

Ali Ul-Haq had decided, quite sensibly, given the circumstances, to paint his ass white and run with the herd.

He had used his contacts in the government to get the building plans and security systems of the Al-Nouri Weapons Facility. The rest was history. Al-Nouri had been breached, and three of Pakistan's nuclear weapons were missing. Ali Ul-Haq had received further compensation once the weapons had disappeared. Twenty million dollars U.S. was a handsome reward for making a few phone calls.

Bolan watched Makhdoom's and Fareed's eyes as they glared at Ali Ul-Haq and wondered what kind of reward they were reserving for a traitor to Pakistan.

Last Bolan had heard, beheading was still the preferred method of punishment for capital offenses in this part of the Indian subcontinent.

"The enemy must know by now that we have compromised Ul-Haq." Makhdoom steepled his fingers in thought. "It appears the weapons may have traveled to Kashmir."

"Yes." Fareed never took his glare off of Ul-Haq. "But why would Hindus wish to take nuclear weapons there?"

"To start a war between India and Pakistan," Bolan said. It was the obvious answer, but no one wanted to think about it.

"To what purpose? Our nuclear arsenal is our deterrence against depredations by India." Makhdoom shook his head. "I am a simple soldier, but no one wins a nuclear war."

"Even the tragedy of the 9/11 attack in your country—"

"The attack on the World Trade Center wasn't a tragedy. If the Trade Centers had fallen in an earthquake, that would be a tragedy." Bolan's eyes went hard. "What happened on September 11 was an atrocity committed by terrorists."

"Hmm." Fareed grunted and nodded. He seemed to like the way Bolan thought.

Makhdoom looked at Bolan thoughtfully. "And how would you define terrorism? War? A crime?"

Bolan shrugged. "That's just a question of language."

Fareed's ugly face split into a smile. "But we are Pakistanis. We love language."

Bolan smiled wearily. "I wouldn't call it a criminal activity, but only because by definition money is not the motivator. If I had to define it…"

Fareed hung on Bolan's words. "Ah?"

"It's war." Bolan shook his head slowly. "Indiscriminate war, conducted for political reasons, against noncombatants, and has no objective."

The three warriors sat in sober silence.

"But I don't believe we are facing terrorists."

"No?" Makhdoom set down his cup. "Then what?"

"True believers."

Fareed sat up straighter. "I do not understand the difference."

"Terrorists lash out, there is no real objective that they can hope to achieve other than killing. True believers have an objective, however mad it may be. I believe the people were are facing have a higher purpose than just lighting off a nuke and killing as many people as they can."

Fareed frowned and set down his cup as if the tea no longer agreed with him. "What is this higher purpose?"

"I don't know. But God help us if we don't stop it."

The Mountain

"ALI UL-HAQ has become a liability, Guruji." Mehtar bowed low and prepared himself to wait for a reply. His guru was deep in his meditations. The meditation cell was a natural pocket of stone deep within the mountain. Exposed formations of mica in the rock ceiling reflected the light of the dozen candles like otherworldly constellations of stars. The room swam with the smell of sandalwood incense. The guru sat in lotus position, wearing nothing but a loincloth of simple homespun. He sat upon a white Siberian tiger skin. It was known throughout the mountain that the guru had killed the great cat with his own hands in the snowy peaks above to make himself a meditation seat as described by the ancient texts. A huge, lobed, all-iron ceremonial ax lay by his left knee.

The guru's bones showed through his flesh in emaciated high relief. He would have looked like a death camp survivor except for the fibered cables of muscle that stretched across his stark bones like separate living entities. His flesh was like an anatomy chart; over the ropes of sinew, veins crawled. Even in repose, Guruji was terrifying to behold.

Mehtar knew his guru was performing *kechari mudra*, or roaming in space. The guru's chin rested on his chest as if he were asleep, but his eyes were open, crossed and glaring ferociously upward like an unblinking lion from the point directly between his eyebrows. He looked like some terrible ancient sage carved out of oak. His crossed eyes stared into the canted flaring eyes of the goddess.

She stood in stone in front of him. Guruji walked in space hand-in-hand with Kali.

"I see him." Mehtar jumped as his guru spoke. "I see Ali Ul-Haq. He is an approver. He tasted the sweetness, and felt the fear, but money was all that moved his heart and fear his tiny mind."

"Truly, Guruji." Mehtar bowed low again. "But what is to be done about him? He has become compromised."

"Young Atta was compromised. He met the fate of all those who waver in their faith."

"Ul-Haq is not a believer." Mehtar picked his words carefully. "Does he deserve proper execution?" Mehtar was very worried about the risk of such a venture. Atta Naqbi had been a believer and had been punished properly, but it had cost much.

"Indeed, not. Ali Ul-Haq is a tainted soul and an unfit sacrifice." The guru raised his chin from his chest. "Let his blood be spilt. Let it stain the red dust of the earth. Let it be done by unbelievers, let it be done by ungodly men, men of his own ilk."

Mehtar breathed an inward sigh of relief. The situation called for brutal, unhallowed methods.

The guru spoke, as he often did, with a disturbing, mind-reading prescience. "Let it be done by men with guns."

"Indeed, Guruji." Mehtar turned his mind to other even more serious matters. "But what of Captain Makhdoom?"

"Muslim warriors have always made fine sacrifices. Let it be so."

"As you will, Guruji." Mehtar glanced up from prostrating himself. "And what of the American?"

A slow smile spread across the guru's lips. "The American...intrigues me."

"Guruji, the American must be Special Forces. Our witnesses have told us he is nearly inhuman in battle." Mehtar considered the report he had just recently read. "And he is tenacious."

The guru nodded as his disciple spoke the obvious. "All these things he must be to have followed the trail so far."

"He will continue to follow the trail," Mehtar warned.

"He will follow his nature." Guruji shrugged his inhumanly broad shoulders with infinite patience. "He can do naught else."

Nervousness betrayed itself across Mehtar's face. "He will come, Guruji."

"And as it should be." The guru's smile was beatific. "We will let him in."

Islamabad

GENERAL AQEEL NASEERUDDIN gawped in white-knuckled terror. The general's pistol sat forgotten in the holster on his hip. Naseeruddin sat frozen as he watched the eyes of his adjutant roll back red-veined in their sockets and his blackened tongue loll from purpled lips. His adjutant hung suspended in the air for a moment and slowly slumped to the floor.

Naseeruddin swallowed with great difficulty. "Shah?"

Lieutenant Shah lay lifeless upon the floor of Naseeruddin's office. It was very obvious that he was dead.

The general's voice shook as he called to him anyway. "Shah—"

The general nearly leaped out of his chair as the phone on his desk rang. His heart fluttered in his rib cage like a dove with an injured wing. Naseeruddin stared at the phone as it continued to ring. His hand seemed to belong to someone else as it stretched out to pick up the phone. His eyes never left Shah's body as he brought the receiver to his ear. "Hello?"

A voice spoke in Punjabi, the language of Naseeruddin's birthplace. The voice spoke softly but with absolute and unyielding command and conviction. "Listen very carefully." The voice sounded very much like God might if God chose to use a telephone. "Your very soul depends upon it."

"Bismillah—"

"Allah cannot help you, Aqeel."

Naseeruddin flinched. "What is—"

"No, you tell me. What is it that lies before you?"

The general went as white as a sheet.

"Do you understand what has just transpired?"

The general's guts turned to ice water. He had heard the tapes of the massacre in the pass. Every general in the Pakistani military had, and all had heard the rumors of the *djinns* that had killed invisibly. Naseeruddin had discounted such rumors. Oh, some nuclear weapons were missing, of that he was fairly sure, and a platoon of the prima donna Musa Company had gotten themselves killed. But he considered the whole mess of missing nukes and slaughtered special forces troopers just one more Byzantine power struggle within the Pakistani armed forces. It was none of his business. General Naseeruddin dealt in tanks and armor. He spent most of his time squeezing bribes out of the warlords in his own district, taking his cut of the heroin trade and running an occasional armored exercise along the border to keep the Indian army on its toes. He wasn't ambitious. Indeed, he was quite comfortable. Naseeruddin had found his niche.

The general wasn't a devout man, either. He enjoyed his liquor and the taste of pork and frequenting houses of prostitution on his many trips out of the country, particularly those with Russian blondes. He had no use for the fundamentalists who were always trying to take over the government and stir up the people. He found them to be a tremendous pain in the ass and in idle moments he thought that they needed a good crushing.

General Aqeel Naseeruddin wasn't a good Muslim. However, he was very superstitious.

Now his adjutant lay slain in front of him in the middle of his office, his dead eyes popping out of his head. Slaughtered by the unseen. The general shuddered. The *djinns* had come to visit him.

The supernatural spoke with him on the phone.

"You are aware that Ali Ul-Haq has been attacked in his fortress in the north?"

Naseeruddin had heard. Someone had spearheaded an attack using airborne troops. That someone was widely rumored to have been General Iskander Hussain. Naseeruddin had even less use for Hussain than he did the Taliban or fundamentalists.

"He was attacked by General Hussain. General Hussain

used members of Musa Company he has co-opted. General Hussain used U.S. mercenaries."

"Truly?" Naseeruddin found this hard to believe.

"Ostensibly, he will say he has done this to secure the missing weapons." The voice paused dramatically. "His true purpose is to secure the entire heroin trade in the north for himself."

Naseeruddin had no problem believing that whatsoever.

"We have further purpose for Ali Ul-Haq. He has a destiny to fulfill. What has happened is untenable."

The general swallowed and tried to think of something to say.

The voice brooked no interruption. It was as horrifying and hypnotic as the body on the floor. He couldn't look away from Shah's body. He couldn't hang up the phone even if he had dared.

"You will kill General Hussain. You will kill Captain Makhdoom of Musa Company. You will capture the American, if possible, but kill him rather than let him escape. You will do this for the good of the nation. You will do it to insure your own survival. You will do it so that your wife, your children and your mistress do not suffer the same fate as Shah."

The general shrank in his chair.

The voice brightened with some awful amusement. "You will do it to secure yourself fifty percent of the profit taken in the heroin trade in the north."

The general didn't brighten. But despite his terror, the lower portions of his mind began to move with the thought of fifty percent of the heroin trade.

CHAPTER NINE

General Hussain's Mansion

"Striker, where on God's green earth did you get this?"

"The Temple of Kali," Bolan replied. He sat in the general's private study and examined the crude but anatomically correct erotic woodcuts from the Kama Sutra adorning the walls.

Kurtzman paused a moment on his side of the satellite link. "Striker, the Temple of Kali is in Calcutta."

"This was a local branch, downtown Rawalpindi."

Kurtzman was appalled. "Striker, we gave a fragment of the fabric you sent us to the boys in NSA. We got called back within thirty minutes. We got a call right from the top. The Pentagon demanded every fiber of that piece of fabric you sent and every shred of intelligence surrounding how it was acquired. The President himself had to give explicit orders that whoever found the fabric, what the operation was, and what auspices they were working under, were on a need-to-know basis, and that anyone who wanted to know would have to come to the Oval Office and ask him personally. We still had to give the fabric up. We sent it to the Capitol surrounded by armed guards. Guys in black helicopters even we don't know about took it and whisked it away."

Bolan sighed. He was very tired. The overstuffed couch along the wall was of much more interest than the sinuously entwined figures on the walls. "So you think some of the top minds over at the Pentagon may have let one of their experiments leak?"

"No. I think it's worse than that."

Bolan perked a weary eyebrow. "How so?"

"I think what you found is something they don't have yet. I may be reading between the lines, but I think it is something they are feverishly working on. I think you found something no one on Earth is supposed to have yet. I think the Pentagon is appalled by what you found. Quite frankly, I think they're scared."

"So what is it?"

"I don't know, but I have a hunch. I went along for the ride to drop off the fragment. Among all the dark suits and sunglasses I recognized someone."

Bolan straightened. "Oh, yeah? Who?"

"A Dr. Allison Austenford. She has a Ph.D. in optics. I've read some of the papers she's published as they relate to supercoherent light."

"You mean, lasers."

"Right, but only kind of. She was into some very interesting and experimental applications of light transferal. Brilliant stuff. Then it gets interesting. About three years ago she dropped completely out of sight."

Bolan leaned back in his chair. He could see what was coming. "She went to the dark side."

"That's right. Black projects. Top-secret, code-word-level clearances with the Pentagon. Then a year ago she left Washington, D.C. and went north."

"North?"

"It took some digging, and I had to call in a few markers, but I found out that Dr. Allison Austenford is currently living—and from that, I suspect gainfully employed—in Natick, Massachusetts." Kurtzman paused for dramatic effect. "That ring any bells for you, Striker?"

It did. Over the past few years Bolan had personally gotten his hands on some very interesting prototypes of some very weird and wonderful ordnance that had come from some very obscure laboratories located in Natick, Massachusetts. "The United States Army Soldier Systems Center."

"Give the man a cigar." Kurtzman was clearly pleased with himself. "I have every reason to believe that Dr. Austenford is spearheading one of the teams working on our Future Warrior Program."

The U.S. Future Warrior Program was dedicated to bringing together the very latest technologies in communications, observation and detection, armament and armor. Their goal was to take the very cutting edges of these technologies and produce integrated, modular systems that would make the U.S. soldier the dominant force on the battlefield for the foreseeable future.

"And she's flying around in black helicopters and commandeering our evidence."

"That's about the size of it."

Bolan considered what he had encountered in the Haji Pir Pass and in the garment district of Rawalpindi. "So what did we find, Bear?"

"Well, temporarily barring the supernatural, I would say you found a working piece of see-through-cell technology."

"What does that mean?"

"We're talking cloaking devices."

"Bear, your talking Trek-geek."

"No, I mean it. Literally, a cloaking device. Or, more specifically, a light-transferring textile."

"Give me a quick rundown."

"Quite simply, the fabric itself transmits light. In this application, a garment made of this stuff would absorb light behind you and transmit to your front and vice versa."

Bolan contemplated this. "So you would be virtually invisible against any background."

Kurtzman was pleased with Bolan. "You win a cookie."

"Bear, has this stuff actually been produced?"

"I don't know, but I'm guessing not. By the way the black project honchos are behaving, I'd say not by us, and until you took your little jaunt to Rawalpindi, our boys never dreamed anyone else might have it, either. We're working on it, but if I had to guess, I'd say we have only the most primitive prototypes, probably just static pieces of the fabric that demonstrate the technology. Certainly nothing that could be applied in the field."

"Who else could have developed it?"

"That's the question. This is very complicated stuff. It's not just getting the fabric to do the job. You need to power it, and if you are going to integrate it into a soldier's kit, it has to be woven or somehow integrated into his uniform, his armor, his helmet, his boots, his weapon—everything. Every exposed inch of the soldier and everything he's carrying." Kurtzman let out a long breath. "The fabric would have to be able to transmit not only everything in front and behind the soldier, but above and below the soldier. Now we're talking about doing it in three dimensions, not just a flat-screen effect, and whenever the soldier passes his arm or his weapon in front of himself, the fabric would have to do double transmission. Theoretically, it's all possible, but the cost, at least currently, would be enormous. Then there's the question of movement. You might be able to make it now so that a static individual would blend into his background, but once you start moving you bring in a whole new set of problems. Distortion effects would be bad, and then there's the problem of any kind of dust or dirt getting on the fabric and sections of your suit no longer transmitting. It's very exciting technology, and it is on the horizon, but currently, in application, it's a nightmare of biblical proportions."

"Yeah, but someone has done it."

"That's why I said cloaking device. You said in the fight in the warehouse you felt enveloped by something. You saw shimmering and distortions. On top of that, the bad guys were already in place and waiting. So I took that mission parameter. Forget about a uniform, helmet, armor, boots and weapons for a soldier moving and fighting on the modern battlefield. You just cut down the requirements to something like a cloak, a blanket or an all-enveloping robe. You put it on at an ambush site of your choosing prepositioned and use it just to sneak up behind someone and strangle them. The technology, as we are projecting it, becomes a lot more applicable. It's not a viable battlefield system, but it could be one hell of an assassination device."

Bolan had felt that piece of fabric around his throat. "And even their weapon of choice is invisible."

"So it would seem."

"Which begs the question. Who developed it if it wasn't stolen from us, and how did it get into the hands of Kali cultists?"

"That is the million-dollar question."

There was a polite knock on the door and Makhdoom stuck his head into the study. "Something is happening."

Bolan stood. "What?"

"Fareed says something is coming up the street."

"What kind of something?"

"Fareed says armor."

"Bear, I'm going to have to get back to you."

"Striker—"

Bolan flicked off the link and followed Makhdoom down the hallway.

General Hussain's mansion was situated on a little hill in the suburbs of the capital. Within the twelve-foot-high clay walls was a decent-size lawn. Behind the house was a swimming pool and a clay tennis court. The nets had been taken down and a Hind gunship sat parked on the hard red clay. Some of his bodyguards had been amusing themselves by playing croquet. Most of them had set down their mallets and had unslung their Bulgarian AK-47 rifles. Bolan followed Makhdoom upstairs. He came into a room where General Hussain and Captain Fareed were peering out the window with binoculars. Fareed glanced up and passed Bolan a pair of WWII-vintage British artillery field glasses. Bolan's eyebrows rose as he scanned the little road that twisted up the hill to the general's gate.

An armored convoy was clanking its way up the road. There appeared to be four light trucks loaded with men carrying automatic rifles. Of much more concern were the three Russian PT-76 amphibious light tanks and the three Chinese-made Type 531 armored personnel carriers accompanying them.

"General, how many men do you have on the premises?"

Hussain did some math. "I would say a score."

"Do you have any heavy weapons?"

"No, why?"

Bolan wondered once again exactly how the man might have made general. "Who would have access to tanks here in Islamabad?"

The rotund little general stroked his mustache in thought. "Why, General Naseeruddin is in command of the armor park here in the capital, but I am not aware of any scheduled exercises."

"Is General Naseeruddin a friend of yours?"

"Oh, no." Hussain's eyes lit cruelly with some past victory. "He has no reason to love me."

"Well, he's coming to call on you. With tanks."

Hussain suddenly shot straight. *"Bismillah!"*

"Yeah." Bolan nodded. He and the general were finally on the same page. "I suggest you get that Hind up in the air and call for more of them."

"Yes, that is a good—" The general was interrupted by the unmistakable thud of a large-caliber mortar. The bodyguards playing croquet scattered in all directions. Two of his men were blown in every direction as the high-explosive shell blasted a ten-foot divot in the general's once immaculate lawn.

"That was a 120 mm," Bolan announced.

"That was my personal pilot and his copilot." Hussain sighed. He looked at Bolan hopefully. "Can you pilot a helicopter?"

"In an emergency."

"Perhaps one will come up," Makhdoom suggested.

The two soldiers laughed.

Hussain blinked in confusion.

Bolan turned to Fareed. "Get your men together. Get gasoline and all the glass bottles you can. Find detergent, frozen orange juice concentrate, anything to thicken it. One-quarter gelling agent to three-quarters gasoline or kerosene." Bolan glanced a final time out the window. The windows rattled in their panes as another mortar bomb detonated somewhere behind the house. "You have about three minutes. Get your best shots on the roof. Have them start shooting anyone who sticks their heads out of the vehicles."

Fareed glanced at his general. Hussain nodded rapidly. "Quickly!"

Bolan jerked his head at Makhdoom. "Follow me."

The two soldiers ran downstairs. Another mortar shell detonated on the lawn as they ran out the back toward the tennis court. Bolan's jaw tightened as he saw black smoke drift across the swimming pool. He and Makhdoom skidded short in front of the tennis courts.

The Hind was in two pieces. The tail boom and rotor lay

crumpled on its side. The front portion of the helicopter seemed nearly untouched save that a ten-foot crater separated it from its tail. The tail section was burning.

The captain narrowed his gaze. "So much for that."

Bolan examined the fuselage critically. "Get as many of the men as you can! And get me the battery from the general's Mercedes!"

"But what—"

"Do it!"

Bolan ran to the shattered helicopter. He yanked open the front weapon operator's cockpit and slid into the seat. A sea of switches, dials and screens densely engraved with Cyrillic writing confronted him. Bolan knew basically what he was looking for. He just had to pray the batteries hadn't been smashed. He began flipping switches, relieved as lights blinked on across the controls. A rough, glowing green diagram of the front of the helicopter's nose and stub wings filled one of the screens. The hard points were all green for go. Bolan began flipping a row switches beneath the screen.

The green lights representing the load-bearing hardpoints beneath the wings all went red at once.

The bolts holding the Swatter AT-2 antitank missiles released and the four missiles fell to the ground, followed by the external fuel tanks. Bolan winced as the rocket pods dropped to the clay with a clang. He vainly wished he could somehow get his hands on the 23 mm revolving cannon but he didn't have the time or the tools.

Bolan jumped out of the broken helicopter as Makhdoom ran back with Fareed and a dozen of Hussain's men. The men Fareed had put on the rooftop were firing their weapons. That meant the oncoming armor was within rifle range.

Time was running out.

"I brought the battery," Makhdoom gasped.

"I brought jumper cables," Fareed rumbled. His green eyes

surveyed the shattered aircraft. "But I fear they will not be enough." His eyes met Bolan's. "The enemy is upon us."

As if the enemy commander had heard Fareed, the 76 mm cannons of the light tanks began pounding the house. The men on the roof screamed and called upon God as they fired their rifles in vain answer. The chimney blew away in a shower of brick, as did the rifleman trying to take cover behind it.

Bolan snapped open his Emerson fighting knife with a flick of his wrist as he took the cables from Fareed. "Get the rocket pods around to the side of the house."

Fareed stared at the car battery, the rocket pods and the cables as Bolan cut off the clamps and stripped the wires to expose about six inches of copper. "You are a clever man," he said.

Bolan nodded grimly. "Just pray Russian rocket igniters are 12 volt."

Fareed barked orders and the men began manhandling the 57 mm rocket pods around to the side of the house. Bolan pointed at the front gate. "There! Point it there!"

The men set down the 32-round rocket pod with a groan. Bolan straddled the six-foot-long pod and attached the two remaining claws of the jumper cables to the Mercedes's battery terminals. He jammed one of the stripped ends down the exposed socket. One of the surviving men on the roof waved his rifle and shouted in Urdu at the top of his lungs while Bolan worked. The soldier needed no translation.

The tanks had arrived.

Makhdoom scanned the perimeter. The clank and whine of tank treads was audible over the mortar and cannon fire. "What should we do?"

Bolan tapped the rocket pod he sat on. "Take cover." He jerked his hand at Fareed. "Give me your jacket."

Fareed stripped off his leather jacket. There was nearly enough leather in it to upholster a couch. Bolan held up the remaining wire. "Run."

The Pakistanis scattered.

The rocket pod was designed to fire single rockets, rippling salvos, or all of its rockets at once. The selector switch was back in the helicopter's weapons suite. All Bolan could do was to jam the wire down into the other socket and pray that the hot-wired pod would deliver.

The wooden gate of the mansion blew apart in an orange burst of high-explosive flame. The clay walls on either side shattered inward as an amphibious tank rammed its way through the narrow entrance. The rifle fire from the roof had forced the tankers to batten down their hatches. The turret turned in Bolan's direction. The muzzle of the 76 mm cannon pointed accusingly at the soldier.

Bolan flung Fareed's leather jacket in front of him like a cloak and jammed down the second wire to complete the circuit.

The rocket pod beneath him made a sizzling sound and began to shudder. The thirty-two rocket motors began igniting one after the other like a string of bottle rockets. Only, the bottle rockets were 57 mm with high-explosive warheads. Heat wash from the rocket exhaust shoved into Bolan in wave after wave like superheated fists. The leather jacket smoldered around him, and the thin metal of the pod housing began to burn his legs. Rocket after rocket hissed from the pod, drawing sizzling black lines of smoke straight into the oncoming tank.

The Russian PT-76 was a light tank, amphibious, and the design was more than fifty years old. The frontal arc of its turret armor was only 14 mm of milled steel at its thickest. Resisting 160 pounds of high explosive in five-pound increments in the space of three seconds hadn't been in the manufacturer's specifications.

The front of the tank disappeared in flashing orange fire. The frontal hull armor buckled and breached, and the last six rockets streamed into the ruptured hull to detonate within the tank itself. The tank shuddered and bucked as its stored 76 mm cannon ammunition cooked off and began exploding.

The PT-76's crumpled turret burst upward from its moorings and rose in the air on a pillar of expanding superheated gas and fire.

Fareed's men gave a ragged cheer as the tank burned and died.

Bolan leaped off the red-hot pod and scooped up the battery. "Bring me the other rocket pod! Bring the fuel tanks and the missiles!"

Four of Fareed's men groaned and manhandled the rocket pod from around the house. Bolan grabbed Fareed's shoulder and shouted over the ringing in his ears and detonation of mortar and cannon rounds. The mortar rounds were now falling on target. The mansion was being reduced. "You saw what I did!"

"Yes!"

"Can you do it!"

"Inshallah! Yes!"

"If they're smart, they won't hit the gate again! The tanks will ram the walls! You'll only have seconds to adjust your aim and you'll only have one shot! Wait for my signal!"

Fareed took the battery and the cables. "I understand!"

Hussain and his six remaining men piled out of the burning mansion. Hussain had a .45 automatic in his hand and a surprising look of grim determination on his face. "What can I do?"

"The fuel tanks! Take four men! Bring the fuel up! Roll them up to one side of the gate if you can. The rest of your men stay with Fareed and follow his orders."

"Yes. Indeed!" The general and his men ran back toward the tennis courts.

"And you?" Makhdoom cradled his AK-47 rifle.

Bolan folded the stock of his weapon and held it in his right hand like a gigantic pistol. He grunted as he took one of the fifty-five-pound AT-2 Swatter antitank missiles from one of Fareed's men. "Doom, you're with me."

Makhdoom folded the stock of his weapon and shouldered a missile.

Bolan turned back to Fareed. The captain had one wire shoved down the hardpoint socket. Two of his men stood ready to rotate the pod wherever the threat presented itself. About a dozen men stood with AK-47s and Molotov cocktails they had made inside the house. "Throw the firebombs at anything that comes through! It won't stop them, but it will keep them buttoned down and maybe screw up their optics!"

Makhdoom translated rapidly. Fareed's men nodded grimly. It was a suicide mission.

Bolan and Makhdoom trotted across the cratered lawn toward the wall. The big American dropped his missile and his rifle and hit the wall in a running jump. He grabbed the top and pulled himself up.

A PT-76 was ten yards away and closing.

Bolan dropped as the tank's heavy machine gun raked the top of the wall where he had just been. He scooped up the missile and took a few steps to one side. He could hear the whine and clank of the treads and the scream of the gears as the driver threw the armored vehicle into ramming speed.

The clay wall shattered apart as the fourteen-ton tank hit it at twenty miles per hour. Two of Fareed's men ran forward and threw their firebombs. The glass bottles shattered and gelled gasoline smeared and ignited across the frontal arc of the tank, but not before the tank's coaxial gun ripped one of the men to ribbons.

Bolan ran in at an angle. He shouted with effort as he hurled the missile into the tank's path. He locked eyes with Makhdoom, thirty yards away. "Shoot it!"

Makhdoom couldn't hear Bolan's words, but his meaning was clear. He dropped his own missile and went prone with his rifle. Bolan emptied his rifle on full-auto into the side of the tank. It did no damage whatsoever but the enemy could hear the bullets hitting and through the periscope could quite possibly see him doing it.

Bolan flung himself down as the tank turret and its coaxial machine gun began to track him. The tank rumbled forward and from Bolan's perspective the antitank missile disappeared underneath the behemoth's bulk.

Makhdoom's rifle ripped into rapid semiautomatic fire.

The distance was only thirty yards. Several of the rounds impacted the missile. The rocket motor burst into flame and shoved the warhead sideways as it ignited. A split second later the shaped-charge warhead detonated. The missile lay on its side, but the jet of superheated gas and molten metal shrieked through the tank's drive wheels and two of the tread links fused and broke. The tank began to spin in a circle with only one active tread.

The tank rammed to a halt as the driver cut the engine, but the turret continued to spin toward Bolan.

Bolan was up on his feet. He charged the tank and jumped on top of it as the machine gun ripped into life.

Makhdoom was up. He ran forward and jammed his own missile warhead up against the side of the ruined treads. He leaped back and unloaded his rifle into the side of the missile.

The rocket motor exploded and a second later the shaped-charge warhead sent its armor-piercing jet burning up at an angle through the belly of the tank. Bolan jumped off the tank as it shuddered. He and the captain ran as the tank began to rock and burn as its stored cannon shells cooked off.

The wall shattered behind them as the third tank breached the garden.

Bolan knifed his hand down at Fareed as he ran. "Now! Now! Now!"

All thirty-two of the rocket tubes were pointed directly at Bolan and Makhdoom. They charged forward as Fareed rammed the wire into the rocket pod socket.

Bolan and Makhdoom dived into a mortar crater as the rockets began whooshing out of their tubes. The rockets sizzled by inches over the heads. Behind them the tank took the full salvo across its frontal arc. Its armor failed just like the first.

Bolan rose up through the smoke and stench of rocket exhaust as the tank burned and exploded behind him.

Fareed pumped his fist in victory.

"Bismillah! Makhdoom roared. "You dance closer with the Devil than any man I have ever met!"

Bolan picked up his rifle and clicked in a fresh magazine. "We've still got two trucks and three mortar-carrying armored personnel carriers."

The soldier turned and was pleased to find General Hussain and his four men straining as they rolled a 238-liter external fuel tank from around the other side of the house toward the gate. Even Hussain heaved and groaned against the huge, teardrop-shaped liquid weight.

"You know, he's really blossoming under fire," Bolan observed.

Makhdoom muttered something in Urdu under his breath.

Bolan glanced up. The surviving man on the roof was shouting and pointing toward the gate. "One of the armored personnel carriers—with a truck behind it—is coming for the gate," Makhdoom translated.

"Is the carrier open or closed?"

Makhdoom yelled at the man and then nodded at Bolan. "Open! Men with machine guns all over it!"

Bolan figured that would be the mortar carrier. His plan just might work.

"Hussain!" Bolan roared.

The general looked up as the Executioner charged forward. Bolan pointed at the gate. Hussain and his men heaved at the fuel tank in all-out effort. Bolan skidded in line with the ruptured entry. One of the Type 531s was, indeed, rumbling down upon the gate. A Russian heavy machine gun was mounted on the front. It was one of the mortar carriers. Its huge upper trapdoors were open and lined with men aiming automatic rifles. Behind it was a two-and-a-half-ton transport truck carrying half a platoon of armed men.

Bolan sprayed a long burst at the armored vehicle and dived behind the wall. The wall erupted like a string of geysers above his head as the .61-caliber machine gun tracked him blindly. Bolan rose up. Hussain and his men heaved desperately against the fuel tank. They weren't going to make it. Bolan waved them off. "Run!"

Hussain and his men abandoned the tank and ran. Bolan broke into a dead sprint for the gate.

"Striker!" Makhdoom shouted.

Bolan ran past the open gate, spraying his rifle to the side. The Type 531 was yards from the gate. Bullets cracked like supersonic hornets as the enemy guns sought him. Bolan kept running and vaulted the fuel tank. His lungs burned as he tried to make as much distance as he could.

The edge of the battered gate shattered inward as the armored personnel carrier rammed into a hard turn after Bolan. The front of the truck came though and riflemen were already deploying off the sides.

The soldier dropped and brought up his rifle.

The armored personnel carrier rammed into the fuel tank. For a moment the vehicle rolled the tank ahead of it with its nose. The tank was teardrop-shaped for aerodynamics. It didn't roll evenly on the ground. The fuel tank spun and its narrow end crushed beneath one of the treads. Bolan burned his entire magazine into the container as it began to go under the vehicle.

Two hundred and thirty-one liters of enclosed aircraft fuel ignited.

The Type 531 armored mortar carrier disappeared behind

a thirty-foot wall of flame. Fire rose in a column and then fell to earth once more. The interior of the open APC and the truck behind it were engulfed in sheets of burning aircraft fuel. The sizzling rush of the conflagration was eclipsed by dozens of inhuman screams.

Bolan ran for his life.

Behind him a sudden clatter of thud-hiss sounds signaled impending Armageddon. The Executioner stretched out in a dead sprint for the fountain in the middle of the lawn. The burning fuel was not enough to set off the stored mortar bombs in the APC.

But it was more than enough to ignite the increments.

The increments were the charges in the base of each mortar bomb that hurled them into the air out of their tubes. They weren't explosive, but they burned incredibly hot and used expanding gas to shove the mortar bomb out of the tube like a bullet from a gun. The increment propellants weren't being confined by the mortar tube. They were firing off loose. The interior of the APC was already burning. Superheated gas was erupting upward out of it as the increments of the stored mortar bombs went off. The armored walls of the carrier focused the heat and fire into an inferno. Within that burning maelstrom, somewhere between thirty or forty 120 mm mortar bombs were leaping around like fish.

Not surprisingly, one of the 14.5-kilogram warheads detonated.

Goldfish scattered as Bolan dived into the fountain.

A second warhead detonated, followed by a third and a fourth and a fifth, until the sound of detonations blurred into a single, sustained cataclysmic roar as nearly a thousand pounds of high explosive fulfilled its function. The blast waves expanded the burning aircraft fuel outward in an overpressure fireball that lit the sky above shades of Halloween orange and chimney red. Bolan squeezed himself under the lip of the fountain, covered his ears with his hands and squeezed his eyes shut as the world came to a violent end.

A final detonation shuddered the fountain. The Executioner waited, holding his breath. Moments later the surface of the fountain began splashing as blackened pieces of armored personnel carrier, weapons and humans rained from the sky. Bolan's lungs contracted in his chest, but he sat tight and counted several long seconds after the last splash before he stuck his head up out of the fountain. He let his breath return to normal before he peered over the edge.

The mortar carrier was gone. Bits of it were scattered all over the lawn and the street outside the wall. Little of it was recognizable. The mansion gate was gone, as were major portions of the wall that had once surrounded it. The front half of the troop truck was utterly gone; the back half had been reduced to only three or four pieces of any significant size. The men who had manned the vehicles were in little better condition. Black smoke covered the lawn like fog and bore the horrific stench of high explosive, aircraft fuel and burned human flesh. Bolan glanced back. The mansion was burning out of control. Dimly, Bolan heard sirens wailing in the distance.

He yawned against the ringing of his ears and fished his rifle out of the fountain as he stood. The tanks were gone. No more mortar bombs were falling from outside the walls. The enemy had probably gotten one hell of a lot more than they had bargained for. Bolan trotted back to the edge of the burning building. Makhdoom and Fareed stared at him unblinkingly.

"You are the bravest man I have ever met," Fareed pronounced.

Makhdoom stuck out his hand. "Are your superiors aware that you are insane?"

Bolan took the offered hand. The captain grabbed his elbow as Bolan wobbled. Even with the stone fountain sheltering him, he had taken a beating. "Did Hussain make it?"

"I am here." The general and his four men trotted around from the back of the house. Hussain was missing his eyebrows, but other than that he seemed to be in a very good mood. "You shall receive a medal! I will ensure it!"

"Thanks." Bolan steadied himself. "We need to get out of here. Someplace safe." The soldier shook his head at the burning mansion. He'd lost his satellite link and, whoever the enemy was, if they were smart they would be watching the U.S. embassy in case he came calling. "We've got to—"

Someone was screaming twenty feet above.

Fareed's man on the roof had grimly stuck to his post. A great deal of the roof was burning. Fareed's man now hung from the eaves by his hands. His eyes were wide as he looked over the remains of the walls and he was kicking his feet for emphasis.

Fareed shook his head. "Oh, no."

The remaining Type 531 APC crashed through the wall. It was buttoned down and a pair of .30-caliber machine guns raked the ground ahead of it from an enclosed turret. Bolan was out of loose rocket pods, antitank missiles and fuel tanks. The mansion was burning. In the open ground Hussain and his riflemen would be slaughtered.

He did have about fifteen men and one half of a Hind gunship.

"Run! Get to the helicopter!"

"What?" The Pakistanis stared at him as if he were insane.

"Get to the chopper! Point it at the side of the house! Do it!"

Bolan knelt by the side of the burning mansion and began firing at the APC. The Pakistanis charged back around the house for the tennis courts. Bolan didn't look back. He fired another burst at the carrier. He wanted it moving straight toward him. The carrier commander obliged. The sloped nose of the 531 yanked around to point straight at Bolan. Its twin guns ripped into life. The big American jumped back as masonry flew with .30-caliber strikes. Bolan dropped prone and gritted his teeth as he fired another burst around the corner. The twin .30s responded. He rolled back behind cover and his teeth clenched as sparks flew from his rifle barrel and the AK-47 was hammered from his hands. His hands buzzed and ached. They were bleeding and nearly failed him as he pushed himself up.

Bolan ran exhaustedly for the back of the house. He stopped at the far corner and pulled his Beretta with shaking hands as he turned. The corner of the burning house sheered away underneath the APC's prow. Bolan snapped off five quick rounds to let the driver know he was still around. He ducked as the .30s ripped into life once more. The 531 was lightly armored and it was nimble. It could do 65 kilometers per hour and it was currently red-lining on flat, grassy ground.

Bolan ran.

Ahead of him the Pakistanis were heaving on the Hind airframe. It was resting on its wheels but even blown in two, they were still wrestling with nearly nine thousand pounds of aircraft. The nose of the helicopter was slowly turning toward the corner of the house as the Pakistanis hurled their strength against it.

It was turning too slowly.

Bolan ran on. He was out in the open, out of ideas and completely exposed.

Behind him stonework shattered as the APC turned the corner on the burning mansion the hard way. Bolan kept his eye on the nose of the Hind. He noticed with mild surprise that Hussain was in the front cockpit.

The general shot Bolan a happy thumbs-up with his left hand. He did something below the windscreen with his right. The 27 mm twin-barrel revolving cannon clacked once as it revolved and chambered a round.

Bolan threw himself down as the twin .30s opened up behind him.

The Hind's 23 mm cannon began jackhammering. The supersonic cannon shells boomed in a continuous stream over Bolan's head. His eardrums seemed to compress and meet in the middle of his brain as if he were being stabbed with an ice pick through each ear.

The cacophony ended as abruptly as it had started. Bolan opened his eyes and lifted his head painfully. The APC and the Hind had exchanged fire. Hussain sat smugly in the Hind. His windscreen was spalled and lead-smeared, but other than that the front of the Hind was intact. The massive Russian helicopter had been designed to withstand direct hits from U.S. 20 mm antiaircraft guns.

Bolan turned his head.

The Type 531 sat unmoving. Its armor had been designed to protect the occupants from rifle fire and shell splinters. The Hind's 23 mm cannon had punched 75 holes into the frontal armor of the APC. Her machine guns were silent. Black smoke oozed from the honeycomb of cannon strikes.

No one was climbing out.

Bolan lay back in the grass and gazed wearily up into the blue vault of the sky. The Pakistanis cheered rabidly and gave thanks to God as they pulled General Hussain out of the cockpit and carried him around on their shoulders. Bolan sighed.

He needed backup.

CHAPTER TEN

Florida

"The Thuggees of Kali." Carl "Ironman" Lyons walked down the pier. The only thing more achingly blue than the water off the Florida Keys was the sky above it. "Can you believe this shit?"

"I don't want to believe this shit. I thought we had taken care of that shit. A long time ago." Calvin James sighed. "But if the big man says it's for real, then it's real."

Lyons and Calvin James had been to India before. They had met and fought the Thuggees, or at least some very scary facsimiles thereof. Bolan needed men from that mission, and Lyons and James were the only two men available at the moment. More than that, the big guy apparently needed backup. Carl Lyons had been struck by inspiration, and he and James had come shopping for backup in the Florida Keys.

Two of the most dangerous men on earth left the pier and went to the parking lot. They found the space with the same number as the fishing yacht they had just checked. An ancient beige Jeep was up on blocks. A redheaded man of massive proportions struggled with a block and tackle and what appeared to be an equally ancient V-8 engine suspended over the engine compartment. He wore khaki shorts and Mexican rope-soled sandals. A brown U.S. military-issue XXL T-shirt with cut-off sleeves strained across his massive chest and shoulders. A Miami Dolphins baseball cap was turned around backward on his head. Beneath it the tight coils of red hair were bleached almost orange from long days out on the water. Arms like firehoses wrestled with the engine. The arms were burned a permanent deep-water rust from the harsh Florida sun.

Big Red was a man who would never tan.

A cooler of beer sat in the shade of one of the oversize tires. Tim Buckley's "Greetings From L.A." blared from a boombox perched on the rollbars. Lyons noted with approval that the big man's once massive girth no longer strained the front of his T-shirt the way it once had.

"Hey, Red. You lose weight?"

"Jesus H. Christ!" The big man nearly leaped out of his sandals. His green eyes flew wide at the sight of Lyons. "You!"

Trevor Burdick had once been a gunnery sergeant in the United States Marines. He had made Force Recon and served with distinction in Grenada and Operation Desert Storm. He had been wounded there, transferred to Ordnance and stationed in Korea. He had been trapped behind a desk and fallen into trafficking weapons on the black market. Many of those weapons had belonged to Uncle Sam. A man Trevor Burdick knew only as Striker had yanked him out of that situation and forced him to serve his country once more against a predatory Japanese business consortium. A while back Striker had shown up in front of his fishing boat and given him the opportunity to serve again.

Striker was without doubt the most dangerous human Burdick had ever met, but the man he knew as "Ironman" was the scariest. Burdick stared with some trepidation at the blond man in front of him. He had seen him action. Ironman was a stone-cold berserker. Burdick topped him by nearly half a foot and a hundred pounds. Burdick was Marine Recon and used to being the biggest, meanest thing on two legs in any gathering. He could meet Ironman's ice-blue eyes only with difficulty.

Ironman was that intense of a guy.

Burdick didn't know the lanky, black man standing beside him, but he seemed like an exact opposite of Ironman. He was utterly relaxed and at ease. He was like a cobra, stretched out and enjoying the Florida heat.

Burdick had been around some very bad dudes and just looking at the man, Burdick knew he would strike like a cobra. Only there would be no coiling or flaring of hoods. You would be on the ground, dead or unconscious, before you even knew you had been hit.

Now Ironman and his equally dangerous-looking friend were standing in his parking spot.

Burdick wiped sweat from his brow. These men hadn't come calling for a couple of beers or to book a fishing trip on his boat. They were here on business. They had business with him. Burdick was scared and excited at the same time. He wiped at the grease on his fists with a rag. "How you fellas doing?"

Lyons smiled. "You busy, Red?"

Burdick glanced at his Jeep engine hanging suspended in midair and the sea of parts and tools laying everywhere. "Um…nope?"

"Good. Good answer. You got any beer?"

"Um…yup." Red fished out a couple of longnecks and cracked the caps off from under the bumper of his Jeep.

Lyons took a long pull from one of the beers and cocked an eyebrow. "Light beer?"

"Yeah, well, you know." Red patted his newly reduced stomach. "Been beach running in the morning and hittin' the weights at the Y at night."

Calvin James sipped the beer and wiped the sweating bottle across his brow. "Hear you're a real wizard with languages."

Burdick cracked himself a beer and nodded. "My high school French, German and Spanish teachers called me a goddamned idiot savant."

"Hmm." James was something of a linguist himself. "Anything else?"

"I picked up some Arabic in the Gulf. Learned some Portuguese last year in my spare time when I had an idea about sailing down to Brazil." He shrugged with false modesty. "Been learnin' some Russian, recently. Mostly from my girlfriend."

"How's your Hindi?"

Burdick considered that question, and more importantly what it might lay behind it. "Uh…real thin."

Lyons nodded. "You can pick some up on the way."

"On the way?"

The black man shrugged. "To India."

"India." Burdick took a long breath and let it out. "What's happening in India?"

"The Thuggees of Kali." Lyons sipped his beer. "Heard of them?"

"No."

"They serve the Hindu goddess of death. They strangle people. They've learned to turn themselves invisible."

"Yeah, I've seen that. On a rerun of the *X-Files*."

He saw that the Ironman wasn't laughing. Neither was his friend.

"They also seem to have stolen some Pakistani nukes."

"Okay." Burdick turned off his stereo. "So, you're telling me all this because…?"

"The big guy dropped a dime. Said he needs backup." James finished his beer with a smile. "And you're the biggest, dumbest, redheaded Marine we could find."

"A left-handed Gemini with a bad moon rising, as I remember." Lyons grinned in rare humor.

"The big guy." Burdick looked back and forth between the two men. "You mean, Striker."

"Yeah." Lyons checked his watch. "Striker."

"He's in India?"

"No, Pakistan."

"Pakistan."

"Right."

"Oh."

"But there's a strong possibility that the wind is blowing in that direction."

"Oh."

"You look like you're in shape, Red." Lyons finished his beer. "Let's go."

Islamabad. The Christian Quarter

"I HAVE some people coming."

"Oh?" Makhdoom glanced up at Bolan as he ran a cleaning rod down the barrel of his rifle. "Have you cleared this with General Hussain?"

"No." Bolan sat on a sack of potatoes in the café cellar storeroom. Makhdoom had called on his connections in the Christian community. It was as safe a place as any to hide when invisible assassins, goddesses of destruction and the Pakistani II Armored Corps wanted you dead. Bolan stroked a whetstone across the edge of his rifle's folding bayonet. "But they're charming people and I think the general is really getting off on all of this."

"Yes." The captain unlocked his own bayonet and held the blade up to examine the edge in the light. "He is finally getting to play soldier."

Hussain had gone back to military headquarters and was

quite rightly pitching a fit at the highest levels. He had been attacked in his own home by tanks from the Pakistani II Armored Corps. The vehicles involved were the direct responsibility of General Aqeel Naseeruddin.

General Naseeruddin had gone missing.

Bolan suspected that the general's sudden disappearance might have coincided exactly with the ignition of about a thousand pounds of high-explosive aircraft fuel. The attack on the mansion had been more than political assassination attempt. It had been an all-out armored assault. Even with most of his vehicles knocked out, he had kept on attacking, as if his life had depended on it, and Bolan believed Naseeruddin had hit the mansion in person to make sure the job was finished, and finished right.

Naseeruddin had been gotten to, and Bolan had a good idea by whom.

Makhdoom set down his rifle. If it hadn't been finished in dull blue it would have sparkled. "You believe the warheads are now in Kashmir."

"Yeah."

"Well then, you shall have to cross the disputed border with India."

Bolan clicked open his rifle's folding stock and oiled the hinge. "Yeah."

"You know—" Makhdoom stroked his mustache in mock thoughtfulness "—my government has an extensive intelligence network in Pakistan."

"So I have long suspected." Bolan grinned.

"And you shall have to go undercover."

"Yeah."

"That will be very difficult for a Westerner."

Bolan sighed. "Yeah. Difficult, but not impossible."

"Yes, but it would be better if you had some assistance. A translator, at least, and someone you can trust."

"Yeah."

"Did you know, that as a member of Pakistan's special forces, one of the tasks I have been trained for is deep-cover operations in Kashmir?"

"Really."

"Yes, and in fact, I was born in Kashmir, in the city of Srinigar."

"I didn't know that."

"Indeed."

"Well, I am thinking about going into Kashmir. It will be illegal. The Indians will shoot us as spies if we are caught." Bolan grinned as he clicked his bayonet down and refolded the stock. For a high-powered assault rifle, an AK-47 could fold into a fairly small package. "You want to go to Kashmir with me?"

Makhdoom checked his watch. "I have no previous engagements."

Stony Man Farm, Virginia

"WELL, WELL, WELL." John "Cowboy" Kissinger looked up from his workbench. "If it isn't Big Red."

"Nice to see you, too." It occurred to Burdick that he didn't know this man's name, either. Burdick held his blindfold in his hand. All he knew was that he had been flying in a helicopter for hours. He glanced around at the racks of weapons on the wall. Some were ancient, some were modern and highly modified. Others looked as though they had been beamed straight from the twenty-fourth century. Burdick had no idea where he was.

Kissinger glanced over at Calvin James. "Where're you gentlemen headed?"

"Pakistan, and maybe into India. We may use the cable news team bit for initial cover, so we need walking-around-town weapons onsite, on arrival, as well as full warloads delivered to the embassies of both countries and to at least two safehouses."

"You've got it." Kissinger smiled at Burdick. "I suppose you want a left-handed .45."

"Well…yeah."

"I don't have much in stock for port-siders like you, but it would be easy enough for me to machine a few polymer-framed Para-Ordnance pistols into lefties for you."

James smiled as Kissinger began to speak in weaponese.

"Of course, with a polymer frame and the 14-round magazine, some people would complain about the recoil and the grip being too thick." Kissinger stared at the bunch of bananas Burdick called a hand. "But I don't suppose you'll have those kinds of problems."

Burdick held up his red-knuckled soupbones and smiled back. "Nah."

"And you're partial to M-1 rifles and Browning Auto-5 shotguns, as I recall."

"Yeah, and don't worry about trying to modify it for me. The United States Marines never made any allowance for it, so neither do I generally, except in my pistols."

"I suppose you'll want a knife."

"Well, yeah."

"Here, I was building this up for Gummer, but I can let you borrow it."

Kissinger tossed Burdick a folding knife. The big Marine caught the knife and snapped his wrist as though he were throwing a Frisbee. Three and three-quarter inches of stainless steel clacked open as if it had been spring-loaded. Burdick smiled at the elliptical, wasp-waisted knife. "Grohmann, Canadian boat knife." Burdick remembered a man with the handle of Gummer from before. The man had been a dead shot with a rifle and had an unhealthy fascination with explosives. "I didn't know they made folders."

"I slimmed the handle down and added the pocket clip. Let me know how you like it."

Burdick clicked the knife shut and made it disappear.

Kissinger nodded at Calvin. "Your equipment will be in Pakistan before you are. I guarantee it."

CHAPTER ELEVEN

Srinigar

The motor-rickshaw careened through midtown traffic. A thousand similar brightly covered three-wheeled vehicles swarmed in all directions, making way for trucks and automobiles and forcing mopeds and scooters and pedestrians out of the way. Bolan sat back and enjoyed the ride as their vehicle's ancient brakes shrieked and Makhdoom swerved them around a trumpeting elephant.

Crossing the border had been remarkably easy. Beyond the border was the actual line of control. All along the line, tanks and armored vehicles patrolled and hilltops were studded with strongpoints and dug-in artillery. However, as was the official border, the line of control itself was porous and people poured across it in both directions. Bolan had darkened his face several shades with skin dye and wound a scarf around his head. He wore the traditional local baggy trousers and *shalwar qamiz,* or longshirt, as well as the universal, thin *chador* blanket, which served as a shawl, pillow, jacket or knapsack, folded and draped over one shoulder. The shapeless cotton clothes were very comfortable in the heat and an amazing amount of hardware could be concealed beneath them. Unfortunately, Bolan had no hardware at the moment. His blue eyes had already drawn some stares, but as long as he kept his mouth shut, he could pass. Until further notice he was Makhdoom's mute cousin. If it came down to a police interrogation, he was also retarded.

Bolan watched a pair of Sikh policemen standing in the middle of the road attempting to direct traffic. Both men carried five-foot rattan staves as well as Sterling submachine guns. Both India and Pakistan were on a war footing and had been so for years. Kashmir was a pressure cooker that was continually blowing its top.

"Nice town," Bolan observed. It was true. The lake-rimmed city was amazing and the surrounding Vale of Kashmir was beautiful beyond words. It had once been the number-one tourist destination in India. The violence that tore the province apart was tragic.

"Indeed. The traffic is not bad today." Makhdoom narrowly avoided running down a pair of old men yanking on the reins of a recalcitrant camel. "There is a cricket match today, so anyone who can is watching a television or listening to the radio."

"Where're we headed?"

"To a contact of mine. He is expecting us." Makhdoom suddenly whipped the three-wheeler down a side street and parked. They walked into a café that was nearly empty. A radio in the back blared with the sound of radio announcers and the cricket game. In the kitchen the staff alternately cheered or moaned every few seconds. A thin man in a western-style suit sat in the corner drinking coffee from a Turkish-style *ibrik*.

The man rose as Makhdoom and Bolan entered.

The thin man had a knife scar on one cheek. He and the captain grinned at each other and pumped hands. Makhdoom gestured to Bolan. "This is…Mr. Striker."

Bolan smiled. It would do.

"Striker, this is Inspector Agha Sattar. He is a good friend of mine from back in our school days."

"A pleasure to meet you."

The three of them sat, and coffee was poured. The inspector put on a poker face. "How is it I can help you, old friend?"

"We have had a…problem in Pakistan. We think it may have wandered into your jurisdiction, if it has not already been in place here."

The inspector rubbed absently at the knife scar on his cheek. "What kind of problem?"

"We need to examine the records of murders within Srinigar within the last year, and if possible all of the province of Kashmir and Jammu."

Sattar lost his poker face. He burst out laughing. "Are you serious?"

Bolan leaned back in his seat. Even he had to admit was an awfully tall order. Kashmir was a war zone.

As the 1980s ended, many thousands of Kashmiris who had crossed into Afghanistan to fight as religious volunteers in the jihad against the Soviets had come home. They had come home hardened veterans, and they had come home with their guns, their fanatical devotion to Islam and the attitude that India, like the Soviets in Afghanistan, was an unwelcome, hostile, infidel invader. In 1989 a spasm of violence had erupted from one end of Kashmir and Jammu province to the other that had yet to cease. Over the past thirteen years the fighting had claimed more than a hundred thousand lives. The threat of all-out war between India and Pakistan waxed and waned year by year like the incoming and outgoing tide, but disputed land between the two Asian powers constantly seethed with religious riots and political unrest. Acts of terror were commonplace throughout the besieged state, and nowhere was the violence more evident than in the capital city of Srinigar, where bombings, beheadings, kidnappings and random shootouts were daily occurrences.

The inspector shook his head. "Do you have any idea how many murders there have been in Srinigar in the past year? And those are only the ones that have been reported. There are parts of the province where there is open warfare, parts where the police do not go, only the military will go, and only in tanks, and you wish to see police reports about murders? Do you have any idea what our case log is like? The sheer size of it?"

"We're looking for cases of a particular kind of murder."

Sattar scowled. "What kind of murder?"

"Strangulations." Bolan caught the inspector's eye and held it. "There will have been no witnesses. The bodies will have been found later. Circumstances as to how the person could have been murdered, the time, situation or surroundings may be anomalous."

"Well, the murder method of choice in the city of Srinigar is an AK-47 rifle, followed closely by large amounts of black market Russian or Chinese high explosive and tribal-cutting implements of all sizes and descriptions. Ruling those out does significantly cut down on the cases we have to work with." His eyes narrowed. "But there is more you are not telling me."

"None of the victims will be women."

The inspector frowned. "You are looking for some kind of serial killer?"

"Serial killers," Makhdoom corrected.

The inspector folded his arms across his chest and waited for the punch line.

Bolan laid the cards on the table. "The Cult of Kali is active within India again. We believe they are here, in Kashmir."

The inspector gazed at Bolan shrewdly. "And you have followed them here from Pakistan?"

"Yes."

"Forgive me, but I find it difficult to believe that a Hindu death cult could operate, much less flourish, in a modern Muslim state. Further, if my recollection serves me, the Cult of Kali was based out of Calcutta, in West Bengal, which is several thousand kilometers from here and on the other side of India. Kashmir is full of Muslims and Sikhs, all of them armed and militant, both of whom would take a very dim view of the cultists' activities."

"You make very good points, Inspector. The Cult of Kali operated out of Calcutta in West Bengal, and in what is now known as Bangladesh. Both are areas with high concentrations of Muslims. The Thuggees were deceivers, famous for posing as Muslims, and if, indeed, they are operating today, in Kashmir, the endless rounds of violence would only act to shield their own activities."

"That is an intriguing theory, my friend, and I must admit, like many in India, I was told as a child that if I did not eat my spiced spinach *palak* and cease tormenting my sister, the Thuggees of Kali would come for me in the night." The inspector leaned back and regarded Bolan dryly. "I did not much believe it then, and I'm having a hard time believing it now."

"And you, my old friend." Sattar turned a hard gaze on Makhdoom. "You and I have known each other all of our lives. I have worked hard to be a good police inspector, and I have worked hard and at great risk in the underground to serve the faith in this disputed land. I find it very strange that you would come to me now with fairy tales."

The captain's jaw set. "I do not bring you fairy tales."

Sattar shook his head dismissively. "Even if I were to divert myself from my already immense caseload, and find some cases of strangulation among the burnings, decapitations and mutilations, you would have to show me conclusive evidence."

Makhdoom's voice dropped low. "My brother, I have seen the bodies." He pulled down the collar of his shirt to show the fading bruises around his neck. "I have felt the strangler's cord around my throat, and would have died had this man not saved me."

Sattar's eyebrows flew upward. He paled as Bolan pulled down his own collar.

Bolan's voice was as cold as the grave. "They're here."

"They are," Makhdoom continued. "They have three of my country's nuclear weapons, and God help us all should they put them to use. I implore you, old friend. Aid us."

"Very well, I shall look into the matter." The inspector met Bolan's blue eyes and flinched at the determination he saw there. "But I do not think I will like what I find."

U.S. Embassy, Islamabad

"HE'S IN KASHMIR?" Carl Lyons frowned. They had just spent twenty-two hours on three different planes to reach Pakistan, and Bolan had gone and jumped into a hornet's nest without them. Aaron Kurtzman sat on the other side of the satellite link with a "What can you do?" expression on his face.

Both Lyons and James turned as Trevor Burdick began humming the song "Kashmir" by Led Zeppelin. The big man reddened and stopped. "Sorry."

Lyons suppressed a grin. Burdick was already proving to be worth his considerable weight. The big man had spent the past twenty-two hours with earphones in and absorbing CIA language school tapes like a proverbial sponge. By the time they had reached Asia, he had been chatting up the India Airlines hostesses in Hindi. When they had touched down in Islamabad, he'd charmed his way through customs in ultrapolite

Urdu. He wasn't quite ready to lead an interrogation, but Trevor Burdick's high-school teachers had been correct.

When it came to languages, the giant redheaded Marine was a savant.

There was a knock on the door of the secure communications room. Lyons blanked the screen but left the audio on as Burdick opened the door. Big Red stood in front of the door and blinked once. He wasn't used to being stared in the eye. He had an inch or so on the man filling the door frame, but the other man had about twenty pounds on him.

The two giants measured each other.

The visitor spoke in voice like cracking slate as he offered his hand. "I am Captain Ghulam Fareed. I am your liaison officer with General Hussain. I am to assist you in any way possible while you are here in Pakistan."

Burdick took the offered hand. Knuckles whitened and tendons strained as the two titans tested each other's strength. Big Red's lazy smile became a grimace of effort. "Glad you're on our side, Captain."

"Indeed." Fareed's own green eyes blazed as his jaw flexed and his knuckles creaked. "As am I."

Calvin James leaned over and spoke softly to Lyons. "It's like watching Neanderthal meet Cro-Magnon man."

"Yeah." Lyons nodded as he watched the big men play big-man games. "Which one's which?"

By some mutual subliminal signal the two men stopped trying to fracture each other's hand. "Call me Red."

"Red, yes, thank you." Fareed turned toward Lyons and James.

Behind him Burdick flexed his fingers to bring the blood back into his hand and silently mouthed the words, "Jesus Christ!"

Ghulam Fareed's green eyes measured Lyons. "You are in command while Striker is in Kashmir?"

"Yeah, that's about it." Lyons nodded.

"You have weapons?"

"We have some prepositioned here in the embassy armory, but we haven't armed up and we don't quite know our mission parameters yet. I'm hoping you can give us a debriefing on the situation. Our information has been sketchy, and we've been in transit for nearly a day and a half."

Fareed bowed slightly. "My armory is open to you. Under General Hussain's authority I am authorized to requisition you anything you require. You may ask me anything you wish. However, questions that broach Pakistani national security I must clear with the general."

"Understood, Captain, and thank you." Lyons motioned to James. "You and Red take our friend downstairs and get him some coffee. I need to make a couple of calls."

Lyons clicked the monitor back on and Kurtzman's face filled the screen. "So, is Captain Fareed as big as they say?"

"He's a freakin' human wall." A hint of a smile ghosted across Lyons' face. "But it's good to have King Kong *and* Godzilla on your side. What's the situation on your end?"

"Striker is in Srinigar. He hasn't gotten back to me since he checked in at the capital, but I've been informed by General Hussain that Captain Makhdoom has. Makhdoom is pursuing leads using a contact he has in the local constabulary. They're looking for strangulation-style killings. It's a hell of a long shot in a war zone like that, but it's all we have at the moment."

"How solid are the Pakistani allies of ours?"

"General Hussain is a real yahoo, and a wild card, but so far the man has come up aces for us in the support department. According to Striker, Makhdoom and Fareed are rock-solid."

"Where is Striker now, exactly?"

"Makhdoom was born in Srinigar, and he seems to have a lot of contacts. He and Striker rented a houseboat on Lake Dal, called *Persian Gulf*. I've been waiting for him to make contact. Meantime we have a safehouse set up for you downtown. Once you get there we— Carl!"

Lyons's head snapped backward. His eyes flared as his ca-rotid arteries cinched shut. A brutal knuckle of hardness com-pressed his throat, cutting off his air and threatened to crack his trachea. Battle instincts took over and he instantly dropped and went for the shoulder throw. His vision exploded in agony as whatever was behind him countered the maneuver with a knee to his kidney.

"Carl!" Kurtzman watched Lyons across the video link as he staggered and flailed like a drunk or a madman, his face unmistakably purpling from strangulation. "Carl!"

The force behind Lyons shoved him into the desk. He was pinned front and back and could get no leverage for a kick or a strike. The Able Team leader seized the flat-screen monitor and swung Kurtzman's image back over his shoulder like a 22-inch flyswatter. Plastic shattered and sparks flew. The ten-sion eased on Lyons's throat for a split second and a sip of air passed into his burning lungs. He dropped the shattered rem-nants of the computer monitor and used the moment's slack in the strangling cord to pivot.

The blow started in Lyons's feet. His legs cork-screwed themselves against the floor as his hips torqued. Lyons's shoulders snapped in line with his hips and torso as his stiff-ened fingers rammed forward like a blunt spear. The stran-gling cord around his throat choked off his martial arts *kiai* into a sound like a cross between ruptured steam engine and a dying wolverine. The blow landed with perfect precision.

Only years of intensive training prevented Lyons from shattering his fingers as something soft and shimmering en-veloped them and they suddenly met the hard trauma plate of body armor.

Lyons was body-checked back against the desk and the gar-rote went tight again. His throat was brutally yanked to one side as his hands clawed for a pair of scissors and missed. Against his will he was spun away from the desk. The knee came into his back again with blinding force. Lyons's vision began to go black. His hands found the shape of a human arm and he tried to get purchase for a wrist break, but the enemy was locked in, and pressure around his throat was implacable. Lyons clawed for a face but the reach was awkward and all his hands found was an invisible, shimmering softness.

Lyons's knees buckled as his brain began to die.

"Ironman!" Burdick stormed through the door. Lyons could barely make out the wild surprise on the big man's face as he tried to determine what was happening. Burdick's face split into an ugly snarl as he figured it out. He moved straight at Lyons, scooping up a heavy oak chair with ridiculous ease along the way.

The pressure on Lyons's throat suddenly eased as Burdick came into range. Lyons fought his instinct to fall forward and threw himself backward. His back met the shape of legs and hips and for a moment he had his assassin pinned against the desk.

Lyons ducked.

Burdick roared with effort as he scythed the chair in an arc six inches above Lyons's head.

Wood splintered and cracked and one of the chair legs flew across the room. A human foot hit Lyons in the back of the head as the pressure around his neck suddenly ceased. The window in front of the desk shattered outward.

Lyons let himself collapse forward onto his hands.

Burdick stood holding a pair of broken chair legs. He tossed one away and retained the other. He knelt beside Lyons, the club cocked in his left hand while his eyes scanned the room. "You all right?"

"Yeah." Lyons spoke with effort. "What did you see?"

"Fareed got a call on his cell. General Hussain wants a meet within the hour and Calvin sent me back to tell you. I heard banging around and a shout out in the hall. I came in and found you flailing around the room like you were having a conniption. Then you reached back and your hands disappeared." Burdick waggled his club. "That's when I figured it out and rearranged the furniture."

"Glad you did."

"I saw a pair of legs and feet go out the window ass over teakettle."

Lyons rubbed his throat and tried to swallow. "What's out there now?"

Burdick leaned out the shattered window. The room was on the third story. "Nothing. There's nothing out there at all except some garbage cans."

Lyons took a few moments just to enjoy breathing again.

"Jesus." Burdick scanned the room again. "Invisible fucking assassins. You know, I really didn't believe it when you told me."

Lyons shook his head. To tell the truth, neither had he. He had believed in some kind of improved camouflage or personal stealth technology, but the enemy had apparently walked right past the Marine guards and into a U.S. embassy and waltzed right into the secure communications room sight unseen. Lyons grimaced. The enemy had been sitting in the room with them—with himself, James, Burdick and Ghulam Fareed, and the four highly trained soldiers hadn't noticed a thing. The enemy had caught him absolutely flatfooted and nearly taken him out. Lyons took that personally. He picked up Burdick's discarded chair leg.

There could be another one in the room right now.

Lyons's knees wobbled as he pushed himself up. Burdick grabbed his arm and hauled him to his feet.

The ex-Marine let out a long breath. "You know, there could be a hundred of those fuckers here in the embassy and we'd never know it."

"I was just thinking that myself." Lyons bent and a picked up three feet of thick, gray, silky material that lay upon the floor. He ran it through his fingers and found the lump in the middle that had nearly cracked his larynx. He worked the lump with his thumb and forefinger and a shiny metal disk came up out of a slit in the fabric.

The disk was a very old, heavy, silver rupee coin.

Burdick glanced over Lyons's shoulder. "You seen that before?"

"Yeah, I've seen it before." Every worst suspicion was being confirmed. He looked at the smashed computer monitor on the floor. "I've got to call Aaron."

Lyons suddenly straightened. The enemy had been right in the room with them. They had heard every word that had passed between him and the computer expert. If they were clever at all, they would have been transmitting.

"We've got to get hold of Striker."

CHAPTER TWELVE

Lake Dal

Bolan watched the sun set over the lake. The bloody sunset turned the waters of the lake purple and the mountains behind it into a fire of pink alpenglow. There was a reason why travelers had been mystified by the beauty of Kashmir for thousands of years. There were reasons why every famous Indian actor in Bollywood had kept a palatial houseboat on one of the lakes. Bolan considered the police files they had gotten from Inspector Sattar. Last month's murder rate alone formed a mountain on the table. There was a reason why the famous and wealthy of India had taken their money and gone to the beaches of Goa in the past ten years. Many of the houseboats were unrented and the hotels were filled with Indian army officers.

Kashmir was a bloodbath, and there was no end in sight.

The houseboat *Persian Gulf* was palatial. With the tourist trade all but dead they had gotten it cheaply. A few rupees more had gotten them a speedboat and a couple of Waverunner personal watercraft attached to it. Bolan turned from the rail and the setting sun. Makhdoom sat on the sofa sifting through the mound of reports. The majority were hand-typed and in Urdu or Hindi. Without a computer and translation software there was little he could do to help.

Bolan sat by the sofa and unslung his weapon. He shook his head at the weapon. It was a German Schmeisser MP-40 submachine gun…or a reasonable facsimile thereof.

The weapon wasn't an ancient relic of some lost German patrol that had gotten lost in the Russian steppes during WWII and wandered south. The weapon was so new it gleamed. It was a "Peshawar Special." There was a village in the Northwest Frontier Province named Daram Adam Khel. It neighbored Kashmir but was within the borders of Pakistan.

But it was beyond Pakistani law.

The village and everyone in it specialized in one thing, and that was the manufacture of firearms. The majority of them were made by hand in the hundreds of closet-size gunsmithies lining the village's single street. The bestsellers were copies of AK-47s and U.S. M-16s, but it was said you could give a gunsmith of Darra any handheld firearm, even one he had never seen or heard of, and within ten days he could make you a copy. Once he had made the sheet metal templates defining the size and shape of every part, he could start grinding them out one every three days. There were few lathes and milling machines in the village, and those who had them used them to create antiaircraft guns and automatic cannons. For the majority of the work, anything that couldn't be drilled or punched out of sheet metal was forged by hand.

It was said that between four hundred and seven hundred weapons were produced in Darra daily.

Bolan ran a hand over his weapon. The best work of the smiths stayed at home, but Makhdoom had connections. The MP-40 Bolan held in his hands would have made Hugo Schmeisser proud. It had literally been made by hand. The fit of the parts was glass-smooth perfection and the finish was lustrous gunmetal-blue. The weapon also had the benefit of being untraceable. There were no maker's marks or serial numbers on the weapon. The only hint of its origin was the inscription "God is Great!" in Arabic on the barrel. Makhdoom had acquired handguns and heavier weapons, as well, and had them in place at the houseboat on arrival.

"Here."

Bolan glanced up as the captain tapped a photograph from the file in front of him. "I have found a third case of strangulation."

Bolan leaned over. A naked man lay on the stones of the lakeshore. His flesh was bloated and blue. Bolan could tell from the photo that the victim had been under water for some time. The mottling around his throat was still very evident despite his decomposition. "What does the report say?"

"It—" The captain paused as his cell phone rang. He clicked it open and listened for a moment before handing it to Bolan. "It is for you."

Bolan took the phone. "Striker."

Carl Lyons's voice came across the line. "We've been trying to get hold of you for hours. The satellite exchange here is nuts."

"What have you got?"

"What we got was hit, right here in the embassy. Someone came in like Casper the Friendly Ghost. I nearly got ended right in the middle of the secure communications room. Advise you assume your location is compromised."

Bolan casually let his hand drift over the grip of his weapon. "How long ago was this?"

"About four hours. Like I said, getting a call through anywhere through all these mountains and valleys on a good day is nuts, and Pakistani telephone exchange is right out of the stone age. Where are you now?"

Bolan kept his voice conversational. "Here on the boat. The lake is beautiful."

"Just you and the captain?"

"Yeah."

"You armed?"

"Oh, yeah."

Lyons voiced dropped low. "Striker, you have got to assume one or more of these assholes is on the boat with you right now, and I mean like two feet away, waiting for one of you to go to the bathroom or take a nap. Get the hell out of there."

"I understand. We're going to do some research here and catch some z's. I'll get back to you in the morning." Bolan clicked the phone off and handed it back to Makhdoom. He yawned, stretched and checked his watch. "You want some tea? I'm going to make some tea."

"No, I am fine." Makhdoom peered closely at Bolan, clearly wondering why he wasn't sharing what had been said on the phone.

Bolan slung his weapon again and rose from the couch. "Tell me more about the case you've found."

The captain shrugged and allowed the conversation to change. "Well, it is interesting. For one, the victim was a police inspector. It appears…"

Bolan walked into the kitchen. The houseboat wasn't the largest on the lake, but it was opulently appointed. A servant and a cook normally came with the premises, but Makhdoom had given them both a thick wad of money and put them on paid leave until further notice. Bolan put on a kettle to boil and then opened a couple of cabinets until he found what he was looking for. He walked back into the central room of the houseboat with three small sacks of flour in his hand. He clicked the switch on the ceiling fan to full with his elbow on the way in.

Makhdoom read from the report. "The inspector himself was looking into a murder, the strangulation of a government official he—"

"What kind of tea do you like?" Bolan interrupted.

The captain looked up. "I told you, I do not wish any tea."

Bolan nodded. "I recommend the Schmeisser."

"What?" Makhdoom blinked, but his hand went toward his weapon instinctively.

Bolan flung the flour sacks toward the ceiling fan in the middle of the cavernous central room. He shrugged the MP-40's sling from his shoulder and caught the pistol grip in his hand in one motion. The submachine gun came up as Bolan twisted his body like a lunging fencer and extended the weapon. The flour sacks exploded as the Executioner ripped each one with a brief burst. The room became an instant snowstorm.

"Bismillah!" Makhdoom rose, his eyes flaring as if he thought Bolan were insane. Bolan pointed his weapon directly at him. Casper the Friendly Ghost had literally risen up behind the captain, billowing outward like a powdered jellyfish in the fallout. The shape of a strangling cord made a smoking line through the air as it whipped for Makhdoom's throat.

"Down!"

The captain dropped like the highly trained soldier he was and the cord slapped the side of his head with a puff of flour.

Bolan squeezed the trigger of the homegrown subgun and fired. The undulating shape in front of him shuddered and seemed to smoke as flour flew from it with each hit. Bolan burned half of his magazine until the fantastical shape collapsed to the floor. He pivoted on his heel and whirled his smoking muzzle on a second shape in the corner. Five rounds hammered the apparition and Bolan's MP-40 clacked open on an empty chamber. The shape in the corner collapsed inward on itself and fell forward. Bolan ejected his spent clip and reached for a reload.

A cord whipped around his neck from behind and cinched tight. A knee blasted into Bolan's spine with sickening force.

Makhdoom rolled up from the floor with his own Schmeisser leveled.

"Hold!" a voice shouted in English just over Bolan's shoulder. "Hold, or I shall snap his neck!"

Bolan's empty Schmeisser fell from his hand as the cord twisted and tightened. He could barely sip air past it. He could feel the immense strength of the killer who held him and knew the threat was real.

"Release him!" Makhdoom snarled. The captain's eyes flicked back and forth around Bolan's head and shoulders. The killer behind him hadn't been caught in the flour storm.

"That shall not happen," the Thuggee stated. "But there is yet a chance he may live."

It was a very cryptic remark, but Bolan didn't have the time to ponder it. A lot could be hidden beneath the traditional baggy, flowing Kashmiri garments Bolan wore. His hand blurred for his sash. The strangling cord crushed his arteries and began to twist for the neck break in response. Bolan's vision darkened, but his hand carried out his implacable will. The barrel of the Peshawar Valley copy Webley revolver whipped over his right shoulder.

The .455-caliber report was cannonlike in the confines of the houseboat. Bits of unburned powder and muzzle-flash burned Bolan's cheek and his right eardrum seemed to compress into the middle of his brain. Blinking lights danced in front of his already oxygen-starved vision.

Bolan was nearly pulled from his feet as the strangler behind him fell, cord in hand. The soldier ripped the cord free and staggered back against the doorjamb, covering himself with the smoking revolver.

The powder of the flour dust was settling on everything in the room like a very fine snowfall. As it fell, it defined a man-size shape at Bolan's feet. At one end of the shape no flour was needed. Between the world wars the British army had decided that the .455 Webley round was too powerful and too inhumane and switched to a .38. The crumpled bloody lump topping the figure was disrupted in red ruin the way that only a .455 caliber, 265-grain soft-lead bullet could disrupt a human head.

Makhdoom traversed the muzzle of his weapon around the room again warily. His face was ugly to behold. "Truly, these worshipers of death begin to weary me."

Bolan sucked air until he trusted his knees. He was getting damn sick of them himself. Thrusting his revolver back in his sash, he scooped up his Schmeisser and smiled wearily as he reloaded. "Nice workmanship."

Makhdoom held up his own whitened weapon. "I buy only from Suleiman Sultan Ruifi. He's the best." He looked around again at the bullet holes in the walls and the white flour coating everything. The ceiling fan had done a fine job of dispersal. "We may lose the deposit."

His eyes traveled toward the ceiling and the deck above. "There may be more of them."

Bolan considered. "I don't think so. I think they would have joined in if there were, but I'm willing to bet we're under observation." Bolan thought about the words of the man who had held him. "I have a hunch that they might have wanted to take us alive this time."

"Yes, and they have failed."

"Yeah, and that tells me that they'll probably go to Plan B."

"Plan B?" Makhdoom shook flour from his head. "What is Plan B?"

"From what little I know, the followers of Kali won't spill blood. It's taboo, and it ruins the acceptability of any sacrifice. Spilling blood, except in certain ritual circumstances, makes the Thuggee who did it profane."

"Yes, I see, and as we have seen, they are not above getting others to stain their hands for them."

Bolan nodded. "That's right."

"You think we are going to get hit again."

"I would say almost immediately."

The roar of engines out on the lake spoke in answer.

Bolan went to the walk-in closet and pulled out a B-40 rocket launcher. He handed the weapon to Makhdoom and took out the second. The B-40 was a Chinese copy of the Russian forebear of the RPG-7. It had no optical sight, which made it easier for the craftsman of the Peshawar Valley to reproduce. Bolan tossed Makhdoom a reload and the two soldiers walked to the patio rail of the houseboat. A pair of speedboats were flying past the docks out to where *Persian Gulf* was anchored. Bolan shouldered the primitive rocket launcher. It had crude iron sights and a hopeful recommended range of one hundred meters.

Bolan faded back from the deck. "Give them a few bursts from your gun. Suck them in."

Makhdoom unlocked the folding metal stock of his submachine gun and aimed out across the lake. Fire stuttered from his muzzle and smoking brass shell casings flew across the deck.

The ornately carved interior of the *Persian Gulf* began to chip and burst apart as automatic rifles fired in response. The captain threw himself down and fired another burst between the rails. "Here they come."

A speedboat screamed toward them in the aquatic equivalent of a drive-by shooting. Three men with FN rifles hammered away at the houseboat on full-auto. A second speedboat came in like a wingman fifty yards behind. Bolan lay prone as the distance closed. At thirty yards he popped up on one knee. Ignoring the high-powered rifles chewing the *Persian Gulf*'s interior apart, he lined up his sights.

The speedboat began to peel away at twenty yards as the second boat began its run.

Bolan estimated the speed at forty-five miles per hour and led the prow of the speedboat by about five yards as he squeezed the trigger. Flame screamed from the gas-escape valve on the left side of the launcher like an angry teakettle. Backwash blasted into the houseboat's interior as the rocket left its launch tube.

The rocket accelerated to 800 feet per second and coincided neatly with the speedboat amidships. The shaped charge warhead detonated and the open interior of the speedboat lit up yellow-orange as the superheated gas blasted through the hull. Its throttles were full forward and it continued on across the lake at full speed burning, spinning out of control.

The second speedboat peeled off well out of range. Makhdoom fired a long burst from his weapon to help speed them on their way. "They'll be back. We need to police up the bodies and get to shore. I will contact Sattar and have him meet us with a dozen men. Then—"

The deeper sound of a chugging diesel was becoming distinctly louder.

"No time." Bolan left the rail and walked across the houseboat and back to the stern. Most everything above four feet in height was riddled with bullet holes. The draperies and the sofa were already burning from the rocket's launch. Bolan peered out the small kitchen window rather than going out on the back deck.

A houseboat a little larger than *Persian Gulf* was chugging toward them across the waters. Bolan listened a moment to the sound of its engines. They sounded big.

Bolan suspected outrunning them was out of the question. Makhdoom joined him, cradling the two B-40 launchers. He had reloaded Bolan's tube. He handed off the weapons and glanced out the window. "They do not seem to be in a hurry."

"No, I bet they're talking to the guys in the surviving speedboat."

"Telling them we have rockets."

Bolan nodded grimly. "That's what I'm thinking."

The surviving speedboat cruised in a large arc some eight hundred yards away. Bolan shouldered his weapon and waited. His worst suspicions were confirmed as the oncoming houseboat came to a halt a hundred and fifty yards away.

Makhdoom shook his head angrily. "How do they know the range!"

Bolan glanced back at the cloaked bodies littering the burning, well-floured mess of the main room. "Those guys watched us unload our ordnance. They probably sent a full report."

"Bastards."

"Yeah." Bolan stepped out onto the back deck and shouldered his weapon. He aimed it up into a high arc and pulled the trigger. Rocket exhaust seared the deck and the antitank grenade ascended upward on a tail of fire. Bolan could hear shouting and consternation aboard the enemy boat.

Bolan grimaced as the rocket fell five yards short and formed a hissing geyser as it detonated into the lake. "Damn."

The opposing houseboat chugged in a deep circling motion and brought its starboard broadside to *Persian Gulf*. Like a wooden ship from the days of sails, the houseboat threw open the three wooden shutters along its starboard like gun hatches.

The muzzles of three KPV Russian heavy machine guns rolled forward to point accusingly at the other houseboat.

Bolan threw himself flat as the .61-caliber machine guns opened up like God's own jackhammers of vengeance. *Persian Gulf* was being blasted apart. What didn't fly apart in splinters burst into flames. The 14.5 mm round had been taken directly from the Russian's WWII antitank rifle, and the enemy seemed to be using both high-explosive and armor-piercing incendiary ammunition.

It would take little more than a minute for the heavy automatic weapons to reduce *Persian Gulf* to the waterline.

"How many more rockets do we have?"

Makhdoom shouted above the incessant roar of destruction. "Three!"

"Fire one at them in thirty seconds! The second the same! Do whatever you want with the third!"

"Fine!" The captain shook his head at the insane American. "And just what are you going to do?"

Bolan began stripping off his baggy garments. "I'm going to swim over and board them."

"You are mad!" Makhdoom jerked his head toward the back of the boat. "What about our speedboat! The Waverunners!"

Bolan eyed Makhdoom narrowly.

The captain grimaced. "Our invisible friends will have already disabled them."

Bolan nodded. He slung his MP-40 across one shoulder and his bag of spare magazines across the other. He crawled to one of the bedrooms as the machine-gun bullets blew up or burned all they struck over his head. Bolan slithered into one of the bedrooms and beneath the window. "Where's the speedboat?"

"Circling to portside! Toward you!"

The Executioner flung open the window and slid over the side. The cold, mountain waters of Lake Dal closed over Bolan's head and clenched his naked flesh. The sun was setting behind the enemy boat. He would have to surface at least once, and would have to hope his head was lost in the glare. Bolan passed back beneath *Persian Gulf* and stroked smoothly toward the enemy boat.

He began running out of air much too swiftly. The repeated stranglings he'd taken over the past seventy-two hours had robbed him of wind and endurance. Bolan counted seconds and kept kicking. His lungs were fire in his chest, but he forced himself to stroke ahead another few seconds. He kicked to the surface and breached as lightly as he could. Com-Bloc green tracers streaked in straight lines overhead. They smashed into *Persian Gulf* and exploded or burned. From out of the carnage a shape roared up from within the houseboat and whooshed up into the sky. The rocket arced through the air and fell toward the enemy boat. Bolan didn't wait to see where it would land. He sucked air and dived back down into the dark waters.

The water ahead thudded and lit up orange for a brief moment.

Bolan swam directly toward the flash of light and waited for the bullets to tear through the depths and bite into him. Bolan's vision shadowed as his brain became starved for air. As he rose, he could see the dark bulk of the houseboat above him and the stuttering strobe of the heavy machine guns. Bolan breached directly beneath them and gasped air into his lungs. He took a few breaths as the guns hammered two feet above his head, then submerged and swam beneath the enemy houseboat's belly.

Utter exhaustion was beginning to overcome him. Bolan breached up into the dying daylight and gasped for air. He grabbed the side of the houseboat and wearily worked his way toward the rear deck. He needed time to steady himself, but if Makhdoom was still alive he was probably hiding in *Persian Gulf*'s bilge by now. Bolan unlocked the folding stock of his weapon and clicked it into place. He took a deep breath and heaved himself over the rail. The guns paused a moment as the crews slid in fresh belts of ammo into the feeds. Bolan waited for the crescendo to continue and then stepped in out of the breeze.

The layout was similar to *Persian Gulf*. The back deck led into the kitchen and then to a large, central room. Bedrooms were in the back and each had access to the rear deck. The central room was dominated by the three heavy machine-gun emplacements and the weapons pointing out the opened windows.

The sound of Bolan's 9 mm Schmeisser was lost in the continuous roar of the big guns. The effect wasn't lost on the nearest crew. The soldier gave each a burst through the back without mercy. He tossed away his weapon and yanked the dead gunner out of his seat. One of the crew from the next weapon over looked up in shock as a naked American elevated the KPV's four-and-a-half-foot barrel out of the window and traversed down and around to bring the muzzle level with its sister weapons.

The crewman screamed and yanked at his gunner's shoulder.

Bolan depressed his thumb trigger and the crew-served weapon began spewing high-explosive and armor-piercing rounds. The soldier burned fifty rounds into the nearest gun and crew, but there was no need to conserve ammunition. The 600-grain bullets were traveling at over 3,000 feet per second. No human body could contain them or even offer more than token resistance to their trajectory. Any bullet that didn't smash and mangle the neighboring gun flew through its operators to strike the weapon and crew behind it. Bolan raised his muzzle slightly and ripped the rest of the magazine into the third gun position to make sure.

The KPV suddenly clacked open on a smoking, empty chamber.

Bolan scooped up his MP-40 and clicked in a fresh magazine. A man with a pair of binoculars swung down from the rooftop to see why the firing had stopped and where all the smoke was coming from. Bolan shot him down as he came in through the kitchen. For a moment there was dead silence except for the crackling of the woodwork and tapestries as they caught and burned from the incendiary rounds.

Bolan cocked an ear as the roof of the houseboat creaked

above him with a footstep. He raised his weapon and put a burst through the ceiling. He heard a grunt, and the ceiling thudded as someone fell. Bolan swiftly made a recon of the rest of the houseboat. He climbed up on the rail and peered across the roof. A man with a pistol lay unmoving. Blood stained his pants and shirt, and his jaw had been shot away by Bolan's burst.

The speedboat was pulling away into the sunset at top speed.

Persian Gulf was a full-on inferno. Bolan was pleased as a figure suddenly burst onto the fiery deck and flung himself into the lake. Bolan watched their old houseboat burn down to the waterline as Makhdoom swam toward their new one.

They were definitely going to lose the deposit.

CHAPTER THIRTEEN

US Embassy, Islamabad

"You ready?"

James, Burdick and Fareed nodded. They were going into Kashmir as a cable news crew to link up with Bolan. They were dressed as civilians, but they were armed to the teeth. The CIA station chief at the embassy had provided them with a van, camera equipment and all the right papers.

Still, driving across the border was going to be difficult.

Lyons rolled his eyes as someone knocked on the door. Last-minute door knocks were like phone calls at four in the morning. It never meant anything good. He raised a bemused eyebrow as something good came through the door.

It was a stunning redhead.

Two Indian or Pakistan men followed her. They wore plain clothes, but the way they carried themselves screamed special forces soldier. Lyons remembered Kurtzman's report he'd read on the flight and extended his hand. "Dr. Austenford."

The woman took Lyons's hand and shook it once. She glanced at his team. Her body language spoke volumes about how she felt about what she saw. "You're the team commander."

"Yes, ma'am. That would be me."

She gestured to the two men flanking her. "This is Sergeant Ramathorn Rhadak, 16th Air Wing, and Corporal Veeshal Patel, 75th Regiment." The two men accompanying the doctor had obviously been chosen for their physical appearance, probably their languages skills, and the fact that they knew which end of an M-4 carbine was the business end.

"I'm Ironman." Lyons nodded at his team. "That's Chicago, Big Red and…" He paused as he came to Fareed.

The captain flashed a smile. "My name is Ghulam."

The two soldiers kept their poker faces, but clearly weren't happy. Ironman and his team stank of deep, dark and spooky operations, which they abhorred.

Dr. Austenford didn't look pleased, either. "I have been assured of you and your team's full cooperation."

Lyons gave his most winning smile. "We aim to please."

"I want personnel reports on every member of your team and their qualifications. I want a similar report on this operative 'Striker,' as well as a situation report on everything that's happened within the last forty-eight hours."

"I can debrief you on the last forty-eight hours." Lyons kept the smile on his face through sheer force of will. "Personnel reports are on a need-to-know basis."

"I need to know." Dr. Austenford's eyes went arctic. "And my orders come straight from the President."

"So do mine." Lyons's face went stony as he folded his arms across his chest. "When I receive verified orders to reveal personnel files, it will be my pleasure to deliver them to you."

Austenford flushed. "Give me five minutes."

"Take all the time you want."

Sergeant Rhadak set a suitcase on the desk and opened it to reveal a secure communications link. He had it fully operational with the oiled speed of long practice. Austenford took a seat, put on a headphone set and began rapidly typing. She typed responses to whatever she was being told with machine-gun speed. She suddenly shot up straighter in her seat and her eyes flicked to Lyons. Her fingers began hammering the keyboard with more vigor. Her hands froze as she went rigid. Several long moments passed. She punched a final key and slammed the link shut.

Lyons kept the smile off of his face through force of will. "How else may I assist you, Doctor?"

The scientist's voice was a study in controlled anger. "I would like that situation report, typed and in my hand within half an hour." She spun on her heel. "I'll read it on the way to Kashmir."

The doctor and the two soldiers left the room as a unit.

"Hoo-ee!" Burdick shook his head after the door closed behind them. "You pissed her off but good."

"Yeah." Lyons wasn't laughing. There was now a serious new wrinkle in the plan. He believed he already knew what the lay of the land was going to be. The President wanted the Pakistani nukes found. Austenford and the Pentagon wanted the light-transferring textile technology. It was a double agenda, and double agendas sucked. It was just such situations that got civilian scientists put in charge and led to international incidents and goat-screws of monumental proportions. Lyons knew what had to be done. It was very simple. Search and destroy. Find the Kali cultists, open a can of whoop ass on them and everything would fall into place.

He doubted whether the Pentagon could be convinced of such a rational plan.

He needed to get on the horn with Kurtzman, ASAP.

Burdick reached into the minifridge and found a bottle of Kingfisher ale. "You should never piss off a redhead."

Lyons turned. "Oh, yeah?"

"Oh, yeah." Burdick nodded as he twisted off the nontwist

cap. "They're stubborn, vengeful, controlling, and have long-ass memories." He grinned as he took a long pull on the Indian ale. "Trust me. I know."

Embassy Parking Garage

DR. AUSTENFORD SAT in the open back door of the CIA-supplied van. She jerked upright as Lyons appeared at her left elbow.

"I'm sorry I startled you—" Lyons stepped back as two shapes lunged protectively on either side of the doctor, baring their fangs.

"Sadie! Schatzie! Sit!" The dogs vibrated with aggression but rooted their butts to the bed of the van. "Down!" The dogs lay down and rested their heads on their paws. "Settle!" The two dogs rolled over and the doctor rubbed their bellies. "Are you my good dogs? Are you my babies?"

The two dogs shuddered like squids beneath the doctor's hands.

Lyons smiled at the control the doctor showed over her animals. Sadie appeared to be some kind of Rottweiler-German shepherd mix. Schatzie was a giant schnauzer with the bristling mustaches, beard and eyebrows of a Napoleonic Hussar. "Countermeasures?"

"Our frontline of defense. Cameras can be fooled, sensors can be jammed, you can play tricks on the human eye, but a dog's nose...now that is just about the most sophisticated sensor on Earth." The doctor's eyebrows narrowed dangerously. "Whoever these assholes are, they're not ready for Schatzie and Sadie."

Lyons suddenly decided he didn't want to be on the good doctor's bad side. "Listen, I think you and I got off to a bad start."

"Oh, we sure did." Austenford stood. Lyons had to admit to himself the woman had command presence, and he wasn't used to women tall enough to nearly look him in the eye. "But sooner or later I rub everybody wrong, usually from the get-go."

She suddenly looked at him mischievously. "You like my dogs?"

Lyons nodded. "Very much."

"I have more." She pulled out an aluminum suitcase and flipped the latches. She took out one of about two dozen thin metal tubes about as big as a beer bottle. "Know what these are?"

Lyons took the cylinder and noted the pin and cotter lever. "These are paint grenades. Banks sometimes put them in money bags during transport. If the wrong person opens the bag, the grenade detonates and sprays nonsoluble paint in all directions. Permanently staining the money and the perpetrators for future identification."

"Very good, Mr. Ironman. These have been modified to work like a hand grenade. Pull the pin and toss it to mark anyone or anything you think might be in a room that you can't see. Just make sure you're outside of the five-yard marking radius or you're going to have a Smurf blue complexion for a very long time. I've also had some 40 mm grenade versions worked up for the standard U.S. grenade launcher."

Lyons grinned. "Lady, I thought only me and a few people like me had access to toys like this."

Austenford matched his grin. "Buddy, I work for the Future Warrior Program. I've got toys you wouldn't believe."

"What else you got?"

"A few other weapons you might be interested in." The doctor blew a lock of red hair off her brow. "Listen, we have to work together. I'm a controlling kind of gal, I'll admit it. But I've been informed that I don't have to know who you are, all I need to do is thank God I've got you on my side."

"I appreciate that, and I'll be truthful. I don't like going into combat with civilians. Striker has already been hit about half a dozen times. I nearly got whacked right in the embassy. You sure you want to go into a combat zone?"

"I have to. We have to find the nukes, and we have to find out the who and how of the enemy using light-transferring textiles. If their stuff is as good as we think, it could affect the balance of power in land warfare and special operations in the side of our enemies for the next half century."

"I can appreciate that."

Austenford cocked her head. "But?"

"But can you shoot?"

The doctor's grin went feral. "Did I mention I'm a director on the Future Warrior Program? I get to play with all the toys."

Lyons ran his arctic-blue eyes appreciatively up and down the doctor's five-foot-ten frame. He was betting she could shoot. He held up a manila folder. "I've got that report you were asking for."

Srinigar

BOLAN RAISED his Schmeisser.

He regretted the twenty-four hours of downtime, but it had done him a world of good. He had actually grabbed three square meals and a full eight hours of shut-eye. His throat was still a mass of bruising, but he could speak without croaking and he felt half human. The fact remained that they had lost all the police files from Inspector Sattar and the bodies of the three Thuggees and their light-transferring technology when the *Persian Gulf* had burned and sunk.

They were back to square one.

He flicked off the safety as someone knocked on the door a second time. "Who is it?"

Bolan lowered the muzzle of his submachine gun as Carl Lyons spoke through the door. "Ironman. You decent, Striker?"

"Come ahead." Bolan nodded to Makhdoom and the captain shot the bolts on the heavy oak door. Lyons came in followed by a small army. He was glad to see Calvin James and Ghulam Fareed. Bolan's eyebrows rose slightly at the sight of Burdick. "You pulled Red for this one?"

"You said you needed backup. I brought the biggest backup I could find."

Bolan rose and extended a hand. "Been a long time, Red."

Burdick shook hands with him. "Good to see you in the pink, Striker."

"How's your Hindi, big man?"

Burdick didn't answer. He just looked over at James, shook his head. "The man is uncanny."

Two men of South Asian descent stood beside a nearly-six-foot knockout. The woman wore a long dress and shawl of local manufacture and a scarf over her head like a respectable local woman. She stripped the scarf away to reveal hair several shades a bloodier red than Burdick's.

Lyons gestured at the strangers. "This is Dr. Austenford, our invisibility specialist. These men were tagged by Special Operations Command to assist with the mission. Sergeant Rhadak is SAR and Corporal Patel is Army Rangers, demolition specialist."

Patel held out his hand. "Call me Boom-Boom. My friends do."

"Ramathorn Rhadak," the sergeant offered. "But call me Ramrod. It's easier."

Bolan shook hands with Boom-Boom and Ramrod. The doctor whistled and a pair of very large dogs loped through the door. The doctor was measuring Bolan. She seemed to like what she saw. "I'm glad to finally meet you. All I've been getting are cryptic reports with the name Striker on them."

"I like your dogs. That's an excellent idea."

"Oh, you don't know the half of it." The doctor snapped

her fingers and the dogs snapped to attention. "Schatzie! Sadie!" She pointed at Bolan and Makhdoom. "Friends!" The two dogs rose and shoved their noses into the men's crotches.

"Search! Sweep!" The dogs loped through the house in a sniffing pattern of every room. Bolan was impressed. The dogs now knew the scent of everyone on the team and identified them as pack members. Anyone they sniffed out sitting invisibly in a corner was very likely to get ripped apart.

Makhdoom finished meeting and greeting and turned to Bolan. "Quite a little army you have here. What do you intend to do with it?"

"I don't know." Bolan watched the dogs come back wagging their tails. "Invade India?"

The Pakistani special forces officer smiled. "I have been wanting to invade India for a long time."

CHAPTER FOURTEEN

"Two teams." Bolan checked his gear. Lyons had brought him a full war load along with Austenford's highly modified equipment from the labs of the Future Warrior Center. "Ironman, you keep your team the way it is. Work the news team gig for whatever it's worth. Take one of the dogs. I don't know how you'll explain her, CNN mascot, whatever, but the enemy will most likely layer their next attack, and you'll need that dog's nose."

"Roger that," Lyons agreed. Having been nearly strangled to death in a U.S. embassy secure room, he considered Sadie, the wonder dog, a definite asset.

"I'll stick with Makhdoom and Fareed. We're going to try to look like locals and see what we can find." Bolan glanced over at Schatzie. Explaining a giant schnauzer in Kashmir was going to be very interesting. Most Muslims, and Hindus for that matter, considered dogs unclean animals. "Doctor, you keep your men close and go with whichever of us you think is getting you where you need to be."

Austenford racked back the action on a silenced Walther PPK. "Fine." Boom-Boom and Ramrod were checking over their suppressed Mk 23 SOCOM pistols.

"We're going to try to get hold of copies of the police files we got from Inspector Sattar. We had a couple of leads, but they went down with the ship. Any questions?"

Everyone seemed to have their mantra tight. "I have a question for you, Doctor. Are you sure this isn't something that escaped out of your lab?"

"All I have to go on is that fragment you acquired in Rawalpindi." Austenford's brow furrowed. "But on that alone, I would have to say that our lab hasn't been breached. We've just been flat out-topped. Someone out there is several steps ahead of us."

The doctor tucked her weapon away. "While we're asking questions, are you really sure about this Kali connection?"

Bolan rubbed the bruises on his throat. "We have the same MO. We have a couple of abandoned places of worship, and one witness, recently deceased, who corroborated it. The enemy risked a great deal to take out our witness. We haven't found any four-armed idols yet, but my gut instinct is yes. It's a Kali cult."

Austenford frowned. "I'm having a hard time believing in some fanatic Hindu cult stealing nuclear weapons from Muslim countries and getting their hands on light-transferring textile technology that is a generation ahead of the stuff in our labs."

"Positively anomalous, isn't it?" Bolan checked over a suppressed 9 mm Colt submachine gun. It mounted a thermal-imaging sight on top, and someone had slaved a high-pressure paint canister beneath the barrel. Bolan glanced up at Calvin James. "Can you shed any light on it?"

"Well, to begin with, not all Thuggees were Hindus. The cult is believed to have originated in the Bengal region, where there is a large Muslim population. Large numbers of Muslims converted to the Kali cult over the centuries."

Makhdoom and Fareed snorted in disgust at the idea.

"The Thuggees often used passwords and secret signs

based on Islam," James continued. "'Greetings, Ali my brother' is one of the more traditionally well-known. There were others, most based on the Islamic Prophet Ali. Shi'ite Muslims hold Ali as one of the highest prophets. So did the Ismaali assassins of Persia. Not surprisingly, the largest concentration of Ismaalis left in is India. Of course, tens of thousands of Muslims fled East Pakistan when it was overthrown by the Hindus and became Bangladesh. Most of them moved to Pakistan. Judging by what we've seen, I'd say a significant number of Kali cultists followed the migration. I'm thinking we have active chapters of Kali on both sides of the Indian subcontinent."

Bolan mulled all that over. "On your mission, didn't the cultists have a charismatic leader?"

"Oh, yeah, but he was a fake. A gangly little guy, but he had the gift of gab and he could make people believe."

"If the Kali cult is suddenly active again, using modern gear and stealing nuclear weapons, something or someone must have energized it."

"A new leader." James nodded.

"Yeah, I'm talking full-on messianic figure. If he exists, there must be rumors of him, at least on the street level."

"You're talking street level, like on the streets of Calcutta."

"Yeah, I don't how much more we can get done here. Even if we can get copies of those reports, I'm thinking everyone involved will have cleared out by now and taken the weapons with them."

Bolan turned to the captain. "Doom, did you get hold of Sattar yet?"

"No. He is not answering his phone at police headquarters. At the desk they say they have not seen him." Makhdoom clicked his phone shut. "He has not answered his cell phone in four hours."

"You know where he lives?"

"Yes, I do."

Bolan nodded. "Let's roll."

IT WAS TOO QUIET.

Bolan ran his thermal-imaging sight over the yard. Nothing showed up. Nothing was moving. The two teams had met up at inspector Sattar's house with the dogs. The inspector lived in a suburb near the Jhelum River. The ground was marshy and the little streets were lined with water-loving trees. His house was set back to one side near the end of a cul-de-sac. It had the street to its front and the river to its back. There were no streetlights to speak of away from the center of downtown. Bolan didn't like it.

Calvin James's voice echoed the sentiment in Bolan's earpiece from his sniper-hide on the roof of an empty and shot-up house across the narrow street. "Nice place for an ambush."

Great minds thought alike.

Bolan kept his sights on the house as he spoke softly to Makhdoom. "What do you think?"

The Pakistani stared unblinkingly at the house. His homemade MP-40 now sported a similarly homemade Peshawar Special sound suppressor. "I fear for my friend."

Bolan feared the worst, as well. He put his thumb to his throat mike. "Ramrod, what have you got on the east?"

The SAR operative spoke from his side fence. "Nothing moving, Striker."

"Red, what have you got on the river?"

Burdick answered from where he and Fareed hid in the trees watching the side and back of the house. "Nothing, Striker. River is quiet."

Austenford cradled a suppressed FN P-90 Personal Defensive Weapon. "What do you think?"

Bolan smiled thinly. "I'm interested in what Sadie and Schatzie think." He took the dogs' leads and handed Sadie's to Makhdoom as he gave the orders. "The captain and I are going in. Cover us."

Bolan and Makhdoom left the cover of the van and crept forward under the starlight. They took the low wall surrounding the front of the house in a silent vault. They crouched in the shadow of the wall for long moments listening. Bolan spoke low. "Sadie, Schatzie, search, sweep!"

The two men let go of the leads and the dogs ran a search pattern around the front yard. Bolan waited until they came back wagging their tails before he approached the front door.

"Do it."

The captain put his boot into the door and it splintered backward out of its frame. Bolan stepped with the muzzle of his weapon in front of him. He flicked the light switch and nothing happened. He pressed the thumb switch on his carbine and the mounted light burst into life.

"He had a wife and children?"

Makhdoom held his Schmeisser in one hand and played a flashlight around the living room with the other. "Yes, but he sent them away yesterday to stay with relatives in Baramula."

Bolan thumbed his throat mike. "Chicago, what do you have out on the street?"

"No movement, Striker," Calvin James replied. "Quiet, real quiet."

"Ramrod, Red, take the back door. Boom-Boom, Fareed, cover them."

Bolan and the captain stood shoulder-to-shoulder and waited. Burdick's voice rumbled in Bolan's earpiece. "We're at the back door."

"Come on in, then hold position."

"Affirmative, Striker."

"Schatzie, Sadie, search and sweep!" Bolan and Makhdoom dropped the leads and the dogs ran across the living room sniffing in all directions and then disappeared down the hall.

Burdick spoke again. "Striker, K-9 team has made contact."

"We're coming ahead."

"Wait!" Burdick paused a moment. "Come ahead slow, something is up with the dogs."

Bolan stopped in the hallway. Schatzie and Sadie were moving their heads back and forth and making unhappy noises at the closed door to the master bedroom. Bolan's nose wrinkled at a faint smell he had become all too familiar with in his life.

The stench of death washed into the hall as Bolan kicked the door. Guttural blasphemies snarled from Makhdoom's throat as his light played on what was left of his friend. Bolan had seen the human "turkeys" the Italian Mafia had carved and left as an example to anyone who would defy them. He had seen Colombian "neck-ties" and every assorted atrocity used by organized crime.

This was his first calling card left by the goddess of death.

The goddess had been painted on the wall crudely but with great attention to detail. Bolan had downloaded any number of Kali images before he had lost his computer, and this one ran to type. Kali stood six feet tall, her skin was dark blue and she was naked except for a necklace of human skulls and a string of human hands about her waist. Her two-foot-long bright-red tongue fell from between her fangs to loll between her pendulous breasts. Blood besmeared her lips and bosom. Of her four arms, two hands were curled in mudras—or symbolic and holy hand gestures to encourage her worshipers. In a third hand she held a sword on high and in the fourth a severed human head. She danced upon a corpse. The painting was fairly crude, but the artist had captured the spirit of his subject.

Kali's red eyes seemed to fall upon you wherever you stood in the room.

There was one other significant difference. The dark blood staining Kali's lips, tongue and breasts was real. Two of the human hands that formed her skirt were real and had been affixed to the painting with nails. The corpse she danced upon was real and lacked both of its hands and its head. The painted hand of Kali held up Inspector Sattar's head as a bloody trophy where it had been nailed.

"If Allah wills it…" Bitter tears spilled down Makhdoom's face. His voice was terribly quiet. "There shall be a reckoning."

Calvin James spoke in Bolan's receiver. "Street is still quiet, Striker. What's your situation?"

"We're too late. The enemy got here first."

"Damn. Is it bad?"

"Yeah." Bolan gazed bitterly upon the human sacrifice. "It's bad. Ironman, you need to come in and bring the forensics kit from the van. I need fingerprints, paint samples—the works—and we don't have much time."

"I'm on it."

Bolan turned to Makhdoom. "You all right?"

"No. I am not all right." His eyes never left the corpse of his friend. "Do you know the word, *badal?*"

Bolan had heard the word. He had crossed the border between Pakistan and Afghanistan in the past and had seen the results of tribal feuds that had spiraled out of control for generations. *Badal* was one of the four pillars of *Pashtunwali*, the moral code of Pathan society. *Melmastia* was hospitality, shown to all visitors without expectation of reward, no matter what its cost to you, and even to the point of laying down one's life for one's guest. *Nanwatai* was the total submission of the vanquished to the victor. If done with absolute humility and sincerity, honor was restored to the vanquished, and then the victor was expected to be magnanimous. *Nang* meant honor, most prominently the honor of the women belonging to the tribe, clan or family. *Nang* was defended to the death. *Badal* was the final pillar of Pathan honor.

"It's a Pashtun word." Bolan gazed at the bloody goddess adorning the wall. "It means revenge."

"Not entirely. It is more than just revenge." Makhdoom gazed long upon the bloody goddess adorning the wall and the bloody trophy she held. "*Badal* means one's obligation to avenge."

"I didn't know you were a Pathan."

"My family moved to Srinigar two generations before I was born. *Pashtunwali* ruled our lives in the mountains of the north. In Kashmir my family became sophisticated city people, but we never forgot that we are Pathans. Before the Prophet Mohammed, all praises onto him, there was the *Pashtunwali,* and always will there be, until the end of time, or the end of the Pathan people."

Bolan's eyes fell from the goddess to her victim. "*Badal,* then."

"Yes." Makhdoom's face was terrible to behold. "*Badal.*"

Lyons entered the room with his forensics kit. He took in the horrific scene with a single stone-faced glance. Then the former L.A.P.D. detective went to work collecting evidence.

"Striker!" Burdick spoke from his position covering the river behind the house.

"What have you got?"

"I don't know." Bolan could hear the click of the big man's safety flicking off. "Something, maybe nothing. I don't know."

"What did you see?"

"Movement, maybe. At the river's edge. I don't see anything now, but with these shitheads we're dealing with…"

"Hold your position. Chicago, can you see Red?"

"Got him covered," James replied. "How do you want—wait!"

"What is it?"

"Vehicle, coming down the road. Two of them. Civilian cars. They have light bars, Striker! Police vehicles!"

Lyons looked up from his work. "This is going to be fun to explain."

Makhdoom checked his weapon. "If it's really the police."

Bolan ran the possibilities. The enemy were deceivers. They could be wolves in cops' clothing. But if the enemy was invisibly watching the house, it was they who could have called the police just to mess with Bolan and his team. Lyons was right, their weapons, their presence, and ritual sacrifice would be real fun to explain to the Indian authorities. The van was parked in a cul-de-sac.

And Burdick thought he had movement on the river.

"Red, Ramrod, hold positions. Boom-Boom, I need you here. Chicago, cover me." Bolan turned to Makhdoom. "We're Americans, but you're Pakistani special forces. If this goes sour, it's an international incident, but you'll most likely be shot as a spy. Link up with Red and pull a fade on the river if this goes official."

The captain clearly didn't like it, but he nodded and moved toward the back of the house.

"Striker," James radioed, "they're pulling up beside the van. Two vehicles. Eight men getting out. Big guys, wearing turbans. They look like Sikhs."

That jibed. Sikhism was a religion, but ethnically most of them were Punjabis, and they were a tall and brawny people. They had the reputation of being pugnacious and not taking crap from anybody. Sikhs were very often soldiers and policemen in Indian society.

Bolan and Patel walked out of the house with just their pistols tucked beneath their shirts. The eight men had surrounded the van. One man was tapping on the window with his *lathi*, a five-foot fighting stick made of rattan. It was the traditional billy club of India, and lethal in trained hands.

Austenford was smiling, shaking her head and not opening the door.

"Can we be of some assistance?"

The Sikhs turned. Bolan could see the police badges they

wore on chains around their necks. A very large, bearded man in a turban loomed over Bolan. "And who are you?"

"A guest of Chief Inspector Sattar's and this—"

Boom-Boom began to speak in Hindi with the policemen. Bolan didn't know what he was saying, but he produced some official-looking documents that caused confusion among the ranks. The big man turned to Bolan. "I am Inspector Arjan Singh. We had reports of a disturbance at the inspector's house, an anonymous report. He is not answering his phone. Now we find strangers on the premises. You can understand our concern."

"Of course. We are concerned ourselves. We have been unable to contact him, either."

The big man raised an eyebrow. "The inspector is not here?"

Bolan shook his head. "No."

"Perhaps we should look inside."

"Very well."

Corporal Veeshal Patel spoke in Spanish. *"¿Habla Espanol?"*

"A little," Bolan replied in kind. "Why?"

Both of Inspector Singh's bushy eyebrows rose. "I am sorry, what did you say?"

The Ranger continued in Spanish. "These guys aren't Sikhs. I don't think they're cops, either."

Bolan spun. He ripped the heel of his hand up in a vicious uppercut that unhinged Singh's jaw. The man beside him viciously lunged his *lathi* like a bayonet at Bolan's solar plexus. The soldier made no move to block. He took the hit on his concealed body armor. Bolan stepped forward and slammed the steel toecap of his boot into his attacker's shin with bone-cracking force. His right hand pistoned into the man's solar plexus a split second later. The man threw up and fell as his xyphoid-process broke and perforated his diaphragm.

Bolan knelt and swung his fist up like a ball and chain be-

tween the legs of a third attacker. The man gagged in agony.
The Executioner continued the move, standing and lifting his
opponent up into a fireman's carry. He flung the agonized attacker into his comrades.

A strangling cord whipped around the big American's
throat and cinched tight.

His attacker pressed a knee into Bolan's back to tighten
the strangle. The soldier reached back and found the strangler's hand. He pried his attacker's thumb open and the
man screamed as Bolan broke first one and then the other.
The knee slipped from Bolan's back and he whipped the
back of his head into his attacker's face. He ripped the cord
from his attacker's mangled hands and drove his foot into
the side of his knee. The crippled assassin fell mewling to
the street.

Boom-Boom was fully engaged. One man tried to strangle him while another tried to beat him to death with a *lathi*.
Two men with sticks rushed Bolan. The door to the van flew
open and Austenford shoved her silenced PPK forward. The
little pistol chugged three times in rapid succession and one
of Bolan's opponents dropped. The second man swung his
stick like a baseball bat toward Bolan's head.

Stick fighting was simple if you didn't have a stick. You
had to counter the instinct to stay away and try to dodge. You
closed with your opponent and lunged into the arc of the
blow. The center of the hurricane was the only safe place. Japanese karate men called the technique "grasping the thunderbolt." The caveat was, you had to do it without getting your
head taken off in the process.

Bolan lunged as the stick blurred for his temple. He seized
the man's wrists and torqued his hips. The deceiver flew over
his shoulder and into the van with spectacular force.

Austenford's little pistol clacked open on a smoking empty
chamber as she shot Ramrod's last opponent in the temple.

Bolan surveyed the crippled and killed at his feet. "Chicago, what do we have on the street?"

"Nothing moving but you and yours, Striker. Damn, you fight ugly."

"Red, how are we doing on the river?"

"I'm linked up with Makhdoom. I don't see anything moving, but I don't like it. Something's wrong."

"Striker!" James's voice rose in warning.

Bolan pulled his pistol from beneath his shirt. "What?"

"The trunks! Of the cars!"

Bolan whirled on the two sedans the fake policemen had driven. Both trunks were open. Bolan and Ramrod went back-to-back.

The invisible had just made an appearance.

Austenford raised a whistle to her lips and blew. Sadie and Schatzie came blasting out of the house at a full gallop. "Sadie! Schatzie!" The doctor barked orders. "Get some! Get some! Get some!"

Schatzie, the giant schnauzer, bore down on Bolan like a seventy-pound, mustached thunderbolt. She veered off at the last second and lunged to Bolan's right. The dog slammed into something and appeared to hang flailing in space with its teeth clenched around something invisible.

The invisible something screamed as Sadie attacked, as well. The dogs fell to the ground savaging whatever lay beneath them and a pair of feet and legs suddenly flailed into view. Bolan joined the dog pile. He slammed down the steel slide of his Beretta as if he were splitting wood where he felt a forehead beneath him. The invisible figure stopped struggling.

"Striker!" James warned. "Lookout! The car!"

The driver's-side door of one of the sedans slammed shut. Although no one appeared to be behind the wheel, the car roared into gear and leaped forward. Bolan heaved up the unconscious body beneath him and staggered to put the van between himself and the oncoming car. The car ran over its former occupants without a qualm. Glass flew and metal screamed as its bumper smashed into the front corner of the van. The car fishtailed past, bullets striking sparks off the hood as James engaged from the roof. Bolan ripped open the passenger door of the van and threw in his suspect.

The sedan screamed around in a circle at the end of the cul-de-sac and revved up to ramming speed. Bolan leveled his Beretta 93-R and began methodically putting bullets through the driver's side of the windshield. Patel fired his SOCOM pistol from the other side of the van. Bolan waited to the last moment, watching the car's tires to see which way it was going to go.

The car jinked left, and Patel went to dive out of the way. The Ranger yanked to a stop.

"Patel!"

The shot, crippled and run-over men at Patel's feet clutched his legs and held him in place. Patel fired his pistol into the crippled assassins clasping him. Bolan ran around the front of the van as the sedan roared past. Patel flew thirty feet as the car hit him dead-on at forty-five miles per hour. Once more the driver of the sedan crunched over his own people. Bolan fired the 93-R dry as the sedan became nothing but taillights in the distance.

"Patel's down! We are blown at this location! We are extracting!" Bolan ran to Patel, but already it was too late. Only tendons and skin held the shattered Ranger together. Bolan grabbed the corpse and carried it to the van. "You all right?"

Austenford had been inside when the van had been hit. Her scalp was bleeding, but she had already slid behind the driver's seat. The front bumper was crumpled, but the engine started when she turned the key. "I'll live."

Burdick, Fareed, Ramrod and Makhdoom came pounding around from the back of the house. Lyons came out the front a moment later. They piled into the van with the dogs. Ramrod's face was tight as he saw what was left of his team member. "Look at that."

Bolan looked. Someone was visibly sitting in the passenger seat. The slumped form of a man in a silver-gray monk's robe sprawled unconscious. Whatever had powered his light-transferring textile garment had cut out. The men piled into the van, and the doctor pulled it around. James came loping out of the darkness and leaped through the sliding door. Burdick slammed it shut, and the van pulled away from Inspector Sattar's house.

"You, asshole—" Burdick glared at the robed figure "—are in a shitload of trouble."

GET FREE BOOKS and a FREE GIFT WHEN YOU PLAY THE...

Lucky 7

SLOT MACHINE GAME!

Just scratch off the silver box with a coin. Then check below to see the gifts you get!

YES! I have scratched off the silver box. Please send me the 2 free Gold Eagle® books and gift for which I qualify. I understand I am under no obligation to purchase any books, as explained on the back of this card.

366 ADL D34F   **166 ADL D34E**

FIRST NAME

LAST NAME

ADDRESS

APT.#   CITY

STATE/PROV.   ZIP/POSTAL CODE

7	7	7	**Worth TWO FREE BOOKS plus a BONUS Mystery Gift!**
🍒	🍒	🍒	**Worth TWO FREE BOOKS!**
♣	♣	♣	**Worth ONE FREE BOOK!**
🔔	🔔	🍒	**TRY AGAIN!**

(MB-04-R)

DETACH AND MAIL CARD TODAY!

The Gold Eagle Reader Service™ — Here's how it works:

BUSINESS REPLY MAIL
FIRST-CLASS MAIL   PERMIT NO. 717-003   BUFFALO, NY

POSTAGE WILL BE PAID BY ADDRESSEE

GOLD EAGLE READER SERVICE
3010 WALDEN AVE
PO BOX 1867
BUFFALO NY 14240-9952

NO POSTAGE
NECESSARY
IF MAILED
IN THE
UNITED STATES

CHAPTER FIFTEEN

Uri

Bolan's hand closed around his Beretta 93-R pistol as someone knocked softly at the door. The team had bugged out of Srinigar and driven east for several hours over some of the most treacherous mountain back roads Bolan had ever seen at two o'clock in the morning. They had arrived at the city of Uri several hours before dawn and gone to a teahouse used as a haven by Muslim guerrillas.

Makhdoom seemed to be on a very friendly basis with the proprietor. They had taken the suite of tiny rooms above the teahouse and grabbed some sleep. Bolan's hand relaxed around his weapon and he slid it back under his blanket. "Come in, Doctor."

Austenford entered. She had discarded her traditional garments and was wearing an oversize Navy SEALs PT shirt as a nightgown and apparently not much else. It clung to her tawny form in all the right places. She smiled suspiciously. "And how did you know it was me? You always expect redheads at your door at four in the morning?"

"I smelled your perfume."

"You are good." Her eyes narrowed. "And I've known some guys who are good."

Bolan put down his book and sat up on the bed of rope. "Couldn't sleep?"

"No, I can't. I'm kind of worked up. This is the first genuine use of light-transmitting textiles in the field, and they're not mine." The doctor sighed as she sat on the bed. "And I'm nine thousand miles away from a lab that's of any use to me."

Bolan nodded. "Must be frustrating."

"It is. I guess I'm still all amped up from what happened tonight, too. That was my first firefight."

"You could have fooled me."

Austenford grinned and flexed her bicep. "Not bad for a girl who just turned forty."

"I pegged you for thirty-five."

"Hmm." The doctor grinned in bemused suspicion. "You're sweet."

"You must work out."

"I don't have time to work out. I work in a lab, for the Pentagon. When I have any time to myself—" the doctor shrugged "—I play golf, drink Cosmopolitans, and sleep with Special Forces soldiers."

"Nice regimen." Bolan nodded respectfully as he admired her form. "It seems to be working."

"Thanks. It was my first firefight, but I've had some training. In my line of work they make it very clear to you that you could be the subject of kidnapping. I took some steps, consulted some old boyfriends and picked up a few tips." She peered at the book Bolan was reading by the light of the oil lamp. "What's that?"

Bolan held up the book. The doctor read the title. "'*Kali: Black Goddess of Dakshineswar.*'"

Bolan tossed the book aside. "Light, bedtime stuff."

"You're really buying into all this Kali cult action?"

"You didn't see what was left of Inspector Sattar," Bolan countered. "Be glad you didn't."

The doctor's voice grew somber. "Your friend, Ironman, told me about it. It's horrible."

"Yeah, and they can turn invisible, and they have nukes." Bolan looked deeply into the doctor's eyes. "Who could have manufactured suits like that, besides you?"

"Well, I can't, and that's kept me tossing and turning for three days." The doctor's brow furrowed in thought. "The Russians, possibly, but they're really just too bankrupt to make the attempt. Chinese, possibly, but if they are, we have no records of any scientists they have who are capable of it. The Japanese have the wherewithal, I suppose, but our intelligence has received no inkling that they are working on it, and we have our ears to the ground."

Bolan looked at Kali's leering face on the book he had tossed on the table. "The Indians?"

"No way." Austenford snorted. "They just don't have the facilities."

Bolan's instincts suddenly began talking to him as he stared at the goddess's bloody gaze. He found himself considering a few past missions. "You know, I've operated in Northern California once or twice, and just about every other high-tech engineer in the Silicon Valley is from India."

"Jesus! You are good! I've been thinking Chinese-Russians-Chinese-Russians and chasing my tail." Austenford sat upright on the bed as her mind took the idea and ran. "But that could be it! Right in our own backyard. I guess it was ego that kept me from seeing it. I knew my lab hadn't been breached, and I didn't give anyone else back home the credit. That's possible. That is a genuine possible lead. In the morning I need to..." The doctor suddenly snapped around from her ramblings and looked hard at Bolan. "Wow, you have a brain and everything."

"And everything," Bolan agreed. "What do I win?"

The doctor cocked a mischievous eyebrow. "Do you know what I like about Special Forces guys?"

"They play with your toys?"

"Well, yes."

"But?" Bolan asked.

"Yes, the butts are nice. Running a million kilometers every morning, swimming a thousand more at night, wrestling crocodiles. Yup, nice butts, but the coolest thing…" The woman's eyes grew luminous in the lamplight. "Strong hips."

A slow smile spread across Bolan's face as the SEALs shirt rose up over Austenford's head and was flung into the corner. It was all she was wearing. Bolan examined the curves of her body as her pale skin glowed rose-color in the lamplight.

Cosmopolitans and golf were treating the doctor well.

"But as for what you win…" Austenford's breasts dragged across Bolan's chest as she leaned over him toward the lamp. Her lips pursed and the tiny room went pitch-black as she blew out the flickering flame. "Brains get you in the bonus round."

The Cellar

BURDICK SHOVED his face into the captive's. "You're in trouble, shithead." The captured Thuggee flinched back as far from the redheaded giant as his bonds allowed. The man was a large man with very large hands. He had the dark skin and aquiline features of a Dravidian from the south of India. His brow was a massive raised welt where Bolan had pistol-whipped him. Bolan had to admit that Burdick was right.

The killer was in a lot of trouble.

Makhdoom surveyed the man coolly. "Perhaps we should give him to General Hussain." The captain's nose wrinkled in distaste. "He delights in these sorts of activities."

Bolan didn't want Burdick to beat the man into oblivion,

and Bolan had little use for battery acid and jumper cables or the people who employed them in interrogations. He nodded to James. "You ready?"

The former Navy SEAL medic tapped the bubble out of a syringe. "Let's do it."

The captive thrashed, but he was securely bound. And with Burdick and Fareed holding him down, he might as well have been locked in a vise. The Thuggee suddenly went still and sneered as James approached with the needle. "And what is that?"

"You're going to sing like a bird," Burdick stated.

"I, who have heard the nightingales singing in Paradise?"

Everyone turned as the prisoner spoke for the first time. The Thuggee seemed preternaturally calm as he watched the needle. "What is that to one who has tasted the sweetness of Kali?"

James expressed a slight amount of fluid from the syringe and a faint garlicky smell filled the room. The former SEAL medic slid the needle into the captive's arm and injected him with 500 cc's of thiopental sodium.

The Thuggee watched the proceedings with amusement.

Bolan watched the man's eyes.

"Truth serum" wasn't the wonder drug films and books made it out to be. It didn't make people tell the truth at all. A good description of thiopental sodium would be an "ultra-fast-acting barbiturate producing general anesthesia." Psychiatrists and veterinarians used it every day in their practice. What it did in humans in small concentrations was loosen them up, make them lose their inhibitions and become very communicative. It couldn't make an individual tell the truth if they didn't want to. Bolan had felt its effects himself. A man of will, particularly with training, could resist interrogation under it. But the drug still had its effect. It would certainly help a man make mistakes in cross-examination. Its greatest effect was as an anti-inhibitive. Human nature was on Bolan's side. The fact was, humans liked to talk, and what they loved to talk about most was themselves. In Bolan's experience, fanatics, in particular, just couldn't shut up about themselves or their causes.

Bolan doubted the man was going to reveal where the nukes were or give up his organization, but Calvin James was a master. Bolan had every hope that over the course of a friendly conversation Calvin could make the man slip up and give out some important clues.

James smiled. "How do you feel?"

The Thuggee smiled back. "I feel fine."

"Not quite the sweetness of Kali, huh?"

"No, to feel Kali's embrace is to know all, to be all." The Thuggee smiled condescendingly. "What do you know of Kali?"

"She's a soul sister." James grinned. "Black like me."

Bolan suppressed a smile. Another way to get someone talking was to piss them off.

The Thuggee regarded James as if he were speaking to a little child. "Kali is dark as night. Dark as the sea at night. Look upon the sea from a distance and it is dark and girds the world. Approach the sea and it is clear and colorless at your feet. Try to hold it in your hands, it is formless. You cannot hold it, you cannot truly see it, but you can step into it, let it envelop you, drown in its majesty and become a part of it. Such is Kali."

"Beautiful metaphor," James agreed.

"It is not metaphor. It is the truth. The sea can also be a dark destroyer. Unstoppable, rending all the works of man. We live in the fourth cycle, the dark age, the end time." The Thuggee's face was serene. "Now is the time of Kali."

Burdick leaned in close and spoke softly in Bolan's ear. "I don't like it. This guy's way too salty."

Bolan agreed. He watched the captive's eyes and he didn't like what he saw. Most people at least initially tried to clam up and fight the drug. The Thuggee was utterly relaxed and his eyes were clear. He was drugged, bound in a cellar in a Muslim safehouse in Kashmir and surrounded by his enemies.

Yet the Thuggee was acting as though he was in control of the situation.

"We had little time to prepare Inspector Sattar." The Thuggee's eyes widened. He regarded James and the rest of the men in the room with exaltation. "You all shall feel the sweet pain of sacrifice as Kali takes your flesh and souls."

Makhdoom's knuckles cracked as he made fists. Bolan put a restraining hand on the captain's shoulder. The Thuggee's eyes slid to Bolan's. There was genuine power in the man's dark gaze. Bolan gazed back impassively.

The Thuggee's smile was beatific. "You, dark one, however, shall taste the sweetness of Kali."

James shot Bolan a quick grim look. It wasn't working. The interrogation was going FUBAR.

"Kali has four hands," the Thuggee continued. He ran his burning gaze over Fareed, Burdick, Makhdoom and James. "In one hand she holds the severed head of sacrifice, so shall you four be." His eyes fell once more upon Bolan. "Two arms she holds out to her worshipers, in that exalted embrace shall you find yourself."

Makhdoom shook his head in disgust. "I say we give him to Hussain and his secret police. They'll—"

"In Kali's fourth hand she holds a sword," the Thuggee interrupted. "I am that sword." He bowed his head. His eyes crossed and his terrible gaze regarded a place between his eyebrows. "Behold."

The muscles of the Thuggee's exposed arms contracted like cables across his bones.

"Shit!" Burdick roared.

Three plastic police cuffs held the man's forearms to the arms of the chair, and two more pairs held his ankles to the chair legs. Four of the six straps exploded like springs from the Thuggee's arms as he rose. The arms of the chair snapped away as he took the other two restraints up with him.

"Bismillah!" Fareed threw his arms around the man in a bear hug. Bolan had learned that Fareed had been a former heavyweight wrestler on the Pakistani national team.

The Thuggee snapped his shoulders contemptuously and sent Fareed flying backward. The cellar shuddered as Fareed bounced off the wall. The blazing eyes of the Thuggee were terrible to behold.

Burdick was closest as the rest of the team converged. The big Marine lunged, hurling all of his three hundred pounds behind a wild left-hand lead. His massive fist collided with the Thuggee's jaw like a train wreck.

The man didn't blink. His head moved all of an inch with the force of the blow. He spread the tapering fingers of his huge, spatulate hand and slapped Burdick across the chest with the sound of a frying pan hitting a side of beef.

Burdick's barrel chest folded under the blow. His face went dead-white as the blood drained out of it and he collapsed to the floor. James blurred into his attack before the Thuggee could pull back his hand. Beyond his SEAL close-quarter battle tactics, James was black belt in Tae Kwon Do. Using his favorite combination of hand and foot strikes, he could hit a man twelve times in just under four seconds. He got off a round kick to the head and a knife-hand strike just under the ear before Bolan and Makhdoom could pile on.

The prisoner caught James's spear-hand before it could hit his throat, and his huge hand squeezed. The bones of Calvin James's left hand broke in the Thuggee's grip. The Phoenix Force warrior grimaced and swung his right hand around like an ax in a killing blow to the temple. The Thuggee released the broken hand and backhanded him to the floor in a sprawl.

Makhoom hit the Indian in a flying tackle. The Thuggee

didn't budge. He seized his adversary in his hands like a sack of potatoes. He pivoted and flung him into Fareed as the captain rose from the floor, and the two Pakistanis went down in a tangle of limbs. The prisoner turned for his final prey.

He found himself staring into the cold black muzzle of a Beretta 93-R machine pistol.

The Thuggee's eyes were still crossed and staring into whatever terrible place he was drawing his power. The remains of the chair snapped apart around his legs as he took a step forward. The Beretta barked once in the Executioner's hand. The Thuggee's crossed eyes suddenly regarded a bloody black hole between his eyebrows.

He fell bonelessly to the floor.

The cellar door crashed open on its hinges. Ironman came through with his automatic shotgun in his hand and Ramrod right behind him. Lyons surveyed the scene and then looked at Bolan. "Problem?"

"Yeah." Bolan holstered his pistol. "We lost our suspect."

Makhdoom rose shakily and hauled Fareed to his feet. He gazed with great foreboding at the dead Thuggee. "I am not sure if we ever truly had him."

Bolan nodded. It was an ugly assessment and probably very accurate. He went over to Burdick. "You all right?"

The big man sat wheezing and pale against the wall. "Jesus…he didn't even blink. I hit him with my best shot. My Sunday best and…" Burdick shook his head in pained wonder. "He bitch-slapped me."

James rose with a groan. He cradled his broken left hand against his chest and rubbed his jaw with his right. The entire left side of his face was swelling up spectacularly. "You ain't the only one, Red."

Burdick's face clenched as he tried to take a deep breath. "So what do we do now?"

The Thuggee was dead. Bolan really only saw one plan.

"We're done here. I want to get the doctor on a plane, ASAP, and get her into a lab. I need Bear working on leads in the U.S."

Makhdoom rolled his arm painfully in the shoulder that had bounced against the wall. "And what are we to do?"

Bolan surveyed the dead Thuggee. They had met the deceivers, and the hired goons and muscle, but the dead man at Bolan's feet had made a mess of nearly the entire team with his bare hands. The "Sword of Kali" was the hardcore that awaited them. There was really only one choice. "It's time to invade India. We're going to Calcutta."

CHAPTER SIXTEEN

India Airlines Flight 717

Bolan examined his team. They had taken a beating and the long ride back to Islamabad hadn't helped. Flights from Pakistan into India were very heavily screened, so they had been forced to fly to Saudi Arabia and then take an Air India flight to Calcutta. The fatigue was starting to show. Calvin James's hand was in a half cast and the left side of his face didn't look human. Burdick's ribs were taped where the Thuggee's hand had cracked three of them near the top of his sternum. If it weren't for Burdick's huge size and the masses of meat armoring his torso, Bolan suspected the Thuggee might have slapped Burdick's heart right out of his chest. A giant hand-shaped bruise sat like a blue-black spider over his heart as a reminder of how close death had come. Makhdoom and Fareed were bruised and stiff, but otherwise all right except for exhaustion. A single fact remained.

One unarmed Thuggee had ripped through his team like a whirlwind.

They didn't make the news like karate or kung fu, but most regions of India had their own indigenous martial arts traditions, frequently embedded in religion. Bolan had experienced far too many times the nearly superhuman abilities religious fanatics and highly trained martial artists were capable of.

Bolan looked over at Lyons. It was past midnight and the rest of the team was sacked out in their first-class seats. Lyons sat up drinking a beer. His right hand slowly closing and opening again into a fist. His arctic-blue eyes stared straight ahead into the middle distance as he thought Carl Lyons-type thoughts. Bolan smiled wearily. Carl was genuinely sorry he had missed "the fun."

Bolan checked his watch and pulled an aluminum attaché case from under his seat. It was time to check in to see if Kurtzman had anything for him. He plugged in his earpiece and typed in the correct codes. Kurtzman's face instantly popped up on the eleven-inch flat screen. So that his words wouldn't be heard by the other passengers in first class, Bolan typed his question.

What have you got for me, Bear?

"Not much." Kurtzman responded through Bolan's earpiece as he flipped through some files. "We used some contacts in the State Department to float the idea that there might be a revitalized Kali cult operating in India. The idea was universally scoffed at."

Bolan had expected that.

What have you got on other fronts?

"Well, the U.S. intelligence presence in India isn't strong. India just isn't on our front burner. Most of what we do have revolves around watching their nuclear arsenal."

But…

"But we may have found someone who might be able to help. England's intelligence community has a much stronger presence there. We've called in some favors with MI-6. They have cooperated with Indian intelligence and helped train some of their operatives in modern espionage techniques. We can at least get you an introduction and 'please show all professional courtesies to' with a RAW agent. Beyond that you're going to have to win hearts and minds, and I warn you, they're not going to like what you have to tell them. They're probably going to think you're running some sort of bullshit U.S. capitalist-imperialist game."

Going into a country cold and telling them they had a problem was always an ugly way to make friends.

What's RAW?

"Research and Analysis Wing. They have several unique commando units. They answer directly to the director general of security, rather the Indian army high command."

They're spooks and paramilitaries.

"That's right, and frankly we don't have a whole lot of information on them, other than that they are mostly an external intelligence agency. Sorry we couldn't get you anything closer to their version of the FBI."

Bolan shook his head as he typed.

No, it's good. You go to internal intelligence sources with a problem, and they go territorial on you. They're usually bloated and bound and gagged with red tape and interservice rivalries.

He thought of the United States and how the FBI, DEA, ATF and every other domestic service were constantly butting heads.

> External services are leaner, meaner and have a lot more leeway. When you present them with an internal problem, they want to fix it rather than worry about looking bad. It's not perfect, but it's not a bad back door to get inside.

"Well, I'm glad you're happy. When you get to the airport, send the rest of the team ahead. We didn't tell them about your team, and we sure as hell didn't tell them you had brought Pakistani special forces with you."

Bolan looked over at the two Pakistanis. They had shaved their beards and mustaches and their documents said they were Punjabi businessmen returning from the Middle East. Both men had been trained to penetrate and engage in covert operations in India, but the moment Indian intelligence found out who they were, it was going to hit the fan. Bolan grimaced. The fact was Pakistani intelligence had an extensive network in Bangladesh and the West Bengal. It was an asset Bolan couldn't afford to give up, and Captain Makhdoom had made it plain he was going to Calcutta, with or without Bolan's cooperation.

> Will do. Who do I make contact with, and where?

"Go to the Captain's Club in the airport and someone will contact you in the bar. That's all we have at this point. It's sketchy, I know, but it is a public place, and MI-6 insists the contact is kosher."

> Will make contact, and report back from embassy. Out.

Calcutta

THE AIRPORT WAS the nightmare Bolan had heard. The air-conditioning appeared to be off throughout the terminal. The moment they had stepped off the plane they had been assaulted by such incredible, boiling humidity that the soldier longed for the searing heat of Pakistan's desert plateau. The humidity wasn't helped by the shoving, shouting, screaming of humanity packed to the rafters. Calcutta had changed its official name to Kolkatta, but few people used the new name except for government officials. Few people used the official name for the airport, either. Netaji Subhas Chandra Basu was too long for visitors and locals alike to use in conversation. Everyone called the airport by its unofficial name, "Dum-Dum." Dum-Dum because the airport was once the site of the British arsenal that had invented the flat-headed rifle bullet, whose brutal stopping power was designed for use against "indigenous resistance."

The team had broken up on debarkation. Makhdoom and Fareed had gone to meet their own people in the city. Calvin James had paired up with Ramrod. They would pick up Sadie and Schatzie from customs and sweep the safehouse the CIA had set up for them. Lyons and Burdick were going to meet the local CIA talent to see if they could pick up anything useful.

Bolan shouldered his way through the throng of humans. Kurtzman had sent ahead full warloads to the safehouse and to the embassy in the capital, so the soldier had avoided picking up any bags.

Burdick showed up through the mob at Bolan's elbow. "You going armed to the meet?"

Bolan spoke softly as he continued to push through the herd of humanity. "No, but we have guns waiting for us in the cars."

"Take this." Burdick pressed a shallow oval of steel and rosewood into Bolan's hand.

The Executioner palmed the knife. "How did you get that through customs?"

"You don't want to know."

Before Bolan had slapped Burdick across the right side of the line, the big Marine had specialized in smuggling arms. Bolan kept the smile off his face as he slid the blade it into his pocket.

Burdick was right. He didn't want to know.

The big ex-Marine broke away, his body mass making a hole through the press of people like an icebreaker pushing through the icepack in the Arctic. He grunted over his shoulder. "Luck."

Bolan scanned the area and caught sight of the sign for the Captain's Club. Command presence was a luxury won in the face of death, and it worked in Bolan's favor now. As he made his way through the steaming, sweating throng, anyone who made the mistake of meeting his gaze quickly made way.

The soothing embrace of air-conditioned air enveloped the Executioner. He made his way to the bar, which was full of businessmen and men of medium to minor importance from more than a dozen countries. They hobnobbed, being served drinks by Indian hostesses and exchanging business cards as they waited for their limousines to page them or their flights to board. Bolan scanned the room and made his way toward the most beautiful woman in the room.

There might not have been a pair of bigger, darker eyes on the planet. They were widely set apart beneath coal-black brows. Her features were slightly Western, with a long straight nose and high cheekbones. Her chin and cheeks could almost have been sharp except that the effect was softened by lips that could only be described as perfect.

One corner of those sensuous lips turned up just slightly as Bolan approached. "Mr. Belasko?"

The woman rose from her seat and extended her hand. She wore a spectacular sari of purple, black and gold, and one cinnamon-skinned shoulder was scandalously exposed. Her body was like an elongated hourglass of broad shoulders and hips and a languorous waist that stretched between them. The immaculate drape of her traditional garment did little but accentuate the figure beneath.

Bolan took the woman's hand. Just about every intelligence agency on earth kept a few beautiful women agents around. In some kinds of missions they were extremely useful. They often took a man off balance, and men would let small things slip to a beautiful woman who was paying attention to him that he wouldn't with a man.

It looked like the Research and Analysis Wing had pulled out their biggest gun just for him.

"My name is Bijaya Khan." The woman's fathomless dark eyes stared deeply into Bolan's. She spoke her English with a perfect Oxford accent. "Welcome to India."

"I see you already know my name." Bolan released her hand and took a seat. "Call me Mike."

"I doubt it. However, you do come with some very unique recommendations and MI-6 seems to be very fond of you." Her dark brows veed slightly. "Though trying to find out anything about you of any consequence has proved impossible."

"Sorry to be so mysterious. May I buy you a drink?"

"I do not drink, unless a mission requires it." The woman's full smile suddenly lit up the room. "But you are a guest in my country and it would be inhospitable of me to leave you drinking alone."

"That's very decent of you."

"Yes," the agent agreed. "I will allow you buy me a French '75, a double."

Bolan grinned. It would be hard to find a more expensive drink than champagne and cognac over ice. It was pretty much the ultimate brandy and soda. Bolan motioned to a waitress and ordered himself a Cobra lager from Bangalore, as well. The Indian agent smiled benevolently until the drinks arrived. It was the kind of smile that most men would do just about anything to keep. She waited until the waitress left.

"So what can the Research and Analysis Wing do for you?"

Bolan examined the woman's beautiful face. RAW wouldn't have sent her to a meet with an unknown U.S. agent with an unknown agenda unless she was an absolute ringer as a field agent. She had been sent to charm all possible information out of him. Bolan saw no use for using charm. The woman had been hit on by pros all her life. Besides, she was an intelligence agent, and she was used to being lied to and not told the whole truth.

Bolan decided it was cards-on-the-table time.

"The Cult of Kali is active, again."

Her brows narrowed slightly. "You will have to be more specific. Untold millions of Indians worship Kali. My mother offers her devotions at the Kali Puja every year."

"I mean the Thuggees, Miss Khan." Bolan believed the agent knew exactly what he meant. "The Cult of the Deceivers."

The huge dark eyes widened in bemusement and disgust. "Really."

"Yes." Bolan opened his attaché case and removed a file. He opened it to a picture Lyons had taken of Inspector Sattar's demise.

"The work of some sick fanatic. You should have taken it to the police." Agent Khan's face set. "And for that matter, how did you come by this photograph?"

"The man in the photograph is Police Inspector Agha Sattar, of the Srinigar City Police."

Alarm registered on Bijaya Khan's face.

Bolan pressed home. "I first encountered the Thuggees in Pakistan. In the Hajir Pir Pass. They had a temple there. They had wiped out a Pakistani special forces group."

"Pakistan!" Every ounce of blood drained from the

woman's magnificent complexion. "What would they be doing in Pakistan?"

"Stealing strategic nuclear warheads. They have three of them."

RAW Agent Bijaya Khan looked as if she might throw up. Instead she reached down and drank half of her double French '75 in a gulp.

Bolan sipped his beer and waited. He knew he'd hit paydirt. The look on the agent's face told him Indian intelligence community was already aware they had a problem. Other than the make-up of his team, he had put all of his cards on the table. It was time to see what Indian intelligence was willing to reveal.

"You are sure of this."

"I've seen the bodies. I've seen the sacrifice. I've felt the strangling cord around my own neck, and I've met with Pakistani intelligence. They are desperate to contain the situation."

Khan visibly steadied herself. "Would you do me a professional courtesy?"

"Sure."

Bijaya took out a cell phone. "Please excuse me for a few moments. I must make a phone call."

"I've been on three planes in twelve hours." Bolan nodded helpfully. "I'll go wash my face."

"Thank you."

The Indian agent began punching buttons as Bolan rose and went to the rest room.

Inside, an ancient Sikh sat on a stool. A tray of colognes and rolled scented towels were on the counter beside him. He smiled ingratiatingly at Bolan. *"Sahib?"*

Bolan shook his head, but put a few rupee notes in his carved wooden bowl. Bolan went to a sink and ran cold water. He splashed some onto his face and cupped his hands to snuff some through his nose. The sting of the cold water brightened his senses, but he was still exhausted and not in the best shape to bargain with Indian intelligence.

However tired he was, he'd definitely hit the target. Bells would be ringing all the way up the chain of command. The question was whether he could—

Too many battles. Too many beatings. In too little time. Bolan saw the figure behind a half second too late. The strangling cord hissed through the air and wound around his throat with practiced aplomb. Behind Bolan, one of the bathroom stall doors slammed open and a second attacker dived into his legs to pin him against the sink counter. Arms wrapped around his legs. The strangling cord cinched tight, and the coin within it pressed against his trachea with hideous efficiency.

Bolan overrode every instinct in his body. He ignored the silken garrote around his neck and didn't struggle against the helper holding him in place. As his vision constricted, he slid the knife Burdick had slipped him from his pocket and flicked his wrist. Three and three-quarter inches of Canadian stainless-steel clacked open.

The man holding Bolan's legs screamed as the knife whispered across his eyebrows and scored his face open the bone. With his last vestiges of consciousness Bolan whipped the point back up and stabbed over his shoulder. The Grohmann knife slid into an eye socket and jammed into his strangler's skull.

The strangling cord went limp, but the dead man still held it. Bolan fell backward as his assassin collapsed.

The strangler's assistant stumbled to his feet. He was a big man in a business suit, and he clutched the red ruin of his face as he stumbled for the door. Bolan struggled for breath as he rose to one knee. Colors washed across his vision. Bolan reversed the knife in his hand and took it by the blade. The folding knife wasn't an ideal missile, but the elliptical blade was blissfully point-heavy and the range was point-blank.

The knife had no time to revolve as Bolan threw. The big

man screamed and fell against the doorjamb as the blade flew like a dart and sank between his shoulder blades.

Bolan rose. Three and three-quarter inches of steel wasn't going to penetrate any vital organs, but it had slowed the man's flight. Bolan rose and followed the man as he staggered out the door.

People screamed as the wounded killer lurched into the bar. Bijaya Khan was on her feet. She shouted above the clamor in Hindi, and screaming people began throwing themselves to the floor. From beneath her sari she produced a .25-caliber Colt pocket pistol. She shouted something once at the Thuggee as she took the pistol in both hands. The man roared like a wounded bull and seized a bar stool.

A Sikh bouncer plunged for the Thuggee and was swatted to the ground for his trouble.

The tiny pistol snapped spitefully as Khan fired as fast as she could pull the trigger. Her diminutive weapon clacked open on empty as the huge Thuggee came on, oblivious to the seven holes in his chest.

The Thuggee jerked as Bolan yanked the knife out of his back. The killer's back bowed as Bolan grabbed his head by the hair, and he went limp as the Executioner sliced the razor-sharp steel across his throat. Bolan let the dead man fall to the floor. "Did anyone run out of the bar?"

"What?" The Indian agent frowned as she ejected her spent magazine. "Yes, I believe so, several."

Bolan knelt and cleaned his knife on the dead man's jacket. "Detain everyone still inside for questioning, anyway."

Bijaya slid a fresh magazine from under her sari and shoved it into the butt of her pistol. "I do not understand. You said you took three flights to get here. How could they have followed you?"

"They didn't follow me." Bolan made his knife disappear. "They followed you."

CHAPTER SEVENTEEN

Traffic in Calcutta was Armageddon.

Schatzie, the giant schnauzer, stuck her head out the rear window. Her mustaches flowed in the wind and her tail thumped against the back seat as she took in the unforgettable smell of downtown Calcutta.

Bijaya Khan smiled as she whipped her car through traffic with fluid aggression. She now wore a thoroughly modern pantsuit. A pair of motor-rickshaws in the lane behind them broke formation and forked around the car, blaring their horns. Bolan watched Chaos Theory at work and could detect only two rules of the road in force. One was that all traffic should attempt to occupy the center of that road, and two, that to slow was to falter, to brake was to fail and to stop was defeat.

Khan leaned on her horn with vigor. One of the few indigenous cars produced in India was the British 1954 Morris Oxford, which the Calcutta plant continued to roll out to the original 1954 specifications. Bijaya had the windows of her Morris open and the radio blaring Indian techno-pop at skull-splitting decibels. "You said we needed a private talk!" The agent grinned. "No one can hear us here, and I doubt anyone can follow us!"

Bolan had to agree. Except for impending vehicular manslaughter, rush-hour traffic in downtown Calcutta was probably the safest place in the world to take a clandestine meeting.

The Indian agent leaned out the window and shouted something that sizzled at a man pulling a rickshaw directly across traffic. Bolan watched as two men leaped out of their cars, both of which were attempting to occupy the same lane behind a stalled bus, and began a fistfight. The bus suddenly belched blue smoke and lurched forward. Both men leaped back into their cars instantly in a race to get back in traffic.

"The assumption of immortality is required to drive here." Khan smiled.

Bolan watched vehicles of every description honking, swerving and shooting by in all directions. Every vehicle seemed to be loaded to twice its capacity.

Khan seemed to read Bolan's mind. "Oh, there are rules of the road here, but they are unofficial."

Bolan watched a family of five drive by on a wheezing, ancient Italian scooter. "Oh, really."

"Yes, the caste system is still very much in effect. It is simple. You must give way to cows, for religious reasons, and elephants, for survival reasons. Then, depending upon where you are in the food chain, and in descending order, you must give way to heavy trucks, buses, official cars, camels, light trucks, buffalo, Jeeps, oxcarts, private cars, motor scooters, auto rickshaws, goats, bicycles, goods-carrying bicycles, that is, hand carts, rickshaws, bicycles, passenger-carrying bicycles, that is, dogs, and then pedestrians."

Bolan smiled, but Khan didn't appear to be joking. "You know, in the United States pedestrians have the right of way."

Khan took her eyes off the road and looked at Bolan with extreme seriousness. "I have heard of such things, but one hears many wild rumors about the United States, and one never knows what to believe."

Bolan watched a tractor come head-on with a twenty-foot load of cotton bales. At the last second Khan swerved and leaned on her horn shouting at the three Sikhs driving it. Apparently, honking your horn meant you had no intention of stopping, even if you could.

Bolan entrusted his fate to Karma and got on with the business at hand. "We have a mutual problem."

"We certainly do."

"You're aware of the revitalized Kali Cult."

"We have had our suspicions. You have not only confirmed them, but surpassed them in spectacular fashion." The agent took her car onto a broad avenue where traffic flowed a little more sanely. "This is the Chowinghee Road."

Bolan watched the amalgam of British Colonial architecture and modern buildings slam into one another along the boulevard.

"It was once little more than a pilgrim path through the jungle."

"A path to what?"

"To that." Khan pointed to a spired temple of whitewashed wall and tile that rose up in the midst of the middle-class neighborhood. "The Kalighat, the Temple of Kali." Khan pulled over and parked. "That building next to it is Mother Theresa's Home for the Destitute and Dying."

Bolan glanced at the building. The crippled, the lame and the obviously dying were lined up around the block. All hoping to be admitted into this final refuge that was already jammed to the rafters. Khan reached across the big American and opened the glove box.

His eyes swept over an antique, nickel-plated Webley-Fosbery .455 revolver. "That's a swanky piece you have there."

"It's my car gun." Khan smiled serenely as she opened the action and checked the loads. "It scares the shit out of suspects, and I do not like the way my .25 failed me in the airport." She made the massive revolver disappear into a shoulder holster beneath her jacket and slid a handful of cartridges into her pocket. Her eyes flicked around Bolan's face. "You colored your skin for this mission?"

"Yeah. Why, is it rubbing off?"

"The blue eyes are unusual, but you will do. Here." She pulled out her cosmetic case and drew a line of paint down Bolan's head. "Now you're *Kshatriya*."

"Warrior caste?"

"Very good."

"I thought Gandhi had made the caste system illegal."

"There is what the law says, and then there is what is. The caste system permeates India still from top to bottom, Muslim, Hindu and Christian. The Sikhs and Buddhists are the only ones who have truly attempted to reject it, and even they lapse. I, myself, am a Christian, but any Indian I meet would want to know what caste my people were before they converted. You cannot escape it."

Bolan was mildly surprised. "You're Christian?"

"Yes, many of the operatives in the Indian intelligence service are. The government is run by the Hindu majority. Sikhs and Muslims are considered good soldiers, but not completely trusted with national security matters, and as I said, the caste system permeates everything, which can unconsciously or even consciously affect Hindu operatives. In many ways Christians make perfect agents. We are loyal to the government, and with training, we can blend in with anybody."

Bolan eyed the woman shrewdly. "But your people were warrior caste before they converted."

"Of course." Khan snorted at the obviousness of the question. She quickly painted a round red dot on her forehead. "By the way, we are married." She opened the door. "Let's go. Don't say anything. Only Hindus are allowed within the temple, itself. I'll do any talking."

Bolan checked the loads in his Airweight Centennial revolver and slid two grenades from the knapsack at his feet into his coat pockets. "Schatzie, stay, guard."

The giant schnauzer sank back into one of the footwells of the back seat and disappeared from sight.

"Good dog." Bolan and Khan climbed the steep steps and removed their shoes before they entered the temple. The architecture of spires and domes was beautiful. "This temple was built in 1809, but there has been a temple to Kali here since ancient times. It was here that the Thuggee would come to worship before going out into the land to carry out their depredations."

As they stepped inside, a shaved head priest in a saffron colored *dhoti* clasped his hands in front of him and bowed. Bolan and Khan bowed back and walked down the incense-scented gallery.

Khan spoke softly. "Do you know Kali's origin?"

"I've mostly been researching Thuggee behavior."

They came to the end of the main gallery and beheld the goddess.

Bolan examined the statue. Kali was plumper, her limbs more rounded and her face less gaunt. The goddess's tongue was much shorter, and her mouth didn't have fangs. The painted statue was festooned with garlands of flowers and there were offering bowls at her feet.

"She doesn't look so bad here."

"Devout Hindus worship Kali as an aspect of the divine mother. She nurtures, she protects. Only the Thuggees worshiped her as a demon, using her as an excuse to commit their crimes. Such worship is considered depraved."

"But it happened."

Khan frowned. "Most Christians would consider the Spanish Inquisition an atrocity in God's name, but it happened, and nearly all Christians fail to understand true Hindu cosmology.

Kali is but an aspect of Durga, and everything—gods, angels, demons, men, the universe—is but an aspect of the One.

Bolan nodded. "Atman, the Universal Self."

"You have been doing some reading." Khan gestured at Kali. "Many Hindus consider Kali a metaphor for certain aspects of the world and the universal order. Kali comes from the ancient word Kala, which means both 'black' and 'time.' The 'devourer of time' is one name by which she is known. She is often worshiped as the dark mother from which everything sprang, and into her dark formlessness which all returns."

"Like a black hole."

Khan raised an eyebrow.

"Many modern physicists believe the universe started with a singularity that exploded in the Big Bang, creating the expanding universe we know now. Many also believe that in the end the universe will collapse back into that same singularity state. Your culture seems to have come up with the same theory ten thousand years ago." Bolan shrugged. "No one does metaphysics like Hindus."

Khan's bell-like laughter rang through the gallery. "Well, you are right about that, and you are very shrewd. Most Christians simply see a death goddess with four arms covered with blood and are appalled. In the West there is a certain cultural abhorrence of death. To those in the East it is considered just a natural part of life. To us, a goddess of death is by no means considered evil. Kali saved Heaven and Earth, you know."

"I didn't know that."

Bijaya gazed upon the goddess. "Yes, there are many Kali origin myths. In a common one, the gods and devis were locked in a life or death battle with an army of demons, led by the demon king, Daruka. They were so powerful that not even all the gods arrayed could stand before them. The gods called upon Lord Shiva for help, but he was so deep in his mediations that he could not be reached. At the forefront of the battle stood the warrior goddess Durga. As the tide of battle turned and the demons threatened to overwhelm her, her brow furrowed, her face blackened, and out of her terrible desperation and need Kali sprang from her brow, fully formed, armed with a sword and skull-tipped staff. Kali slew Daruka and his demon army in an immense, unstoppable slaughter. In celebration, she drank the blood of the fallen and, drunk with carnage, she began to dance. She reveled in the blood and slaughter and the feel of the dead beneath her feet. Her dance became ever more frenzied, a dance of destruction. The gods could not dissuade her, and Kali's dance threatened to end the world. The dance awakened Shiva, and only when he threw himself beneath her feet and she realized she was dancing upon her husband did she stop."

Bolan glanced at Kali's feet and saw that she stood upon the figure of a man.

"Worshipers of Kali believe that her dance has only been stopped temporarily. A great deal of Kali worship is simply appeasing her and averting her wrath. Many believe that one day she will resume her dance of destruction and end the world. The painting on the wall, where you found Inspector Sattar, depicted Kali in *jagrata,* her most terrible, fully awakened aspect."

"Her aspect that will end the world."

"Yes." Khan let out a long sigh. "Though many Hindu scholars and priests believe that is only a metaphor for liberation of the soul. They say she does not bring death, but the death of death."

"You know a great deal about it for a nice Christian girl."

Bijaya smiled. "My father was a Christian, and Anglican. His family converted more than a century ago during the English Raj. Father insisted that I be baptized, and I went to church every Sunday. But my mother was a Hindu, and it was in days spent with my aunts and cousins that I heard all the stories every good Hindu girl knows."

"So what brought Kali to the attention of RAW?"

"There have been…murders."

"Murders committed by Thuggee methodology."

"Yes, and investigations into the murders came up with nothing, or worse, missing investigators."

Bolan met Khan's eyes. "The Indian government and security forces have been penetrated by the Thuggee."

"One could get into a great deal of trouble insinuating such a thing. RAW is an external security force. We are associated with the military. Our main focus is espionage and intelligence gathering. Our operations are primarily directed against Pakistan and China. What you are suggesting is an internal security matter. For RAW, it would be as if your CIA approached the FBI and told them that they had been penetrated by the Ku Klux Klan. They would not appreciate being told that the Klan's activities were being ignored or even aided and abetted by state and federal law enforcement."

Bolan had been right in the middle of that kind of debacle before. "It's my experience that the revitalization of a religious movement generally centers around a charismatic leader."

"That, too, has been the subject of our search. We have heard rumors of such. Of a man who is said to speak directly with the goddess. A man who is Kali's instrument upon this earth. A man who is said to interpret Kali's dream of the world as she tosses and turns toward her full awakening."

"Sounds like a real nutcase," Bolan opined. "What else do you have on him?"

"Nothing." Khan stared bitterly at the offering bowl on the altar. "Our investigations have met with open ridicule and stonewalling from internal security, and we have already lost three agents." The agent slid a roll of rupee notes from her pocket and slipped them into a bowl.

They walked from the gallery and bowed to the priests as they left the temple and descended the steep steps. "I do not know how we will find them, and if what you say is true, time is running out before something terrible happens."

"We don't have to find them."

Bijaya gasped. Her hand went under her coat as Bolan pointed at the car. A sheet metal jimmy was stuck halfway down through the window frame of the driver's door. The glass was broken. Schatzie was in the front seat. Her nose and her brow were cut where she had rammed her face through the glass. Darker, dried blood colored the giant schnauzer's mustaches. A shred of silver-gray fabric was still clenched between her canines.

Drying blood spattered the car door and formed a trail down the sidewalk away from the car for a few feet and disappeared.

Bolan reached through the broken glass and scratched Schatzie behind the ears. "If all else fails, they'll find us."

CHAPTER EIGHTEEN

"Goddamn…" Trevor Burdick was as subtle as a brick through a window. He stopped short of openly drooling, but Lyons had to admit that the man was right. The woman Bolan walked in with was beyond beautiful. Bijaya Khan was hauntingly, electrically, mind-emptyingly erotic. "Glad to see you safe, Striker. We were starting to get worried."

"Had to take Schatzie to the vet." The giant schnauzer had lost her right eyebrow and her left mustache to the vet's razor. Fresh stitches covered the bright pink swathes of bare skin. A plastic cone surrounded her head to prevent her from scratching her wounds. Schatzie hung her head despondently. On some deep instinctual level the dog knew how ridiculous she looked.

Burdick shook his head. "The Doc is gonna kill you when she sees what you did to her dog."

Bolan glanced around the safehouse. "We need this place beefed up, full countermeasures."

Lyons rose from his seat. "You think we're going to get hit?"

"I'm counting on it." Bolan nodded toward the Indian agent. "This is Agent Bijaya Khan, Research and Analysis Wing. She's our contact with Indian intelligence."

Burdick leaned over to Calvin James and murmured low, "Bijaya Khan, agent of RAW. It just gets better and better."

"Keep it in your pants, Red." James, himself, had to struggle to keep his gaze professional. The Indian spy was about the longest, tawniest thing he'd seen in a career that had spanned the planet.

Bolan examined the safehouse closely. It was crumbling Victorian and probably well over a hundred years old. "We threw down the punk card when we visited the Kali temple. I think they're going to pick that card up and hit us with everything they've got."

James nodded as he looked around the house. "The doors are thick, the walls solid." He gestured with his cast at the huge multipaned windows. "But those suck. Instant entry."

Bolan took out a wad of rupees and tossed it to the former Navy SEAL. "Take Red, go shopping. Fix it." He turned to Lyons. "Get hold of Doom. We're going to need everyone for this little party. I've got the feeling they're going to try to take us out. They're not going to hold back."

Lyons stared hard. "And you want prisoners."

"Yeah, I do. The enemy is going to have all the cards on this one. Even if we win, the police are going to come storming down in force. A bunch of Americans with guns will instantly get arrested despite Bijaya's vouching for our character. If we end up in custody, we end up dead. Just like the prisoners in Ul-Haq's dungeon. I want prisoners, and I want a bolt-hole out of this place. Get hold of Barb and The Bear. We need a secondary hide, and somewhere close by."

Lyons folded his arms across his chest like an iron Buddha. "One thing is bothering me."

Bolan glanced at Lyons. Not a whole lot bothered the Able Team leader. "What's that?"

"Twice, now, the bad guys have made noises about taking you alive. I don't like it."

Burdick rumbled in agreement. 'Yeah, that kind of freaked me out, too."

Bolan kept his eyes on Lyons. "What are you saying?"

"I'm saying we've got guys who can turn invisible. Religious death-freak guys who have taken a personal interest in you. I'm saying maybe you should let me take care of the shenanigans here in Calcutta."

"And I thought Hal was a mother hen. But thanks for your concern. I'll take that under advisement, but we're going to need every gun here."

"You think they're going to hit us that hard?"

Bolan shrugged. "What would you do?"

"I'd stomp us like bugs at the very first opportunity," Lyons stated.

Bolan turned to Khan. "What can you do for us on your end?"

"Little, I am afraid. RAW is an intelligence gathering agency. My superiors will not move without more evidence, and to move they will have to involve Internal Security." Bijaya let out a long breath. "By cooperating with you, RAW has unofficially declared war on Internal Security. If Internal Security has been compromised, any aid I request may be working for the enemy."

Bolan had suspected as much. "What kind of opposition do you think the Cultists can muster here in Calcutta?"

"I do not think the cultists can pull in army units as they did against you in Pakistan. If they are going to assault you here, they will have two primary resources from which to draw other than their own ranks. First are the *goondas,* they are Indian equivalent of hooligans, street criminals and thugs within the city. They are often for hire to strong-arm people, to commit robberies, or even to pillage and riot in mob strengths. They are usually poorly armed, most often with clubs, bladed weapons and occasional handguns."

Bolan nodded. "What else can they pull?"

"The other source they could draw on are the *dacoits,* highwaymen, bandits who rob travelers between cities and in the mountains. Some of them are family crime dynasties whose clans have been active for centuries. In recent times they have engaged in drugs and gun running. They have had a history of being Kali cultists under the British Raj. They, on the other hand, are often heavily armed."

Bolan weighed the odds. It didn't sound good, but at least there wouldn't be tanks this time. "Carl, we're going to need some light support weapons. I want force multipliers, ASAP."

"You've got it."

Bijaya looked around the safehouse. She seemed to be weighing its defensibility and finding it wanting. "Is there anything else I can do?"

"Yeah." Bolan really needed a nap. "Be seen. Be seen coming here."

"WE HAVE SEEN THEM, Guruji." Mehtar was breathless with excitement. "They have come to us, as you predicted."

The guru looked very different in an immaculately tailored Western suit. He didn't look out of place at all in the beautifully furnished office surrounded by computers and sitting behind a magnificent arc of mahogany desk. Neither did he did look surprised. "They visited the temple."

"As you said they would, Guruji. We followed the woman from the RAW office here in the city. She is, indeed, the one who was making inquiries about our activities. As you predicted, it was she who made contact with the Americans."

"And where are they now, Mehtar?"

"They are in a house. One we suspect that is a safehouse used by the CIA. The house is here in the Kalighat neighborhood, between Tolly's Nullah and Jalindas Park."

The guru's smile of triumph was terrible to behold. "Then they are but two blocks from here."

"Indeed, Guruji." Mehtar beamed with pleasure. "You have but to stretch forth your hand."

"We shall not take them unawares." The guru steepled his fingers on his desk. "Indeed, they shall be expecting us."

"All is in readiness. The men are amassed. They understand their tasks and await your orders. The gold has been spread among the bandits. The Kale, Shinde and Hira clans have come down out of the Rajmahal Hills and infiltrated the city, and they have brought weapons as you have asked. All is in readiness. With your word, Kali's will shall be done."

"Yes…" The guru stared off into some terrible place he shared with the goddess of death. "Kali's will be done."

"The American commando," Mehtar cautioned. "Perhaps it would be better to kill him and be done with it. I fear it will be very difficult to take him alive."

"You are wrong, Mehtar. Taking him in Kali's embrace shall be easy."

Mehtar didn't doubt his master, however he was surprised. "Easy?"

"Yes." The guru steepled his fingers once more and peered into the middle distance. "I have changed our objective, and you shall modify your plans accordingly."

Mehtar's eyes went wide as his guru explained what he wanted him to do. Mehtar's smile grew as cruel as his master's. The American would embrace Kali.

He would have no choice.

"IT HAS BEEN three days." Ghulam Fareed raised his bulk up from the couch and stretched. "You are sure they will attack us here?"

Bolan watched the local Calcutta news impassively.

"Very well." Fareed sighed. "I shall go spell Ramrod on roof duty."

Time was weighing heavily on the team's hands. The tropical heat and humidity was oppressive. There was no air-conditioning in the one-hundred-year-old house, and the makeshift fortifications hadn't helped air circulation. In the past forty-eight hours the glass doors had been covered with a layer of chain-link fencing bolted behind the curtains, and all the first-floor windows and doors had been buttressed with three feet of sandbags. The airy, Colonial-style home had been turned into a dark, sweaty bunker. Cabin fever was running high, and the sharp edge of Bolan's team was becoming dull with waiting.

Bolan watched the news and allowed himself a single beer for the day.

Fareed scooped up his rifle and stomped toward the stairs.

Bijaya wiped her canned iced tea across her brow. "Tell me that man is not Pakistani special forces."

Bolan sipped his beer and sat glued to the screen. Bolan had admitted nothing, but Bijaya Khan was an intelligence agent. She knew full well that Bolan was cooperating with Pakistanis in her country. She had grudgingly accepted it, but with tempers fraying in the heat Bolan didn't want another harangue about it.

Burdick watched the television, as well. His grasp of Hindi had become nothing short of frightening.

Khan blew a lank lock of dark hair from her brow. "You could be wrong, you know. About them hitting us here."

"I could," Bolan acknowledged, "but I'm not."

The Indian woman's impossibly dark eyes narrowed. "How do you know?"

"He has an instinct for these things." Lyons ran a rag over his South African Neostead shotgun. The pump-action assault shotgun had twin-feed tubes mounted over the barrel. One six-round tube was loaded with marking paint projectiles. The other tube was loaded with lead. A laser sight was mounted on the carrying handle over the receiver. Lyons had long ago learned to respect Bolan's battle instincts. You lived longer if you did. "We'll get hit, all right."

"There." Bolan pointed at the television screen.

On the screen an Indian news anchor was speaking in Hindi. Behind him were scenes of rioting in downtown Calcutta. It appeared to be a spontaneous religious riot. A large group of Hindus had gone into a Muslim neighborhood with clubs and swords and begun torching and looting. Similarly armed Muslims had flooded from their homes and responded in kind. Bolan didn't speak Hindi, but he could tell the story by what he saw. The riot was spreading throughout the city.

"That's their diversion. The riot is going to tie up almost all the city police." Bolan rose from the couch. "We're about to get hit. The invisibles are already in place."

Bolan's cell rang right on cue. Ramrod spoke from his perch on the roof. "We've got trouble."

"There's a riot coming this way?"

The SAR sergeant paused. "How'd you know?"

"Go to tactical communications." Bolan clicked his phone shut and began shrugging into his armor. He nodded at everyone else in the room. "They'll be here in minutes."

"You are one scary dude," Burdick observed. The giant Marine grabbed his Mossberg Marine Corps Close Quarter Battle shotgun and racked the action.

"Go wake up Doom and Chicago. Tell them they're coming."

"Right." Burdick roused his frame off the couch.

Khan opened one of her suitcases and pulled out a wooden box. She flipped the lid, and inside were a matched pair of the ancient nickel-plated revolvers. They lay in red velvet like dueling pistols. She took a massive revolver in each hand. "My great-grandfather was a *Risaldar* major in the Bengal Lancers. These pistols were presented to him by Lord Kitchener himself."

Bolan eyed the weapons. They were museum pieces, but

there was nothing obsolete about what the blunt-nosed .455 caliber all-lead Webley bullet would do to a human, and Khan held the pistols with the familiar ease of long practice.

Makhdoom and James were hunching into their armor and festooning themselves with weapons as they came into the living room. Makhdoom racked the action on his Peshwar Special Schmeisser. "The enemy is upon us."

"Yeah, the rioters are going to be a cover. I doubt we'll have to work too hard to drive off the *goondas*. The *dacoits* will be another matter. The enemy knows we're here and knows we're armed. Whoever they pulled down out of the hills will be hard chargers."

Ramrod spoke in Bolan's earpiece. "Striker, we have about two minutes. The crowd is coming this way. There's hundreds of them."

Everyone was wearing their tactical communications and had heard. "Jesus Christ!" Red glanced at the shotgun in his hands. "Hundreds?"

Bijaya nodded. "The *goondas* will have rounded up transients, street youths and the like to swell the mob. There will be large numbers of relatively innocent among them."

Bolan grimaced. "All right, we're going nonlethal."

Burdick shook his head. "Nonlethal? Against hundreds? Are you nuts or—"

"The car's outside, Red." Bolan reached into his pocket and threw the keys on the coffee table. "You've got about forty-five seconds to get the hell out of Dodge. You didn't bargain for this when you signed up. No hard feelings."

"Well, hell, I wasn't saying that. I was just sayin'—"

"Say something constructive, or shut up."

"Um, yes, sir." Burdick shut his mouth and then suddenly opened it again. "You know, I been readin' up on India."

Lyons shook his head. "This had better be good, Red. We're running out of time, and you're pissing off the man."

Burdick flushed but continued. "Well, the festival of Holi is next week, ain't it?"

One of Khan's perfectly sculpted eyebrows rose questioningly. "Yes?"

"I been reading it's traditional to fling paint and pigment on people during the festival."

"Yes…" Khan's frown deepened. "It is considered a blessing."

Bolan began to smile.

Even Lyons was smiling. "God, I love Marines."

Bolan thumbed his throat mike. "Everyone load up with the marking rounds. First the tear gas, then the paint. Don't go to lead unless you see gunfire."

"Affirmative," Ramrod replied. "Thirty seconds, Striker. They're coming down the street."

"Roger that. Everyone into position." Bolan picked up one of the three Mechem South African 40 mm grenade launchers Dr. Austenford had been kind enough to send along to the Indian subcontinent. Bolan cracked open the action and slid six CS tear-gas rounds into the revolving cylinder. "Ironman, Red, with me. Doom, go up to the roof with Ramrod. Take something with a 40 mm tube with you. Hammer anything that comes over the garden wall. Bijaya, keep an eye on the back. Let us know if anyone comes from the park side."

"Right."

Bolan nodded at the door. "Gentlemen."

Lyons and Burdick each grabbed a launcher, and the three warriors went for a walk. As they stepped into the front garden, they could already hear the sounds of rioting. The rising and falling animal roar of the crowd was punctuated with high-pitched screams and the sound of breaking glass. Bolan stepped out onto the street. A hundred yards down the road a rolling mass of humanity filled the street from sidewalk to sidewalk. Various lengths of rattan staff were the universal bludgeon of the Indian subcontinent, and it rippled in waves above the crowd. Bladed weapons glinted among the forest of clubs. Bolan scanned for firearms but didn't see them. The horde was throwing bricks and stones at houses as they passed, but they weren't taking the time to break into the affluent middle-class homes of the Kalighat neighborhood. The mob was moving swiftly down the street. Whoever was running this end of the riot had an agenda.

Someone at the forefront of the mob pointed a staff at Bolan and screamed. A hail of rocks flew threw the air but fell well short of the mark. Bolan raised his launcher and began firing. Lyons stepped out onto the street with him, and the huge six-round cylinders of the 40 mm grenade launchers smoked and rotated as they both fired as fast as they could pull the trigger.

Ramrod spoke from his perch on the roof. "Striker! We have hostiles coming through the park!"

Bolan kept his eye on the crowd as they roared in outrage. The mob turned into screaming gray shadows in the suddenly expanding gas cloud. "Range!"

"They're 150 meters and closing!"

"Smoke 'em!"

Up on the roof Ramrod and Makhdoom's single-tube launchers boomed simultaneously.

"Red!" Bolan broke open the action of his launcher and began reloading. "Lay down some assistance on our flank!"

"Roger that!" Burdick turned and clicked his sight two notches upward. He shouldered his launcher and began rapidly arcing gas grenades over the house and into the park beyond.

Bolan and Lyons distributed twelve more grenades in rapid succession. They shot the gas canister in higher and shorter arcs to make the mob walk the final hundred yards through as high a saturation as possible. Bolan cracked open his empty weapon. Smoke boiled out of the cylinder. The barrel of the 40 mm launcher was already burning hot to the touch.

Burdick plucked hot brass from his own empty tubes and began sliding in the special marking rounds. The giant Marine's smile was savage as he snapped his weapon shut. "Can we Smurf 'em?"

Bolan reloaded his own weapon. "Wait for it...."

The roar of the crowd was now much more ragged and underscored by the sound of scores of people coughing and choking as they ran forward. The shapes of the mob began to solidify through the gas, bruising it like a cloud about to erupt into sudden rain. The mob was charging.

Lyons clacked his fully loaded weapon shut. "Now can we Smurf them?"

Bolan raised his weapon to his shoulder. "Wait for it..."

The crowd broke from the gas in a ragged wave, choking, weeping and screaming for vengeance.

"Smurf 'em!"

Bolan, Lyons and Red began to fire directly into the crowd. The sounds of the eighteen grenades firing on rapid semiauto shuddered the air like sticks of dynamite strung like firecrackers. During the Vietnam War, the U.S. had developed a personal defensive munition for the 40 mm grenade launcher. They had replaced the high explosive with thirty rounds of buckshot, turning the grenade launcher into a giant shotgun. Austenford had taken the same principle but filled the grenade with marking-dye submunitions.

A weekend paint ball warrior would have considered it the mother of all munitions, except that the paint balls in the grenade exploded out of the grenade in all directions at just under the speed of sound. They were less than lethal, but only just. Austenford had designed them to mark an entire room where an invisible opponent might be hiding, and not only mark them visually, but mark the hell out of them physically, as well.

Bolan, Lyons and Burdick hit the crowd with more than half a thousand rounds in three seconds. The choked roars of rage degenerated into screams of pain. People howled and fell as limbs were hammered, torsos brutally bruised and heads broken open.

It all occurred in exploding bursts of brilliant, electric blue.

"It's goddamn surreal," Burdick remarked.

"Reload and retreat! Fire three more rounds of gas each! Right up to the door of the house!" Bolan barked. "Send the last three back over the house into the park!"

Gas bloomed up in front of the mob again as the soldiers pulled a fade back to the house. Ramrod and Makhdoom continued to fire from the top of the house. Fareed and Khan stood on the porch with weapons in hand. Bolan locked and barred the gate, but he didn't delude himself that it would withstand much of an assault. He tossed his spent launcher inside and withdrew his Beretta.

A screaming man came vaulting over the garden wall with a staff in hand. The rattan *lahti* was bound with brass on both ends. Bolan clicked down the folding foregrip of his machine pistol and moved to meet him. The rattan club swung down at Bolan's head in a furious arc. The soldier blocked, and the force of the blow shuddered down his arm as the club slammed to a halt against the short steel strut of the machine pistol's foregrip. The steel-reinforced toe of Bolan's boot rose up in an equally ugly arc between his attacker's legs. The *goonda* howled in agony and fell to his knees clutching himself. Bolan mercifully pistol-whipped the man unconscious to the lawn.

"Ramrod! What's the situation!"

"You've got a mob in the park." The sergeant's voice rose with urgency. "A few have tried to come over the back wall, but we blasted them back with marking shells. The gas isn't stopping them. We are running out of gas and marking grenades. They're throwing bricks and stones. There's a lot of screaming. I think they're working themselves up to try again!"

"Expend all your gas! Full saturation! Then—"

An immensely fat man somehow heaved his bulk over the wall. He rolled over the top and thudded down into the garden. The fat man rose up howling in incoherent rage. His eyes rolled back in his head and spittle flecked his lips. He hurtled forward howling like a dog drunk on slaughterhouse blood.

He hurtled forward with an Indian sabre in each hand.

Burdick charged forward to meet him. His grenade launcher was gone. In his hands he held his Mossberg Marine Corps shotgun in a high guard. His bayonet was fixed, but the plastic sheath still covered the blade. Burdick skidded short and let one of the Indian's blades swipe past him. As the fanatic raised his second weapon, Burdick rammed his sheathed bayonet into the Indian's voluminous belly with all of his bulk behind it. The giant Hindu let out an explosive gasp, and his blades fell from suddenly nerveless fingers. Burdick whipped up the butt-end of his shotgun in a blow that unhinged his opponent's jaw.

The big ex-Marine took a step back as three more men came over the wall. "Jesus! Can we use lead yet, please?"

"You heard the man." Lyons held his shotgun at the ready. The tube filled with 12-gauge marking projectiles was still selected, but Lyons's finger hovered over the selector switch. "Wait for it."

Khan stepped past them. She scooped up the fallen staff of the first intruder and strode forward. Two of the three men carried staves like her own, and the third carried a cleaver.

Bijaya Khan suddenly began spinning her commandeered staff around her body like a deranged drum major. The brass tip of the staff smashed the cleaver from the lead attacker's hand and broke the bones that held it. The man had no time to scream before the staff whipped down across the crown of his head, splitting his scalp and crossing his eyes into unconsciousness. Rattan staves clacked and blurred as Khan met and blocked the other two men's attacks. One fell gasping from a thrust directly over his heart. The second man took Khan's staff in the side of the neck with a blow that would have decapitated him if she'd been swinging a blade. The blow crushed his carotid artery and nerves and dropped him convulsing in agony to the ground.

Khan scooped up the fallen weapons and stepped back to stand shoulder to shoulder with Bolan and Burdick.

Metal tore as the screaming crowd managed to rip the wrought-iron gate off its hinges. Lyons and Burdick began firing marking rounds into the mob that spilled in as fast as they could pump the actions of their shotguns.

"Get back in the house." Bolan took one of his last two tear-gas grenades and a marking grenade from his belt and pulled the pins. He tossed the gas grenade into the middle of the lawn and hurled the marker directly into the mob. Gas bloomed, and the throng screamed, staggered and blossomed blue as the grenades detonated.

"Ramrod! Doom! Empty two sacks! Front yard!"

Bolan and Khan retreated into the house while Lyons and Burdick fired their shotguns dry. There was a strange jingling sound from above, but no one stopped to watch. They leapt through the door, and Bolan dropped two-by-fours through the add-on brackets they had bolted to the doorframe. Within seconds new screams rose above the bloodlust. Screams of surprised pain.

Lyons had done a great deal of shopping within the last seventy-two hours. Mostly in hardware and building supply stores. Besides sandbags, beams and chain link, Lyons had also bought six pounds of six-penny nails and a pair of spot welders. He and Burdick had spent four hours welding the nails in groups of four so that however one threw them on the floor one nail was sticking straight up supported by the other three. Ramrod and Makhdoom hurled nearly five hundred of the makeshift calthrops down through the gas into the front yard.

The fact was that the vast majority of the common people in India still wore sandals.

The entire tenor of the attacking throng changed as members of the mob impaled their feet on the two-inch nails and fell screaming and choking to the ground to be pierced by more.

James shook his head at Lyons. "That is some great medieval shit, Ironman."

Lyons nodded without taking his eyes off the door.

Whoever had organized the riot had whipped the *goondas* and the mob they had recruited into a genuine frenzy. Screaming rioters pushed past their hobbled fellows and began to hurl themselves against the house. Lyons knelt beside his gear bag, shucking blue shells into his shotgun. His face was grim. "We're running out of the good doctor's toys."

Fareed jerked his head at the television. "The riot downtown is on all the stations. The fact that there is a riot here in Kalighat has not made the news yet."

Bolan keyed his throat mike. "Ramrod, Doom, throw the rest of the spikes around the sides and back of the house. Drop any remaining gas you've got."

"Affirmative, Striker."

The enemy had planned their attack to a T. The police were occupied, giving the attackers here time to mount a genuine siege, which would ultimately force Bolan's team to open up with lead. Dozens of "innocent" rioters would be wounded and killed. Bolan and his team would be forced to flee Calcutta or be arrested. Either scenario would suit the enemy's objectives. Bolan wasn't going to play into either. James was right.

They were going medieval.

"So." Burdick loaded his last marking rounds. "What's the plan?"

Bolan took one of the extra *lahti* staves from Khan. "Repel all boarders."

"You *are* nuts," the Marine affirmed.

"Well, then." Khan dropped the extra staff and the saber on the couch and marched off to the kitchen. "I will put on a kettle of tea for our visitors."

James bent down and picked up the saber. The Chicago knife-fighter smiled as he examined the three feet of curved steel. He perked an eyebrow as staves and fists began pounding on the doubly boarded windows around the house. "Charlie's in the wire."

"All that floor-to-ceiling glass in the back is the weak point. We concentrate there. Fareed, Red, Ironman, you're with me. Chicago, get Doom down here. Keep an eye on the front of the house, and take the dogs. Do whatever you have to do."

The men nodded and moved.

"Ramrod, what have you got left?"

"Bullets."

Bolan considered. "Calvin, grab the smoke grenades. Throw them around the house, they'll contribute to the mess."

"Got it." James began to gather beer-can-shaped grenades from the gear bags.

The team strode to the back of the house. The back had been reinforced with sandbags, beams and chain link, but it was shuddering under the blows as the mob surrounded the house. Lyons scowled at the unmistakable sound of a nail shrieking as it ripped out of fresh wood. "They're pulling away the first layer of planks."

No one said anything as the noise outside mounted. There was the sound of wood shattering around the side of the house. Bolan nodded at Burdick. "That's the guest bedroom, paint anyone blue who tries to crawl through the window."

Burdick ran to the hallway.

Wood splintered in front of their eyes. The wood broke inward to expose the chain link behind it. More of the first layer of planks tore away. Someone was ramming a bench against the barricade. The wood broke, but the chain link shivered and bounced against the blows.

Burdick's shotgun began booming down the hall.

Wood shattered at the front of the house.

"I need help here!" Makhdoom roared.

"Fareed! With me!" Bolan bolted for the front of the house. The front door was half shattered inward. Only the hinges and one of the two-by-fours held it up. A potted palm tree from the house across the street had been used as a battering ram. Makhdoom was ramming the steel strut of his submachine gun's folding stock into the face of a shrieking *goonda* who hung halfway inside. The head and shoulders of another *goonda* shoved through the failing door. His face was blotched with blue paint and he struggled to stab with a knife. Bolan swung his staff in a wicked arc and shattered the man's collarbone. He hung in the doorway pinned as the press behind shoved and tried to extrude him through like a screaming sausage. He suddenly popped through with a shriek, and another screaming man replaced him. Ghulam Fareed swatted him into silence with a two-by-four.

"It's like fucking *Night of the Living Dead!*" Burdick roared. His shotgun had fallen silent. He was using his blunted bayonet and buttstock to keep the enemy from crawling through the window.

Another piece of the front door broke inward, and clawing hands and heads shoved through weeping from tear gas and bruised and blasted blue from the marking projectiles. Bolan swung his staff in clubbing blows. "Ramrod! Reinforce Red!"

Bolan jerked aside as a sword thrust through the disintegrating door.

Khan's voice shouted above the cacophony. "Move!"

Bolan, Makhdoom and Fareed jumped back. Khan tottered forward with a gigantic stockpot in her hands. She let out a snarl of effort and hurled twenty quarts of boiling water and detergent through the shattered door. The howls rose to screams of agony once more as the boiling soap clung and blistered flesh. The press eased slightly as the front of the mob sagged and slipped on suds into a squirming pile.

Khan ran to the kitchen. "I have two more!"

Planks broke in the study. Bolan moved. "Hold them!" Bolan stuck two fingers against his lips and let out a piercing whistle. "Sadie! Schatzie!"

Bolan ran past the guest room. Hands and arms flailed in the shattered window, but it was at shoulder height. Any head that showed itself got thrust or clubbed with a Mossberg shotgun backed by three hundred pounds of ex-Force Recon. Bolan braked in the study door. He could hear the sound of the dogs charging down the hall behind him.

Two planks had been yanked out of one of the narrow windows. The breach was barely big enough for any normal human being to crawl through. Bolan scanned the room with his staff held in front of him. Tear gas oozed through the window. Bolan was out of marking grenades. His instincts hammered up and down his spine.

"Sadie! Schatzie!" Bolan stepped out of the doorway. "Get some! Get some! Get some!"

The two dogs hurtled past. Sadie lunged at nothing and was swatted aside. Schatzie's veterinarian cone had been removed, and she hit a split second later. It was payback time for the giant schnauzer and she sank her teeth into something and began brutally savaging it. Sadie bounced up and lunged. The two dogs hung in midair like bizarre, writhing and snarling ornaments on an invisible Christmas tree. Their heads shook back and forth as their teeth rent and tore into the unseen. The air around them seemed to shimmer. The light-transferring fabric was becoming distorted from the ripping, violent movement.

Bolan strode forward.

He chose a point directly between the two flailing dogs and swung the brass-capped staff with all his might. The staff impacted and bent with satisfying impact. The staff rose and fell like a trip-hammer as Bolan beat the unseen Thuggee into oblivion. One of his blows missed and the dogs suddenly dropped down. They continued savaging something lying on the floor. Bolan continued the beating.

"Chicago! Bring the restraints! I have one!"

"Affirmative! On my way!"

"Ironman! Ready the bolt-hole! We are out of here!"

"Affirmative, Striker!"

James ran in and threw down his saber. He opened a gear bag and yanked out padded medical restraints. Feet flailed into sight and Sadie lunged and sank her teeth into an ankle. Bolan found the shape of a head and pinned it down brutally. He rammed the tip of the staff down into the side of the Thuggee's neck.

Bolan yanked away the robe as the man went limp. Silvery gray fabric shimmered into his hand as the system turned off. "Sadie! Schatzie! Back off!"

The dogs released and backed up, baring their fangs at their prey. He was a big man, like the first they had captured. James swiftly hog-tied and trussed him like a Christmas goose.

Lyons's voice spoke across the com link. "Bolt-hole is ready!"

"Affirmative!" Bolan and James hoisted their captive. "Everyone extract to the living room! We are—"

Khan's twin .455 revolvers detonated like cannons in rapid fire from the front of the house. A submachine gun snarled. Bolan and James nearly dropped their burden as the house shuddered down to its foundations with a massive detonation.

"Ironman! Was that you!" Bolan knew the answer even as he asked.

"Negative!" Lyons came back. "Front of the house!"

Bolan dropped his end of the Thuggee. "Chicago! Get this guy out of here!" Bolan pulled out his Beretta and ran down the hall. Smoke and dust filled the air. In the foyer Makhdoom was rising to his feet unsteadily. The *goondas* and mob members in the doorway hung limp or twitching across the two crossbeams that remained, stunned by the blastwave.

"Where's Fareed?"

Makhdoom blinked and shook his head dazedly.

Bolan shook him and moved his mouth in exaggeration as he shouted. "Fareed!"

"Kitchen!" Makhdoom gasped. "Helping Bijaya!"

Bolan ran to the kitchen with the hounds at his heels.

Most of the outer kitchen wall was gone. Smoke, dust, gas and the stench of burned high explosive filled the air. Someone had used a satchel charge to breach the house.

Lyons's voice rose in Bolan's earpiece. "The back is about to fail! We go to lead, or we get out of here!"

Bolan knelt beside Ghulam Fareed. The huge Pakistani lay limp among the rubble. The blast hadn't killed him, but it apparently had stunned him enough. The carbon fiber collar had been ripped away from under the neck of his shirt. A red silk scarf had been twisted around his throat. His eyes were rolled back in his head, and his face was a cinotic blue.

Bijaya Khan was gone.

"Striker!" Calvin James clapped his hand on Bolan's shoulder. "We've got to go!"

Bolan searched for a suitable weapon. They had stacked the tools in the kitchen. The soldier picked up a shovel they had used to fill sandbags. "They have Bijaya."

"Goddamn it! That's the draw! We go out there, and they'll be waiting!"

"I know. Take that cultist and make him talk!"

James nodded. "You got it." He turned and ran down the hall. Bolan tied a bandanna around his face and hefted his shovel as he walked across the rubble and emerged out of the house and into hell.

Moaning bodies lay everywhere. No one had told the *goondas* or their recruited mob about the plan to breach the house with an explosive charge. Some staggered about drunkenly. Others ran in all directions. The air was a horrific mix of smoke, dust and tear gas, all shot through with billowing streamers of red, purple and green marking smoke. Bolan gritted his teeth. His eyes began to burn as he moved through the atmosphere of some far-flung hostile planet.

Behind him the hissing crack of cutting charges whipped the air. In the living room they had torn up the floorboards and dug a hole in the foundation to expose the sewer. The charges had breached it, and his team would be extracting to the Hooghly River. Anyone trying to follow would have to deal with the white phosphorous grenades James and Lyons would be using to break contact.

Someone ran forward out of the smoke and gas, screaming and pointing accusingly at Bolan. The Executioner slapped him silent with the shovel blade. Others noticed and moved in with knives and staves. Bolan was no longer in the mood to be merciful. He moved through the remaining hostiles, his shovel blurring in a bone-crunching dance of destruction. He broke heads and reaped the limbs of anyone unfortunate enough to cross his path. His eyes were burning out of his skull, but Bolan had been exposed to tear gas and worse before. His iron will kept him moving forward unerringly through the hellish slaughter ground.

He burst through the gate to find the mob running in all directions. Bolan squinted and blinked away tears. Outside the garden walls the gas was rapidly dispersing. Down the street Bolan saw a black Ford Falcon.

Bijaya Khan's limp form was being piled into the back seat by four men.

Bolan drew his Beretta.

Two *goondas* with swords charged at him howling with bloodlust.

Bolan pulled back the shovel and suddenly knelt as he flung it. The shovel revolved once as it flew through the air and scythed the lead *goonda* off his feet. The second man tripped and staggered over his falling friend. Bolan slammed the slide of the Beretta into his temple and dropped him.

The Executioner broke into a dead sprint as the exhaust pipe belched blue smoke and the tires suddenly screeched on the pavement. He stretched his legs out but his burning lungs were failing him.

The car began to pull away.

Bolan stopped and knelt. He raised the Beretta, and a snarl spit from between his teeth. His gun wavered in his hands as his lungs choked and burned. His sight picture blurred as his eyes continued to tear and film over.

With Khan in the car it was no longer a shot he could risk.

Bolan rose.

The Cult of Kali wouldn't harm a woman, but it was very clear they knew people who would. They would make contact, either through the American embassy or with Khan's superiors at RAW. They would offer a trade. Bolan knew exactly what that trade would be. He holstered his Beretta as the mob howled for blood behind him.

Bolan tasted bitterness as he ran for his life.

CHAPTER NINETEEN

Bijaya Khan yanked at her bonds. Smoky torchlight lit the room from a pair of sconces. The space looked as though it had been hewn from the earth with picks. The air was musty, fetid and dank, and smelled of human excrement and blood. The floor was wet and the ceiling dripped in many places. A burlap sack had been yanked down over her face once she had been thrust into the car, but Khan was a trained intelligence agent. They hadn't driven far, and she had felt the car take many turns, many of them doubling back on themselves to make a circle. They were still in the Kalighat district, or very close, probably near or even under the river.

She ceased her struggles and glanced around her surroundings again. The water seeped from the ceiling in many places. Small stalactites had formed dripping spikes from above and the miniature cones of matching stalagmites poked up out of the floor. Parts of the cell fell into blackness outside of the light of the torches. The tomb was very old.

The steel chains that held her to the wall weren't.

They were freshly oiled and gleamed with newness, as did the bolts in the wall that secured them. The only way in or out of the room was through a modern steel door sunk into a poured concrete frame incongruously set into the cave wall. Khan shook her head and yawned to open her jaws wide against the ringing in her ears. Blood caked her brow and chin, and her lower lip was split. Every muscle in her body ached as though she had been beaten with a hammer, but her injuries were miraculously minor and had come from being bounced off the kitchen wall by the explosion rather than any of the attentions of her captors. She had, however, been stripped of her weapons and everything she had been carrying, including her concealed .25 pistol. She was vaguely thankful that she hadn't been stripped of her clothes.

Khan rolled her shoulders and flexed her fingers to try to bring back feeling into her numb hands and arms. Sooner or later someone had to come. Khan's father had been a Christian Bengali, but her mother had been a Hindu from the lush Malabar Coast of Kerala. She had spent her summers growing up in that tropical paradise with her mother's family, and in the cool of the evenings she and her cousins had diligently practiced the ancient martial art of *Kalari Payat* in the courtyard under the exacting, baleful gaze of her grandfather. Khan's arms were numb from being chained over her head, but her legs, bruised as they might be, were still lethal weapons.

All she needed was one error in judgment by her jailers.

She relaxed in her chains and concentrated on her breathing. An hour passed until the bolt in the door shot. A short bullet-headed man with a broken nose and the physique of a wrestler came in bearing a pink sports bottle and a bowl of something. The guard closed and locked the door behind him and shoved the keys in his pocket. He walked up to her and pulled open the sports bottle's spout with his teeth. Khan arranged a look of fear on her face. "Listen, please, I—"

The guard muttered monosyllabically in Bengali as he thrust the spout between her lips. "Drink."

Khan struggled to swallow rather than choke as water was

squeezed down her throat. The guard's thick fingers continued to squeeze the plastic bottle until they met in the middle. He tossed the bottle aside and Khan abandoned any attempts at conversation for the moment as he shoved the bowl against her mouth and tipped it. "Eat."

Khan downed the watery, split pea *dal* that the guard didn't spill down her chin. She jerked in her chains as he unceremoniously slid his free hand up under her shirt and grabbed one of her breasts. He shoved the bowl hard against her mouth and pinned her head against the wall. "Eat."

Khan ate while the man's hand roamed. It took little acting to shudder beneath the man's unsubtle touch. She ate. The lentils were undercooked and the *dal* had far too much turmeric and not enough coriander, but she didn't know where her next meal might be coming from and knew that whatever lay before her would require strength. She considered her options and let out a choking sound as she emptied the bowl. The guard tossed the bowl away as he applied both hands to unhooking the front of her bra.

"Please…" Khan moaned. "I'll do anything you want."

The guard smiled with unpleasant familiarity. "Of course you will."

"Please…you don't have to hurt me."

The guard's smile was grotesque in its pleasure. "I will hurt you if I wish."

Khan grimly calculated the man's brutal face. His nose was already broken, and she didn't fancy her chances of winning an exchange with his scarred brow. The guard gave up on the clasp and his callused hands yanked against the elastic. He smiled with childlike delight as it tore apart in his hands.

"Ah…" He turned his head slightly as he glanced down at the glory that spilled into his hands.

He also exposed his left temple.

Khan snapped her head forward. Stars exploded behind her

eyes as the frontal arc of her skull crunched into the thin bone of the guard's temple. The guard reeled erect. She couldn't afford to let him stagger or fall out of reach. She snapped her instep up between his legs and smashed his turgid organs. The guard moaned and fell against her as he dropped to his knees. Khan hung in her chains as she yanked her knees up to her chest. The man wept and gagged with pain, but he struggled to get a foot beneath him to stand.

Khan let him get half turned so that he presented his back. She scissored her thighs around his throat in a hanging figure four and vised down on his carotids.

The man grabbed at her ankles and thighs to break the lock. He was immensely strong, but he had a concussion and crushed testicles, and Khan's current workout regimen consisted of waking at dawn and engaging in two hours of an exceptionally arduous form of Ashtanga yoga. The guard's hands were reduced to feeble pawing within seconds. She held him until he went limp and continued to hold him until both his weight and hers became unbearable against her shackled wrists. She eased the guard to the floor belly-up at her feet.

Khan allowed herself a brief, savage smile of exultation and got down to business. She spent long moments worming her toes down his front pocket and fighting with the jammed folds until her toes closed around the ring of keys. She fished the keys out and hung in her chains for a moment. She folded her body in two in a leg lift that brought her foot up to her right hand. She chose a key and grimaced. She didn't have the leverage to reach the tumbler. She needed slack. There was no footstool to be found in the underground dungeon so she stood on the guard's Buddha-like belly and gave herself an extra two feet of height. The key slid in the first time and her right hand came free. She swiftly freed her other hand and stepped down off the guard and began rifling the rest of his pockets.

She leaped up and whirled around in a wide-open fighting stance at the sound of two hands clapping in applause.

"Oh, good." The voice that spoke from the shadows was deep and melodious. "Oh, very good."

Khan shot a look at the door and gauged her chances as a figure stalked to the dim periphery of the darkness. He was big, she could tell that, and she could tell that she wouldn't reach the door and unlock it in time. She opened her stance even more. Her posture was firmly balanced yet freely extended. *Kalari Payat* was known as a "brave" or "honest" style of martial art. It had no secret techniques. One either learned to focus and move the energy residing in the body or one didn't. For those who couldn't, the moves were little more than an exotic but beautiful dance. For those who could focus, the dance transformed into a whirlwind of killing blows.

Khan's dark eyes blazed. She was utterly relaxed. She was utterly focused. If the man in the shadows didn't have a gun, he was dead. She exposed her dazzling white teeth in defiance. He might just be dead even if he did.

She kept the consternation off her face with effort as the man presented himself. He was six and a half feet tall and wore nothing other than a blindingly bleached white linen loincloth. His face was sculpted in the classic Aryan features, but his skin was dark like a Dravidian. Thick black hair shot through with a few strands of gray fell to shoulder length like the mane of a lion. He was emaciated yet disturbingly muscled. Like a Greek god that had spent six months in a death camp. His hands were huge. The man moved with an equally disturbing ease, and each gliding step he took through the shadows seemed to cover more ground than even a man of his size should. He, too, was utterly relaxed. His eyes were utterly focused upon her.

His eyes were utterly crazed.

They drank her in unblinkingly from beneath the wings of

his black eyebrows as he stalked forward. For an instant his eyes and face softened as he looked pityingly at the dead guard. "Ah, Ramanand, always it was your fleshly desires that failed you."

His terrifying gaze suddenly locked back on Bijaya. "But you, Bijaya, a woman warrior, the very image of the Goddess Durga, Mother from whom Kali sprang, Kali, who is mother of us all. Your beauty is her blessing onto us…"

Khan struggled in the grip of the terrible gaze. The black pools of the man's eyes seemed to expand and fill the room. She spoke with great effort through clenched teeth. "Jesus saves…asshole."

"Ah, the carpenter of your father." The huge eyes filled the universe but his lips parted in a condescending smile. "But your mother came from Kerala. You, Bijaya, came from Kerala, and there…there they know the Dark Mother well, do they not? Sunday mornings in plaid skirts and stiff sermons of a white savior cannot strip away what you have known in your heart since you were a child, can it?"

The mellifluous tones of his voice seemed to creep like fingers through her brain.

Images of her mother's sacrifices to the small idols of the gods came to the woman's mind unbidden. One of those many idols had been of Kali. Her sinuous, black, bare-breasted form seemed to rise up in front of her. All Hindus gave Kali her due during the festival time of the *Kali Puja*. Khan shook. But that was just one aspect of creation. What this man was into was an abomination.

"Listen to me…" The man's voice was irresistible as it insinuated itself into her consciousness.

It occurred to Khan that the food had been drugged.

"No…" The voice crept warmly into the recesses of her will, melting her thoughts into mush. "You have not yet tasted the sweetness of Kali…"

Khan resisted. She fought back by focusing on a single, diamond-hard thought. She wasn't going to fall for the bullshit of some dimestore fakir with a correspondence course certificate in hypnotism.

Khan yanked herself free of the voice. She ran three skimming steps to close the distance. Her voice rose from the pit of her belly and ripped from her throat like the scream of a leopard as she leaped into her attack. Her right foot snapped toward her opponent's groin as the fingers of her left hand spread and shot forth for his eyes. Even before the two blows landed, her cupped right palm was already torquing around viciously to concuss and rupture his eardrum.

The man's huge dark hands caught her in midflight and bore her to the floor with childlike ease. Before Khan could react, his hands pinned her forearms and his knees pinned her thighs. He pressed his forehead against hers to gently but inexorably hold her head to the ground and prevent a headbutt. She was perfectly pinned. She hadn't noticed before, but the ground he stood upon wasn't crushed rock or the cones of infant stalagmites but a wide circle of soft and scented sand.

Khan was a trained field agent and in her training it had been made very clear to her that she was a woman, and just what she might have to expect if she was captured. By force of will Khan shoved her terror into a corner of her mind where she could use her fear rather than be ruled by it. No matter how powerful this man was, if he wanted to play in the sand, sooner or later he would leave her an opening that would ruin his whole day.

"Oh, no, Bijaya…" His dark eyes bore into hers. "No man who worships Kali in his heart could do such a thing. All women are of Kali's image. All are the avatar of the Dark Mother of us all. Ramanand betrayed his faith, as I knew he would, and he has paid for it. I am Brahmin, and a priest of Kali. My sexual energy has been subsumed to a higher purpose. Kali is the only lover I aspire to."

His dark eyes seemed to meet in the middle to become a single black ocean that Khan's will was drowning in. He lifted his head, but his eyes held her in place as easily as the silken vise of his hands. A pair of women approached from either side. They wore the saffron saris and brow paint of priestesses. They were exquisitely beautiful.

"Fear not." The man's smile was angelic except for the terrible light that burned behind the darkness of his gaze. "We bring you a gift." He nodded at the priestesses. "Ashalata, Kalyani."

The women knelt on either side of Bijaya. Ashalata bent forward, smiling sensuously. The smell of scented flesh mixed with the burning incense.

A huge dark hand closed around Khan's jaws, partially opening her mouth and holding it open. Ashalata pressed her lips to Khan's. She snarled helplessly. Ashalata held something between her teeth, and the RAW agent tasted the sweetness of raw sugar dissolving between their mouths.

Khan struggled violently as her gums began to tingle. She had read everything recorded from the days of the British Raj when they had tried to stamp out the Kali cult. She had read the reports of officers of the British East India Company. She had reviewed the myths and legends.

"Yes." The man read her mind again. "I bring you the Sweetness of Kali."

"The Sweetness of Kali" was metaphor for the consecrated sugar Kali devotees took during ritual worship. No sources knew what exact drug or combination of ancient drugs the sugar was laced with. Only wild rumors circulated about what the inner sanctum rituals of initiation might be, but all sources quoted the same legend. Once one tasted the sweetness of Kali, once one was truly initiated, one never turned back.

You were hers, forever.

Glorious warmth flushed through Khan's veins. Her eyes rolled and her struggles weakened. Her skin tingled as if a hundred hands caressed it. Her fingers and toes clawed into the sand as if to keep from falling off the earth as the electric hand of the goddess herself seemed to caress the core of her being.

Khan's will crumbled as utter ecstasy rolled over her like a tidal wave.

Ashalata leaned back. Her face rapturous with the drug she had shared. Kalyani bent down and pressed her lips to Khan's. The woman didn't resist. Her lips opened of their own accord and she gladly accepted Kalyani's gift.

Bijaya Khan gave herself over to the unbearable rapture of the four-armed goddess of death.

CHAPTER TWENTY

"It's been three days." Burdick scowled at the beer in his hand and put it down without drinking. They were back to the waiting game again. The big man heaved a sigh and looked at Bolan. "What do you think?"

Bolan sat with his fingers steepled against his chin meditatively. Long ago, in a different kind of war, his first training as a warrior had been as a sniper. There were a fair number of crack shots on the planet, but what truly made a master sniper was his ability to wait and to observe. "I think it's getting close to time for them to make contact."

Burdick shook his head unhappily. "I know you've got some eerie ass instincts, but I'm worried. I've read the same shit that these Kali assholes won't hurt women, but—"

"But these mothers are religious fanatics," Calvin James finished. "And that kind can rationalize whatever kind of twisted shit their agenda requires."

The former SEAL was saying what they were all thinking. "Big Red is right. I don't normally like intelligence spooks, either, but Bijaya danced in the jaws of the serpent with us, and when the jaws snapped shut on her she fell with a .45 going off in each hand. That spook had my respect. We get her back, or we get her some payback. Same goes for Fareed. He gets payback. We make the magic happen on these bastards."

"Yes, vengeance for Ghulam Fareed." Makhdoom had radiated cold, burning intensity since they had withdrawn through the sewers. He had carried Captain Fareed's massive corpse all the way through the sewers to their new hiding place. He wouldn't leave his body in the hands of demon worshipers. It was in the Calcutta morgue, and only massive CIA intervention was keeping the circumstances quiet until the body could be transported back to Pakistan. "But our first duty is to the living. The woman must be rescued. If she still lives."

Bolan silently agreed. By helping them, Khan had put her career and her life on the line. She had known the risks, and the RAW agent's love for India had decided for her. The risk was worth it. Now she was in the enemy's hands. Fareed had gone into enemy territory to serve Pakistan, and he had paid the ultimate price.

"She's alive. They'll make contact." Lyons grunted. He stared at Bolan meaningfully. "We all know what they really want."

Bolan nodded. He was well aware of that. "Calvin, what have we gotten from our friend downstairs?"

James snorted in disgust. "I don't know what these freaks are on. They're high on Kali or high on something, but at the same time they are absolutely lucid. I know what you said about battery acid and broken glass, and I know it was metaphor, but shit. I don't think blowtorches and needle-nosed pliers would work on these assholes. Maybe it's yoga. Maybe it's some messed-up martial arts training. Maybe it's just goddamn faith. Faith can move mountains. I don't know what to do. I've drawn some blood and hair samples and sent them back to be analyzed for anything exciting. But short of jumper cables and broken glass, I am running out of ideas. This guy is a rock, and only triple restraints designed for the mentally deranged are keeping him contained."

Burdick glanced down the neck of his beer bottle and didn't like what he saw. "So we go for the trade."

"We agree to the trade," Lyons corrected. "Then, like Calvin said. We make the magic happen."

The satellite link on the table chimed right on cue. Bolan leaned forward and punched a button on the laptop slaved to the com link. Aaron Kurtzman's face popped into view. "We've been contacted."

Burdick slammed his beer on the table and looked Bolan with vague trepidation. "Dude, you freak me out."

Bolan ignored the freaked-out former Marine. "How were we contacted, Bear?"

Through the U.S. embassy in Delhi. The CIA station chief got a message mentioning Striker, Ironman, Big Red. The CIA guys in India have orders to give you whatever assistance they can, and those are code names they got in the dossier we sent them when you hit India. The communication mentioned some other small details the cultists could only have gotten from Agent Khan."

"So they want to trade for their guy we have in custody, or do they want me?"

"They want their man back, and they are willing to give up Bijaya for him. Though they did mention you. They want to talk."

Bolan smiled thinly. "Talk."

"That's what they say. You come alone, no guns. You let their man go and they'll let Agent Khan go. Then all they want is a meet."

"Meeting them alone means a snatch, Striker." James's eyes turned warily toward the floor and their captive below. "And you let that freak in the cellar loose, he will go berserker mode and become part of that equation."

"And no guns?" Lyons folded his arms across his chest. "You remember what happened when you guys went hand-to-hand with one of these psychos in Uri."

Bolan knew all of that. "Or they'll do what, Bear?"

"They were kind of vague about that." Kurtzman's brow wrinkled. "They talked about letting her go anyway, but it was menacing the way they phrased it."

"Yeah." Lyons' eyes narrowed. "Like letting her go naked and handcuffed on the docks at midnight next to a container vessel loaded with women bound for the Sudan. They don't have to hurt her, they can just let someone else do it. Like Calvin said, they can twist their fanatic shit to fit."

James was more than unhappy with the situation. "They can turn invisible. There is no way in hell we can back you up and know whether we've been spotted or not."

"Yeah." Bolan sighed. "Looks like they're calling the shots."

"Jesus!" Burdick was appalled. "You're not actually thinking about going along with this?"

"I'm thinking about it."

"Alone!" The big man waved his arms in mounting outrage. "Without any guns!"

"Thinking about it."

Burdick's arms fell helplessly to his sides. He suddenly cocked his head. "You got a knife?"

"Several." Bolan glanced up at the big man. "Why?"

"Here." Burdick reached into his pocket and pulled out the Canadian folder. "Take this one anyway, for luck."

Bolan took the boat knife and nodded at the massive ex-Marine. "Thanks, Red."

South Park Street Cemetery

BOLAN WHISTLED in the graveyard. It wasn't an ideal situation. The cemetery was large and, except for a bit of rolling ground, the terrain was wide open. The enemy could easily see his approach, and they had hundreds of tombstones and mausoleums to hide behind. Hindus traditionally cremated the bodies of the dead. Hindu scripture referred to Kali as the Goddess of the Burning Ground. The graves here were of Christians, many of them old with the names of the English colonizers. Others were Muslim and Jewish. Bolan didn't fool himself.

He was in enemy territory.

The cemetery gate had presented no obstacle. Bolan wheeled his burden along one of the cemetery paths. The Sword of Kali fanatic stood in a dolly, trussed and bound like Hannibal Lecter after an escape attempt. Bolan walked along, extending his senses out to all sides. There were no clouds in the sky. There was no moon, either, but the stars were bright and the glow of the Calcutta night made for decent visibility.

"Favored One."

Bolan stopped at the sound of the voice. He propped up his trussed cultist and turned. A man strode forth from behind the marble mausoleum of an ancient British mausoleum. The man was as tall as Burdick, but a long dark coat concealed his form. It was hard to make out his features in the gloom.

The man held Bijaya Khan by the hair. Bolan could see the white cloth that gagged her and the white cord that bound her hands. He nodded at the bound man in the dolly. "I brought your boy."

"So I see," the man said. His speaking voice was spectacular in its depth tone.

"I came alone."

"You have people waiting for you, but they are out of sight of us and out of rifle range. I, too, have people, but they are also at discreet distance. None shall interfere with us here."

"Good. Let her go."

"Do not be so hasty," the man intoned. "There is much—"

"Deal is a deal." Bolan pushed the cultist off the dolly. The

Thuggee twisted and jerked in his bonds, but he was bound like a cocoon. He toppled forward like a tree and helplessly fell face-first to the gravel path. Bolan put his boot between the Thuggee's shoulder blades and pinned him in place. "Let her go. Now. Or I kill him."

The man shrugged. "Very well, she is of no particular importance." He opened very large hands and let Khan free. She staggered forward and fell into Bolan's arms. The Executioner kept his eyes on his opponent as he removed her gag. "Are you hurt?"

Khan shuddered. "I am not…hurt."

"Can you walk?"

She nodded and stood up wobbly but under her own power. The giant in the shadows took a step forward. Bolan produced the folding boat knife and opened it with a snap of his wrist. The elliptical Canadian steel gleamed in the starlight.

The man stopped.

Bolan slashed the cord binding Khan's wrists. He took one of her hands and stepped off the bound Thuggee and began to back away.

The man extended a huge, open hand and beckoned. "Wait."

Khan stopped dead. Bolan blinked as he actually felt the compulsion to stop at the sound of the man's voice.

"We must speak."

Bolan didn't stop.

His will had been forged in battle on every continent on the planet. His War Everlasting had cost him more than most other men could bear, but the blood, anguish and loss had given him hard-won gifts, as well. Mack Bolan, by free choice, had become a man apart. He felt the inhuman will of the other man and his own rose of its own accord. The eyes were the windows to a man's soul, and something was communicated between the two men. The Thuggee's eyes were black pits, offering nothing but an endless dark descent into madness. Inhuman power gained at the price of insanity. Bolan's burning blue eyes revealed a mind, body and soul honed to razor sharpness. He was a man who had chosen a path that brought him face-to-face with the event horizon of human evil. He had dedicated his life to staring into the terrible place and telling it no.

The Executioner raised his knife.

He had to kill this man, but first he had to get Khan clear. Bolan shook his head. "We have nothing to say to each other."

The point glittered between them. Bolan had no illusions. If this new Thuggee was anything like the last two they had captured, he had grave doubts about taking him in hand-to-hand combat.

But he did have a few cards up his sleeve.

"No." Once again the towering apparition seemed to read his mind. "Kali favors you, Blessed One. Her grace falls upon both of us, Brother. No harm will come to you from my hand."

Bolan's blade never wavered. "Good to know."

"I come in all humility," the Thuggee continued. "I have brought you a gift."

Bolan released Khan and his left hand drifted to his side. He pressed the small black box clipped to his belt underneath his shirt. It sent a very simple signal. Anyone monitoring would receive one click or two. Bolan clicked once.

He had the package.

His team would be descending on the cemetery like wolves from the surrounding neighborhood. Bolan played for time. "What gift is that?"

Bolan backed up, dragging Khan with him as the giant knelt over the fallen Thuggee. He rolled the man over and brushed away the gravel imbedded in his bloodied face. "Tungesh, are you injured, my brother?"

"No, Guruji." The bound Thuggee glared bloody murder at Bolan. "I am unharmed."

"Guruji." Bolan made a mental note of that.

"Good. Very Good." The giant Thuggee looked up from his charge. "Oh, yes, your gift." His smile shined in the darkness. "I have brought you the Sweetness of Kali."

Bolan began backing away. "I don't want it."

The great Thuggee's smile was beatific. "It is already yours." He bent over the bound deceiver. His huge hands went to the front of the heavy canvas restraint-mounting garment and closed around the padded neckline.

The sound of tearing fabric was very loud in the cemetery as the Thuggee tore the front of the reinforced straitjacket from collar to hem in three convulsive heaves.

Bolan thrust the knife into Khan's hands and shoved her in the direction of Park Street. "Run!"

The woman bolted.

The fabric belts shackling the Thuggee's legs presented little more of an obstacle.

Bolan's first and best instinct was to run, as well. It was ugly, but this was possibly the best opportunity he would have. His team was closing.

He had to delay the two Thuggees until the cavalry arrived.

The Thuggee named Tungesh was a big man. The man he called Guruji lifted him to his feet like a child. The freed Thuggee stood in the shredded remnants of his restraints like a mummy in tattered wrappings.

"Tungesh, my brother. Sword of Kali." The Guru pointed a long tapered finger at Bolan. "Bring him. There is little time."

Then the Guru turned and disappeared into the darkness.

Tungesh's lungs pumped his breath like bellows in through his nose and out through his mouth. He lowered his head and his eyes almost crossed as they regarded Bolan from the point beneath his brows. The soldier snarled and dropped into a fighting stance.

Bolan broke and ran, sprinting through the graves. Tungesh roared like a bull. Khan was a hundred yards ahead. She was still running, but her stride had faltered to an enfeebled trot. Bolan followed her path and kept himself between her and the pursuing Thuggee. He might be sworn not to hurt women, but Tungesh had gone high on life and only God knew what he might do if he got his hands on Khan rather than Bolan. Bolan wove between marble Stars of David and Christian crosses. He risked a glance back. Tungesh was taking the tombstones like an Olympic hurdler and closing quickly. Khan might make the wrought-iron fence, but Bolan wasn't sure if she could climb it in her condition. Bolan knew he wasn't going to make the fence.

Not a chance in hell.

The Thuggee was right on his heels and closing. Bolan vaulted the four-foot bullet shape of a gravestone and spun. Tungesh didn't even alter his stride as he sailed over the granite marker. When Tungesh was six inches from touchdown Bolan's boot connected with his sternum in an apocalyptic heel kick. Tungesh flew backward and half uprooted the tombstone in its anchorage. His facial expression didn't change as he bounced off the granite marker like a rubber ball and his hands shot forth for Bolan's throat. The big American brought his arms up between his adversary's forearms and momentarily deflected them off target.

Tungesh's eyes flared in slight surprise as Bolan's hands wrapped around his neck. The Executioner flexed his wrists once violently as the Thuggee grabbed his forearms to rip away the chokehold. Bolan vised his hands down and the flat snapping sound of electrical arcing and burned ozone filled the space between the two men.

Tungesh went rigid as he felt the ace Bolan had up each sleeve.

Dr. Austenford had wanted intact light-transferring textile

samples, and both she and Bolan had wanted prisoners. Part of the Indian warload delivered to the Calcutta safehouse had been electrical stun guns. Calvin James's jury-rig had been crude, but they had taped two of the stun guns to Bolan's forearms beneath his leather jacket. They had cut holes in the palms of his leather gloves and strung leads from each gun into his palm. Beneath the leads he wore rubber garden gloves. When he snapped his wrists back, he activated the switches on both guns. Bolan held the Thuggee's throat in a death grip. There was no off switch.

Tungesh's body jerked and shuddered in Bolan's grasp as the stun guns drained their batteries into him at 400,000 volts per gun.

Bolan vised his thumbs down and cracked Tungesh's trachea. The Thuggee made a single, guttural "cluck" noise and fell down dead at Bolan's feet as he released him.

The crackling arcs suddenly faded and died as the batteries bled dry. Bolan turned and ran. He ripped away his gloves as he sprinted for the fence. Khan was painfully trying to climb her way over the decorative wrought-iron spearheads topping each rail. Bolan hit the fence running. He put a foot on the middle brace, and Khan cried out as he heaved her over his shoulder. The blunt fence tops tore at his leather jacket, and then he fell free to the sidewalk outside. The woman's added weight jarred him down to his heels on landing. Bolan set her back on her feet. He grabbed her hand and dragged her into a staggering run down the street.

"Move!" Bolan roared.

Khan wept with exhaustion as she whipped herself to greater effort. Park Street had been the agreed extraction point. A tan Land Rover was screaming down the lane toward them. A pair of motorcycles tore along either side of the cemetery in a flanking movement behind them. The Land Rover's tires screamed as the driver spun the wheel and yanked up the parking brake into a bootlegger's turn. Burdick flung open the back gate. He cradled his Mossberg shotgun in both hands. Makhdoom stood up in the sunroof scanning the surroundings over the muzzle of his Schmeisser. The Honda Nighthawk motorcycles converged onto Park Street. Carl Lyons and Ramathorn each rode tall in a saddle with an Uzi in hand.

Bolan shoved Khan into Burdick's arms and dived into the back of the Land Rover. "Hit it!"

Calvin James stood on the accelerator. The Land Rover lunged back the way it had come, and the two motorcycles fell into formation like outriders. Bolan sagged, gasping, to the bed of the cargo area. Khan dropped against his chest shuddering and sobbing. Burdick's brutal face loomed over them. His brow creased with concern. "You okay?"

"I think so." Bolan took long breaths. He eyed Khan as she shook. "I think so."

The big ex-marine suddenly grinned. "You rescued the package, man!"

"Yeah." Bolan slowly relaxed. "We did."

"You met the enemy?"

"Yeah, I think I met that charismatic leader Calvin was talking about."

Burdick raised an auburn eyebrow. "Was he as scary as those other two assholes?"

Bolan put an arm around Khan's shoulders and stroked her hair as she wept. "Scarier."

CHAPTER TWENTY-ONE

The Harley-Davidson roared. Pedi-cabs and auto-rickshaws made way at the last moment for the grim-faced warrior astride the ancient iron horse. A motorcycle was the only way to get anywhere fast in Calcutta. Bolan let the thunder of the fifties vintage Duo-Glide's engine do his talking for him rather than leaning on the horn. Calcutta's famed midtraffic fistfighters stayed in their vehicles when Bolan locked his gaze with theirs. Man and machine cut through the late-afternoon rush hour like Moses parting the Red Sea.

The traffic was horrific but that was to Bolan's advantage. He spent a good forty-five minutes losing himself and any tail he might have picked up in the snarls of downtown Calcutta before he broke away and pulled his motorcycle through Tiretta Market. He slowed to a crawl, jostling with the horde of hawkers and buyers haggling over vegetables, dried fish and meat in the market place that had been named for the friend of Casanova who had been forced to flee Venice. Once more the press made way for the massive motorcycle and the man on it. Bolan suddenly crossed an invisible dividing line and found himself in Chinatown.

Bolan glanced around and recognized nearly everything.

Chinatowns were the same all over the world. He found himself surrounded by Chinese restaurants, markets and shops, and a new throng that all shouted, bartered and did business in Cantonese. Bolan stopped at the Nanking Restaurant and picked up a bag of food he had ordered an hour earlier and paid an exorbitant price for a six-pack of Tsing Tao beer. He drove past the restaurant and pulled down an alley and then two more.

As was every alley in Calcutta, it was hip-deep in rotting garbage. Sunset hadn't yet fallen, but the crumbling buildings were tall and close set, and the alleys between them were already growing dark. It hadn't rained in a week but the immense potholes were still lakes of opaque, foul-smelling mystery moisture. It grew worse every turn Bolan took deeper into the maze. Here in the back streets people lived in lean-tos and huts made of sagging cardboard, damaged pallets and plastic bags. Beggars and cripples leaned against crumbling walls. Half-naked children played in the puddles, while their mothers burned small fires of filth to cook whatever they had in scavenged pots. Every eye Bolan met was huge with hunger and quiet desperation. Almost every face and limb he saw was marked with the ravages of disease or malnutrition. Many were missing limbs. Bolan had seen some of the worst poverty on Earth, but the city of Calcutta had a lock on the top of the list.

It had been a long time since Bolan had seen a leper.

The man sat on a block of concrete a few yards away from Bolan's destination. The leper's hands were wrapped in rags and out of the stained pieces of cloth he seemed to have about seven fingers between them. A crutch leaned against the wall beside him. His feet were completely covered, and the rags around them nearly stained black from hobbling the streets he called home. Most of his head was wrapped to conceal the corruption of his flesh. One eye was patched over with filthy gauze. The remaining one was riddled with red veins but appeared to be functional. The stained bandaging wrapped closely enough against his face to reveal that he didn't have a nose. His lips were ragged shreds barely discernable from the stained and torn bandaging around them.

Bolan parked his Harley.

The Executioner brought his hands up in front of his chest in a prayer position. *"Namaste."*

The Hindi greeting was ancient and, literally translated, meant, "I recognize the divine within you."

The leper grunted in bemusement. Leprosy was hideous in its capriciousness. Out of the destroyed face the tattered lips parted to reveal a dazzlingly white smile. He pressed what was left of his hands together and greeted Bolan in return. *"Namaste,* Handsome One."

Bolan nodded toward his motorcycle. "I need someone to watch my bike."

"I can watch it." The leper turned his one eye on the Harley. His English was flowing, and almost feminine. The wheezing breaths he had to take by mouth between sentences marred the effect. "It is beautiful."

Bolan eyed the leper doubtfully. "I was thinking of a couple of boys."

"I am your boy." The leper revealed his flashing smile again. He held up the fore and little finger of his right hand. There were no fingers between them. "I am *Hijra.* All I need are these."

Bolan accepted the implication. *Hijras* were eunuchs, and usually transvestites. They were almost always of the Untouchable caste. In India's multistratified society they were considered third-gender and to possess occult powers. They were shunned wherever they went, but the belief that they could cast misfortune or curse made most give them a few rupees to be rid of them. While they were openly shunned, in private they were often sought out as prostitutes. They told fortunes at fairs and festivals. Perversely, women who were desperate for children would seek their blessing for fertility. The man in front of Bolan was a karmic triple threat. He was an Untouchable. He was a leper and he was *Hijra*.

No Indian would risk having those two fingers pointed at them in the sign of the Evil Eye.

Bolan looked at the fading light above the tops of the buildings. "I may be here for a while."

"I have no previous engagements." The single bloodshot eye walked up and down Bolan's frame. "Do you have any cigarettes?"

Bolan reached into his pocket. He had the occasional cigarette, but had given up smoking long ago. But most of the world still hadn't. Cigarettes were useful as social icebreakers and minor bribes. Bolan almost always carried a pack. He struck a match and lit up. Bolan took a drag and then placed the cigarette between the ragged lips.

The leper leaned back. His single eye closed in bliss as he breathed in. Lepers felt no pain. As the disease advanced, they could hardly feel anything at all. The leper could clearly still taste tobacco and enjoy his addiction as the smoke filled his lungs. He breathed with deep satisfaction. "Marlboro."

Bolan wrapped the pack of cigarettes and the matches in a few rupee notes. He pressed them into the hand with the most fingers. Bolan took his takeout from one of the motorcycle panniers and set a box of vegetable chow mein on the concrete block beside the leper. He put one of the fortune cookies on top.

"You're hired."

"You are generous. My name is Tipu."

"Mike."

"Mike. I like it. So American." The leper's dazzling smile had probably once earned him his living. The single eye regarded Bolan pointedly. "You have come to see the beautiful lady."

Bolan nodded. "Yes."

"I was once as beautiful as her. I was much sought after. I was seventeen and they said I would someday be *hijra rani*, a eunuch queen." Tipu sighed out a long stream of smoke. "You know, I took every precaution. I was very particular about my clients. I was worried about AIDs." He shook his head sadly at his corrupted flesh. "Karma is strange."

Tipu suddenly looked up at Bolan. His single eye bore into Bolan's. Tipu spoke with quiet, startling force. "The woman within is in terrible trouble."

"I know."

"You are in even more terrible trouble. You are strong, but it is all around you. You should not have come here."

Bolan nodded. Nothing good had happened in India, and it was going to get far worse before it was over.

Tipu held up his hand again but with only his forefinger extended. Bolan knelt and let the leper touch him between the eyebrows. Tipu spoke a few words in Hindi and then nodded. "A blessing."

"Thank you, Tipuji."

The leper smiled at the honorific. "Go to your woman. I shall smoke cigarettes and watch your beautiful motorcycle."

Bolan walked on down the alley and stopped at a narrow, peeling, blue-painted door. He knocked three times, and then twice.

Bolts stepped back and the lock turned. The door cracked open and Bijaya Khan smiled wanly. Bolan read her body language and didn't like what he saw. Her perfect posture was gone. Her shoulders were hunched as though she had been beaten with a stick. Dark circles of exhaustion marred the flesh beneath her eyes. The flinching, haunted look in her dark eyes hinted at a darker bruising within. Her feet were bare and she was wearing a scandalously short, black satin robe with golden Chinese dragons on the front.

She held one of the .455 Webley-Fosbery revolvers cocked in her hand.

Bolan put up his hands. Both held takeout. "I brought chow mein and beer."

"Good." The revolver sagged to her side as if it weighed a hundred pounds. "I have not eaten today."

Bolan followed her up a rickety stairway as narrow as the door. The door at the top of the landing was open. It was a steel security door. Things changed when they stepped inside. A sumptuous Persian carpet covered the floor of the one-room studio. The floor was hardwood and several tasteful tapestries depicting Indian mythological epics covered the walls. A queen-size futon set to face east dominated a good portion of the room and a kitchenette the other. Fresh flowers were spread in vases around the room.

Bolan shut the steel door and turned the bolts. "A safe house?"

"Yes. One I established privately for myself. Few people would look for a Christian Indian spy in Chinatown. The front of the building is a storehouse belonging to a Chinese tea merchant. I pay him well to keep a low profile here."

Bolan glanced around at the décor. It was eclectic but simple, and matched the beauty and taste of the woman who owned it.

Khan uncocked her weapon and set it on the nightstand. "I'll be just a moment."

Bolan wandered around the tiny space as the woman went into the bathroom. Everything was very neat. A King James Bible lay on the nightstand beside her massive revolver. Over the bed hung a portrait of an imposing-looking man in turn-of-the-century British uniform. He sat formally with a lancer's helmet crooked in his left arm, his right hand resting on the hilt of a saber.

The weapon hung beneath the portrait. The hilt was the

standard brass basket of a British officer's sword. In the last century an Indian swordsmith had removed the narrow, shallowly curved blade of the English saber and replaced it with the wide, near crescent moon curve of an Indian *tulwar*. The sheath was wrapped in red velvet with brass fittings. The luster of the velvet and the gleaming state of the brass bespoke of generations of loving care.

Khan emerged from the bathroom. She had brushed her hair and the judicious use of cosmetics had smoothed away the rough edges of her exhaustion. Bolan handed her a beer. Her eyes closed as she took a long, slow pull from the bottle. "God I needed that." Her eyes moved to her kitchen cabinet. "I have whiskey."

"Beer will do."

Khan went and got plates and chopsticks and set places at her tiny table in the breakfast nook. She started pulling out boxes of food. She nodded appreciatively at the browned squab with roasted salt and pepper and the cold asparagus salad. "You have excellent taste."

"Thank you. The Nanking has an excellent menu."

Khan frowned. "You said there was chow mein."

"I gave it to a leper."

Bijaya blinked. "Really."

Bolan shrugged. "He's watching my hog."

"I do not know what that means." Khan managed a genuine smile. "And I am not sure that I wish to."

Bolan sat and tucked in. All the small bones made eating squab a lot of work, but the flavor was exquisite. Khan lost some of her lethargy and attacked her food with vigor. Bolan watched her eat and read her signals. He waited until she was full of food and beer and had relaxed.

"How was it?"

"It was bad. I need a drink." Bijaya had drunk three beers but she rose and poured a pair of stiff Scotch and waters over ice. Bolan joined her as she sat on the bed. Her hand shook enough to rattle the ice in her drink as she took a long gulp. "Not 'bad' the way you are imagining. I was not tortured or…raped, but there are worse things."

"I understand. I've been captured before, it—"

"No, you do not understand." Khan trembled with the effort of controlling her emotions. "You met him, in the graveyard."

"The leader?"

Khan shuddered. "Yes. He's their leader. The guru of the new cult."

Bolan waited.

"He…got inside my head." Khan stared into a place more awful than words. "It is good that I know almost nothing about you or your organization. Because he now knows everything about me and mine."

Bolan took her hands in his. "Listen to me. No matter how good you are, in this line of work you get tagged. I have the scars to prove it. Flesh heals. The worst wound closes and the ugliest scars fade with time, but here—" Bolan touched her forehead with his finger "—the scars are for life. You can't go back. You can't pretend it didn't happen, but if you're strong enough, you can turn it. Make it a strength. A long time ago some very bad people got inside my world. They took just about everything I cared about. I could have folded up, or run. Instead I took the path I'm on now. My old life is gone. I can't ever go back, and I had to leave every last shred of it behind. I wouldn't wish what happened to me or the path I've chosen on anyone. Not even on my worst enemy, but I wouldn't go back either. I just go forward."

"You do not understand. My career is over. I am…damaged goods." Khan's hands fisted into the bedsheets. Her knuckles went white. "I am already on suspension. I'm going to be debriefed again tomorrow. My superiors must decide how much damage I've done, and what is to be done with me."

"Bijaya—"

"I—I couldn't stop him, I just couldn't stop him, I couldn't…"

Khan broke.

She fell against Bolan bonelessly, sagging as the pent-up anguish and exhaustion shattered the remaining vestiges of her self-control. She made no sound but she shook uncontrollably. Bolan could feel her tears against his neck. She wept for a long time. The blinds faded from yellow to red with the last rays of the setting sun before she finally pushed herself away and slid her robe from her shoulders. Her black hair fell down across her perfectly sculpted collarbones. The fading red glow of the sun through the blinds fell on her cinnamon skin. Bijaya Khan's face belonged on the cover of fashion magazines. The glory of her body belonged in the centerfold of more male-oriented literature. Her dark eyes glowed from within as they stared into Bolan's.

"People might think I'd be taking advantage of you," the soldier husked.

"The only person taking advantage here is me."

CHAPTER TWENTY-TWO

Safehouse, midnight

"What are you saying?" Carl Lyons stared at the link.

Dr. Austenford's face and auburn hair filled the screen. "I don't think the Chinese or the Russians could have done it. Nor the Indians, not exactly."

"Well, that means the light-transferring textiles came from your lab or from 'not exactly', which is it, Doc?"

"I think they may have come from an Indian-owned company in the United States, in the Silicon Valley, California."

"Home of the start-up."

"That's right." Austenford warmed to the subject. "And a lot of the start-ups out there are Indian owned or have Indian engineers. The Indian State of Karnataka has emerged as their equivalent of California's Silicon Valley. The universities of Bangalore, Mysore and Goa are pumping out quality engineers and they have invaded the United States—Northern California in particular. Very high-tech, cutting-edge stuff."

"Well, now that is interesting. You have a list of likely suspects?"

"Yes, yes, I do." Austenford's smile was cruel. "And it is mercifully short."

"Tell me you have a top three."

"I've got a number one with a bullet, blondie." Austenford typed some keys and information began to scroll down Lyons's screen.

A second window opened to reveal the home page of an official Web site. "Coherence."

"Yes, as in 'coherent light.' They produce lasers. I should have thought of it sooner, but their applications are so left field of mine it didn't register. I went over their company prospectus. Coherence is doing excellent business in the commercial sector. The only black mark they have is in their research and development wing in Santa Clara. They've branched off, and are supposedly working on communication lasers for military applications. This top-secret stuff is supposedly a flop, and has been falling deep into the red for five years running."

"Isn't that a little odd?"

"It's more than odd, it's almost a joke in the industry, and it would be financial suicide for a company the size of Coherence except for one thing." The doctor raised a challenging eyebrow. "Can you fill in the blank, Mr. Ironman?"

Lyons produced a rare smile. "Except that the project has investors on the Indian subcontinent who keep pumping rupees into the project."

"Give the man a cigar."

"Doesn't anyone consider this strange?"

"No. Most people just consider it stupid, but people throw money at pipe dreams all the time in the high-tech sector. Sometimes those pipe dreams pay off in the billions. I work for Uncle Sam, Ironman, and I can't begin to tell you some of the weird and wonderful ways your tax dollars are being spent."

"You don't have to."

"I'm sure I don't. So, no, no one considers it strange. On the whole, Coherence is in the black and moving forward. The majority of the investors are happy and as long as the Indians keep bleeding cash into that little top-secret side project, its profitable, too."

"Who's in charge?"

"The CEO of Coherence is solid. It's the VP in charge of the project who might interest you."

"Yeah?"

"It's time to go split screen, Ironman, your friend Mr. Bear has more." The flat screen monitor split and Aaron Kurtzman's face appeared. "Who we have is this."

Kurtzman clicked more keys. An Indian man's face appeared on the screen. His long hair was swept back from a wide brow in a ponytail. He had the piercing black eyes and the aquiline nose of a hawk. His face descended to a wolflike jaw. The man was cruelly handsome. His face was inset into the text of a two-year-old *Forbes* magazine article entitled "Incoherence at Coherence." The man in the picture was described as the embattled vice president of ROD. The text detailed the travails of the man as he lead the one failing department of Coherent into a deeper and deeper boondoggle while the rest of the company moved forward. The man had declined to be interviewed but had given *Forbes* a prepared statement that spoke of "greater vision" and "vindication at the cutting edge of the next generation of laser communication technology."

The man's name was Dr. Kalidas Kaushal.

"We've got a bio on him. He was born into a wealthy textile family in Calcutta, and his original given name was Sugata. He attended the Indian Academy of Sciences in Bangalore, where he was also captain of the cricket team. He got his master of science degree there, and then came to California and got his master of engineering at the University of Davis. He got his M.B.A. at Santa Clara University."

"So far he sounds like a real professional college geek."

"Yeah, six-foot-seven professional college geek, but can you guess what happened next?"

"I don't know, he disappeared?"

"He went back to India for vacation. Things get very sketchy after that. All we have at that point is he got involved with an uncle of his named Jagmoan."

A picture appeared on the screen of a little bald, bearded man of indeterminate old age wearing a *dhoti*. Brahmin caste marks were painted on his forehead and he wore garlands of prayer beads the size of golf balls around his neck. A younger, ganglier Kalidas towered over him with an arm affectionately across his shoulders. Both men were smiling happily at the camera.

"Uncle Jagmoan was a real black sheep of the family. A genuine religious ascetic. He had been a priest for a time at the Temple of Kali before he got into esoteric, tantric practices and became a guru. Sugata seems to have fallen under the uncle's influence. There was a big stink about it. Sugata became a real true believer. Uncle Jagmoan initiated Sugata into his sect and renamed him Kalidas. Now, can you guess what the name Kalidas means?"

"Dunno." Lyons examined Kaushal's face with the trained eye of cop. He didn't like what he saw. "Slave of Kali?"

"He's good." Austenford beamed. 'He's real good."

"So, Uncle Jagmoan was a Thuggee?"

"No, and that's the weird part. He seems to have been legit, or at least legit as far as a cult leader can be. His disciples practiced severe physical austerities, but what he preached was love and kindness." Kurtzman sighed as he usually did when he was confronted with things his mighty intellect couldn't prove or disprove. "There were rumors he could levitate during meditation."

"Great, so they're levitating and passing out flowers at the airport. What happened next?"

"Kalidas and Uncle Jagmoan went into the jungle on religious retreat and disappeared. Kalidas staggered out of the trees ten years later. He claimed his uncle Jagmoan was a fake. He claimed that their religious community in the jungle had been nothing more than a cult of personality. Kalidas told tales of ritual sexual abuse and orgies, financial scams involving donations and money laundering. He said that commune had been attacked and wiped out by the local *dacoits* his uncle had schemed with and double-crossed."

"What did the police find?"

"They investigated. There really was a commune in the jungle. The place had been burned out, bodies everywhere, including that of Uncle Jagmoan. Kalidas was the sole survivor. He was interrogated and cleared of any part in it. The family took Kalidas back. He kept his new name but cleaned up his act. He went back to California and got his Ph.D. at Stanford and got intimately involved in the Northern California hightech boom of the 1990s."

The West Bengal State Police report scrolled out of the printer and Lyons rapidly scanned the official record of the commune massacre.

Kurtzman cocked his head expectantly at the former Homicide Detective. "So, Carl, what do you make of it?"

"It wasn't a massacre by local bandits. It was a hostile takeover, and an internal one. I'm buying Uncle Jagmoan. I'm betting he really was into peace and love and the whole bit." Lyons examined the picture of the gnomish little man again.

Lyons was a black belt in Shotokan karate, and in his travels he had met some masters who were capable of some incredible things. There was one thing he had learned in his studies.

It was always the little, goofy-looking old men who could eviscerate you with their little finger.

"Hell, maybe he could levitate. Who knew, but he had

something that Kalidas wanted, and when he got it, or thought he had it, he killed his guru, and took over. Kalidas was the one who got in with the local *dacoits*. He was the one who took over whatever underground remnants of the Thuggee cult were still in West Bengal and turned it into the high-tech whatever it is assholes we're facing today."

Austenford stared out of the screen with awe. "Jesus."

"Yeah, back to the high-tech part of it. You're telling me these assholes in the research-and-development wing at Coherence could be producing popcorn poppers or light-transferring textile smoking jackets and no one would be the wiser?"

"That's how top secret works." Austenford heaved a sigh. "Unless someone demands an audit, and as long as the money keeps rolling in, that just doesn't happen very often."

Kurtzman's face was grim. "One man did."

Another police file began printing. This one with the department heading of the Santa Clara County Sheriffs.

"A rival VP at Coherence. A Harvard man. You know, the real go-getter type. He seems to have crossed Kaushal's path. I contacted some friends in high-tech community in the Valley. This guy had had it in for Kalidas from the get-go. He didn't know why Kaushal was there, didn't know what he was doing, and didn't like, either. After the article in *Forbes* came out, he demanded that the project be canceled. Called it an embarrassment to the company. When the board wouldn't cancel he demanded an audit. Can you guess what happened to him?"

"He was found strangled."

"They found him in his palatial house in the Saratoga Foothills. When the police searched the residence they found an attaché case full of cocaine and guns. They chalked it up to some side deals with the wrong kind of people."

"And Kalidas and his little side project have just kept bubbling along."

"To this very day." Kurtzman confirmed.

Lyons shook his head. "He can't keep that shit up forever."

The lines across Kurtzman's brow only deepened. "If they're ultimate plan was to use the technology to get their hands on nukes, then maybe they don't have to much longer."

"I think I need to drop in on this Kaushal."

Kurtzman nodded. "I figured you'd say that. I have full warloads en route to the Bay Area as we speak. Dr. Austenford will be on a plane ASAP to meet you there to give any technical support you need, or if you need her as a prop for an undercover insertion."

"Good. Got it. I've got to drop a dime on the man. Ironman out." Lyons clicked the laptop shut and speed-dialed Bolan on his cell. Lyons waited while it rang. When he got the voice mail he paged and then dialed again, using the emergency number.

Bolan wasn't picking up.

"Calvin! Red!"

Calvin James trotted into the room with a rifle in his hand. "What's up?"

Burdick pounded into the room a moment later.

Lyons took his .357 Colt Python from the table in front of him and checked the loads. "Striker's in trouble."

Chinatown

BOLAN ROLLED OVER as his phone rang. His internal clock told him it was somewhere around midnight. His eyes roved Bijaya's gorgeous form by the low-burning candles on the two nightstands.

"Oh, God." Khan groaned and slapped at the phone where it lay on the nightstand. "Just kill it."

"I need to answer that." Bolan reached across her as the phone fell to the carpet and stopped ringing. "I need to check in."

"Kiss me first."

Bolan smiled. "Make it a quick one. The boys will worry."

"The boys will figure you were getting laid, and they'll be right. If you still have anything left." Khan held her hand up to her face and recoiled as she sniffed. "Oh, Jesus, dragon breath. Too much Scotch."

"I can live with it. Pucker up."

Khan opened a drawer and broke open a small tin. "Breath mint?"

"No, thanks."

"Well then come here, sex machine." She smiled and popped one into her mouth.

Bolan pressed his lips against hers.

Khan held the mint between her teeth. Bolan almost pulled away as saccharine sweetness melted between their mouths.

Khan thrust her tongue in Bolan's mouth eagerly. His gums and tongue tingled but not with the menthol-like taste of mint. It was far too sweet, and he brought up his hands to push her away.

Khan seized Bolan's hair and rolled on top of him, violently holding the kiss.

Bolan continued the roll off the bed and landed on his feet. He grabbed Khan and broke the kiss by hurling the woman away from him. The Executioner shook his head savagely and spit. His entire mouth tingled. He had read the reports and rumors from the eighteenth century to the modern day. He knew what had been done to him. He seized the open bottle of Scotch off the table and took a hefty slug. He swirled it around in his mouth and spit it out to the floor.

Agent Bijaya Khan lay on the floor in a heap. She laughed hysterically. "You are hers now."

The sweetness of Kali tingled across Bolan's skin.

The door to the studio opened and large men began to file in. The five men closed the door behind them. They looked at Khan on the floor and then at Bolan. Smiles crossed their faces. The man in the lead passed his hand in front of his face in ritual greeting. "Greetings, Ali my brother."

The man came forward. His arms open in welcome. Bolan shook his head savagely. His vision skewed and tripled. The smiling man warped and smeared across Bolan's perception.

"Come brother, Kali's embrace is—"

Bolan closed his eyes and lashed out, smashing the Scotch bottle across the face of the man by instinct. He opened his eyes and lunged again.

A second Thuggee screamed as Bolan rammed the jagged crown of remaining glass into his neck. The other three bore down up Bolan, grabbing for his arms. A Thuggee leaned close, hissing in Bolan's ear. "Listen, brother! While you still can! You have tasted deep of the sweetness of Kali! Far deeper than any first-time initiate. There will be darkness before you awake in the warmth of Kali's light! You will need a guide! Without a guide, there shall be madness beyond your—"

Bolan yanked his arm free and ripped an uppercut into the Thuggee's jaw. Bolan focused on his anger to steady himself. He shook himself free and leaped back on top of the bed. He reached for his guns, but a Thuggee dived on top of them. Bolan drove his foot into the side of the man's head but he went to the floor with guns clutched to his chest. The two bloodied Thuggees rose. They began chanting something.

Bolan knew what the chant meant. O brethren take the name of Kali. There is no refuge save in her.

Bolan reeled as he stood on the bed. The sound of the chant crawled through his brain. The light in the room was changing. Every time one of the Thuggees moved, smears of color marked his path through space.

A Thuggee watched Bolan's reactions. He smiled even as he wiped blood from his face. "O Brother, thou art hers."

The Thuggees came for him.

Bolan reached back. His hand closed on the brass hilt of the one-hundred-year-old *tulwar* of Khan's great-grandfather. The three-foot crescent of steel rang from its sheath, as sharp as the day it had been forged as Bolan lunged from the bed.

A Thuggee shrieked as his reaching hand was lopped off at the wrist.

The deceivers produced short, brass-shod lengths of rattan and charged. A club thudded into Bolan's stomach and another truncheon slammed down across his shoulders. He ignored the blows as he slashed a Thuggee across the eyes. The deceiver screamed and raised his hands. Bolan slashed open his stomach and then cut his throat. Bolan's victim fell, raining blood in all directions. The clubs of the Thuggees pounded like hail. Bolan dropped to one knee as a club crashed into the side of his neck and another bounced off his brow. The Executioner lashed out, half blinded with blood in his eyes. His saber's blade bit deep under his opponent's kneecap. The Thuggee collapsed to his hands and knees screaming. Bolan rose up with a roar. He raised the *tulwar* high and chopped it down like a butcher's blade. The edge crunched with brutal finality into the Thuggee's spine.

Paralyzing pain radiated across Bolan's chest as a brass-headed club rammed into his solar plexus. He staggered back as he took another blow to the temple. The pain helped focus him against the drug. Fingers flew as he slashed at the fist that swung a club at his neck. The club fell from the Thuggee's maimed hand, and his head flew from his shoulders a moment later. Bolan's world exploded into stars as he took a blow between the eyes. Blood poured down his face in a torrent. Everything in front of Bolan narrowed into a dark tunnel lit by purple pinpricks. Another blow clipped his jaw and nearly dropped him to his knees.

Bolan slashed and the blade met flesh. He charged forward, ramming the Thuggee off his feet and bore him to the floor.

He whipped the *tulwar* overhead and swung it down once, twice and a third time. Bolan rose, reeling. Bone splintered as he yanked the blade from the Thuggee's forehead.

His phone was ringing on the emergency line.

He was out of opponents.

The spray of arterial blood painted the walls of the small studio in gruesome tapestry. He undoubtedly had a concussion and, freed of action, the drug continued to crawl through his mind. His opponents were butchered meat at his feet but Bolan could still hear the chant in his brain.

It took Bolan a moment to realize the chant was coming from Khan. She pressed herself up naked from the floor. Bolan reeled on his feet. The room swung in and out of focus, but he kept the *tulwar* between them. The woman reeled in the grip of the drug herself, but a heavenly smile crossed her bloody lips. Bolan's phone no longer rang but Khan chanted on. Twice she fell against the wall, smearing the spray of Thuggee blood. She staggered to her small closet and turned to regard Bolan.

There was nothing left of Bijaya Khan in the black eyes that gleamed at Bolan. The woman was utterly in the grip of possession. Bolan raised his blade as she slowly swung open her closet door.

It was exactly like the painting on the wall in Srinigar, except that it had been painted with exquisite artistic ability. Kali covered all seven feet of the door. She was gaunt, skeletal, terrible, yet the width of her hips and the spill of her breasts were horrible in the offered fertility. He bloody tongue crawled across her fangs and hung down nearly to her belly. Her red eyes bored into Bolan's. In her hand she held a severed head and her raised foot stood upon a headless body, ready to begin the dance of destruction.

Ghulam Fareed's head was nailed to her hand. The Pakistani's giant's body lay headless on the floor. Bijaya knelt naked before the horrific image in supplication. She turned and smiled at Bolan. The perfection of her cinnamon skin smeared with coagulating human blood. She opened her bloody hand out to Bolan.

"Come to her...come to me...come to Kali."

Bolan's blood hammered thickly in his temples. His vision doubled and tripled again, and his heart smashed in the cage of his ribs as if it might rupture. His limbs shook uncontrollably. Sweat burst out across his skin in rivulets in malarial fever heat, mixing with the blood running down his face and limbs. Khan chanted to him, offering herself, clad only in blood and darkness as the goddess of death looked on. Bolan's blood moved like molten lead into his lower body, responding to what the woman offered. She gazed in rapture and rose, opening her arms wide to him.

Bolan suppressed the scream rising in his throat as Kali stepped from the door behind her.

The three-foot, blood-drenched tongue flicked forward lasciviously. The huge, canted, red eyes burned at Bolan with scarlet hunger. The goddess offered her dark flesh in terrifying pantomime of Khan. In one hand Kali held Ghulam Fareed's head high in bloody triumph. The other three arms opened out to Bolan in unholy embrace. Bolan's last rational act was to let the scream go. It tore out of his throat in animalistic defiance.

The three-foot, razor sharp blade of the *tulwar* hissed around in a terrible arc.

CHAPTER TWENTY-THREE

Chinatown

Carl Lyons and his team stormed the safehouse. They piled out of the CIA Land Rover and beggars and cripples flung themselves aside as the team of grim-faced, heavily armed men smashed open the rotten downstairs door. Flexible charge cut the upstairs steel door off its frame and Lyons's boot sent it flying off its hinges. He hadn't known what he would find. All he knew was that Bolan wasn't responding.

What he found inside the safehouse was a slaughter yard.

Large and small portions of human beings were scattered around, including heads, hands and limbs. The floor was a sea of drying blood. Lyons had started his career as a homicide detective for the L.A.P.D., and he scanned the scene with a detective's eye. He made it five victims. Either they had been run through a harvester or someone had taken them out with a very large, very sharp implement. He took in the empty sword sheath on the wall and considered the vacant blade a good suspect. The larger pools of blood were still tacky.

This could have happened minutes ago.

The rest of the team filed into the room with their weapons ready. Burdick cleared the bathroom while Calvin James and Ramrod walked the perimeter.

"Bismillah." Makhdoom's face was terrible. Lyons looked over at the closet and saw Fareed's head nailed to the door and his decapitated body lying on the carpet. The goddess Kali was painted on the door in horrific glory.

"Bismillah!" the captain repeated.

Lyons went over to the closet where Makhdoom stood. Behind Fareed's body, Agent Bijaya Khan lay naked on the floor. She was covered with blood, but didn't appear to be wounded. Her eyes were rolled back in her head so that only the whites showed. Foam flecked her lips and her mouth mumbled something between a chant and a prayer.

"Jesus Christ…." Burdick loomed over Lyons's shoulder and looked leerily at the headless corpse and the naked, writhing agent next to it.

"What's she saying, Red?"

"Uh…" He listened a moment. "Crazy shit. 'He is hers, he is hers…'" Burdick clutched his shotgun and grimaced distastefully. "'He is mine.' She's chanting them interchangeably."

James knelt by the nightstand. "Found something." The former Navy SEAL held up a little tin of mints. He snapped on rubber gloves and fished out a dark brown lump from among the mints and sniffed it. "It's raw sugar."

Burdick's craggy brow furrowed. "The consecrated shit the reports talked about."

"That's what I'm thinking." James stared at the lump of sugar like he held a poisonous snake. "The Thuggee blood and hair samples we sent back from Kashmir came back with traces of some unidentified cocktail of hallucinogenics. I'm betting this stuff is laced to hell and gone with the same stuff."

Burdick stared down regretfully at Khan as she tossed and mumbled. "Well she is hopped up to hell and gone on something, and it ain't good."

Ramrod knelt on the other side of the bed. "Found his phone, found his guns. Her pistol is just under the bed on your side, Chicago." The SAR sergeant glanced over a chair. "There's the big guy's clothes." He shook his head. "They've got him."

Lyons stared at the empty sheath on the wall. "I'm not so sure."

"Yeah. I hear you." James surveyed the carnage. "But they got to him."

Everyone looked back at the image of Kali painted on the door. A ragged two-foot hole had been hacked out of the door that would have corresponded to where her head should have been. "Striker wouldn't waste his time hacking off the head of a cartoon in a normal frame of mind, and he's not a minty-fresh kind of guy, either." He glanced at the empty cartons of Chinese takeout. "I'm thinking Bijaya got indoctrinated when she was captured. She could've slipped it to Striker via the food, but that wouldn't be the most certain vector for a hallucinogenic you need to dissolve across mucous membranes."

Lyons took a blanket off of the bed and wrapped the naked, shuddering agent and carried her from the closet. "You want to slip a hallucinogenic across someone's sensitive membranes, I'm thinking Bijaya's about all the vector you need."

"You may have a point," James conceded.

Ramrod looked around the room again. "So where is he?"

Burdick stood staring into the distance. He held two fingers to his earpiece. He had been monitoring the local police band on the way over.

Lyons laid Khan on a relatively bloodless section of the bed. "Red, you got something?"

"Yeah, I think so. Just a minute." Burdick peered at the ceiling while he listened. "It's kind of sketchy, but I think it may just be Striker."

"What are they saying?"

"There's been disturbance here in Chinatown."

Lyons peered out the window to the street below. "They talking about here?"

"No...a few blocks away."

"What kind of disturbance?"

Burdick frowned. "Possible escaped lunatic."

"Description?"

"White, naked, armed with a scimitar." The big ex-Marine let out a heavy sigh. "And raving about the goddess Kali."

BOLAN REELED in dark delirium, the bloodstained blade of the *tulwar* a blackened crescent in front of him. The denizens of Calcutta's dark back alleys melted before him, making way. Those with night errands, of drugs, sex or other illicit diversions, the nonnatives, screamed and ran. The true dwellers, however—the beggars, the cripples, the prostitutes, those who made their home in the deepest, ugliest bowels of Calcutta— didn't run. They looked into the white warrior's crazed, bloodshot eyes. They beheld the well-used butcher's blade clutched in his hand. They heard the name of the goddess raved in both terror and rage upon his foamed lips. In the foulest back streets, the signs were well known. Some pressed their hands together in *namaste,* recognizing him, others made the sign against the Evil Eye, but all whispered in awed reverence in his wake.

"...Kalidas...Kalidas."

Slave of the goddess Kali.

He had been chosen. He had been taken.

Bolan heard their murmurs. He slashed at any form that threatened to come too close. He heard his name being spoken behind him, beckoning. He almost recognized it, and almost turned, but the imperative of rage and terror propelled him forward. He had killed the goddess Kali. He had cut her face to ribbons with the *tulwar* in his hand, and she had risen up after him, laughing in Bijaya's voice, inexorably following him into the dark depths of the city.

Kali was coming to claim him.

All he could do was run.

Bolan's blood burned out of control in his body. Within the Executioner's mind, thoughts and visions, dark and ugly beyond reckoning, twisted across his sight. Somewhere deep within Bolan's besieged psyche he knew what was happening, he knew that hallucinogenics could be fought, controlled, but that voice was but one whisper among the gibbering, screaming cacophony of insanity shrieking through his intellect. Every hand he saw was black with blood, every pair of eyes watching him stagger through the alleys glowed red with the goddess's gaze. Opponents beyond counting in his War Everlasting against human evil rose up in front of him, rotting from the filth and sewage. They reached out for him, to drag him down. The *tulwar* rose and fell as Bolan slashed the phantoms down, only to rise again. The goddess of death called the death dealers on to herself and sent them before Bolan, to bring him down, to bring him on to her.

The Executioner staggered through the slums, burning in the black hell of Kali's embrace.

LYONS STRODE the streets. His team formed a phalanx behind him. They had left Chinatown, but the slums of Calcutta twisted and wound endlessly. None sought to impede them.

"Jesus!" Burdick recoiled from whatever he saw as he shone the flashlight mounted on his folding shotgun down a passageway. "He could be anywhere!" Burdick glared savagely at the street people squatting in the squalor or peering out of windows in the shanty huts. "Goddamn it! If he's in the same shape as Bijaya any of these shitbirds could have rolled him!"

"Keep cool, Red." Lyons continued to scan the twisting alleys all around them. "Keep looking."

Burdick was right. They had found Bijaya Khan eye-rolling, twitching and frothing at the mouth. James had administered 400 milligrams of Benadryl. She was sleeping now, with Ramrod standing guard over her. With luck her body would metabolize whatever the hell the Thuggees had given her. Lyons shook his head as he thought of Bijaya's condition and then Bolan. In his time as a cop Carl Lyons had seen people on some very bad hallucinogenic jags. The carnage in the safehouse indicated that Bolan was on the mother of bad trips.

Makhdoom and Burdick grabbed random inmates of the back alleys and waved thick wads of rupee notes, demanding any information on the sword-armed white man roaming the streets. Most bowed and shook their heads, others lurched away making the sign of the Evil Eye.

"You, Americans…"

Lyons turned at the sound of a voice speaking in English. He was confronted by a man dressed in rags. The leper sagged against the wall, leaning on single crutch. His breath came out of his mouth in exhausted, gurgling gasps. "You…you are friends…of the Handsome One, of…Mike."

Lyons blinked once. "Who are you?"

"Tipu. My name is…Tipu."

"How are you involved?"

"Mike, he came to see the beautiful lady. He asked me to watch his motorcycle. He gave me some money and food, some cigarettes. He was kind. The Thuggees came but I could not warn him, they beat me aside. When he came out, he did not recognize me…I saw his eyes…I saw he had been…taken by the goddess. I followed, as best I could, but I could not…"

The leper collapsed to the ground. Fresh blood stained the rags wrapping his feet. His crippled pursuit of Bolan through the streets had cost him dearly. Lyons took a knee beside him. "You did good, Tipu. You did real good."

Tipu smiled. His fingers shook around a pack of cigarettes.

Lyons took the pack and lit a cigarette for him. The leper coughed and breathed the smoke in deeply.

"Tell me, Tipu. Where is Mike?"

The leper pointed at a dilapidated building across the alley. "He went in there. I was just too tired to follow. He has not come out. The people who lived there, they have."

"Rest here." Lyons nodded to James. The former SEAL medic checked Tipu over and then gave him water from a canteen. He came back to the team. Burdick stared back at the bloodied bundle of rags that had once been a man.

"Anything we can do for him?"

James shook his head. "He's a wet-leper, and advanced. He's also tubercular and living on the streets. He's about to lose one or both of his feet. When that happens he'll quickly lose a leg. When he loses both legs, well…" James let out a long breath. "Unless he gets put in a clinic and his condition is stabilized, Tipu's race is just about run."

"He damaged himself for Striker's sake. I say we make that happen." Lyons glanced over at the building across the alley. The smashed-out windows and the holes in the crumbling walls stared back like blackened eye sockets. "But first we bring the big guy in." Lyons looked to James. "How do you want to play it?"

The Phoenix Force commando was grim. "We don't know what this consecrated shit is, but it's powerful. Bijaya was nearly catatonic when we found her, but still hallucinating. By all indications Striker is having a violent psychotic episode. We're gonna have to treat him as though he's flipped out on PCP. He may not recognize any of us. We may not be able to talk him down, much less convince him to take his Benadryl and have a nap. If it comes to a physical confrontation, pain or significant injury probably won't stop him."

James produced two syringes from his medical kit. "We

need to get both of these shots into him. Each one is 4 cc's of Thorazine."

Lyons stared at the needles. "Isn't that a lot?"

"It's a dangerous dosage. I won't shit you. But he's psychotic, he has a scimitar, and we have to knock his ass out, and keep him out long enough for his body to metabolize this mystery shit running through his veins."

Burdick glanced over at the building. "And how the hell are we supposed to do that?"

"It's simple."

"Really?"

"Yeah, you guys dog pile his ass and hold him down while I shoot him up, twice, and the bigger the muscle group I can get the needles into, the better." James was clearly unhappy with the plan, as well. "And we all try not to get our heads cut off in the process."

Makhdoom folded his arms across his chest. "And we hope that he does not go into shock and die."

"That is the situation." James confirmed.

"Well, I don't know jackshit from Thorazine." Burdick stared unhappily at the syringes. "But ain't there another way than needles?"

"Well, given a few minutes, I could distill the Thorazine into a gel, cut it with aspirin and Vaseline and we could administer it as a suppository." James regarded the big Marine dryly. "You want to volunteer for that mission, Red?"

"Uhh…" Burdick considered the logistics. "Syringes sound good."

"Uh-huh." James nodded. "That's what I thought."

Lyons led his team to the building. There was no door, just a ragged hole in the wall where the door and the door frame had been knocked or rotted out. The building seemed to have been a small textile factory or warehouse. The inside was dark except for a few smoldering fires made of waste of the squatters. The smoking lights did little to illuminate, and threw bizarre shadows across the piles of rubble, exposed beams and rebar. Most of the second floor was gone. The place was eerily quiet save for the crackle of the burning trash. The squatters seemed to have fled since Bolan took up residency.

Lyons stood in the gaping doorway. "Mack! It's Carl! You in there? We're here to help!"

His voice echoed eerily in the empty expanse. He considered tactics. They couldn't walk the streets of Calcutta with assault rifles, so their heavy weapons were back in the Land Rover. Not that any of that mattered. They had to take Bolan alive and unharmed. Mack Bolan was the most dangerous man on Earth. He was psychotic and he had a sword. Both Lyons and James were black belts, but James had a broken hand. Burdick was a brawler and whatever hand-to-hand Makhdoom had was probably aimed at killing and disfiguring people. Having been a police officer, Lyons was the only one truly skilled in arrest-and-control techniques.

He was going to have to take point.

"Red, give me your shotgun. Everyone, put the pistols away. Red, Doom, stay tight. Chicago, hang back and pull a fade. If Striker comes out swinging, try to blindside him."

"Roger that." James faded off to one side and disappeared into the dark as the team entered.

"Mack!" Lyons held the folding shotgun low and in as nonthreatening a manner as possible. "Mack! It's Carl! Let's go home!"

Only silence answered.

They advanced deeper into the dark. The smell of human waste and rot was overpowering. Makhdoom paused and knelt beside a sputtering fire. "Look here."

The Pakistani captain held up an unburned piece of plastic.

There were drops of blood on the plastic and they ran as he held it up.

The blood was fresh.

"He's here. He's—"

"Shit!" Burdick roared.

Bolan was upon them. He came out of nowhere. Loping silently on bare feet, he bounded out of the dark clad only in blood. Lyons had only a fraction of a second to meet Bolan's burning blue eyes, but in that moment, by the lurid red light of the dying fires, Lyons saw all he needed to.

Mack was gone.

The *tulwar* in the Executioner's hand hissed down like the Grim Reaper's scythe.

Lyons shoved up the folding shotgun desperately. The shock of the blow rang down both of his arms as the Indian steel cut through the folding stock, the barrel and finally stopped on the shotgun's feed tube. Lyons torqued the shotgun savagely, trying to twist the wedged saber from Bolan's right hand.

The Executioner's left hand whipped around with liquid speed. Colors detonated behind Lyons's eyes as Bolan's ridge hand chopped into his temple. Lyons's knees buckled and he sat in a pile of rubbish against his will.

James flew out of the darkness as if he had wings. His flying thrust kick sent the *tulwar* and the shotgun mated to the blade spinning from Bolan's hand into the darkness. Bolan let the weapon go. James couldn't quite stop the forward momentum of his flying kick in time. Bolan clotheslined him with a crushing blow beneath the clavicles that smashed him stunned into the ground.

Bolan raised his heel to stave in James's face.

"I got him!" Burdick roared like a bull as he piled into Bolan like a runaway train. "I got him! I—"

Bolan spun like a fullback breaking a tackle midfield. Burdick slipped off the Executioner as if he'd been oiled and flew out of control across Bolan's hip. The big ex-Marine roared again as he landed in the smoldering fire.

Bolan continued his spin to confront his next opponent.

Makhdoom pistoned two jabs into Bolan's jaw and then drove his foot into his belly. He seized Bolan by the throat and swung his boot up between the Executioner's legs. Bolan twisted his hips and took the kick on the thigh, his own hands shooting forth like blunted spears and ramming into the carotid nerves and arteries on either side of Makhdoom's throat.

The Pakistani commando dropped as if he'd been shot.

Lyons lurched to his feet and Bolan closed the distance in a fluid leap. The Able Team leader managed to block one blow and then another but the head shot he had taken had rocked him. Only Lyons's soft body armor kept his sternum from breaking as Bolan's fist blasted into his chest. He didn't see the soldier's snap kick to his groin. His vision went white as he collapsed, vomiting, to the broken concrete floor.

Burdick was up. He tottered toward Bolan, cocking back his massive fist. Before he could swing Bolan's fist, elbow and open hand coincided with Burdick's skull in a whirlwind of blows that drove the big man to his knees.

James's forearm slammed up under Bolan's jaw and vised his throat. He stabbed a syringe down into the meat of Bolan's trapezius and shoved down the plunger. You didn't try a one-handed strangle on a man like Bolan even under the best of conditions. It had been a conscious sacrifice to get the needle in. James paid for it as Bolan's shoulder throw sent him sailing out of control into a concrete column.

Makhdoom rose up only to be smashed back down.

Lyons pushed himself to his feet. His legs were rubber beneath him and his groin was an aching pit of agony. He had failed. The mission was FUBAR. As team leader he had only one responsibility left.

He couldn't let Bolan kill his team.

The stainless-steel .357 Colt Python revolver suddenly gleamed between them.

Bolan's bloodstained teeth were clenched in a rictus of bloodlust. His eyes were empty pits in his skull. He was utterly unaware of the syringe standing up out of his shoulder and seemed equally oblivious of the gun. Lyons thumbed back the hammer as Bolan stepped forward for the kill.

The soldier's knee wobbled beneath him and he nearly fell.

"That's it, Mack." Lyons retreated several steps. "Come on, this way."

Bolan followed Lyons, stalking him, but his eyes had lost some of their insane focus. He swung his head back and forth as if to clear it as he stumbled forward. Burdick hauled himself up, blood pouring from his split eyebrow. Bolan's horrible focus returned as Burdick received his undivided attention.

"Hey!" Lyons raised his revolver and pulled the trigger. The muzzle-blast was deafening in the enclosed space. Nesting birds exploded into flight from the rafters. Bolan's head whipped around at the sound. His eyes met Lyons's in a killing rage, unaware of Burdick going into motion on his flank.

The three-hundred-pound, left-handed ex-Marine threw everything he had into a blindside haymaker for Bolan's jaw.

Bolan's head rubbernecked on his shoulders. He turned and blinked dully at Burdick. James was on his feet with the second syringe in his hand. Lyons fired his pistol again and once more Bolan's attention was distracted. Burdick threw his arms around the Executioner in a bear hug and bodily lifted him up off of his feet.

"Do it!" Burdick snarled. "Do it quick!"

Bolan thrashed savagely in Burdick's grip. God only knew who or what Bolan thought was attacking him but he fought as if Satan himself was trying to drag him down to hell.

"Goddamn it, I can't hold him!"

Lyons barely avoided a foot to the face as he dived in and pinned Bolan's leg against Burdick's in a bear hug of his own. "The quad!" Lyons roared. "In the quad!"

For a scant second they held the leg immobilized and James slid the needle into the flesh of Bolan's thigh. His free leg clouted Lyons in the jaw and sat him back. James's face fisted in pain as Bolan's foot swung around and he took the blow on his casted arm. Burdick groaned with pain and exhaustion as he lifted Bolan higher, like Atlas trying to hold aloft an Earth gone mad.

Slowly, Bolan's struggles subsided. His eyes rolled as he lolled in the giant Marine's grip. Mumbled incoherencies bubbled from between his foaming lips, before his head fell against his chest and he went limp. Burdick dropped him to the floor, his knees buckling. He sat hard. Burdick fell backward into the dust, staring up at the broken skylights.

"Jesus Christ...." he gasped. "Jesus...H. Christ...."

Lyons groaned in wordless agreement as he clutched his aching groin and sagged back against a broken beam.

James held his forearm and his cracked cast against his chest. A choking sound was coming out of his mouth. Lyons looked over and saw James laughing.

Lyons shook his head wearily. "And?"

"And I was just thinking..." James wheezed, trying to catch a breath.

"What's that?"

"I was just thinking it was a good thing we didn't try the suppositories."

Laughter spontaneously burst out of the Pakistani commando lying on the ground. A matching groan of amusement came from the massive Marine lying across from him. Lyons's team clutched their battered ribs as mirth rolled over them uncontrollably. A weary smile crawled across Lyons's face unbidden.

"Calvin?"

The former SEAL could barely breathe. "Yeah?"

"Just make sure he doesn't die." Lyons looked over at Bolan's motionless form. "We owe his ass for this one. We owe his ass big-time."

CHAPTER TWENTY-FOUR

Bolan rose from the black goddess's embrace like Orpheus arising from Hades. The dark gray neuroleptic fog slowly parted in his consciousness. Numb, thoughtless limbo gave way to massive pain throughout his body and nightmare in his mind. Bolan always awoke lucid and aware. Cobwebs clung to the corners of his awareness; he felt disconnected from his surroundings. He was aware that something was wrong with him beyond the staggering ache and pain in his flesh.

The Executioner cracked open his eyes in careful slits.

Once again he was startled to find that he couldn't determine where he was.

He was on a bed. He didn't move or struggle. His limbs were bound. A familiar voice spoke to his left. "How do you feel?"

Bolan turned his head and groaned at the pain that it cost him. A blond man with hamburger meat for a face regarded him. "Carl."

The hamburger patty smiled. "Good to see you back." Carl Lyons lost his smile. "What do you remember?"

Bolan looked hard at Lyons's face and realized he was the one who had inflicted the damage. Image after image began suddenly vomiting up in an avalanche of ugliness from the back of Bolan's brain. Throughout the horrific ride there had been a part of his mind that had been aware of all that was going on, but it had been lost in the schizophrenic horror, unable to make itself heard. But it had been able to observe. Memory after memory, horror after horror, piled on with ever-increasing clarity.

"I don't know what was real and what wasn't." Bolan suppressed a shudder as he reviewed his trek through hell. The armies of the dead and damned in front of him, the goddess of death a hell hound on his trail. They would be nightmares he would carry the rest of his life. "But I remember everything."

"I'm sorry to hear that."

"Did I kill anybody, Carl?"

"Five Thuggees who deserved it."

"Besides them?"

Lyons shook his head. "None that we know of. The locals knew enough to stay out of your way."

Bolan considered sitting up and thought better of it. "How long have I been down?"

"Ten hours. Calvin still hasn't identified what you and Bijaya were hopped up on. We've sent samples we found at Bijaya's studio back to the U.S. for lab tests."

"How's Bijaya?"

Lyons shook his head. "She was a zombie when we found her. Calvin thinks the cult deliberately gave you two a hotshot of whatever that stuff was. You both took a massive dose, but you weigh a lot more than she does. The drug hit her a lot harder. Calvin knocked her out with Benadryl and has her on a sedative drip. He's going to keep her unconscious for another twelve hours."

Bolan sagged back into his pillow. "How did you find me?"

"Tipu followed you. We found him."

"Tipu."

"Yeah, and he messed himself up pretty bad doing it, too. You must have made a hell of an impression." Lyons raised a swollen eyebrow. "Handsome One."

Bolan inhaled a long breath past his aching ribs. "I don't think anyone had been kind to him in a long time."

"Calvin found a leprosy clinic here in Calcutta. There's a waiting list." Lyons shrugged. "Meantime we set him up in an apartment, got a doctor to come and clean him up, and start him on a battery of drugs to eradicate the bacterium and stabilize his condition. Calvin says he'll never have a normal life, and what's left will probably be short, but we can make him comfortable and keep him in clean clothes and cigarettes. It was the least we could do for him."

"You're a good man, Carl."

Lyons flushed slightly. He wasn't totally comfortable with compliments, either on the giving or receiving end.

Bolan cracked a smile at the man's embarrassed, punched-out face. "But whatever you do, Tipu still ain't gonna call you handsome."

Lyons snorted. "Calvin suggested a Thorazine suppository. Next time we won't talk him out of it."

Bolan began to understand his numbness and disorientation. "Thorazine?"

Lyons looked away again. "Yeah, about 8 cc's."

"You know they call that stuff the chemical lobotomy."

"Yeah, well you should have seen yourself, Mack. Naked, raving, waving Grampa Khan's meat cleaver around like you were collecting for the Red Cross. You needed lobotomizing, and fast."

"Is everyone all right?"

"Traumatic bruising mostly. Red got some second-degree burns when you threw him in the fire. You rebroke Calvin's hand. Doom may have a light concussion." Lyons shrugged. "I spent the night with a sack of ice on my crotch. I'm peeing blood and may never have children again. Other than that we're tip-top."

Lyons unbuckled Bolan's restraints. He rubbed his wrists while the big ex-cop took a file from the bedstand. He took out a photo. "Recognize this asshole?"

Bolan needed only single glance at the Coherence VP. "That's the asshole from the South Park Street Cemetery."

"I was hoping you'd say that."

"So we have a line on him."

"Yeah, the Bear and Dr. Austenford put their heads together and came up aces."

Bolan stared into the face of the man who had plunged him into hell. "Where is he?"

"We're working on that. Most likely here in Calcutta or in Santa Clara, California."

"Silicon Valley?"

"Yup."

"That's where the nukes will be."

Lyons stared in surprise. "I thought he wanted to blow up Kashmir."

"He'd love to, and that's likely to happen anyway, but I think this Kaushal wants a hell of a lot more bang for his buck."

"Like what kind of bang?"

"Like an exchange of nuclear weapons involving the Superpowers."

Lyons shook his head. "Last time I heard India and Pakistan weren't considered global superpowers."

"No, but the United States is."

"I don't follow."

"They have three nukes. Probably in California. Off the top of my head, let's say L.A., San Francisco and a random third city all go up in flames. United States military satellites will recognize the detonation patterns being made by Pakistani equipment. The government of Pakistan will claim that they had nothing to do with it, but that won't matter. No sitting American President could turn the other cheek to a nuclear strike on the Continental United States. If we didn't respond with a nuclear strike of our own, at the very least we would have to invade Pakistan to secure their nuclear stockpile."

Lyons nodded. "And Pakistan would never go for it."

"No, any Pakistani government that agreed to U.S. occupation would fall instantly. The new leaders would declare jihad against the United States, and quite probably resort to tactical nukes to repel the invasion. We would respond in kind. India would almost certainly get involved, with or without our good wishes. If there's anything left of Pakistan as a nation after that, they'll use their strategic arsenal. That could easily suck in China, Russia and God only knows who else in the Middle and Far East."

Lyons stared at Bolan long and hard. "You just came up with that after ten hours on Thorazine?"

"Power nap, good for the brain." Bolan pushed himself up and swung his legs to the floor. He sat a moment and waited to see if he would faint or throw up as colors crossed his vision in a massive head rush. Lyons surveyed him critically. "Maybe you should have another one of those power naps, maybe two."

"We don't have the time." Bolan rose and steadied himself against the wall. "We have a Calcutta residence on Kaushal?"

"Oh, yeah. Local CIA is keeping tabs on it."

"Is he there?"

"They think someone is."

Bolan pushed off the wall and took a deep breath. "Let's roll."

The Temple

"BECAUSE YOU LOVE the burning ground, I have made a burning ground of my heart."

"…a burning ground of my heart." Intoned the disciples.

Kalidas Kaushal knelt in front of his god, hands clasped in front of him in supplication. His inner circle of disciples arrayed behind him in a circle. Kali stood in all of her terrible glory before them. She was seven feet of black marble upon a massive altar of similar stone. The ebony marble was shot through with streaks of pink that turned the already gaunt, "fully awakened Kali" into a veined horror. The skirt of desiccated human hands about her waist had been cut from the arms of living sacrifices. Her necklace of human skulls was equally real. The head in her hand and the decapitated body beneath her feet were "freshened" weekly. The immense, multifaceted rubies embedded the statue's eye sockets reflected the torchlight, glittering in bloodthirsty approval upon her believers.

The hand that normally held a sword now held an all-iron ax. The double-lobed blade and iron shaft weren't balanced for battle. It wasn't a weapon, but the tool of an executioner. The ax had been designed for the sole purpose of swiftly and efficiently removing a human head. The edge of the blade was stained with recent use.

Kali held the ax aloft in terrible triumph.

"Because you love the burning ground…" Kaushal opened his arms. His offerings to the goddess of death stood in front of the altar, each wreathed in garlands of flowers.

The three tactical nuclear warheads gleamed in the torchlight.

" I shall make a burning ground of the world."

"…a burning ground of the world."

"Such is the order of sacrifice, first man, then horse, then bull, then ram, then goat, then ewe…" Kalidas sang the litany of sacrifices as his flock repeated. "Man is foremost of animals, and his sacrifice the most pleasing to the Gods."

"Man is the foremost sacrifice, most pleasing to the Gods."

Kaushal gazed upon the thermonuclear weapons.

"Let the time of Kali come…let the sacrifice be made."

"…let the sacrifice be made."

He let the chanting subside before he turned. "Mehtar, you bring news."

Mehtar stood at the entrance to the inner temple. "Yes, Guruji."

"You bring news about the American."

"Yes, Guruji." Mehtar swallowed with difficulty. "Things have not gone as…planned."

"Oh? I believe things have gone exactly as planned." The smile didn't leave Kaushal's face. "You believe the American is not among us, Mehtar?"

"No, Gurji." Mehtar shook his head in confusion. He had fully expected not to leave the inner temple with his head still affixed to his neck. "The American is free. All was prepared as you ordered. Yet somehow he was not captured, and he has killed Bhuvan, Asoka, Rhuka, Razi and Deskichar."

"All five, truly." Kaushal beamed. "And how did he kill them?"

"We have made discreet inquiries with the police. Their bodies have been identified. Some were beheaded, other missing limbs." Mehtar's face grew ashen. "It appears the American killed them with a bladed weapon. He—"

"He killed them with a sword." Kaushal gazed upon the ax in Kali's hand. "Not with guns or explosives, but with a sword. Tell me, Mehtar, where was he last seen?"

"There was word of him in the streets, naked, in the slums behind Chinatown, carrying, as you say…a sword. Our spies tell me that his people came for him. There was a battle, and they took him away unconscious. He is among them now."

"No, Mehtar." Kaushal smiled upon his disciple as if he were explaining something very simple to a small child. "He is not among them."

Mehtar blinked. "He is not?"

"No. He is not among them." Kaushal turned back to gaze upon the nuclear warheads and the goddess of death looming over them. "He is among us, now."

CHAPTER TWENTY-FIVE

Bolan's boot knife rang from its sheath. Cold sweat stung his eyes as they flew open. His hands had found his guns gone and they had instinctively drawn the blade. His lips were pulled back in an animal snarl of rage. Bolan lunged to his feet with the blade in front of him, his blue eyes blazing as Kali's rotting legions came for him.

"Whoa, big fella!" a big voice boomed. "Steady!"

Bolan blinked. There were no demons or undead. He was standing in the living room of the safehouse.

Trevor Burdick stood from the chair he had been sitting sentry in. He was wearing his com link and his body armor and he held his Marine Corps specification close-quarter battle shotgun loosely in his hands. The bayonet was fixed but the sheath was still around the blade for less than lethal combat. The sheathed blade wasn't quite pointed at Bolan. Schatzie and Sadie flanked Burdick, vibrating at attention as they waited for the order to attack. He eyed Bolan carefully. "You know where you are?"

"You let me sleep."

Burdick's shoulders sagged with obvious relief. "Yeah, well, you called the team together, you sat on the couch, you yawned, you closed your eyes, and then you were gone. Calvin said it was for the best and to let you be."

"Calvin usually knows best."

"Sorry about your guns. Calvin told me to take them. They're in the closet." Burdick scowled ruefully. "I missed the knife. He's gonna be pissed."

Bolan put the blade away. "How long?"

"Eight hours." Burdick's eyes wandered over to a bedroom door. "Bijaya woke up a little while ago. I think you'd better talk to her."

"How's she doing?"

"She's tough." Burdick sighed in admiration. "I mean, considering what they must have done to brainwash her like that. I guess it's a miracle she's not a basket case. Whether she still has a career in intelligence, the Ironman says that may be another matter." Burdick shook his massive head. "The CIA office in Dehli is getting more and more frantic demands from RAW to know her condition and whereabouts."

"What have you told them?"

"Nothin'. Calvin said she was in no condition to be debriefed by her people and Carl agreed with him. So we sat tight and let her sleep. Here." Burdick turned and poured a steaming cup of coffee from a hot plate. "You look like you could use it."

The coffee was brewed in the Indian style, thick with cream and sugar that was added at the beginning and sizzling with caffeine. Bolan downed it in a gulp. "Thanks, Red. Thanks for babysitting."

"No problem, Chief. Ramrod is on watch upstairs. The rest of the team is sacked out. We all needed it. Why don't you go see to your ladyfriend? I'll be right here if you need me."

Bolan poured a fresh cup of coffee and knocked twice on Bijaya's door.

"Come in."

The Indian agent sat in bed. The late afternoon was warm but she had the blankets pulled up around her. Her face was pale and drawn. Despair radiated from her in palpable waves. Her arm was in a sling.

"How are you holding up?" Bolan held out the cup. "You all right?"

Khan's hands shook as she took it. She turned bloodshot eyes up to Bolan as he sat on the edge of the bed. "I will live with it."

Bijaya Khan was far from all right. Bolan looked down at her cast. "What happened to your arm?"

"You broke it when you threw me against the wall. I did not feel it at the time. Calvin set it." She looked off into the distance. "I wish you had killed me."

Bolan smiled. "Maybe next time."

"Your friend, Big Red, has my guns." She stared bitterly into the coffee. "He was nice about it when I asked, but he does not think I can be trusted. Not to hurt the team or myself."

"I trust you. What we went through, we went through together. We're in the same club, and it's over now."

"No." Khan looked as if whatever fragile composure she was holding on to could shatter in an instant. "It is far from over, for both of us."

"Tell me about it, anything you can."

Her knuckles went white around the mug. "This…guru…"

"Kalidas." Bolan nodded. "Kalidas Kaushal. We have an ID on him."

"If he were here now, and he told me to kill you—" she turned despairing eyes on Bolan "—I would do it. I could not stop myself."

"You believe that."

"I know it to be a fact."

"All right." Bolan accepted the statement. "Then I'm just going to have to kill him."

"This man, Kalidas…he is more than just a terrorist."

"I know."

"You do not." She grabbed Bolan's hand fervently. "What do you know of Indian religious practices?"

"What I've read, what I've heard. Not much."

"Since ancient times, India has always had its fakirs, its gurus, men and women who could perform supernormal acts."

"All cultures do." Bolan had run into the inexplicable before. He had fought martial artists and members of violent cults who could turn off pain or withstand horrific wounds. "In the U.S. there are devout Christians who handle serpents, speak in tongues and eat poison and broken glass."

"In India such things are almost a science, and acts such as those child's play. In the practice of yoga alone, thirty-four powers are specifically named."

"I've heard a bit about it, but never seen much of it, besides people lying on beds of nails and burying themselves alive."

"I never much believed in it myself. However, in my land, through yogic practice, such powers as the ability to read minds, influence the minds of others, superhuman strength, these are considered signposts, indications of progress of a disciple's spiritual evolution. However, for a true disciple, wishing to experience enlightenment and liberation, that is all they are, signs. To focus on them, to become attached to them, to use them for personal gain, is failure, to stray from the path. Many of the ancient texts say much worse, that attachment to any such powers, particularly the mental and spiritual ones, can lead to great mental, physical and spiritual harm. They can lead to—"

"Insanity." Bolan finished. He had looked into the eyes of Kalidas Kaushal. "You believe he has these kinds of powers."

"Some of them, perhaps. I felt his personal power, even before I was drugged. The drugs undoubtedly help him cement his hold. Afterward, I was his…slave. A slave of Kali." Her gaze fell down to the bunched blankets. "I think I still am."

She looked up and met Bolan's eyes squarely. "I fear, so perhaps are you."

Bolan's blue eyes went arctic. His battle instincts smothered the angry denial and forced him to consider the unthinkable. He had, indeed, felt the compelling power of Kaushal's voice. He had felt the sledgehammer force of his gaze. Even with his adrenaline running and a blade in his hand, it had taken effort of will to resist them. He had received the man's gift. He had tasted the sweetness of Kali from Bijaya's own lips, and that gift had plunged him straight to hell. It had taken several of the most dangerous humans on Earth and potentially fatal dosages of psychoactive drugs to drag him back from the point of no return.

The point of no return.

Bolan considered that. It was said that once one tasted the sweetness of Kali one never returned. The lead Thuggee had said he had received a far greater than normal dose. Bolan had to face the fact that Bijaya might be right.

He might be damaged goods.

"Kaushal might have a foothold," Bolan conceded coldly. "But, slave? That's something he's going to have to earn."

Khan didn't answer, but the look in her eyes said it all. She no longer trusted herself, and she no longer trusted him.

"Get some rest if you can. We're going to make a move, one way or the other, and soon."

Khan nodded numbly and curled herself into a fetal position on the bed. She was weeping as Bolan closed the door.

Bolan's team was waiting for him. They stood in a grim-faced phalanx. "We assault Kaushal's residence here in Calcutta immediately."

Burdick looked skeptically at Lyons. Lyons turned to James, and the men exchanged frowns. Ramrod looked searchingly at each of the three men in turn. Makhdoom's eyes never left Bolan's. The look on the Pakistani's face was severe.

Khan wasn't the only member of the team having a crisis of faith.

Lyons locked eyes with Bolan. "You sure you're up to that?"

The two men stared at each other. Lyons didn't back down an inch.

James sighed. "Mack, we don't know what that shit did to you. What it could still be doing to you. We don't know what that shit was, and I don't like it. I let you rest here in India because I didn't want to move you, but now that you're up and around and lucid, I'm thinking we need to get you back to the Farm. I'm thinking we need to do a full blood workup. I know you don't want to hear it, but you might need therapy, chemical and psychological. I know Bijaya does."

Bolan accepted James's assessment at face value, but his eyes stayed on Lyons. "Carl." The ghost of a smile crossed the Executioner's lips. "You know this is mutiny."

Lyons's expression didn't change. "You didn't answer my question."

"I feel like shit, Carl, but the Thorazine wore off hours ago. I don't feel any effects of the drug, and I appreciate your concern for my well-being."

"I don't give a shit about your well-being." Lyons stood like the living embodiment of his nickname. "What I care about right now is the team. I'm trying to decide whether you're a liability or an asset."

"Then make up your mind. You've got three seconds to decide and then I'm leading this team."

Lyons gave Bolan the once-over as if he were reading his aura. He suddenly shrugged. "You're the man."

Bolan glanced around the assembly. "Anyone else have any objections?"

James clearly had at least a dozen but he was keeping most of them to himself. "You sure this is a good idea?"

"We're going into the heart of this man's darkness, Calvin, and you're going to need everyone. Even me."

"Fine. I object, for the record, but that said, let's grease this asshole and go home."

"Everyone arm and armor up for full assault. We meet back in this room in fifteen minutes. I assume you have already come up with a war plan. I want to roll in thirty."

The team broke up and went to go equip themselves.

"Red."

Burdick turned. "What's up, boss?"

"Come here a sec."

Burdick scooped up his shotgun and loomed over Bolan. "What's up?"

"You're still an outsider here."

"Yeah, like I don't know that." Burdick frowned. "But I thought I was starting to prove myself."

"You have, that's why I need to ask you a personal favor."

Burdick scowled. "I am not staying behind to baby-sit Agent Khan. I've proved myself and, like you said, you need every warm body, including fat old ex-Marines."

"That's not what I'm asking."

Burdick peered into Bolan's eyes and didn't like what he saw. "This ain't a happy favor, is it."

"No." Bolan's voice dropped low. "I've known Calvin for a long time. As teammates we're tight. Carl, I've known even longer. We go back to things you don't know about. Things you never will."

"Yeah, I figured. The blood-brother vibe is real deep with you guys. Frankly, I envy it."

"That's right, and because of that, they could hesitate, fatally, for the whole team. As for Ramrod and Doom, they're on the other end of the spectrum. They're extremely capable, but if things go wrong they could hesitate for a completely different set of reasons. You land right in the middle, Red."

"What're you saying?"

"I'm saying if the shit hits the fan, you're just courageous enough to do the right thing, and do it in time to save the rest of the team."

Burdick straightened to his full height. "I think I know what you're saying."

"So say it out loud, Red." Bolan's voice was as cold as the grave. "Say it so we both know."

Burdick raised his Mossberg shotgun slightly. "You're saying that if it even starts to look like you're going back to the dark side, you want me and old painless here to put you down easy before you can turn on the team."

"That's right. You're going to be my wingman on this one. You watch my back, Red, and you watch it good."

Burdick took a long unhappy breath and then let it out. "All right."

"Are you down for this?" Bolan held Burdick's gaze implacably. "If you aren't, you let me know now. No shame."

The hulking ex-gunnery sergeant held out a hand the size of a bunch of bananas. *"Semper Fi."*

Bolan smiled.

Burdick had invoked the Marine Corps motto.

Always Faithful.

Bolan took the offered hand and shook it. *"Semper Fi."*

James stuck his head back in the room and looked askance at the two warriors. "You two having a white-boy moment or something?"

"Yeah," Bolan stated. "But we're done."

"Good, 'cause Carl's just off the horn with the Bear."

"And?"

"And it's our boy, Kaushal. We've found him." James shrugged. "He's in California, big guy, just like you predicted."

CHAPTER TWENTY-SIX

Moffett Naval Air Station, Sunnyvale, California

Bolan took advantage of the plane flights to sleep. The team had rented a commercial jet in Calcutta and flown to Diego Garcia. From the tiny British-owned island in the middle of the Indian Ocean they had commandeered a U.S. Air Force KC-135 tanker and flown the fourteen thousand miles to California nonstop. All told the trip had still burned more than twenty-four hours they couldn't afford, but it had given Bolan's team desperately needed downtime. Calvin James had insisted on giving Bolan a sedative. It had left him feeling foggy on landing, but his sleep has been mercifully devoid of nightmares.

When he could sleep no more Bolan had read everything Kurtzman had dug up on Kalidas Kaushal. He agreed with Lyons's assessment and combined it with everything Khan had told him. The math kept coming up ugly. Whether Kalidas Kaushal had genuine occult power or just heightened power of personality was irrelevant. What was relevant was that he was one of the most mentally and physically dangerous opponents Bolan had ever faced, and he had the means, the will and the intention to start World War III. By introducing the drug into his system, Kaushal had landed the first blow between them. The soldier was still reeling from it, and by the perpetual look of concern on Calvin James's face, the blow had set him up for a potential knockout.

There was also the added factor that Kaushal was very likely to be clinically insane.

Bolan awoke again as they landed at Moffett Field.

They debarked and Bolan and his bruised and jet-lagged team limped into the cavernous, echoing interior of Moffett Field's dirigible hangar. Inside they found a pair of surveillance vans courtesy of the San Francisco FBI branch office. Three folding tables between the vans were laden with weapons and gear. Coffee was steaming on a hot plate and there was a plate of submarine sandwiches.

Jack Grimaldi sat in a folding chair smoking a cigar with his feet up on a pile of armored vests. Dr. Allison Austenford sat next to him with her feet up, as well. The pair seemed to be getting along famously. Grimaldi ran his eyes over the team and let out a long stream of blue smoke. He looked at Bolan questioningly.

Austenford was a bit more blunt. "You guys look like dog dirt. What the hell happened to you?"

James waved his damaged hand at Bolan and took a seat. "Him."

"Heard a little about that." Concern clouded Grimaldi's usual grinning demeanor as he examined Bolan. "You all right, big guy?"

"No." Bolan sagged into a chair. He wasn't. The past week had been a frenzy of fire missions. Within the last forty-eight hours he had engaged in hand-to-hand combat with nine men. Drugs had allowed him not to feel the blows at the time. He felt them now down to his bones. "But I will be come game time. What have we got on Kaushal's whereabouts?"

"The FBI has been staking out his place and the Coherence R & D facility." Grimaldi tapped a map of the Santa Clara Valley in front of him with a pair of red circles drawn on it. "Dr. Kaushal arrived in California seventy-two hours ago. He spent the night in his house in Los Gatos. Went to work the next morning and came home. He went to work today at the Coherence R & D laboratory in Palo Alto and still hasn't left."

Bolan checked his watch. It was 6:30 p.m., Pacific Standard Time. "The doctor's working late."

"Yeah," Grimaldi said with a grin. "And on a Friday."

"How about his research team?"

"That's the funny part, they're all working late tonight, too. Everyone else at Coherence R & D has gone home except for the janitors."

"Palo Alto." Bolan frowned. "That's where Stanford University is located, isn't it?"

Grimaldi checked his map. "Uh, affirmative."

"Then Kaushal has had years to set this place up to his specifications." Bolan glanced at the tables heaped with weapons and then at Austenford. "You bring us any new toys?"

Austenford grinned and stood. She picked up an M-4 A-1 carbine. A 40 mm grenade launcher was attached under the barrel and its topside rail interface system was festooned with optical equipment. "The flashlight and Aimpoint electro-optical sight are standard issue." She tapped a flat plastic box with a pair of lenses mounted just behind the front sight. "The laser-infrared illuminator has been modified."

She picked up a remote and pointed it at wire frame ten yards away. A length of silvery gray fabric was suspended within the frame. A pair of wires were clipped to the fabric and led to a black box on the floor. "This is a piece of light-transferring textile you gentleman captured. We still don't know how the enemy made it work, but we have been able to power it up." The doctor clicked a button on the remote.

"Good God!" Burdick's jaw dropped.

Every member of the team had fought enemies wearing the fabric, but this was the first time they had seen it powered up from the get-go.

The fabric was gone. The frame appeared to be empty. The two electrical power wires seemed to be levitating in space. Austenford brought the carbine to her shoulder and aimed at apparently nothing. "Now here's your latest countermeasure."

The carbine's laser sight blinked to life. It appeared to strike nothing and painted a ruby red dot on a six-by-four-foot steel plate set on the wall ten yards behind the frame. However, a tiny red light winked on top of the forward laser sight box and an electronic chime peeped frantically.

"We modified the laser sight to act like a laser range finder." The doctor smiled at her own cleverness as she lowered the weapon. "Just like laser ranging binoculars, the laser sight hits a stationary target and constantly measures the distance from the lens to the target. This happens at the speed of light."

The doctor swiftly shouldered her carbine again and clicked on the laser sight. The ruby dot appeared once more on the plate. The light and chime began their frantic warning once more. "However, when the laser hits the light-transferring fabric, well, there is a transfer. The optical cells in front receive the laser light and transmit the signal to the back and visa versa. That transfer takes fractions of a second that mean nothing in real-time terms. The human eye doesn't notice it, just as we can't see the difference now."

She dropped the muzzle and powered off the laser.

"However, the microprocessor in the sight does detect the difference. It detected a break while it was trying to range."

Captain Makhdoom smiled for the first time since the battle for the safehouse in the Kalighat. "So we can detect them, without carrying around five-pound bags of flour or paint ball grenades."

"It gets better." The doctor suddenly raised the rifle. Bolan's team started and hands went to pistols as the alarm cheeped as the 40 mm grenade launcher boomed and belched yellow smoke. Downrange, the steel target plate screeched and sparked as if half a dozen submachine guns had unloaded into it simultaneously.

Between the doctor and the target plate the frame holding the fabric was bent and twisted. The fabric hung in the frame, clearly visible and torn to shreds. Scores of tiny, twisted, toothpick-size slivers of metal littered the ground in front of the target plate.

"The problem with the paint marking rounds we worked up for you is that they left your grenade launchers and shotguns less than lethal. We have to assume the enemy will have adapted to this." Austenford put down her carbine and picked up a 40 mm grenade from one of the tables. She unscrewed the round blunt nose of the grenade and upended it.

Ugly, finned steel darts tinkled to the table in a heap.

"These are your standard United States military two-inch, .17-grain artillery fléchettes. Normally they're packed by the thousand into artillery shells, also known as beehive munitions. They turn artillery pieces into giant shotguns for close-in, perimeter defense. Choppers use them for the same effect in Hydra antipersonnel rockets." She picked up another grenade. "Each one of these 40 mm munitions is packing 115 darts per round. Coming out of a 40 mm tube we predict a 5.3 yard dispersal pattern at twenty-five yards. They should penetrate soft body armor at that range. From fifty yards out, velocity, penetration and dispersal will become dicey. The secondary benefit of the fléchettes is that as you can see, if you rip enough holes in the fabric, the light-transferring capability is compromised. My advice to you, gentlemen, is to keep your 40 mms locked and loaded, laze constantly and shred any son of a bitch who breaks your beam."

"God…damn!" Burdick was as giddy as a kid on Christmas Day. "Who said 'military' and 'intelligence' was a contradiction!"

"Coming from a Marine, I'll take that as a compliment." The team laughed.

Bolan smiled wearily. He liked the idea, as well. Austenford's technical innovations and tactics were continually keeping him and his team and alive. They had all been through a lot, but they were salty, and in an aggressive mood.

"All right," Bolan said, "everyone arm and armor up. I want to be in Palo Alto in thirty. We are going in hard."

Coherence Research and Development Laboratory

IT WAS 4:00 a.m. Bolan lay on a hilltop with Trevor Burdick at his side. He scanned the target for the hundredth time. The building was a fairly small, two-story affair set in the rolling hills of the South Bay. Cows and horses grazed in the vast tracks that stretched from one high-tech firm to the next. The parking lot was nearly full. The entire research team appeared to be working the wee hours. Even the janitors hadn't left.

A pair of civilian Bell JetRanger helicopters were parked on the roof.

Bolan clicked his link. "You got anything for me, Bear?"

"Well, every member of the janitorial service has a Hindu name. That strike you as slightly odd?"

It did, but Calvin James's voice came across the link before they could discuss it further. "Striker! I have movement, half a klick northeast of your position!"

"How many?"

"I saw one individual, appears to be armed. Moving very stealthily."

Bolan panned his night-vision scope over the area and caught movement. He upped the gain to full power and the scope to maximum magnification. Bolan shook his head slowly.

"Striker, can you make them out?"

Bolan could. It was Bijaya Khan, and she was armed for bear.

Burdick's voice rumbled low. "What have we got?"

"A volunteer." Bolan clicked his mike. "Hold position. I'm going to make contact."

He nodded at Burdick. "Stay put."

Burdick swung his nightscope northeast. He grunted and lowered the rifle. Once again he wasn't quite pointing the muzzle at Bolan. "You sure that's a good idea, boss?"

"We can't just leave her out here, whatever her intentions."

"She already betrayed us once. Even if her intentions are good, she's damaged goods and a liability." Burdick pushed his goggles onto his forehead and looked Bolan in the eye. "Maybe you should let me take care of her."

Burdick shifted uncomfortably under Bolan's gaze. "I mean…like hog-tie her and pick her up after the mission's over and stuff. Jesus, don't look at me like that."

"I know what you mean, Red. But this is personal between us. I'm going to bring her in."

"Well fuck me." Burdick brought his rifle up and angrily resumed scanning the Coherence facility. "I've already got orders to open your goddamn skull to the sky if you go koo-koo for Kali again, and now I've got to baby-sit both of you? Swell."

"You're a good man, Red. I knew I could count on you."

"Yeah, right."

Bolan began moving down the hillside. He deliberately made noise when he moved. He put the hill between himself and the Coherence building and then stood. Khan rose from her crouch behind a tree and came forward.

She pulled up British-issue night-vision goggles. Her hair was pulled back into a single combat braid and she wore a black raid suit. Her antique Webley-Fosbery revolvers were strapped to her thighs. She cradled a Colt AR-15 carbine. A brutally shortened 12-gauge shotgun was slaved beneath the barrel.

"You got here fast."

"It was not hard. As an agent of RAW, I have access to many resources, including preference on commercial and military flights."

"How did you find us?"

"That was the easiest part. This is the logical location, and it is now less than forty-eight hours until the Kali Puja, the festival of Kali, begins. I knew you would be here."

"Do your superiors know you are here?"

Khan tapped her weapon. "There is a large Indian population in California. RAW has assets here. They will know that I requisitioned weapons, but they do not know where I am."

"You didn't give them the full report on Kaushal."

"No, they would not take direct action in the United States. The weapons will have been detonated before they finished debating what to do." She stared up at Bolan defiantly. "My career is over. This is personal."

"You shouldn't be here."

"Neither should you."

"Big Red is worried you're going to slip me another mickey. He wants to hog-tie you and keep you out of it."

"Let him try."

"He has orders to blow my head off if I start to relapse." Khan was silent.

"He'll do you, too, if it comes down to it."

The agent nodded slowly. "Red is a good man, and that is a sensible precaution."

Bolan thumbed his throat mike. "I'm bringing in Bijaya."

CHAPTER TWENTY-SEVEN

The Inner Temple

The thermonuclear weapons were ready. The rituals had been performed. The sacrifices had given up their lives upon Kali's altar. The weapons themselves had been consecrated to the goddess. Mehtar had set the timers and detonators. All that remained was transportation to their final destinations. Kaushal had spent the past twenty-four hours in deep meditation in front of the three tactical nuclear warheads.

His vision of the Apocalypse was terrifying in its completeness.

One weapon would head south for the city of Los Angeles. The second would travel slightly north to devastate the city of San Francisco. The third would take the long journey home, close to where it had been taken from. It would ignite in radioactive fire in the disputed land of Kashmir, setting off the war between India and Pakistan. The two blasts in the United States would ensure the lighting up of the world. Millions would be sacrificed in the opening seconds. In the days to follow that number could grow to billions.

In the days between the first fires and annihilation his devotees would use the light-transferring textile cloaks to assassinate key world leaders. The Earth would become a crematorium, a place of ashes and fire.

The world would become the burning ground of Kali, as had the heart of Kalidas Kaushal long ago.

He recalled his uncle Jagmoan, how the old man had found his spiritual practice faulty, his devotion incomplete. Jagmoan had sent him out into the jungle, to fast and to meditate upon his purpose. It had been there, in the jungle night, rent by the roars of roaming tigers and the screams of the apes that he had first heard the drum and chant. Kaushal had risen from his reed mat and followed the sound. He'd slipped past the Thuggee lookouts and had come upon the circle around the campfire. He had been bewitched by the beauty of the chant and litany, and hypnotized by the drums.

He had screamed out loud in terror when he had beheld the sacrifice of a living man to the goddess.

The lookouts had fallen upon him and dragged him into the circle for ritual strangulation. The priest had noticed Kaushal's Brahmin caste marks and rather than feeling death constrict around his throat, the sweetness of Kali had been forced between his lips.

After that night everything had become very clear.

He'd returned to the commune, proving himself with single-minded devotedness to delving into the mysteries his uncle taught. By night he proved himself to the Thuggees. First as a digger and burier of their victims' bodies. With unflagging fanaticism and clarity of purpose, and cleverness, he swiftly rose through the ranks of the deceivers. Soon he was a true Thuggee, ritually strangling his brother monks, local villagers and travelers beneath the light of the moon. By day he made shocking progress at the commune. The breathing, meditations and austerities his uncle's sect practiced were severe, and could prove injurious if done improperly. They required purity of mind and spirit.

Kaushal took consecrated sugar as his sacrament.

His mind expanded and his progress surged forward. While the rest of the disciples meditated upon peace and light, Kaushal's mind and soul were filled with the ascension of the dark goddess. He buried himself alive for days, resisted fire upon his skin and was able to slow his heart and his breathing nigh unto death. Such things became as parlor tricks to him. Deeper mysteries were revealed to him by day and by night. He took "spiritual outings" out in the jungle, meeting with the Thuggees and local *dacoits*. His spiritual power mounted. Even the local Thuggee priest bowed before him in awe.

Every month upon the full moon another of his uncle's disciples disappeared.

Finally too many monks and commune workers had disappeared to be runaways who couldn't handle the discipline of the spiritual life. Jagmoan had found lumps of the consecrated sugar in Kaushal's hut. He had seen the spiritual power growing in his nephew's eyes. During direct communion, he looked deeper into Kalidas's heart and mind. Kalidas had become powerful beyond imagining.

He was utterly insane.

It had taken all of Jagmoan's own spiritual power to keep his realization secret under Kalidas's gaze.

Jagmoan had followed Kalidas one night and found him strangling one of the village boys who carried rice to the commune. He had returned to the commune to meditate upon what he had to do. Jagmoan was a man of great spiritual progression, but he couldn't help fearing what he'd seen in Kalidas's eyes. He hadn't had the strength to confront his nephew, much less save him.

It would require the authorities, and guns, to bring down his nephew and his new friends.

Jagmoan had lifted his head from his meditations to find Kalidas towering over him. He'd smiled benevolently upon his uncle. The strangling cord had hung loosely in his hands.

Kaushal summoned the *dacoits* and they had fallen upon the commune in an orgy of rape, murder and fire. Kaushal had returned to Calcutta, the city of his birth, and begun to walk the path that would lead to this moment.

Only one thing was missing.

Kaushal smiled as Mehtar entered.

"Guruji."

"Yes." Kaushal rose to his full six feet seven inches of height. "He is here."

BOLAN'S TEAM came in hard.

Khan's shotgun was loaded with barricade-breaching rounds. The 12-gauge boomed and the lock blew off of the front double-glass doors. The heavy panes spiderwebbed as the doors flew back on their hinges. All the lights were on. There was no security guard at the desk. The Coherence lab seemed completely open.

James shook his head. "We're expected."

"Oh, yeah," Lyons agreed. They were all combat veterans. Everyone's instincts were screaming.

Burdick glanced at Austenford. She held an M-4 carbine in one hand and Sadie and Schatzie's leads in the other. "Time to see if your toys work, Doc."

The team played their lasers over every inch of the room. The foyer was plushly carpeted with a vast arc of oak table for the security guard at night and the secretary during the day. No alarms went off on their weapons, but alarm bells were tingling up and down each team member's spine.

There was nothing more daunting than fighting an enemy unseen.

"This is so fucked." Burdick spit on the carpet. His finger twitched on the trigger of his grenade launcher. "My goddamn toes are tingling. This place is crawling with screwheads."

Bolan nodded as he played his laser into every corner. He trusted Trevor Burdick's toes. They were receiving the same signal as Bolan's spine.

The enemy was all around them.

"Laze constantly." Lyons quoted Austenford's advice like scripture. "Shred any son of a bitch that breaks your beam."

Bolan raised his rifle. "Security cameras." The sound-suppressed M-4 stuttered off a 3-round burst and smashed the camera apart. Burdick swung his weapon on the camera above the door they had come in.

"Hi, Mom!" The camera burst into sparking pieces.

"Two-story building." James glanced at the floor beneath his boots. "God only knows what's underneath."

"A temple." It was the first time Bijaya Khan had spoken.

Lyons peered at her narrowly. "How do you know?"

"It will be here. If this is where they produced their cloaks and have the weapons, they will be consecrated to Kali. There will be a temple. Trust me."

Trust came hard in Bolan's business, and she had already betrayed them once. But Bolan trusted her instincts now. "That's where the nukes will be."

The team followed Bolan as he walked past the desk and went to the door that led out of the foyer. A long hallway of office suite doors stretched away. Close by was an elevator. The doors were open.

The team played their lasers down the hall but nothing broke their beams.

"This is so fucked," Burdick reiterated. "You want me to take point?"

"No." Bolan looked at the big Marine meaningfully. "You're my wingman on this one. Remember that."

Burdick scowled. It was a job he wasn't happy about, but he took his place behind Bolan and Khan.

Lyons stepped through the door. The team continued to play their lasers all around him. One by one they entered the hall. Lyons went to the first office door and kicked it in. The interior was a conference room with a long table surrounded by chairs. Once again all the lights were on and it appeared as if no one was home.

He entered the room and the team fanned in behind him.

"This is so—"

"Fucked. We know, Red. Now shut up." Bolan was looking at the dogs. Sadie and Schatzie stood stiff-legged, their hackles standing straight up and their teeth bared. Schatzie let out a low, ugly growl. Austenford let the dogs off their leads. They swept the room sniffing, growling and confused.

Ruby-red laser dots swung along the walls rapidly. Lyons and James panned their beams beneath the table but nothing was setting off the alarms. "Lady…" James continued to pan. "Either your dogs have distemper or your toys don't work."

"They work fine, thank you very much," the doctor told him, but she looked at her dogs and the laser sight mounted on her carbine with grim concern.

Bolan walked to the end of the room with James and Lyons flanking him. They swept the room a final time. "Ramrod, Doom, check the elevator."

The Executioner whipped around as a rifle clattered to the floor in response.

Burdick, Ramrod and Makhdoom were standing on their tiptoes turning purple as they clutched their throats and silently strangled.

Bolan and the rest of the team panned their weapons around the three men but no alarms went off. The dogs barked hysterically, but they didn't lunge at anything unseen.

"Shit!" James dropped his carbine on its sling. Six and

three-quarter inches of double-edge, wasp-waisted steel whispered from its sheath. The ex-SEAL charged in low. His thumb on the blade of the Gerber MkII fighting knife. Bolan and Lyons covered him as he ran to Burdick and spun the big Marine.

James stabbed nothing and his eyes flew wide. "Jesus! There's no one fucking here!"

Burdick's eyes were bugging out of his head as his face went from purple to blue. James grabbed at the big ex-Marine's throat. "Goddamn it, Striker! There's no one—"

James staggered backward, his hands flying to his own throat. His face made a fist as his air was choked off.

"Carl! Get—"

Lyons's carbine fell from his hands. He instinctively twisted and threw a pair of elbow strikes behind him that struck nothing. The veins stood out on his temples as he grabbed at his throat.

"Goddammit…" Austenford's voice rose in mounting panic as she swung the muzzle of her carbine in all directions.

Bolan panned his muzzle toward the ceiling.

The panels covering sections of the overhead fluorescent lighting had been silently slid back. Bolan shone his laser directly over Lyons's head.

The alarm on his carbine chimed and the red LED began blinking rapidly.

His team wasn't being strangled from behind.

They were being hanged.

Bolan tracked his carbine straight up and squeezed the trigger of his M-203. The grenade launcher boomed and belched yellow fire. Fluorescent tubes shattered and a human shape swathed in silver fabric blinked into existence. The length of shimmering strangling cord led from his hands to Lyons's throat. The man's stance on a pair of steel struts set in the ceiling above the lights wobbled as a red stain spread across his stomach. Bolan burned ten rounds from his carbine into the man's chest.

Lyons fell to his knees as the noose was released.

The Thuggee fell with a thud to the carpet.

Makhdoom and Ramrod hung unconscious, seemingly suspended by nothing. Burdick's bulging eyes had seen the Thuggee fall from the ceiling. The big man reached over his head and heaved with every last bit of strength remaining in his three-hundred-pound frame.

A ceiling panel shattered as something fell through it and conference table shuddered with a heavy blow.

"Sadie! Schatzie! Get some! Get some! Get some!" The dogs leaped up on the table and began savaging the unseen. Bolan emptied his magazine into the ceiling above Makhdoom and the Pakistani fell unconscious the floor. Khan pumped three rounds from her shotgun into the overhead lighting above Ramrod. The SAR sergeant collapsed. A second later he flailed as something heavy fell on top of him.

James slammed his cast into something just over his head. His commando knife slashed. He fell to one knee sawing at the visible silvery cord around his throat. A length of similar fabric suddenly dangled over his head.

Bolan dropped his spent carbine on its sling and slapped leather. The Beretta 93-R machine pistol and the .50-caliber Desert Eagle came up spitting flame and recoiling like thunder in each hand.

No man appeared but the chair next to James shattered and the SEAL was swatted to the floor, shattered as something fell upon them both.

A noose slipped around Bolan's neck.

He dropped the Desert Eagle and reached over his head. His hand closed around the cord as it started to cinch shut. He yanked for slack and fired the Beretta upward. The machine pistol rattled off five rapid bursts. Austenford's grenade launcher thumped and a silvery gray figure swathed like a ninja toppled from his perch. Bolan lunged to one side as the Thuggee fell. The deceiver's head bounced on the corner of the conference table with skull-shattering force.

Bolan ejected the nearly spent mag of the Beretta and slapped in a fresh one. "Cut them free!"

Khan and the doctor went to their stricken teammates as Bolan put a 3-round burst into every remaining ceiling panel. No more Thuggees fell through. Half the light fixtures were shattered and glass littered the conference room. The remaining lights in the room flickered crazily. Bolan dropped the spent Beretta and scooped up the Desert Eagle as he strode forward. "Call off the dogs."

"Sadie! Schatzie!" Austenford barked out the command from where she knelt beside Makhdoom. "Back off!"

The two dogs reluctantly leaped from the table. They had ripped enough fabric to compromise the light-transferring cell network. A man lay cringing on the table with his bloodied arms crossed protectively over his face. He started to roll off but Bolan pushed him back. "Relax."

James shoved the dead Thuggee off himself and rose, coughing and gagging. He had cut himself releasing the strangling cord and blood ran down his neck. He had also taken the time to cut the throat of the deceiver who had fallen on him. James's left hand hung at his side; his shattered cast hung in shreds of plaster and gauze. He sheathed his blade and pulled his .45-caliber Heckler & Koch P-9, covering the door into the room. He shook his head Bolan. "God...damn."

Bolan nodded in agreement. The entire team had almost been wiped out in fell swoop. "Red—" Bolan nodded at the Thuggee on the table "—cover him."

Burdick stomped forward and pressed the muzzle of his carbine into the deceiver's gut, pinning him to the tabletop like an insect.

Bolan holstered his pistol and reloaded his carbine and grenade launcher. He swept the laser over every inch of the ceiling, the room and then pointed it back out the door they had
come in. "See how everyone is."

Austenford knelt beside Ramathorn. "Ramrod is hurt." A
dead Thuggee lay next to him. The killer had taken all three
of Khan's buckshot rounds square in the chest. James limped
over and took stock of the moaning, half-unconscious man.

"How bad is it, Cal?"

"His hip is broken." James gently probed Ramrod's abdomen. The front of his uniform pants were wet and dark red.
"He's urinating blood, his bladder may be ruptured. He isn't
critical, but it's bad enough."

Bolan glanced at the ex-SEAL's arm. "How about you, Cal?"

"Oh, it's busted." James narrowed his eyes in infinite wea-
riness as he glanced at the ruins of his cast. "Again."

Bolan looked over at the captain. "Doom?"

The Pakistani was on his feet. He leaned heavily on the
tabletop and heaved ragged breaths into his tortured lungs. His
nose was bleeding. Blood flecked his lips. He continued to
wheeze.

"Doom?" Bolan jerked his head. "Cal!"

James lifted Makhdoom's head. The captain winced as the
medic probed his neck. There was a massive, ugly-looking
trauma on his throat where the heavy coin inside the strangling cord had pressed down.

"Bruised trachea, might even be hairline cracked." James
peered into Makhdoom's eyes. "Can you talk?"

The Pakistani heaved in a breath. "I…still…" The last
words came out in a broken croak. "…can fight."

James looked back at Bolan with a great deal of skepticism
on his face.

Makhdoom fixed his bloodshot gaze on Bolan. *"Badal."*

Bolan nodded. The only way he would be able to make

Makhdoom stand down would be to kill him. Bolan thumbed his throat mike. "Jack, I'm going to need extraction."

"Affirmative, Striker," the pilot replied. "ETA five minutes to your position."

"We have two choppers on the roof. Your LZ will be the front parking lot."

"Roger that, Striker."

James knelt beside Ramrod. "You want me to stay with him?"

"Yeah. If the shit really hits the fan, you get him in the chopper and you and Jack come in as backup."

"The shit has already hit the fan," James said with a weary grin, "but just shout if you need me."

Bolan turned to the Thuggee on the table. Burdick had ripped away the fabric veiling his face. "Where are the rest of your friends?"

The man grimaced but said nothing.

"Last chance. Talk. If you don't, I'll ship you back to Pakistan with Captain Makhdoom."

Bolan's blue eyes were arctic. "And he'll show you what *badal* means."

Makhdoom's hand went to the hilt of his bayonet.

The Thuggee smiled back at Bolan. "You are welcome among us, blessed one."

Bolan shrugged. "Hog-tie his ass."

Makhdoom pulled his bayonet. He raised the M-9 over his head and plunged it down into the deceiver's chest. The Thuggee shuddered as the seven-inch blade sank through his heart. The captain twisted the M-9 bayonet once and then ripped it free. He sheathed the blade and took up his carbine again with a wheeze. "I will capture you another one."

Bolan nodded at Lyons. "Bijaya, take Ramrod's carbine and grenades. Let's do it."

The remaining members of the team deployed back into the hallway lazing up down and all around them. Bolan considered the elevator. "Bijaya, you think the temple will be downstairs?"

"Almost certainly."

Bolan ran his eye over her web gear. "What kind of grenades did you come with?"

"Why, Indian, of course." She reached into her pouch and pulled out a serrated cast-iron lump twice the size and weight of modern grenades. The English had introduced the Mills Bomb in 1918 and it was the prototype of the modern hand grenade. The Indians had been manufacturing them as the Model 36M continuously since WWII with almost no modification. "This one has a four-second delay. I have two more with a thirteen-second delay, for booby traps."

"Let me see that one."

Khan handed Bolan the grenade and he pulled the pin. The safety lever pinged away and he tossed the grenade into the open elevator. "Fire in the hole!"

The team withdrew to either side of the elevator doors. The grenade detonated with a crack and sparks shrieked as shrapnel scored the steel door frames and ripped out into the hallway.

"The elevator is clear, they'll expect us to come down." Bolan smiled coldly. "Give me one of your lucky thirteens."

Bolan took the grenade and looked around the corner. No shredded Thuggees lay dead in the elevator. The slightly hammered buttons showed floors one, two and basement. Bolan pressed the basement button and stepped out of the elevator. Just as the doors closed, he pulled the pin on the grenade and tossed it inside.

"I need these doors open, Carl."

Lyons produced flexible charge from his web gear. He pulled the adhesive strip and pressed the shaped charge explosive into the door into a five-foot hoop shape and pushed in a detonator pin. "Fire in the hole."

The Able Team leader pressed the button on his detonator box and orange flame hissed in a circle as the shaped explosive burned through the doors, melting the metal and blowing superheated gas into the elevator shaft. Lyons put his boot into the blackened circle and a five-foot oblong of door broke apart into two pieces and clanged to the floor.

Seconds later the elevator pinged as the doors opened in the basement. Below them the delayed fuse grenade detonated with a muffled crack. Bolan tossed one of his own M-67 frag grenades through the smoking hole into the shaft. "Fire in the hole."

The team crouched back as fire strobed and fragments hissed in the elevator shaft, striking sparks and vibrating the cables. Bolan leaned into the hole and shone his rifle-mounted light down the shaft. The elevator car was on the basement landing. A dead Thuggee lay on top of the car. Bolan pulled on his gloves and slid himself through the jagged hole in the doors. He grabbed the cables and slid down the twenty feet to the car roof. A few seconds later Burdick thudded down next to him. Khan came down next.

Lyons spoke in Bolan's earpiece. "How do you want to manage the dogs?"

"Let me clear the area down here and I'll send the elevator up. Hold your position."

"Affirmative."

The two men crouched. Bolan took out another M-67 frag grenade and pulled the pin. He nodded at Burdick. Red flipped up the latch on the elevator car hatch and yanked it open. The cotter pin flew away as Bolan dropped the grenade into the hatch. Both men leaned back as the grenade detonated in the car.

Bolan glanced down the hatch without exposing himself.

The inside of the beleaguered elevator car was pitted, scraped and scarred from the multiple grenade detonations, but there were no corpses or blood traces.

Red grunted as he peered down. "Savvy bastards."

"Hold me up." Bolan took one of his remaining grenades and pulled the pin as Burdick grabbed him by his web gear. The Executioner swung his head and shoulders down the hatch and hurled the grenade out of the elevator and into the basement. "Up!"

Burdick yanked Bolan up and two seconds later the grenade blasted shrapnel into the basement.

Bolan dropped into the elevator car with carbine ready and lazing out the door. He took cover behind one side of the door as Burdick dropped down and took the other. Khan appeared a moment later and plastered herself to one side. Bolan thumbed his mike. "Elevator is secure. We'll secure the area and send it up."

"Affirmative." Lyons came back. 'Holding position."

The elevator pinged and the doors began to close.

Bolan shoved his carbine barrel out and the steel doors closed upon it.

They didn't reopen as they should have.

Burdick dropped his weapon and grabbed one of the doors as Bolan grabbed the other. They heaved against the doors with all of their strength, but they didn't budge.

The elevator began to drop.

"Striker!" Lyons's voice rose in Bolan's earpiece. "The car is moving!"

"Ironman! There's another floor!" Bolan snarled as his carbine was ripped from his hands and the barrels of the rifle and grenade launcher warped, bent and broke as they were dragged against the concrete wall of the elevator shaft. Bolan took out his pistols. "We're trapped and heading down!"

"Affirmative! We're on our way!"

The elevator stopped and pinged. "Ironman! Hold position!"

"Affirmative! Holding!"

The doors opened. Bolan, Khan and Burdick took cover on either side of the door and put the outside in a cross fire.

The hidden floor below the basement was hewn out of earth and rock. It was lit in lurid red and orange by flickering torches. The air that came into the elevator reeked of burning incense.

"Striker! What is your situation!"

Bolan and Burdick lazed the smoky stone corridor. "I believe we found the temple."

"You want us to come down?"

Bolan looked up the hatch. Light shone on the basement where the doors were open again. He shook his head grimly. They hadn't just opened up by themselves.

"Negative, Ironman. The shaft is a killzone. They're expecting it. It would take just one grenade to kill all of you as you came down, or they could take you one at a time as you passed the basement."

"They aren't using guns, Striker. We can fast-rope the cables."

Bolan considered. "Ironman, they may not be using guns or grenades, but they're waiting for you to come down that shaft, and nothing good is going to happen when you do."

There was a pause of several seconds. "All right. We will find another way to get to you. Sit tight if you can and keep us advised."

"Affirmative." Bolan and Burdick continued to laze the torch-lit corridor. Nothing broke their beams.

Burdick spit. "These guys give me the creeps."

"You and me both." Bolan looked back at Khan. She was pressed against the wall of the elevator car. She was shaking. "Bijaya, are you all right?"

"No." She had broken into a cold sweat and she stared wide-eyed back at Bolan. "But I will not let you down."

Bolan looked down the corridor hewn out of the earth. The cloying stench of the incense was overpowering. A sound at almost subliminal level caught Bolan's attention.

Burdick's head jerked up a second later. "What the hell is that?"

The sound slowly grew louder. It was rhythmic and pulsing, rising and falling. It continued to grow louder.

It was the sound of drums.

The reverberating drone of chant joined the drums.

"Fine, you sons of bitches!" The immense Marine ripped his bayonet from its sheath and clacked it onto the end of his rifle. "Come get some!"

"No, Red." Bolan put a hand against the wall of the elevator as his knees suddenly went sickly weak. Sweat burst out across his brow as his skin heated and burned with the infection of fever. He shook his head and looked over at Khan.

Spittle flecked the Indian agent's lips. Her eyes rolled back in her head as she sagged and slid to the floor.

"What the—" Burdick started as Khan collapsed at his feet. "Jesus!" He hit his throat mike. "Ironman! We are in deep shit! Khan is down! Striker is— Oh, my God!" Burdick leveled his rifle at Bolan.

The Executioner swayed like a drunk. The interior of the elevator expanded and stretched in sickening parallax. A rapidly failing part of his mind could still do the math. The drums and chanting were sonic triggers. Bolan struggled for control as every shrapnel hole and scar in the walls of the elevator expanded and gaped at him like open graves. He knew what was happening. The incense was laden with the Thuggee's sacramental drug. They were burning into the air that Bolan breathed.

He knew what was happening and he was powerless to stop it.

Kaushal was inducing a flashback.

"Goddamn you, Striker!" Burdick's finger closed around the trigger of the M-203.

The black muzzle of the grenade launcher became a slavering mouth filled with razor-blade teeth in front of Bolan's eyes, ready to vomit forth its deadly, beehive swarm of darts.

"You stay with me!" Burdick roared. "You hear me?"

"Red…" Bolan groaned as he fought for control. He ripped his gaze away from Burdick and the horror show he was becoming. Kali was coming for him and he couldn't stop. He couldn't seize his sanity. It slipped through his discipline like sand through his fingers. Leaving an ugly, empty fist for the goddess of death to fill. Bolan fell to his knees. The torch-lit corridor ahead expanded. The drums pounded loud enough to shake the walls.

The earthen walls of the corridor heaved and convulsed in front of Bolan, dripping like a blood-red womb ready to give birth to the goddess of death in an ascension of radioactive fire. Her birthing pangs had been ten thousand years of agony, fear and death. Her birth cord was the strangling sash of the Thuggee. Her contractions were the tightening of ten thousand years of ritual strangulation

Kali's time had come. She was fully awake. The world would be blood and fire.

The Earth would become her burning ground.

Her dance of destruction would end in a whirling frenzy danced upon the blasted corpse of the world.

There was no stopping it.

Bolan could see the darkness at the end of the corridor coalescing. The flickering shadows becoming sinuous, beckoning arms. The torch lights became the burning bloodlust in Kali's eyes, a hunger that could never be sated short of total annihilation. Every pound of the drums brought her a step closer. Her lascivious form solidifying out from her cloak of black shadow.

Kali was coming.

Bolan took his carbine in his hands. He wasn't aware of the blood that oozed from his pores, sweating in answer to Kali's call. He was not aware of the foam drooling from his lips as he pulled his bayonet and clicked it onto the barrel of his weapon.

Kali was coming for him.

Bolan began to smile.

He would kill her. He would kill her in every form he found her. He could see her incarnation waiting to be birthed in everything around him. She could appear in anyone, in anything. She was infinite, and it didn't matter. He would kill Kali a million times.

He would kill her until the end of the world.

Kali's mouth smiled in answer to the killing fury she saw in Bolan's burning blue eyes. Her four arms opened to him, offering an orgy of blood and destruction. The two-foot tongue fell writhing between her dark breasts, dripping in obscene desire. She offered herself to his bayonet, his carbine, his grenade launcher and all of his weapons, daring him to begin the dance of destruction that hammered in his own heart.

The Executioner rose.

The glittering point of his bayonet reflected in the pinhole pupils of his eyes. There was nothing left in his face that was human. His foaming lips pulled back. Bolan bared his teeth to the gum line in a skeletal smile as demonic as Kali's own. The Executioner stood ready to match the avenging rage of his War Everlasting against the doomsday lust of the goddess of death.

He would show her what killing really was.

Only a vague part of Bolan's mind noted the muzzle of Burdick's carbine as it pressed into the back of his skull, and he didn't care.

CHAPTER TWENTY-EIGHT

Bolan felt the sudden shock in the back of his neck. A few hidden shreds of his rationality accepted Burdick's bullet and were grateful for an end to the pain and madness.

There was no end.

Bolan's vision went white. His limbs locked as fire ripped from the back of his neck and radiated outward, burning through every last artery, vein and capillary traversing his body. Every nerve ending in his being fired pain and seared as if it had been drawn from his body with a scalpel and dragged through jagged crystals of superheated sand. His heart fluttered and jerked like a bird with a broken wing in cage of his chest.

Bolan fell, writhing face-first to the floor of the elevator.

He didn't feel the boot that rolled him over. He did perceive one giant ugly Marine standing over him while he twitched uncontrollably. An M-4 Ranger carbine with attached grenade launcher was pointed at his face. In his other hand Burdick held a dripping syringe of a size fit to tranquilize a horse.

The twin muzzles of Burdick's weapon system never wavered from between Bolan's eyes.

"Tell me you're with me, Striker!"

Bolan groaned. Every muscle in his body flexed and rippled with the hammering ache of tetanus. "What was in that, Red?"

"Well, lookie." Burdick visibly relaxed and took a knee. "The big guy's back."

Bolan's convulsions rapidly subsided. "You drugged me with what?"

Burdick tossed away the spent needle. "Uh, well, Naloxone, Benzodiazepine, Benzedrine, caffeine…a bunch of shit I can't remember. Some kind of Calvin cocktail. Me and the brother had a powwow about my orders while you were packing z's on the plane. He handed me the needle and suggested that if you went to the dark side of the Force, and I had the opportunity, to stick you with it before I blew your brains out. He said there was a ghost of chance it would jump-start you. Something about agonists and antagonists and neuroreceptors. I'm just a left-handed Gemini from Florida. It was all above my high school equivalency exam. He also said it might throw you into a coma, give you a heart attack, or kill you, but at least you'd have more of a chance than with a NATO standard SS109 through the brain."

Burdick removed the muzzles of his weapons from Bolan's face. "How do you feel?"

Bolan's teeth were chattering and his brain buzzed as though he'd drunk a hundred urns of Aaron Kurtzman's coffee. "Like it rained hammers."

"Good, that's real good." Burdick grabbed a fistful of Bolan's web gear and yanked him to his feet. "Can you stand?"

All Bolan wanted was to do was to find an open grave and fall into it.

He put a hand against the wall to hold himself up and stood instead. "Yeah."

"Good. Calvin said there's no such thing as an antipsychedelic, but he said if you hated someone enough and put enough of the right kinds of shit into a needle, you could focus their ass if you were willing to kill them." Burdick raised craggy orange eyebrows at Bolan. "Does your ass feel focused?"

Bolan saw Burdick as if he were looking at the ex-Marine through a pair of binoculars that had been reversed. He had tunnel vision and felt as though thousands of spiders were crawling around the perimeter of the lenses just out of sight.

"Crystal clear," Bolan muttered.

"Fuckin' A. You're a lyin' son of a bitch, but you're pretty salty for a guy who should be dead. You'll do." He grabbed Bolan's carbine from where it hung by its sling and shoved it into his hands. "That's your M-4 weapon system. Hold on to it. You're gonna need it."

Bolan took a deep breath and looked down at Khan. "You gonna shoot her up?"

Burdick scratched his jaw. "Dunno. You nearly vapor-locked. Think I should?"

"What did Calvin say?"

"Well, he did give me two needles." Burdick looked unhappily at the Indian agent as she twitched and foamed weakly in a fetal curl. "But the man didn't look confident, and you outweigh her by about seventy pounds. If I light her up it'll probably kill her, even if she ain't overdosing on that Thuggee shit already."

"Do it."

"Jesus, you really—"

"Do it."

"Um, shit. Okay. Right." Burdick pulled a fresh needle while Bolan covered the corridor and lazed, then slid the needle in.

Khan sat up and shrieked.

"Fuck!" Burdick held the woman down while she went into violent convulsions. "Fuck!"

Bolan kept his red-rimmed gaze and his laser pointing down the corridor. Khan's struggles slowly subsided. "How is she?"

"If she dies this is your goddamn fault!" Burdick felt for a pulse in the now motionless agent. "Okay...okay...weak and thready...but she's alive." He peeled back an eyelid and recoiled slightly. "Goddamn...she is gone, daddy, gone."

Bolan glanced down.

Khan's pupils were blown and two different sizes. Her body was alive but Bijaya Khan wasn't at home. Bolan thumbed his throat mike and got nothing but static. "How long has this been going on?"

"'Bout thirty seconds. Been too busy to worry about it till now."

Bolan sighed as he rapidly switched settings. "We're being jammed across all frequencies."

"Can they do that?"

"Can they turn invisible?"

"Uh...right," Burdick acknowledged. "So what do we do now? Sit tight and wait for the cavalry?"

"This is the elevator to Hell, Red, and we are on the bottom floor. We know they're waiting on the floor above us for someone to try to come up or come down. You want to stick around until they go to Plan B?"

"Yeah, granted, but couldn't wandering around down here be just what they want us to do?"

"Probably, but right now they think Bijaya and I are in La La Land."

"You sayin' you ain't?"

There was a moment of silence. Burdick cleared his throat. "Don't look at me like that."

"Pick her up."

The big ex-Marine scooped up the unconscious agent and tossed her across his shoulders. The two warriors stepped out into the torchlight, lazing as they came.

"SARGE!" Jack Grimaldi dropped the Black Hawk helicopter like a stone to the Coherence parking lot. "Sarge!"

The radio crackled. "Jack! This is Cal! Do not enter the building! We will come to you! We'll link—"

"Cal?" Grimaldi nearly let the remains of his cigar fall from his mouth as the radio went dead. "Ironman? Sarge?"

Grimaldi powered down his bird and turned to a very confused U.S. Army copilot who had been activated and volunteered in the middle of the night. "Anderson? Right?"

"Right, sir. Lieutenant Steven Anderson." He'd had a fascinating, far-ranging conversation with the mystery pilot who had commandeered him and his helicopter but this was the first time the perpetually smiling man had asked his name. "Uh, and you are—"

"You got a gun, Lieutenant?" Grimaldi pulled an Ingram MAC-10 submachine gun from his flight bag.

"Well, yes, sir." Anderson pulled a Heckler & Koch MP-5 subgun from a slot beside his seat. "Why?" He glanced around the commercial parking lot in the middle of the Silicon Valley. "We are in America, sir. Aren't we?"

"Yeah, but we have enemies, Lieutenant. Foreign and domestic." Grimaldi pointed his weapon at the Coherence lab and tapped the windshield with his suppressor. "There's a shitload of them in that building, and rumor is they can turn invisible and they have nukes."

Anderson blinked. "Really?"

"Darn tootin'. Now, I'm going to go make contact with our guys. You stay here and keep the engine running and the doors locked." Grimaldi leaped out of the Black Hawk while Anderson stared after him in disbelief.

Anderson locked the doors.

The ace pilot trotted up to the building and noted the blown-open front doors. He looked around the lobby and went to the door behind the desk. It was open and led to a hallway. There was an elevator with the doors blown open. The air stank of burnt high explosive. He thumbed his throat mike and tapped his earpiece.

Communications were still down.

The last person he'd been in contact with was Calvin James. Grimaldi shouted at the top of his lungs. "Cal!"

A moment later James responded from the first smashed-open door on the left. "I told you not to come in!"

"Can I come in now?"

"Jesus…"

Grimaldi kept the hallway covered as he entered the conference room. The pilot surveyed the havoc that had been wreaked on the room and then the damage to Ramrod and James. "You broke your wing again, Cal."

"Yeah. You want to help me with him?"

The pilot grunted with the Pakistani's weight while James held up the IV.

"Where's Sarge?"

"Down an elevator shaft, last I heard."

"Where's Carl?"

"Trying to find an alternate way down, last I heard."

They divvied up Ramrod's grenades and explosives and then carried him out to the helicopter. Lieutenant Anderson opened the cargo door as Grimaldi knocked with his weapon. They slid Ramrod in and covered him with a blanket. James hung the IV onto a cleat, unpacked items from his medical bag and handed them to the Army airman. "Here's an extra IV. If he wakes up, give him one ampule of morphine and no more. Keep an eye on his vital signs. He's stable but he's got a slow hemorrhage in the lower abdomen that could go bad."

Anderson blinked. "Right."

James rigged himself a sling for his injured arm. He unslung his carbine and handed it to Grimaldi. "You'll need this to laze."

"Oh." The pilot took the weapon eagerly. "Cool."

Anderson stared at the two men in mounting disbelief.

James hefted his P-9 in his good hand. "Lieutenant, we'll be back. We may come running and the LZ could turn hot. These assholes can walk right up to your bird and you'll never see them. So keep the engine running but keep the doors locked."

"Right."

James nodded and turned to Grimaldi. "Let's go find Striker and those nukes."

The ace pilot pressed the laser sighting button and swept the beam across the parking lot. The LED blinked and the electronic chime peeped in rapid alarm. "Shit!" He held down his trigger on full-auto and burned the carbine's magazine in an arc in front of him. He and James piled back into the helicopter and Anderson slammed the door and locked it.

"Get us airborne, Jack!" James jerked his head at Anderson. "Get behind the stick! I'll take care of Ramrod."

Grimaldi was already in his bucket when the windshield in front of him cracked. Something smashed into the lock of the rear cargo door right before James's eyes. The tailboom lurched and there was a clank on top of the cabin.

"Cal?" Grimaldi called back.

"Yeah?"

"We're crawling with them."

James watched the door frame shudder as it was struck by apparently nothing. "No shit."

LYONS CONTEMPLATED the stairs.

Captain Makhdoom was on the same page. "You know they must be booby-trapped."

"Yup."

Austenford held the dogs' leads in one hand and her carbine in the other. "This whole place is rigged like a funhouse."

"Yeah."

Austenford shrugged. "So, how do we get down without getting hammered?"

Lyons came to his decision. "We make our own stairs."

"How do we do that?"

Lyons began to pull blocks of C-4 plastic explosive from his webbing. "Doom, flexible charge."

Austenford grinned delightedly. "This should be fun."

Makhdoom reeled out a length of charge from a pouch. He pulled away the strip covering the adhesive side and pressed a three-foot-diameter hoop onto the floor two yards away from the door to the stairs. Lyons pressed his C-4 blocks together.

"What do you think?" The captain pushed in a detonator pin. "Three? Four?"

Lyons bundled his C-4 together into a brick and put it in the middle of the flexible charge circle. "All."

They moved down the hall and kicked the door on an office. They lazed the walls, ceiling and floors and then locked the door. Lyons held out his detonator box to the doctor. "You want to do the honors?"

"Oh! Gimme!"

Lyons nodded at Makhdoom. "Do it."

The Pakistani clicked his own box for the flexible charge. Nothing happened.

Austenford clicked her own button and was met with nothing but silence.

Lyons took the detonators and went to the door. All radio frequencies were being jammed. The enemy had as many toys as the doctor did, but for every countermeasure, there was a countermeasure. Lyons flicked switches on the two boxes. He opened the door, pointed one box and pushed the red button. The lens in the flexible charge's detonator pin detected the infrared beam and the charge hissed and smoked as it burned its focused explosion down into the floor. It was far from enough to cut through the ground floor of a modern building, but it was enough to weaken it.

The six sticks of C-4 sat in the middle of a burned circle of charred floor as if it had a smoldering black halo. Lyons pushed the button on his second detonator and leaped back into the office as two and a half pounds of high explosive went off in the hallway.

The office shook and fire alarms began to blare. The sprinklers in the ceiling deployed, spraying water in all directions. Sadie and Schatzie barked hysterically at the noise and stench. Austenford gave them both a hotdog from a pouch on her belt. The dogs wolfed down the treats and were instantly all business again. Lyons opened the door and smoke and dust rolled into the office in a wave. He pulled a pair of grenades from his belt and made his way through the cloud to a blackened hole in the floor, noting with satisfaction that it was a good five feet in diameter. He pulled the pins and tossed down the frag grenades. He stepped back from the smoking hole as the black smoke and dust lit with yellow flashes and shrapnel erupted and hit the lights in the ceiling.

Makhdoom had already affixed a rope to a door and he tossed the coil down the hole. He smiled at Lyons. "After you."

CHAPTER TWENTY-NINE

Bolan looked up. The rock-hewn ceiling shook with a low rumble and dust floated down. Burdick quirked an eyebrow. "Sounded like a satchel charge upstairs."

"Carl is up to something." Bolan scraped an arrow into the unfinished wall with the point of his fixed bayonet. "Probably making his own stairs."

The temple was a maze. They weren't lost but it was a labyrinth that had to be threaded, lazing around every corner. Without radio communications it would take Lyons and the rest of the team time to find them. Burdick pointed ahead. "What do you make of that?"

No more side corridors branched out. Ahead stretched a few dozen yards of straight corridor that opened into darkness. "I'd say we've reached the center of the spiderweb."

"Great." The big ex-Marine nodded tiredly. "Let's go kill this bastard."

"Good idea."

The two men lazed their way to the entrance of an unlit cavern. They flicked on the tactical lights affixed to their carbines and shone them around the room. The air stank of incense. The floor was soft, groomed sand. There was only one thing in the room and it stood seven feet tall on a massive black slab of basalt.

The ruby-red eyes of Kali, the goddess of death, stared into the tactical lights. Her two open hands beckoned them to enter. Bolan's shoulders twitched as he stared at the graven image of the goddess. Images of hideousness beyond horror still lurked at the fringes of Bolan's consciousness and the seven-foot goddess standing in front of him let all of those images take one massive step forward into the front of his mind.

Burdick's huge paw slapped down on Bolan's shoulder. "Steady."

Bolan raised his rifle in answer. The ceiling was rock and earth with no visible handholds, but he and Burdick lazed every inch of it anyway, then turned their attention back to the altar. The three metal-encased tactical nuclear warheads lay on their sides beneath the foot of the goddess where she normally stood upon a corpse.

Bolan and Burdick stepped into the inner temple.

"Greetings," spoke a voice from directly behind them. "You are too late."

Bolan spun, but he was too slow. Burdick was burdened with Khan across his shoulders.

The two soldiers rose up in the air and flew across the room as if they had grown wings.

"BASTARDS!" Jack Grimaldi didn't like it when people messed with his ride. He had tried to take off but even as his engines screamed, an underlying howl told him something was wrong with his rotors. There was also an ugly clacking upstairs in the main rotor shaft. His collective and cyclic weren't functioning properly, either.

The windows were spiderwebbing and pocking as if they were being struck with invisible sledgehammers. The unseen was trying to rip its way inside, which precluded opening up the cabin and trying to deploy the door guns. Ramrod was conscious and had propped himself up slightly. His agony was obvious despite the morphine, but he had a 9 mm SIG-Sauer pistol in his hand. James knelt beside him, pistol in hand, watching the crash-resistant windows slowly buckle from repeated blows on both sides of the cabin.

"Jack!" James roared.

"What?"

"Do something!"

"Right!" Grimaldi ran the usual pilot's mantra for dealing with emergencies: *Try A. Try B. Try C...*

He couldn't take off. He couldn't deploy his door guns. He didn't have any guns or rockets mounted outside the helicopter and had no way to use them against an enemy who was crawling on top of and breaking its way into his aircraft. The Black Hawk wasn't specifically a combat helicopter, it was used by U.S. Army Intelligence spooks to play their spooky games. It didn't attack with rockets and missiles. It was designed to gather information, to mess with the enemy's minds.

It did, however, in the course of its duties, expect to be attacked, if not specifically besieged on the ground.

"Right! Countermeasures!" Grimaldi scanned his countermeasures suite. Infrared jammer? Useless. Airborne Radar Jamming System? Equally useless.

"Goddamn it, Jack!"

"I'm on it already!" Grimaldi snarled at his controls, there had to be something. Helicopter Self-Screening System. "Hmm," the pilot mused. He stabbed the button. "Countermeasures away!"

The frame of the Black Hawk shook as thirty 84 mm projectiles burst from their launchers. They exploded in spectacular fireworks-like effects, and clouds of precisely tailored, infrared-blocking gray smoke choked off the outside world in a 360-degree arc around the aircraft. Grimaldi punched the button next to it and rammed his throttles forward. The engines screamed into the redline as a special tank began to inject infrared smoke material into the exhaust manifolds.

The Black Hawk began to vomit black smoke from both engines like an oil rig fire.

Despite the hostile, choking smoke descending on both sides of the airframe a few determined souls were still pounding on the doors.

Infrared Decoy System. Grimaldi smiled. "Flares away!"

The gray smoke obscuring the planet lit from within as one-by-one-inch infrared magnesium flare pellets rippled out of their cartridge dispensers at chest height.

James looked on in awe as a flare exploded as it struck something. The something staggered back as it was struck by a second and a third and resolved into the shape of a man that lay on the ground unmoving as he burned. "Jesus, Jack...."

"Chaff!" Grimaldi exclaimed. Chaff wouldn't have any appreciable effect on a human being but the party was already out of control and everyone loved confetti. "Chaff away!"

The chaff dispenser bricks exploded upward, succeeding in knocking the remaining Thuggee from the roof as millions of strips of aluminized Mylar film blasted up into the air, forming a delightfully dense, glittering, fluttering cloud of tinsel around the chopper. Grimaldi hit the landing lights and then powered up the Nightsun gimballed spotlight beneath the chin of the chopper. He began spinning it 360 degrees on its mount and the seventy-five-thousand candlepower beam began strobing through the smoke.

It was something to see.

The Thuggees were shambling shapes out of nightmares. The self-screening smoke from the rockets produced particularly dense ash designed to foil infrared sensors. The Thuggees were swathed in the light-transferring textile like mummies, only now they were coated head to toe with gray-infrared defeating particulate. Several lay dead and burning where they had been struck by the rockets or the IR flares. The flares spun and sputtered as bright as an arc-welder's torch as they violently consumed themselves in blinding incandescence. Opaque black smoke continued to belch forth from the exhausts. The Thuggees were obviously choking and the attack upon the helicopter had lessened. A few grimly determined Thuggees continued to hammer at the chopper with swathed pickaxes.

The Mylar chaff shimmered and fell through the smog and smoke to fall upon the Thuggees like magic fairy dust, clinging to their sooty forms and sparkling in the strobing spotlight.

Grimaldi grinned as he read his control panel. External Audio Communications. "What have you got in here, Steve-o!"

Lieutenant Anderson clutched his MP-5 and watched his windscreen buckle. "In Iraq we used it to tell the enemy to surrender! Sometimes we'd tell the civilians to stay in their homes or announce rewards for info on the Iraqi leadership. Sometimes we just used noise to intimidate!"

"What have you got right now?"

"I always keep Guns 'N Roses ready!" Anderson flipped switches on the system. "The Republican Guardsman hated that!"

"Hit it!"

Anderson hit the CD changer that was linked to the external communications system and cranked the volume to full. There was a one-second pause while he punched a number into the selector and the system tracked and the end of the world began.

The very airframe of the helicopter vibrated with the bass as the external megaphones thundered out at well over two hundred decibels. The Thuggees beating the outside of the helicopter visibly shuddered and cringed as they were hammered back by a sound system designed to be heard for miles.

The noise was deafening within the chopper; outside by the speakers, it was a heavy-metal Armageddon.

"Go get 'em, Cal!" Grimaldi roared. His smile bordered on the maniacal as he prodded Anderson. "You, go help him."

Anderson clambered wide-eyed out of his seat and back into the cabin.

James had already pulled on a radio headset to protect his ears and goggles for his eyes. Anderson did the same as James helped Ramrod to sit up. "Can you open the door?"

"God…" Ramrod's face was a mask of pain as his broken hipbones ground together and his perforated bladder stabbed. His fist white-knuckled around the latch. "Sure! Say when!"

"On three!" James cradled a carbine in his good arm and nodded at Anderson. "Ready! One! Two! Three!"

Ramrod let out a shout of effort as he unlocked the door and heaved it back on its tracks.

The outside noise exploded inside and smoke poured in. The Thuggees surged. James and Anderson unleashed their weapons on full-auto, point-blank into the crowd of Thuggees. James's carbine ran dry, and he touched off the M-203 spraying fléchettes in an expanding swarm. The Thuggees jamming the door shuddered as they were shredded and felled, dropping their picks and strangling cords. The Phoenix Force commando tossed the spent carbine and grabbed his pistol as he leaped in among the enemy. The German .45 thudded in his hand as he cleared a path.

The world outside was a maelstrom of sound, smoke, strobing light and gray-coated mummified assassins.

Ramrod collapsed against the cabin wall but his 9 mm pistol barked in his hand, shooting at targets on either side of the ex-SEAL. Anderson slammed a fresh magazine into his submachine gun and leaped into the breach.

James's P-9 clacked open on a smoking empty chamber. He hurled the two-pound pistol into the face of a Thuggee and his Mk II whispered from its sheath. The fighting knife was a true dagger, the double-edged blade leaf-shaped and point-heavy. It was useless for almost any utilitarian function. It had been designed during the Vietnam War for the single purpose of killing men.

The External Communication Audio System thundered on like God's hammer reforging reality on the anvil of the Earth.

James's blade glittered in the smoke and fire.

BOLAN'S RIFLE was ripped from his hands before he could rise.

Kalidas Kaushal held the carbine by the barrel and smashed the M-4 weapon system against Trevor Burdick's head. The big ex-Marine fell face-first to the floor. The priest of Kali moved with inhuman speed and grace. Bolan slapped leather for his pistols. Kaushal clamped his hands on Bolan's forearms and the Executioner was suddenly borne aloft and hurled seven feet across the sand. The air burst out of his lungs as he hit the ground ugly and rolled.

The torches in the sconces suddenly flared and lit.

Kaushal had thrown aside his robelike garment of conceal-ment and stood in a white cotton breechclout. His stark physique glistened in the torchlight, a chiseled horror of su-pernatural strength.

Burdick pressed himself up with a groan. Kaushal covered the distance in two strides and slapped the Colt .45 from his adversary's hands. The priest slammed his palms against Bur-dick's chest in a shove that lifted the man from his feet and catapulted him into the rock wall three feet behind him.

Burdick bounced to his hands and knees and collapsed to the sand once more.

"Now." Kaushal turned his attention upon Bolan once more. "You have a destiny to fulfill."

Bolan's boot knife came out of its Kydex sheath with a rasp in agreement. "Yeah."

Kaushal sighed as he read the broken, bloodied intent in Bolan's eyes. "We do not have time for this."

Bolan kept the point of the skeletonized steel between them as they locked gazes. "Let's make time."

"Very well." Kaushal opened his hand and a lump of the consecrated sugar appeared like magic. "The world is a diseased illusion. Kali is the cure. You just require a little more medicine to fathom this."

Kaushal blurred into motion. He moved with grotesque speed.

Bolan lunged to meet him.

The Executioner cut for his opponent's hands, seeking to slice tendons and to take away his sickening strength advantage. Bolan's first and second cut missed as Kaushal's hands moved sinuously, avoided his strokes by inches. One of the priest's hands suddenly closed around Bolan's wrist like a vise and the huge hand squeezed.

Bolan's hand went numb and the blade popped from his fingers as his fist spasmed open. The Executioner drove his free hand like a spear into Kaushal's sternum. His hand opened and rammed up in a palm-heel strike. Neither blow seemed to have any effect on the man whatsoever. Kaushal effortlessly tilted his head to one side to avoid Bolan's finger thrust for his eyes.

"Enough." Kaushal wrapped his fingers around Bolan's throat and lifted him off his feet. He held up the lump of brown sugar that had remained undisturbed in his palm during Bolan's attack. "You will take the sacrament. Do it willingly, and I will have the priestesses guide you toward bliss. Resist, and you shall plunge into nightmare that only your death in ritual sacrifice will release you fr—"

"*Bhen...chod...*" Bijaya Khan could barely stand. "*Bhayn-Chod!*"

Bolan had been in India enough to know that she had said

something about Kalidas Kaushal and his relationship with his sister. Khan reeled on her feet, but her eyes blazed bloody murder. She held a .455 caliber revolver in each hand.

Kaushal discarded Bolan like a rag doll.

The revolvers in Khan's hands detonated like doomsday in the echoing interior of the cavern.

In her weakened condition she could barely control the recoil of the immense revolvers as they rolled in her hands with each trigger pull. She tried to track Kaushal as he literally cartwheeled across the temple. Khan's bullets kicked up sand on the floor and spalled in smears of lead across the idol of the goddess as Kaushal's acrobatics brought him safely behind it.

The hammers finally fell with a click on empty chambers.

Kaushal came out of his cartwheeling and strode back into the middle of the room. Khan threw down her revolvers and staggered toward one of the fallen carbines. The dark priest was much too fast and he took her up helplessly in his hands. "Little sister, blessed one, you, too, require the cleansing of sacrament."

Trevor Burdick bellowed like a wounded bull as he charged across the sand. He didn't attempt to punch or to kick Kaushal. He threw his three hundred pounds into the priest in a flying shoulder block.

Kaushal was moved two feet across the sand. He tossed Khan aside and joined his hands into a double fist over his head. He swung his hands down in an ax handle blow that flattened Burdick face-first into the sand as if he had been struck by a pile driver.

The priest smoothed his hair and checked his watch. "For you, fat one, I shall make a moment to perform the sacrifice."

The priest bent and picked up Burdick by his belt and collar. He effortlessly pressed the ex-Marine up over his head and turned to the altar of Kali. "I consecrate this life to thee, O Kali, in sac—"

The priest stopped in midsentence and stared at Bolan. The Executioner held the carbine that Kaushal had batted Burdick with moments earlier. Kaushal dropped Burdick behind him like a sack of potatoes. Bolan raised the carbine to his shoulder and squeezed the trigger.

Nothing happened.

Bolan glanced at the weapon and noted that the forestock was cracked, and the magazine bent and sticking out of the well at an ugly angle.

Kaushal smiled benevolently and closed the gap.

Bolan slid his finger around the trigger of the M-230 beneath the cracked stock and fired. Pale yellow flame thumped from the 40 mm muzzle with a boom. Kaushal stopped in his tracks and started at Bolan quizzically.

The priest appeared to be utterly unharmed.

Bolan dropped the carbine and backed away, the boot knife back in his hand.

Kaushal took a step forward and stopped. His chin turned down as he gazed at himself. A spot of blood appeared between the plates of muscle. Then a second and a third a fourth. Within seconds he had dozens and then scores of bloody pinpricks. He looked as if someone had tried to carve his heart out of his chest with an ice pick.

What he had was 115 .17-caliber wounds in his chest, all within the diameter of a dinner plate.

Kaushal looked back up at Bolan.

A thin thread of blood leaked from the corner of his mouth.

Kaushal stepped forward.

Bolan found himself backed up against the black basalt altar. A tactical thermonuclear weapon lay at his feet. The seven-foot ebony goddess of death loomed over his shoulder. Bolan glanced back at the goddess as Kaushal closed in. Kali's ruby-faceted eyes glittered down upon him in approval. Her tongue lolled, waiting to taste the blood of sacrifice. Her open hand waited for a head. Her black-iron executioner's ax raised high to descend in the killing stroke of the world.

Bolan reached back and slid the all-iron ax from Kali's slotted-stone hand.

"Thanks."

Kaushal stopped.

Bolan took the ax in both hands and limped forward. Blood now washed down Kaushal's chest. He wore blood down his chin like a scarlet beard. The ax was as heavy as the world but Bolan hefted it back over his shoulder. Kaushal no longer moved with liquid grace and speed. He stumbled back a step in the sand and brought up his hands as Bolan swung the ax.

The blade was double-lobed, almost like an inverted, sharpened heart. The two lobes swept inward to form a double-edged notch of razor-sharp iron, designed to perfectly coincide with a human neck column.

It sheared through Kaushal's left forearm and continued right on through the right.

The sheer weight of the weapon spun Bolan 180 degrees from the follow-through. Trying to stop the stroke nearly yanked him off of his feet. Kaushal fell to his knees at the feet of the goddess. He stared at the stumps of his arms incredulously.

Kali's red eyes glittered in the torchlight. Her two-foot tongue lolling down for the bloody offering before her.

Bolan used his last reserve of strength. His vision darkened as he swung the ax with all of his might. The blade coincided with Kaushal's cervical vertebrae. It passed through the priest's neck with the perfect precision of its thousand-year-old design.

Kaushal's head flew from his shoulders.

His skull struck Kali's outstretched hand, teetering for a moment and then toppling away, rejected, into the sand. His decapitated corpse fell, fountaining blood at Kali's feet.

Bolan could barely stand. He was done. His heart was still

beating but only just. He held on to the headsman's ax only out of instinct as he staggered three steps and collapsed next to Khan. Bolan spent long moments simply breathing. He then pushed himself up to his knees and examined Bijaya Khan. She didn't appear to be physically hurt, but her eyes were half closed, the flesh beneath them bruised with the psycho-chemical sledgehammering she had taken.

Her red-rimmed eyes slid to the black ax Bolan still clutched. "Tell me he's dead."

"Yeah, he's dead." Bolan looked over at Burdick. The big ex-Marine lay on his back a few feet away. He looked like death warmed over but his chest was rising and falling. "Red...you all right?"

"I'm—" blood from internal injuries bubbled across his lips "—a mess."

Bolan knew how the man felt. He didn't want to even begin to think of how badly he was messed up himself—mentally, physically and otherwise.

"How the hell did he sneak up on us like that?" Burdick coughed ugly from bloody lungs. "We lazed. We lazed the goddamn place."

Bolan looked back at the entrance. There was a wide circular opening ten feet above the doorway. He shook his head. "He dropped down behind us."

"Yeah? Well, the headless son of a—" Burdick's train of thought broke into an interrupted gurgle at the explosion. Khan flinched. Bolan wasn't surprised at all as the passageway above the door lit up in yellow flashes and shrapnel tore out across the roof of the temple. Smoke oozed out and seconds later a pair of ropes sailed uncoiling to the sand. Lyons and Makhdoom came flying down the ropes, carbines at the ready.

"You're late."

Lyons's eyes looked at the ancient ax in Bolan's hands and

the headless body by the altar and reserved comment. He went to check on Burdick. Makhdoom lowered his carbine and surveyed the carnage in grim approval. *"Badal."*

Bolan nodded. The obligation of revenge had been satisfied.

Makhdoom ran his laser around the room perfunctorily. "Clear!"

James, Austenford and Sadie and Schatzie entered through the main door. Lyons was speaking quietly to Burdick, who groaned and nodded yes in answer to a question. Lyons opened the pouch where Burdick had been carrying the syringes James had prepared. He noted the two needles were missing, nodded once at James.

James frowned very deeply. He lowered his pistol as he took a knee in front of Bolan. He looked at the bloodstained ax the Executioner held leerily and then peered searchingly into Bolan's eyes. "How do you feel, big guy?"

"You saved my life, again. Bijaya's, too."

"You think I was going to let that jarhead blow your brains out?"

Bolan let the ax fall to the sand. "That shot you cooked up just about did."

The concern returned to James's face. "Yeah, and we need to get you to a hospital."

"Yeah, where's Jack?"

"He and Anderson are still topside. As far as we can tell, any Thuggees that didn't run are dead. The helicopter is in bad shape. Once we regroup, Jack's going to see about hotwiring one of the choppers on the roof and medevacing you, Red, Ramrod and Bijaya to the Stanford Medical Center. I'm going to go with you to advise the doctors about what you two have been dosed with. Carl is going to borrow a car from the lot and drive out of range of whatever radio jammer they are using and call in the cavalry to secure this place. Austenford is going to fly in CIA to secure all the light-transferring material. After that we'll sack out at the safehouse in San Francisco."

Bolan nodded. His team had everything under control.

"Striker." Makhdoom stood staring up at the statue of Kali. The eyes of the goddess stared down upon them all. "And this?"

The Pakistani captain held up a stick of C-4.

"No." Bolan shook his head. "That goes back to India."

Makhdoom stared at Bolan quizzically.

"What was practiced here was an abomination." Bolan glanced up at Kali. "I say we send her back to Calcutta, let her rest in a true temple, let her be worshiped by the truly devout."

"You are a tolerant man."

"The Spanish Inquisition happened. I'm not going to C-4 the Vatican."

Makhdoom grunted thoughtfully and put the explosive away.

"Cal." Lyons still knelt over Burdick. "Red's in a bad way."

James went to Red's side.

Mack Bolan took a deep breath. He stood the executioner's ax up and used the iron haft like a crutch to push himself to his feet. The room spun for a moment but he stood and let his vision clear.

Death hadn't taken him today.

He looked down upon the three thermonuclear warheads and the 150 kilotons of radioactive fury they represented. Their deadly incandescent potential was little more than a flash compared to the devastation that would have followed, a key, that would have opened the door for the burning ground that Kalidas Kaushal had envisioned for the world.

Kali's foot was poised over the warheads, but the dance of destruction hadn't begun this night. The Executioner stared deep into the glittering eyes of the goddess of death.

The old girl was just going to have to wait.